MY NAME IS NOT VIOLA

MY NAME IS NOT VIOLA

A Novel by
Lawrence Matsuda

ENDICOTT AND HUGH BOOKS

Front cover: "Searchlight" © 2015 Roger Shimomura
Back cover: "Portrait of Lawrence Matsuda" © 2015 Alfred Arreguin

Book design Erin Shigaki
Cover design Masha Shubin

ISBN: 978-0-9993646-2-8 Trade paperback

3 5 7 9 10 8 6 4 2

To Karen, Hanae, Kiyoshi,
Matthew, and Jesika Matsuda in gratitude.

Contents

Introduction

Sometimes we don't know the books we need until they've been written. *MY NAME IS NOT VIOLA* is such a book. Lawrence Matsuda has carried this implosive, emotionally freighted cargo his entire life, and now releases it to us.

Patterned on his mother's sorrow-legacy and her determined reclamation of a life co-opted, but not surrendered, the circumstances are emblematic of the lives of 120,000 other Japanese Americans—sixty-two percent of whom were American citizens—wrongly imprisoned in machine gun turreted barracks known by the sanitized name of *Internment Camps*, then after WWII sent to a cruelly ironic freedom with $25 and a bus ticket, no job, no home, and yet expected to start life again from zero.

The heroine, Hanae Tamura, has been taken into a mental institution after release. And no wonder: educated and born in Hiroshima, she inhabits stories of its destruction by the atomic bomb from afar while in the camp. She has entered incarceration with her husband and one child. Then rigors of captivity cause the miscarriage of a second child. Ultimately, she births the son who will tell her all-encompassing story.

This story belongs to all of us who wish to experience the Japanese American heartbeat as it was forced to inhabit a humiliating and hope-sundered invitation to sink, and also, incredibly, for its humiliated sufferers, to absorb a silent mandate from their government to forgive what had been done to them.

The incarceration itself began with Roosevelt's Executive Order 9066 on Feb. 1942, a thinly veiled racist sweep of mostly West Coast Japanese American citizens and their *Issei* families. (One sixteenth or more of Japanese blood made one eligible for the camps.)

How this slow-to-be-revealed period in our history affected the capacity of these betrayed individuals, and hijacked their ability to forgive a country they had loved, is the nucleus of this astonishing and truth-telling book. Now Matsuda, a fine poet, graphic novelist and film collaborator, has given it to us. He has my deepest admiration. Of his story, I want to say: at last!

—Tess Gallagher, internationally known poet,
  fiction writer, film collaborator (*Birdman, Short Cuts*)
  author of *IS, IS NOT, poems from America and Ireland*.

Author's Notes

My Name is Not Viola recounts the life of a Japanese American woman, Hanae Tamura, who was forcibly incarcerated without cause during WWII. The novel explores the physical and mental trauma of being betrayed by the USA government and explores factors that helped her cope with the imprisonment and lingering after-effects.

Hanae was born in Seattle to Toyojiro and Toku Tamura in 1921. She was sent to Hiroshima for an education and returned to graduate from Franklin High School in 1939. In 1942, she married Kiyoshi Yamada and gave brith to two children in camp. Suffering from depression in 1962, she entered the Western State Mental Hospital. There she pondered the similarities between the hospital and her 1942 camp experience. Realizing that she has been forcibly exiled at least twice in her life, she examined the steel grates over her hospital windows. Feeling the weight of her incarceration, she asked herself, *Where did I go wrong?*

To answer her own question, Hanae recalled her childhood and concentration camp experiences. The WWII forced detention of 120,000 Japanese Americans based on race had a lasting effect on her and her children. It left her with pervasive feelings of alienation and mistrust. As a result, her personal challenge was to live a dignified life in America under undignified conditions. To accomplish this task, she drew upon friends, Japanese customs, and Japanese culture for support and comfort.

At Western State Hospital, in 1962, she meets two young Caucasian roommates, Franny and Dutch. The ongoing Cuban Missile Crisis raises fears of nuclear war among the women and Hanae recounts the horrible fates of her Hiroshima relatives who suffered the first atomic attack. The three wonder what would happen to them if Russia declares war. After the missile crisis subsides, Hanae shares Japanese fairy tales with the girls and the threesome see the world through each other's eyes. Each of them experienced past loss, but together they begin to heal. Before Hanae's release, they promise to meet at the Seattle Space Needle on St. Paddy's Day, 1970. When that day arrives, Hanae wonders whether the girls will be there. Nevertheless, she keeps her promise and takes off from work.

Fourteen years after the reunion, Hanae is on her deathbed in 1994. She assesses her life and wonders if she got what she wanted from being alive. To tie up loose ends, she asks her son, Larry, to deliver two photos taken on St. Paddy's Day to Franny. In return, Larry asks if she can forgive the government for the incarceration, thus releasing the burden she carried for decades. She chooses not to forgive, but instead asks him to dance for her at the *Bon Odori* festival which celebrates the annual return of ancestors. Initially Larry refuses to dance. But he changes his mind after she agrees to do something in exchange.

CHAPTER ONE

Western State Mental Hospital, 1962

It was the summer of 1962 when I lifted a crate of vegetables at work. Suddenly I felt a pop followed by a shooting pain that doubled me over. An electric shock ran up my leg. "Ow, that hurts," I said, dropping the produce box with a thud. My muscles twitched and tightened like a wrung out towel.

I was on the floor and tried to stand but could only manage to raise a hand. Feeling dizzy and weak, my rag doll body crumpled on the wet concrete floor. Coworkers gathered around me and the butcher asked, "Hanae, what's wrong? What happened?"

"I hurt my back," I cried. I gritted my teeth. Mr. Saki, the owner, touched my shoulder. "Call an ambulance," he shouted. "This is bad. Someone phone her husband, Kiyoshi, and tell him what happened." As a crowd grew, I heard sirens approaching from down the block. *I feel like a freak at the center of so much commotion*, I thought.

Unable to move, I worried about my family. *How will Kiyoshi manage the boys without me? Who'll cook dinner?*

A Rainbow company ambulance pulled up to the curb. Two medics in whites jumped out and asked, "Where does it hurt?"

I lay in a puddle next to an overturned crate. Embarassed, I adjusted my hiked-up skirt. The medics covered me with a wool blanket and lifted me into the ambulance. Stabbing pains ran up my back and down my leg.

It was a short ride to the Swedish Hospital emergency room. Inside, a strong medicinal odor swirled and made me cough. *Ouch, that hurts!* I thought.

To my surprise Kiyoshi was waiting in the emergency room. His face was pale and twisted. "When did you get here?" I asked.

Before he could reply, the nurse asked him, "Are you her husband, Mr. Yamada?"

He grimaced and looked ready to collapse at the sight of me. But he managed to move close and touch my arm. "Yes, I'm her husband," he replied, "how bad is she?"

"We'll know more after the doctors look at her," she said. "First please sign these forms." She handed him a clipboard. Kiyoshi paused and scanned the papers. He scratched his head and asked, "Hanae what's your birthday? The year, I mean."

I took a breath and thought, *After all this time together?* "1921," I blurted out. "Don't you remember? You're ten years older than me."

In the corner, three doctors discussed the possibility of surgery. I overheard one say, "I would guess it's a couple of ruptured disks that need to be fused."

"Fused?" I blurted out.

The doctors turned and stared at me in surprise.

All my life I've had great hearing acuity. Growing up, crowded places like restaurants or churches used to be an exhausting experience full of overlapping voices. But as I grew older, I learned how to filter and manage them.

To disguise my eavesdropping, I closed my eyes and started mumbling random words like, "coconut" and "cake."

The doctors looked at each other and shrugged.

Fused? I thought, *that's major surgery. How can we afford that?*

"Kiyoshi, come here," I said. "Do we have any savings?"

"Don't worry. We're fine," he replied.

I hope so, I thought.

I drifted in and out of consciousness for a week. Even though I was still weak, they released me because I could walk with assistance. At home, Kiyoshi had rearranged the furniture and created clear paths to the bathroom. I felt useless as the days passed and my world shrank. I worried, *what if there was a fire?* I am not strong enough to escape. I imagined myself dying in a burning bed.

Even my taste buds abandoned me and each bite of food tasted like medicine. Life became a blur as time crawled. My stringy hair smelled sour and I felt like a gerbil living in sawdust. The bedroom air hung heavy. Worst of all, I felt I was not recovering and had nothing to look forward to except more misery. I thought, *I'm in quicksand.*

I cried every day and prayed to God as well as every Japanese spirit I knew. Finally, I thought about ending my meaningless existence. I dreaded the monotonous days and death-like nightmares with soldiers chasing me while my legs turned to rubber. Quickly, the line between dreams and realty faded. I became exasperated and mentally sank deeper into darkness.

This torture was unlike anything I experienced before. In the Minidoka, Idaho War Relocation camp where we were incarcerated during WWII, I had two babies and a miscarriage. But I recovered quickly. In 1948, I had a hysterectomy and everything turned out fine. But this was different. My body ached and my mind was jumbled.

As a distraction I scanned the bedroom: torn wallpaper, worn linoleum floor, steamer trunk stack and brown roll-up blinds. The sunlight bled through the white laced curtains and cast strange shadows on the wall. It was then I realized, *I might as well be dead.*

Suicide was something Japanese did to solve problems. *Why not?* I pondered. *I'm a useless burden. The children will miss me but they'll survive like some of my cousins after the atomic bombing of Hiroshima. At least Kiyoshi and his mother could raise the boys.*

I wondered, *what would be best: pills or a kitchen blade?*

Finally, I decided, *I will use a pair of scissors,* I thought. After I made up my mind, Kiyoshi remarked that he hadn't seen me so cheerful in a long time.

In an instant, Yoko, Kiyoshi's sister, appeared at my door. She brought some fiddlehead ferns. "I preserved these last year," she said.

Yoko was a slender woman who moved like a ballet dancer. Her premature white hair fell to her shoulders. When she approached, I could feel my neck hairs tingle. She had strange abilities to communicate with the dead. Routinely after relatives passed, the family waited for word from Yoko. Within days, she had visions. Usually the dead told her that they were well and not to worry. I imagined contacting Yoko after I passed so my children, Larry and Alan would know I was okay. I thought, *since the boys were Presbyterians like me, I will see them in Christian heaven along with the baby I lost in camp.*

Yoko drew closer and gave me a sideways glance. She raised her eyebrows. I felt her warm breath. She placed her face directly in front of me and asked, "Are you planning suicide?" Even though I knew she had powers, the question startled me. It brought me into the moment. *How does she know?* I wondered.

I hesitated and then nodded. She put down the jars and rushed out of the room. I could hear her arguing with Kiyoshi. Finally, he phoned Dr. Johnson's office.

Yoko reappeared. She examined the surroundings and opened the closet door. Coat hangers screeched across the bar as she pushed them aside.

"Do you have a bathrobe?" She asked.

"Yes, that terrycloth there," I replied and pointed.

"How about slippers?" she continued.

"No, I wear Kiyoshi's socks," I responded.

Yoko had a look that was part disgust and part exasperation. "Never mind," she said as she pulled my suitcase from under the bed and began packing. She grabbed my make-up kit, bathrobe, and underclothes.

"What're you doing? I'm not going anywhere," I insisted.

"Kiyoshi is taking you to a hospital, so get dressed," she snapped.

"No," I said, holding tight to the bed frame, "I want to stay here! I don't want to leave. I just left the hospital."

Yoko replied sternly, "It will only be for a few days." She sat me up and lifted me to my feet.

"Easy, take it easy. Wait a minute!" I said. "Who's going to tell my best friend, Kiku, and people at work where I went?" I asked.

"Never mind," she replied.

WESTERN STATE HOSPITAL ARRIVAL

Rain splattered our 1949 Chevy on the trip from Seattle to Steilacoom. I remembered Highway 99 was the same road Kiyoshi and I took to Copalis Beach on our honeymoon before the war. This time he hardly said a word. Instead, windshield wipers scrubbed and chattered all the way. My body was tired but my mind was like a camera. Outside neon signs blinked red as we splashed through puddles near pawn shops, used car lots, and burger joints. I swiped a clear streak in the foggy glass. Big John's outdoor produce market with wooden crate displays emerged. *That stand looks just like Sumida's at the Pike Place Market where I worked before the war*, I thought. Kiyoshi grumbled about traffic all the way to Steilacoom. He growled after hitting another chuckhole. "Stupids! What's the matter, can't they take better care of this highway?" he barked.

After two hours on the road, we swerved into the turnaround next to the main Western State Hospital building.

"Wake up!" I said to my legs. I flexed my knees and rubbed them to increase the circulation. I cranked the window down and slumped as we approached the main building. I heard hubcaps scraping against the curb. Kiyoshi set the handbrake and swung the door open. He draped his arm over my neck and half lifted me up the stairs, one step at a time.

I must look like a hundred-year-old woman, I thought. When Kiyoshi opened the lobby door, a gust of heavy air rushed out.

"Smells bad," he muttered under his breath.

Inside the reception area, a lumpy corduroy couch sat next to a floor lamp. Magazines overflowed from the wooden rack near a row of stuffed leather chairs lined against the wall. In the center was a teller's cage atop a long Formica counter.

Kiyoshi sat me down. "You'll be okay. Take it easy," he said.

He approached the elderly receptionist. "Good morning," she said as she put down her ivory colored coffee mug and peered over her wire-rimmed glasses. Her gray hair was tied in a bun, a look which complemented her starched blouse.

"I brought the papers from Dr. Johnson in Seattle," Kiyoshi said and then put down my Samsonite suitcase. Wearing baggy khaki pants and a rumpled jacket, he appeared insignificant under the high ceiling. With care, he slid the forms through the slot.

As the clerk examined the documents, Kiyoshi stepped away and peered through the wire mesh windows in the metal double doors. He commented to the clerk, "The halls have copper drains in the center. Why are there so many drains?"

She looked up and said, "I never noticed."

Kiyoshi chewed his lower lip.

I heard the conversation but concentrated on the lobby tile floor designs. Some resembled a scaly creature from a fairy tale, others looked like disconnected Morse code dots and dashes. Patterns emerged and disappeared like optical illusions.

Reviewing the documents, the woman asked, "You're her husband, Kiyoshi?"

He nodded.

The clerk continued, "Hanae is forty-one? Your two children are Alan and Larry, both born in Minidoka, Idaho?"

Kiyoshi blinked, "Yes, that's right."

The metal door swung open with a bang and an orderly pushed a cart through. Kiyoshi craned his neck and looked down the hall. Before the doors shut automatically, I saw a strip of tall wainscoting protecting the lower walls, giving the impression of a long and narrow shower room. The high ceiling was illuminated by widely-spaced incandescent warehouse lights. Steam radiators hissed. I caught a whiff of urine in the air.

Kiyoshi's eyes were downcast when he said to me, "I'm so sorry. I don't have a choice. I can't take care of you alone." He touched my arm and asked, "You okay?"

The clerk date-stamped the papers with a sharp click, "Everything's in order. We'll take good care of her." She picked up her coffee mug and resumed shuffling papers. With a bang of the doors, a burly orderly appeared with a wheelchair. I looked at Kiyoshi and my mind slipped into a fog.

"*Gambare*, be strong," he said as he touched my shoulder. I forced a smile.

THE VISIT

The weeks passed and I improved physically and mentally. The doctors said I was well enough to have visitors, so I phoned Kiyoshi. Finally, the day arrived. Birds were chirping and the air was fresh. I paced the walkway and craned my neck. With butterflies in my stomach, I waited at the turnaround. Sunshine peeked through the clouds when Kiyoshi arrived with Larry. As the car approached, I waved.

Kiyoshi's jaw dropped. He said, "You've lost a lot of weight! Your arms look like sticks poking out of your short sleeves."

"About ten pounds," I replied and embraced him. He stiffened at my touch and Larry backed away since I'd changed so much.

I managed a shaky smile and put my arms around Larry. He recoiled.

I pulled him back and said, "Let's take a look at you. You've grown an inch." I mussed his hair. "Oh, by the way," I continued, "Two nice girls at the hospital liked the pictures of you and Alan. I told them Alan was in California, but they insisted on meeting you."

He frowned and replied, "No thanks."

As if on cue, there was a clatter. Two girls in their Sunday best peeked around the corner and giggled. They were like playful forest sprites wearing fire engine red lipstick. In an instant, they disappeared.

"What was that?" Larry asked.

I chuckled and replied, "That was Franny and Dutch."

"What's a Franny and Dutch?" he continued.

"Just my friends," I said. "They're the ones who want to meet you."

"Ugh," he said. "Those girls are weird. No one dresses like that!"

"They're harmless," I replied and changed the subject. "Oh, I meant to ask, have either of you've been to the Seattle World's Fair?"

Kiyoshi shook his head, "No time," he replied.

Larry's face lit up. "Yeah my friends and I went up the Space Needle, rode the monorail and played games in the Fun Forest," he chirped.

"That's great. Tell me more about the fair later. We're running out of time and I've got so many questions," I replied.

I asked, "How are you two managing? Who cooks and does the wash?"

Larry wiped his brow and said, "Grandma Sachi helps. She's doing a good job."

"That's great," I said, as I thought about how many times I got cross-wise with her.

"Grandma cooks and cleans," Larry said. "But we want you to get well soon. She serves the same thing every day, flank steak and mashed potatoes."

"Larry," I replied, "ask her for Japanese food. She probably thinks you only like American food. She'll do just fine."

"Kiyoshi," I said, "tell her thanks for me."

We walked through the rose garden which was now spindly branches without petals. I was out of step and moved quickly to catch up. Breathing hard, I asked about my best friend, Kiku and Reverend Hori and others at church. Before Kiyoshi could respond, the nurse approached us and said, "Time's up, Hanae."

"So soon?" I blurted. I inhaled and cherished the moment. Then I hugged Kiyoshi and squeezed him tight. His face flushed.

I embraced Larry and put my arm around his shoulder. "Work hard in junior high school," I urged.

"Kiyoshi, I'll get well soon," I declared. "Tell Kiku, I'm fine."

Larry shuffled his feet and said, "Bye, Mom."

Kiyoshi nodded, "See you next week," he said.

On the way to the car, both turned and waved.

I remained on the sidewalk and watched the Chevy drive through the gate. For a moment I gazed at the barren rose garden and tears streamed down my cheeks.

THE SEATTLE WORLD'S FAIR

I headed back to my room and counted steps to occupy my mind. After they left, I felt an overwhelming sense of emptiness. I paced my area and stared at an old *Life Magazine* which featured Century 21, the Seattle World's Fair. The Space Needle filled the full color cover. The celebration energized and sparked pride back home. When the fair opened in April,

I thought it would be better to wait until the crowds had subsided. Now I regretted not attending since I would be here when it closed.

The magazine article read, "After five months into its run, visitors to the fair included the Shah of Iran, Robert Kennedy, former President Nixon, Prince Phillip, the Duke of Edinburgh, Benny Goodman, Johnny Mathis, Nat King Cole, and a host of other famous entertainers. Gracie Hansen's girlie-girlie show on Show Street entitled, 'An Evening in Paradise' was a throwback to Seattle's turbulent past when civic leaders at the turn of the century once boasted about having the world's largest house of prostitution."

I watched the clock hands move and I settled into my daily routine. Western State Hospital was quiet and peaceful with its 1950 small town pace and aura. The three-story brick buildings resembled a college campus with ivy-covered walls. Across the highway were cornfields, fruit orchards, and storage barns that looked like a painting.

I sat on my bed and flipped through the magazine. My legs dangled over the edge and never touched the floor. I felt like a child surrounded by adult furniture. As I slid off the bed, my smock snagged on the rail. I jerked and pulled free and danced on the cold cement. Gingerly I hopped into my blue terry cloth slippers.

"Slippers would be warmer if they were red," I said out loud.

The scent of breakfast drifted into my room. The pungent mist brought flashbacks of my World War II incarceration.

Funny, I thought, *the smell of bacon brings back memories of the Minidoka, Idaho relocation camp.*

The camp breakfast was served from metal tubs heaped full of steaming scrambled eggs and trays stacked with greasy bacon strips. I could almost hear the kitchen pans banging in the mess hall and children playing. I recalled lines of grim faces and residents fending off the dust and sand. Eight thousand people were confined there. There wasn't a day that went by when I didn't think about Minidoka and my miscarriage.

After twenty years, it seemed like yesterday and to this day I still look over my shoulder for fear that we would be taken again. Shopping in downtown Seattle after the war was like being behind enemy lines where danger lurked around every corner. In reoccurring nightmares, armed guards with bayonets marched towards me. Usually I woke before they grabbed me. Once, a dream was so real that I dived out of bed to escape. With a thud, I bounced and rolled on the floor. Kiyoshi woke and asked, "What's going on?"

"Bad dream," I replied. For weeks, I placed extra pillows on the ground in case the dream returned.

In a blink, the bacon smell jarred me back to the present. Inside my room, one concrete wall had grooves that looked like animal claw marks. Near the bed was my wooden nightstand and a four drawer dresser with only a frame and no mirror. It took me weeks to get used to looking at the empty space and not see my reflection. Windows were covered by steel mesh bolted in place. Like the halls, the ceiling was high and the room narrow.

I dropped my face into my hands and remembered how empty I felt before the 1942 evacuation. I cried and cursed President Roosevelt when I packed my silver wedding set and photos of my brother Shintaro, who had died in Hiroshima before the war. I placed the sacred items in apple boxes for storage at the Buddhist Church. I recalled the Baldwin piano I loved to play.

Days before our April 20, 1942 departure, we slept on the bare linoleum in the living room. All the furniture and even the curtains were gone. Grinding truck noises rumbled from the street, and in the darkness, car headlights passed across the living room ceiling. Without furniture, sounds echoed and bounced.

I remembered Dad comforting the family by saying, "*Shikataganai*, it can't be helped." I understood that suffering was a part of the Japanese heritage. But a life of pain was something we had been hoping to avoid in America.

Clutching the wire mesh over the hospital windows, I wondered, *Where did I go wrong?*

CHAPTER TWO

Russell Hotel in Seattle, 1930

As a child, I gazed from my bedroom window. Sometimes I watched the olive drab streetcar churn up Dearborn Street. Its wheels screeched, metal against metal. From my third story perch in the Russell Hotel, I made up stories about the passengers. *Where do they live and where are they going? That one looks like a banker, and she must be a secretary.*

Although I was only four feet four inches tall, I imagined myself as a movie star. Standing erect in front of the full-length mirror, I visualized curls in my long black hair. Then I licked two fingers and swept aside my bangs which cut a straight edge across my forehead. With a sigh I threw my shoulders back and took a deep breath. I raised my eyebrows and rustled my white taffeta dress. My front teeth protruded slightly so I developed a habit of covering my mouth as if to cough or laugh. To strangers, the gesture made me appear sickly or modest.

In the mirror I see a Japanese girl, someone who doesn't want to be sent to Hiroshima, I said to myself as my smile twisted into a frown

I recalled what mother had said. "Too American, must be more Japanese. Need to go to Japan!"

When I turned nine years old, Dad decided I should be educated in Japan and live with my older brother, Shintaro. He was a submarine captain in the Japanese Navy. In pictures he looked like Commodore Perry in a dark uniform with gold buttons. In the photo, he wore a magnificent naval hat shaped like a ship, gold-braided epaulets, and a western-style ceremonial sword.

From the corner of my eyes, I stared at my reflection. The epicanthic slant of eyes, small nose, and front teeth gradually blurred away. My mind played with the fuzzy image until it transformed into shapes and spaces of light between darkness. Hard edges became soft and I refocused. I thought, *I'm a candle, straight and tall with a black wick curled on top.* Amused by the image, I danced like a fairy ready to take flight.

A short straight candle, I thought. Then I wondered, *Am I the only one who can see in this imaginary way?*

I wondered, *What would it be like to live in a real house and not a hotel?* Nevertheless, my room was comfortable and familiar. Dad, Toyojiro Tamura, and mother Toku operated the Russell Hotel, which was a seven-day-a-week responsibility. Mom handled the desk, meals, and maid work with the help of my brothers and me. Depending on the emergency, either one of the boys or Dad would fix leaky pipes or plugged toilets. At night, Dad worked as a janitor at Our House, a Pioneer Square Skid Row dance hall and saloon about a mile away.

Our family occupied four sleeping rooms upstairs; the kitchen and dining room were on the first floor. Next to the lobby was the living area, which adjoined my parents' room. The six boys doubled up in three rooms, but I had my own. *I was hoping for a little sister, someone I could play with. Too many brothers,* I concluded.

I loved my little room with its floral wallpaper and windows with a view. When the wind rose from the southwest, I could smell the sea at low tide. To pass time, I made up a game where I walked the dark hallways. Moving from one light fixture to another, I pretended that I was an actress illuminated by stage lights. I curtsied and bowed deeply to an imaginary audience and raised my right arm, acknowledging their applause.

In my hallway strolls in the mornings, I inhaled the fragrances of breakfast. *The hall is a musical instrument,* I mused. Engulfed in a wave of senses, my feet danced in rhythm. One floorboard moaned low while others squeaked high. Purposely I created an odd symphony as I coaxed pops and creaks from each board.

During my playtime, guests emerged from the darkness under the dangling lights, then faded as their shadows bent. Dust sparkled like fireflies in the sunlight from the hall windows near the staircase.

Meandering the hallway, I wondered, *What is each person doing behind their locked doors?*

Down the hall, music poured from Mr. Yasui's phonograph which played *Honkon no yoru* or Hong Kong Nights with its sad melody. Big band swing music from Chicago by the Benny Goodman seeped from under Mr. Suko's door.

Most mornings, Dad relaxed reading the *Hokubei Times,* lounging in his overstuffed chair. He pulled out his gold pocket watch and cradled it. Patiently, he waited for the Jackson Street train station tower clock bell to confirm the hour.

Aware of the impending plans to send me away, I approached him. For courage, I imagined that I had dimples and ringlets as I knelt on the small rug. In my best childish and modest tone, I asked, "Papa, why must I go to Japan? I like it here in Seattle. All my friends are here."

I took a deep breath. "In Hiroshima I'll be alone without friends. I'll miss Mr. Fujii next door who always shares smoked salmon, and the Japanese guests who tell wonderful stories about Alaska. Sunday I go to the Japanese Presbyterian Church and every day during the week to Japanese school with my very best friend, Kiku. You and Mom speak Japanese so I'm learning here."

I paused and spoke in a very respectful manner, "Anyway, Miss McMann at Bailey School always tells us, "Remember, you're Americans."

I stood straight, laid my hand over my heart and raised my eyes to the ceiling. "Papa," I said, "This is what they taught us." Solemnly I recited the Pledge of Allegiance and smiled, "See, I'm an American."

I folded my hands in prayer and fell to my knees, "So please Papa, please can I stay another year? Pleeeease!"

Dad rose from the chair, which creaked as the cushions whooshed from his weight. He pondered the situation. "My oh my," he said. "The arrangements have been made. Money has been paid. People are expecting you."

He rested his hands on his stomach and slowly drew the pocket watch from his vest. He rubbed the watch between his thumb and forefinger and said, "You must do your duty and obey your parents. That is our way. Never bring shame on the family. Everything you do reflects on our family and every Japanese in the community."

Dad settled back into his chair. "Hanae, your great-great grandfather and family were samurai and retainers of Lord Asano in Hiroshima. For their loyalty, they were granted land in Kakomachi, Hiroshima City, between the Motoyasu and Ohta rivers near a park. You'll stay there with your brother Shintaro and his family."

In America, I thought, *being an individual in the land of liberty, and pursuing happiness was what I learned at school.* I never raised my hand in class to say that duty and family were more important. Besides, I never could have said it in a way that my white classmates would understand.

"Thank you Papa," I said with sadness. My shoulders drooped in resignation knowing that the trip was unavoidable. I realized that I would have to become a real Japanese girl shortly. *At least, when I become an adult, I'll know my cousins in Hiroshima.*

I grasped for a mental lifeline but none appeared. In the movies, a hero on a white horse would save me.

I really don't want to go, I said to myself as Dad continued in a monotone about being descendants of samurai and the importance of duty. But his words were like mosquitos buzzing.

I smiled, until my eyes focused on the spaces between the curtains and on patterns in the linoleum floors. I fidgeted and waited for him to finish. I was a flickering candle as a tsunami gathered strength in the ocean. I wondered, *Will I be swept away completely or will I return as if nothing happened? Papa talks only of my going and never mentions my return.*

So much was left unsaid. I bowed and excused myself. Dad assured me, "Things will be fine." With those words, I realized the full weight of my predicament and instinctively covered my mouth with both hands to stifle the screams.

Shikataganai–it can't be helped–was the Japanese phrase that echoed in my mind along with *gaman*– endurance. If I was a real American like Miss McMann insisted, I would fight and not be quiet. My conclusion was that Miss McMann, although well-meaning, sadly did not understand "duty" in the Japanese way.

Nevertheless, I did not give in. *There must be a way,* I thought.

I hoped for a miracle and prayed to God, *If I stay in Seattle, I promise to go to church every Sunday. Most of all I don't want to leave my friends and Spotty, my dog.*

Spotty was a thin mutt and a good fellow. Every day after school he peeked from his dog house door to greet me. He met me at the front gate with a tail wag until his whole body shook with enthusiasm. Spotty was the only living thing that I could share my secrets with. But he was unreliable and easily distracted by a squirrel, bird, or mailman opening the gate.

Kiku would know what to do, I thought. Kiku, my childhood companion, was like a fire plug full of bottled energy and ideas. She was a tomboy and often wore double braids and jeans. We decided to seek out Reverend Hori at the Japanese Presbyterian Church for advice. He was a dignified man in a black three-piece suit. His solid personality and Christian demeanor commanded great respect, even among the Buddhist community.

Kiku stood by me when the reverend spoke with great conviction, "My child this is God's plan. You must have faith and remember Jesus died for your sins. So let us pray together, *Our father who art in heaven....*"

For a moment I felt a direct connection with God. *If Reverend Hori can't get my prayers answered, who can?* I bowed and thanked the reverend politely, but a nagging feeling remained.

Standing on the street corner, Kiku looked at me sideways. "Was that helpful?" she asked, twisting her face and tugging her pigtails.

"Not really, he was my last hope," I said. I frowned and continued, "Looks like I'll be leaving for sure. Will you write me when I'm gone?"

Kiku replied, "You mail me first so I'll have your Japan address."

"Will do," I said. "And thanks for coming with me, you're a good friend. Thanks again," I said. I tugged her pigtail when we parted.

KOKESHI

On the way home, storm clouds gathered and a light rain fell. Feeling abandoned, I shuffled down Weller Street. *Why pray if God doesn't give you what you want?* Tears poured down my cheeks. *I could have said the Lord's prayer alone.* The Dearborn streetcar rumbled past as I waited for the light to change. An empty soup can lay near the curb and I kicked it with all my might. It clunked and twirled like a top. Eventually, a logging truck flattened the can with a crunch. I stared at the mangled remains knowing the driver hadn't noticed a thing. *Oh I'm just like that can*, I thought.

Trying to feel grateful for Christ dying my sins, I pondered Reverend Hori's message. *There was a cross with Jesus nailed to it in the church lobby. Blood dripped from wounds staining his twisted body and loin cloth. It must have been painful, but how is that going to help me? Reverend Hori missed the point. I don't care about having my sins forgiven. I just don't want to leave.*

Out of frustration, I said out loud, "I can't think of a real sin I've ever committed; maybe a white lie here or there, a glance at my classmate's paper during a test, or listening in on someone's private conversations." Nothing brought me comfort, and nothing made any sense. But the rain kept falling and my shoes were soaked.

Was I the little lamb in the Bible stories or the foolish man who built his house upon sand as the rains came down? I wondered.

After my visit with the reverend, I resigned myself to my fate. I wondered, *What's the weather like in Japan? Should I pack light or heavy clothes? What about my kokeshi?* It was a 12-inch-long wooden cylindrical doll given to me at birth. She had pursed red lips, thin eyebrows, and red kimono. She contained my spirit, so the custom was to destroy her when I died. I willed my spirit into the doll for safekeeping and visualized my thoughts penetrating the figure. *If I leave her in Seattle, at least part of me will still be here.*

With the "clack" of a hammer, I nailed the *kokeshi* storage box shut and wrote "Property of Hanae" on it. To ensure its safety, I took it to the basement and covered it with a canvas tarp. To the casual observer, it looked like a box left behind by a guest who had departed for Alaska.

Out loud I said to the *kokeshi*, "Be safe while I'm away and please guard my spirit."

AT SEA

With one foot in front of the other, I climbed the gangplank of the *Miike Maru* steamship. Shafts of sunlight broke through the clouds over Elliot Bay. The ship rocked gently as the salt water mist mixed with odors of creoste. The hull scrapped the pier's pilings, releasing a milky white cloud of barnacles that floated in the current.

I wiped my eyes and waved goodbye to my mother, father, brothers, Kiku, and friends. Immediately I retreated from the rail and covered my face. *I'll always remember Seattle.* The ship's horn sounded with a deep bellow. I yelled above the noise to everyone, "I'll be back soon." I cradled an armload of gifts and souvenirs for Hiroshima relatives and clutched a small box of smoked salmon cans so tight that my knuckles turned white.

I squeezed my purse to make sure that my cash was safe. The small money was a comfort, an excuse to splurge when I get to Japan.

Paper streamers fluttered from the deck. I thought, *They are my last connection to home.* The ship pulled away and the wind whipped the streamers loose to float on the green waters.

The *Miike Maru*'s horn blasted again and the ship picked up speed. With great care, the tugs maneuvered the ship into the choppy waters of Elliott Bay. The smokestack belched a plume and the captain sounded the horn. The ship turned west towards the Olympic Mountains, past Bainbridge Island, towards the open ocean. The Smith Tower near Pioneer Square grew smaller. I felt adrift, even though I hoped to stay positive on this journey. I sobbed, "Dear God, help me, please." I leaned against the rail and faced the wind.

Walking to the passenger deck, I blew my nose and opened the cabin door. Mrs. Numoto, a long-time family friend was my companion on the trip. She bowed and greeted me with a smile. She was a small, pleasant woman. But it didn't take long for me to discover that her size belied her ability to produce thunderous snores in her sleep. At night gulping inhalations accompanied the ship's upward motions and loud exhalations followed the descent. There was not a moment when things were motionless or silent. The two-week trip became a blur while the ship rocked up and down and side to side.

Nauseated from the motion and exhaust fumes, I felt like I was living in a stagnant pond, searching for a trickle of fresh water and relief. During the day I leaned over the rail and at night rocked in my bunk. I was unsure as to whether I slept or just passed out between meals. My skin turned a light green and I wondered, *Will I ever feel normal again?*

"Eat this," Mrs. Numoto said. She handed me a piece of dried Chinese ginger. "It will help." I sucked the salty morsel, chewed the stringy brown strands, and swallowed the fibers. Between the fumes and rocking, there was no relief. Periodically I felt better, thinking, *Ginger really works until it doesn't.* In the mirror I saw a thin girl with pale skin and black hair who could be mistaken for a sick dog. Like a volcano, my stomach revolted. Spasms exploded with coughs and gags at all hours. This was how I recall the trip: an inescapable teeter-totter, mercilessly slamming up and down.

CHAPTER THREE

Hiroshima, 1930

My heart fluttered when the Hiroshima skyline came into view. Anxious to be on solid ground, I scurried and grabbed my suitcase. The ship glided to the pier and bobbed while the crew secured the thick ropes. I rushed and almost danced down the gangplank until my shoes slipped and I skidded into Mrs. Numoto.

I looked up and saw a city teeming with energy. It was like a carnival of rickshaws, women in kimonos, horns honking, food carts, stores, and workers hauling products. My legs were wobbly. It felt like Hiroshima was spinning. I thought, *Every sign is in Japanese! Why am I shocked that I can't read a word?*

Japanese flags whipped in the wind while people in western suits, navy uniforms, kimonos, and traditional garb scurried. Nevertheless, I felt some comfort from the familiar odors of the sea and creosote.

Oh my, I thought, *I never expected all of this confusion squeezed into a tight space with so many people who all look like me.*

Thank goodness, the ground is steady, I mused. But my legs remembered the trip and wobbled. I looked down and made sure my feet were still under me. Instinctively, I had taken on a bow-legged stride. *Not very lady-like* I thought.

Masa, Shintaro's housekeeper, waved and greeted Mrs. Numoto and me. She bowed deeply, "Welcome back Mrs. Numoto. Hanae, welcome to your new home."

Disoriented and exhausted, I caught my breath. As an afterthought, I returned a bow to Masa. Quickly Masa and I weaved through the crowd and headed for the luggage claim area. Masa chattered endlessly but her words were drowned out by street noise. I gathered my bags and emerged in the sunlight. It was so bright that I had to raise my hand to block the glare. The noise engulfed me in an atmosphere full of screeches, honking, and hollering. I rubbed my eyes. My goodness, I thought, what a lively place.

A weathered rickshaw bounced up to us. *Looks like an oversized toy*, I thought. *Will it actually take us home?*

The driver wore a straw coolie hat, brown knickers, high socks and straw sandals. He bowed and lifted the luggage with a grunt. Masa dusted off the seat and we climbed aboard. Mrs. Numoto bowed and said, "Good luck Hanae, study hard and make your parents proud."

"Thank you for everything, I'll miss you," I replied. The rickshaw lurched up the cobblestone street in rhythm to the sound of sandals slapping stone. Looking back at the station, I raised my arm and waved again to Mrs. Numoto. My teeth chattered when we hit countless ruts and potholes.

Finally, we reached Shintaro's house. It was Japanese construction with sliding shoji screens, straw tatami mats, and a locking front gate. The home was perched on a slight hill near a park between two rivers in Hiroshima City. As the eldest son, Shintaro remained in Japan while the rest of the family settled in America. Dad always planned to return when he retired.

Shintaro was married, but his young wife Fumi and baby, Ichiro, were with Fumi's ailing mother in Fukushima. Being alone and serving in the navy, he couldn't maintain the house. So Dad had hired Masa as Shintaro's live-in housekeeper. She was an older woman, a distant relative and recent widow. Masa had no children and no skills other than housework. If she were left on her own, she would have been relegated to menial service or part-time factory work.

Because of the hard economic times and poor crops, many Japanese farmers were suffering. Some starved and others sold their children as servants. Masa mentioned how lucky she was to have a comfortable home and a decent life.

Her daily dress was Japanese garb—a heavy, dark blue kimono that extended to her feet, and *getas*, the traditional wooden clogs. When she did yard work, she wore an apron and corduroy pants tucked into her boots. For a splash of color, she tied on a yellow scarf, and sometimes an orange scarf while doing housework. She was four feet eight inches tall and slightly overweight with thick legs and thighs. Masa was happy and exuded a cheerful aura. When she smiled, a large gap between her two front teeth appeared.

When Masa did her chores, the house took on a comfortable atmosphere. She cooked with joy and happily shared her secret recipes. *Soba* or buckwheat noodles served in broth was her favorite. She made the dough from scratch and had me roll it flat. With a crispness in her voice, she said, "Be sure the knife is sharp."

The flaccid noodles were draped over a wooden rack to dry and dusted with flour. Masa hummed a quiet melody when she sliced irregular widths purposely. She claimed the variation added extra flavor.

"Factory noodles are not interesting," she insisted. "They do not taste good in your mouth," she continued, smacking her lips. "I'll teach you how to slurp them. Noisy is the Japanese way," she said. Masa pursed her lips and sucked noodles strands held in her chopsticks. The slick sound ended with a small pop. She continued, "Then you take the bowl in your hands and drink the soup."

I chuckled, "Really, is that the way?" I caught on quickly and in a short time both of us were slurping happily, like a couple of cats drinking milk.

I learned other secrets, and extended the cutting technique to fruits and vegetables. Masa also believed that chopsticks and wooden spoons were best for cooking and eating. "Forks and spoons give a metal taste," she said.

Masa's greatest joy, however, was going to the local *sento* (public bathhouse) in the evening. There she met friends and gossiped about the day's events. "We'll go to the *sento* today after dinner," she said with delight.

"Oh boy! This will be something new!" I replied. When we arrived, the reality struck me. I chewed my lower lip and scanned the lobby. I was uncomfortable with the worn wooden furniture and tired looking reception area. There was a musty smell that hung heavy like fog. Over the years, the humidity had peeled the paint and the windows had a permanent haze.

The air was thick with a sweet tinge of incense smoldering at the Shinto shrine. I thought, *I hope there will be individual tubs and curtains.*

Masa stepped up to the counter and pushed two coins to the old woman. The right hand door was for men; the other for women. Each was marked clearly with the appropriate *kanji* or character. Since I couldn't read Japanese, I studied the women's sign so as not to make a mistake and walk into the men's room next time. I grew anxious and my stomach ached fearing what would be next.

"Do we go in here?" I asked pointing to the thick wooden doors.

Behind the changing area was a locker room. There were benches, storage cubbies, and metal hanger hooks. Tile covered the floors and wooden buckets were stacked in the corner. My mouth dropped when I scanned the large open space. *I was expecting privacy*, I thought. *I don't want to do this! I want to run away.*

Almost on the verge of panic, I gasped for air. I chewed my finger nails and worried, *How can I get outta here?*

Masa chided, "Hurry, get undressed and hang your clothes. Shoes go in the locker."

I surveyed the steamy area and there was a woman perched on a wooden stool scrubbing herself. *Oh my*, I thought, *I'm supposed to do that?*

I was amazed at the woman's wrinkles and sagging skin, especially how large and tired her ripe pear-like breasts looked. I stared at the drooping flesh and wondered, *Will I look like that when I get old?*

Without clothes, Masa appeared like a different person. For a moment, I couldn't turn my eyes away. Copying her, I undressed quickly and scrubbed. The feel of my naked buttocks on the cold wooden seat was a shock. I washed and rinsed as the three-legged stool wobbled with each splash.

I can't hide a thing, I thought. In response, I hunched and slipped into a dark corner for cover. *I'm glad the woman is not paying attention.*

I felt ashamed since the Japanese Presbyterian Sunday school teachers taught modesty. Public nudity would have been scandalous.

After scrubbing with a small white wash cloth, I was about to hang it up but Masa said, "Wring out your towel like this."

I twisted it tight and thought, *Oh, this wasn't that bad. Now that I'm clean, I can get dressed.*

Then Masa raised her hand and motioned me to enter another area. It was a steamy room with a swimming pool sized tub. I held the cloth to cover what I could of my body and stepped gingerly on the cool floor into the fog. I pulled my wet hair over my face and watched Masa climb into the steaming pool. The women moved aside and greeted her politely with a nod and smile. She put the towel on her head and migrated to a place where she could sit neck deep. Perspiration dripped off her nose.

I shuffled to an opening at the pool's edge and dipped my right toe.

I hollered, "Wow, owee" and immediately covered my mouth with my hand.

The women swiveled towards my direction, thinking something was amiss. They saw nothing unusual and resumed their quiet conversations. I could hear them clearly although I could not understand everything they said.

"This is Hanae, Shintaro's younger sister from America," Masa said. "She will be going to school here." The women nodded. I managed a tight smile.

Sweat beaded on my upper lip as I navigated the tub and found a cool spot. I hopped and sloshed until I was mostly submerged. I felt less anxious when the water was neck deep. But the heat made my skin feel like a thousand ants crawling. I visualized jumping out and lying down on the cool concrete.

Then it occurred to me, *Oh, maybe, this is punishment for a past sin. Tonight I must pray for being naked in front of strangers.*

Finally, I realized that *If I am to live here, I must do this every day. I don't think I can.*

I draped the washcloth over my head and bobbed to a corner. All my inhibitions and modesty fled as I concentrated on surviving. But the heat caused my consciousness to float, moving higher and higher until I seemed to glide away. My eyes grew heavy. *I'm getting sleepy,* I thought.

Male voices on the other side of the wall startled me. I heard men arguing and singing. I shook my head in amazement.

What's next? I can't imagine naked men singing in a tub. I couldn't believe Dad did this in Seattle, although he must have.

I closed my eyes when the initial shock subsided. *Next time will be better,* I pondered, *but I could never tell Kiku about being naked in front of strangers with men nearby.*

As weeks passed, the granite tubs and shabby *sento* became a daily ritual. I learned to enjoy the hot water, steam, and chatter. The experience drained my troubles and pains. Gradually, I looked forward to the musty and humid atmosphere. Old women with wrinkled bodies became familiar and no longer evoked a second glance from me. Out of shyness, I never spoke much and stayed half-submerged most of the time. I listened to gossip about children who misbehaved and how some merchants were dishonorable. When a person did something wrong, people were quick to talk. I vowed to be on my best behavior lest I bring shame on Masa and Shintaro.

Masa's other pleasures were her pet *koi.* The green pond with multi-colored carp occupied a space near the teahouse. Like a painting in motion, orange and white spotted fish cruised through the submerged vegetation. To my surprise, they raised their heads and approached Masa, all except the silver one. In the murky water, he looked like a shimmering white ghost, a metallic apparition. It had a shiny aura, large body scales, a massive head, pop eyes, nostril flaps, and large mouth. It was aloof and special. *Yurei,* the Japanese word for ghost fitted this dim soul. Imitating Masa, I called the *koi*. But the silver one turned and avoided my outstretched hand.

Because of her caring manner, I called Masa "grandmother." She smiled, revealing the gap between her front teeth. As our relationship grew, Masa nicknamed me *"chibi"* which was an affectionate term for a small child. That made me think of my real mother, which brought sadness.

Back in Seattle, when Mom's chores were done, she told Japanese fairy tales. My favorite was *Hana Saka Jiisan*, which was about an elderly man who loved his dog dearly. An evil neighbor killed it and buried it under a tree. Even though justice was served in the end, I was always emotional, no matter how many times I heard the tale. I couldn't bear for any creature to be killed, especially a faithful dog. Whenever I felt homesick, I asked Masa to tell a fairy tale.

"Hana Saka Jiisan," I begged. The moral of the story involved *bachi* which was like karma. When a person did something bad, they would be punished by the universe. In the story, the mean person met his fate, through circumstances and his own undoing.

Mom and Masa also taught me *haji*, or shame. "One must never do wrong and bring shame on oneself because it stains the family and ancestors," instructed Masa. Big shame required suicide as the only acceptable solution. It was important to practice *gaman*, a samurai value, meaning to "endure." My mother and Masa spoke of these values so that I would never bring shame on the house.

I remembered Mom's lessons when I started school at Honkawa Elementary School nearby. It was a three story concrete building built in 1928 and very modern.

On the first day of school, I primped in front of the mirror and was excited to meet new friends. *I look great in my black and white uniform. It makes me want to march to school like a soldier,* I thought. *If only my front teeth didn't stick out, I would be happy,* I mused.

Masa sent me off and said, "Work hard and make us proud."

I bowed and headed out. The air was crisp and the birds were singing. A crow perched on the neighbor's roof and "cawed" a greeting. The school was surrounded by a fence and a line of trees. I could hear children playing.

Twenty teachers, a principal, and many staff served 800 students. The hall floors were shiny and the walls were spotless. The classrooms were neat and tidy. Like the furniture and clean blackboards, the students were expected to be orderly and immaculate. On the first day, I shared a desk with Michi Ando. She was a bright girl, full of enthusiasm. Her eyes sparkled when she greeted me with, "Good morning."

I lit up, "Good morning, my name is Hanae." Then I covered my mouth.

Michi nodded and smiled politely.

Mrs. Shiga, the teacher, called roll and announced that we would be assigned permanent seats tomorrow.

I hoped that I could sit with Michi. But chances were slim since we would be assigned in alphabetical order. I craned my neck and examined the well-scrubbed faces around me. *Who will be my desk mate?* I wondered.

As a new arrival, I felt awkward and was careful not embarrass myself. Unfortunately, back in Seattle, Mom mixed English into her Japanese conversations. At times I was confused about which words were English and which were Japanese. As a result, I was hesitant to speak. I was afraid of being made fun of by other children who spoke perfect Japanese. That would bring shame on me and my relatives.

In my black skirt, white blouse, and school girl uniform, I thought, *I look like a Japanese student.* But everyone noticed my American gait. To them I was a *gaijin* or foreigner. My classmates saw me as different and were afraid. Behind my back I heard them whisper, *"Gaijin ne."* The words pierced my heart. I cried on the way home. I wanted to kick something out of anger since I couldn't figure out how not to be a *gaijin*.

After school, I studied my daily *kanji* lessons and did chores. *Maybe doing work will help me become more Japanese*, I thought. I lit the charcoal fire, swept the tatami mats, washed clothes, cleaned the screens, and helped Masa with the cooking. Although I missed my family in Seattle, the daily routines distracted my mind. *The scent of incense reminds me of mother praying before the family shrine. How I miss her and everyone back home.* I blinked and shook my head, mentally pushing the sadness away.

Gradually Hiroshima life fell into natural rhythms. The seasons turned with clear demarcations: cold winters and snow-capped mountains; warm springs with cherry blossoms; humid summer days and muggy nights; and then fall, when deciduous trees turned red and released their leaves to flutter and scatter across the walkways. More and more the thoughts of mother and family faded as summer turned to fall and the years passed. *Seattle seems so far away, I thought. I wonder if my friends even remember me? I'll be eleven next year. Oh I need to write Kiku before she forgets me.*

I took a deep breath and let those worries fly away. I thought about Shintaro's return and how it was always a celebration. His submarine took him to Russia, China and Hawaii. On a trip to Seattle, as part of a goodwill mission, he visited Mom and Dad. Shintaro was familiar with the United States, its people and culture. He had studied at the Japanese Naval Academy and taught himself how to read English. His unique background and skills helped him become a captain. Unusually tall for a Japanese and handsome as well, he had jet-black hair, deep-set eyes, and a high-bridged nose. Some people actually thought he was part Caucasian. But his manner was without a doubt Japanese. His commanding presence and ramrod posture demanded respect.

He was descended from samurai, a man to be feared. So any thoughts or remarks about his western facial appearance were never mentioned. Above all, no one ever called him *gaijin*.

As my eleventh birthday approached, my special duty was to prepare crab for dinner. The meat was fragrant and smelled like the sea. The claws and spikes presented a hazard. Pulling every last dollop from the crab was a task I enjoyed. "With these fingers I'll pick it clean," I said out loud. "Masa will be proud of my beautiful crabmeat." Instinctively I knew how to work the picks and mine the chunks like gold.

I understood the value of food. There was an old saying that *Kamisama* or spirits would punish anyone who wasted it and would send dust to lodge in the person's eye.

After his naval career was established, Shintaro asked his wife Fumi and his son to return since her mother was now fully recovered. Fumi was *yasashii*, or very mild and polite in manner. She dressed in a kimono and spoke softly. She was the epitome of femininity and moved effortlessly like a dancer.

When she and her son, Ichiro arrived, Masa's duties increased. Gradually conflicts arose because Fumi began to resent my presence. It was difficult for me to live with her criticisms which she delivered in a quiet and underhanded manner. Her beauty generated credibility. Few disagreed with someone so cultured and attractive. "You must be more graceful," Fumi said to me. "Your clumsiness brings shame on the family."

I thought, *I must improve so they do not gossip about me at the sento. That would humiliate Masa.*

Taking Fumi's words to heart, I worked hard studying and in class I finally answered a question correctly. I was happy and proud. On the streetcar home, I thought, *I'll tell Masa how well I did today.* I unlocked the gate and called for Masa. But there was no answer. I rushed to my room and took off my black and white school outfit. Changing into my everyday clothes, I hummed a happy tune and thought, *In Seattle, Kiku would be fast asleep at this hour.*

Outside I heard strange noises and moans echoing. *This is unusual. What is it?* I searched the rooms to locate the source. Then I heard it coming from the teahouse. I thought, *It might be a ghost or garden spirit.*

Excited, I ran outside and fell awkwardly. It seemed like I twisted and turned in mid-air for minutes. My arm caught a potted bonsai plant on the way down. The ceramic container spilled dirt and cracked wide open, pouring dirt on the grass. *Oh no,* I thought. *I'll get in trouble.* I picked up shards and swept the dirt with my hands. *How can I put this back together so no one will notice?*

After the loud crash, a disheveled Fumi appeared like a ghost. A man's shadow flashed behind her. Fumi's hair was uncharacteristically mussed and her eyes were blood shot. She took a deep breath and glanced back at the teahouse and straightened her kimono.

"What are you doing here, sneaking around?" she demanded. "Never bother me again when I am praying in the teahouse!"

Surprised by her sharp remarks, I replied, "I'm sorry...I thought I heard something. I'm sorry I broke the pot."

I thought of mentioning the shadow because Shintaro was at sea but my mouth felt like cotton. I turned my eyes away. My shoulders crumpled and I stared at the ground. I knew that I had done something wrong, but was too confused to say anything more than "sorry."

Fumi fussed with her kimono and straightened it with a sharp tug. Her face tightened and her eyebrows rose with a hateful look.

"You saw nothing. Understand?" Fumi said. "If you ever sneak around the teahouse again, I will punish you and burn you with incense. I forbid you to go near the teahouse. I don't care what you think you heard. You saw nothing, do you understand?"

I hung my head and lowered my eyes, "*Wakarimasu,* I understand." I trembled and chills ran up my arms. My legs were shaking. My face drooped as I shuffled back to the house. I thought, *Maybe she is right that I am stupid and clumsy.* For days my body held the tension from the encounter. Even the *sento* could not relax my rock hard muscles. I wished I could return to Seattle, or better yet, that Fumi would leave.

For the time being I must stay out of Fumi's way, I thought. Like Cinderella, I tolerated Fumi's demands and criticisms, which grew worse by the day. I remained silent and followed directions scrupulously, even though I felt vulnerable.

Am I a gaijin servant here? I wondered. *That's not why I left Seattle!*

Shintaro was busy and disregarded the growing tension. When he was home, it seemed as though his thoughts were hundreds of feet deep under the ocean. In addition, he developed stomach pains which caused him to visit the doctor.

Masa tried to comfort me but she would never challenge the woman of the house. There was nothing she could do to change Fumi's attitude.

Fumi complained about how poorly I performed chores. "You never slice vegetables thin enough." I cut the greens into irregular sizes as Masa had taught me. But Fumi wanted them cut uniformly and disliked my indelicate approach.

"Your soup broth is too sweet and the onions too strong," she continued. "You aren't special like Shintaro thinks you are. You've a lot to learn."

I bowed politely and picked up a dishrag and walked to the sink. I gritted my teeth.

She came up beside me. "You talk too loud and do not laugh like a Japanese," Fumi chided. "You're not graceful and you play baseball with the boys."

I bowed and replied, "I'll try to be better."

Fumi seemed satisfied and said, "You are such a burden. Why do I put up with you?"

I hung my head and stared at the ground.

Masa appeared and placed her hand on my shoulder. "Remember your ancestors were samurai." There was a kindness in her voice. She continued, We'll pass the sweet shop today on the way to the *sento* and get a treat.

I wiped my eyes and replied, "Thank you, Masa. That would be wonderful."

MOXA

Compared to other girls my age, I was a country bumpkin. To Fumi I was worse. She preferred quiet times and flower arranging. Often, she apologized to her guests, "Please excuse Hanae's cloddish manners." She claimed that I was not a real Japanese, but an American in disguise. Fumi justified her remarks by telling me, "It's for our own good."

The teahouse incident was fresh in both our minds even though nothing was ever discussed. Fumi did, however, remark to a disinterested Shintaro, "Sometimes I have to chase noisy squirrels when I meditate and pray alone in the teahouse." I picked up on the word "alone" since she knew there was a man with her and it was not Shintaro.

On one especially hot summer day, Fumi inspected the tatami mats. "Look at this dust!" she exclaimed.

"Come here and suffer your punishment for being lazy," Fumi said. She twisted my arm and sat me down. Carefully she pinched fluffy *moxa* (dried mugwort) material and formed a small pyramid. She placed it on my index finger and lit it. The material flamed up and raised a small sore.

I tightened my jaws and held back a groan. I refused to cry when I smelled my flesh burn. Mentally I screamed, *Owee.* The pain was intense. It sent my spirit straight to the *kokeshi* doll in Seattle. The punishment was not unusual in Japan but I knew it was not deserved. I clenched my fists and withstood the pain.

After, I soaked my finger in cold water. I was silent but thought about revenge. I prayed the burn mark wouldn't last. This was the first time and last time, I hoped. After all who would want to marry a woman with scars all over her fingers?

If I continued to misbehave, the burns would be like those on a tally stick that showed how bad I was. To hide my shame, I placed my thumb in such a way that the mark was not visible. Shintaro noticed and asked, "What is this?" He was visibly upset, and without further discussion Fumi stopped the punishment.

Nevertheless, she voiced other complaints. Regularly she mocked my dark skin and threatened to hit me with the ivory shamisen strummer. So I resolved to protect myself from the sun. I thought, *I'll carry my red umbrella and wear long sleeves in the spring and summer.*

If it wasn't my skin color, then it was the length of my neck. By most standards, my neck was average as was my complexion. But I didn't argue and wore scarves to de-emphasize the size of my offending neck. Clenching my fists each morning, I checked to see if my neck had grown overnight. *How many more meaningless things will I have to do to please Fumi?* I wondered.

In Seattle, my six brothers occupied much of my parents' time and energy. Consequently, I could run free. But in Hiroshima, Fumi paid close attention to me and her son. Regularly she bragged, "When Ichiro was born, he would never cry but just whimpered when he was wet. I trained him well."

As soon as Ichiro could understand, she would say, "I'll give you away if you don't do better." Routinely she complained in front her friends and offered to give him away as punishment. They understood the ruse and accepted her offer. After they opened their arms, Ichiro rushed to his mother. "I'll be good," he cried, "Don't give me away!" I was appalled. *I'll never use such a cruel trick on my children when I become a mother.*

Observing Fumi, I saw my place in a different light. I concluded that she would never play the same abandonment trick on me. When she made a move, it would not be an idle threat. This thought sent a cold shiver through my body. I lurched and gasped a small breath.

At night I prayed, "God, please help me and give me strength." I sniffled and curled up on the futon. *What can I do to please Fumi?* I wondered.

Hard as I tried, I could do nothing right, and feared even the simplest task like holding a tea cup properly. I worried, *What will become of me if I can't improve? There is no hope. My only choice is to endure.*

I realized that I was not Japanese like Fumi and in Seattle I was not an American like the white schoolchildren. Each day was a challenge. In response to my obvious unhappiness, Masa gave me a special sweet bean cake treat. She said, "The sweetness will take away the bitter."

The friction at home increased and then another incident occurred. On the Thursday streetcar ride to school, a very plain-looking woman smiled and stared at me. I turned, and looked over my shoulder to make sure it was not a mistake. *Maybe she knows me from the sento,* I thought. After a careful examination, I still did not recognize her.

She wore an orange kimono and a red comb in her hair. I got dizzy from the scent of her perfume which hung over me. She smiled and slipped into the seat across from me. I nodded politely and looked away and scooted over. *I should change seats,* I thought. *I'm not comfortable next to this stranger.* Avoiding direct eye contact, I looked down and studied the woman's *geta* sandals as the streetcar bumped and screeched to a stop.

Gathering my books, I bowed slightly and exited. I hit the ground and thought, *This is very strange. Nothing like this has ever happened to me. In Seattle, sometimes white people stared with harsh looks. But this is different.*

After the school dismissal bell rang, I gathered my homework. The other children shuffled out as usual. Realizing the day had passed uneventfully, I took a deep breath and relaxed my shoulders. Briskly walking to the streetcar stop, I thought, I'm happy that woman is not here. Back home I walked up the stairs and unlocked the gate. When the lock clicked behind me, I felt a sense of security and protection.

Masa hummed a tune and stirred tofu in a broth. I smiled and announced, "I'm back." She said, "Welcome home" and continued to stir.

I moved closer. "Something strange happened today. There was this woman on the streetcar," I said. "She sat next to me. I became uncomfortable and it was very weird. I was glad she wasn't on the afternoon streetcar."

Masa didn't look up as she chopped *nappa* with a clack-clack on the cutting board. She raised her glance and asked, "What did the woman look like?"

"She wore an orange kimono and was neat and tidy," I responded. "She was about Fumi's height, weight, and age. Also she wore heavy perfume." The description was useless since it described so many women.

Masa lowered her head and continued chopping. "Never mind," she said as she poured water into a kettle. "Sounds like nothing."

"No, no," I said insistently, "this was very unusual. I wasn't scared but annoyed."

Masa put the kettle on the stove and straightened her apron with a tug. "Okay, on Saturday we'll go to the temple and ask a psychic. When I have questions, I do that," Masa said. "But I'm sure it's nothing."

On Saturday, we caught the streetcar to the temple. In an instant, I visualized the strange woman I'd met a few days earlier. I watched the buildings pass until we climbed a small hill near our destination. We shuffled up a gravel path lined by tall trees. Women selling tea and incense were in booths along the road to the shrine. Before we reached the stairs near the large cast iron bell, Masa said, "There's a fortune teller. We'll ask her."

The female psychic sat cross-legged on a straw cushion. She looked like a beggar with matted gray hair that matched her faded kimono. Masa said to me, "Sit down, please." I knelt on a cushion and Masa dropped two coins that clinked in the bowl. Masa stood behind me and asked, "Please tell us what the future holds for this young girl."

The psychic opened her cloudy eyes and stared. She examined me up and down. "Say something," she cackled. "I want to hear your voice."

I gasped and made a sound barely louder than a whisper. I gulped and cleared my throat, "My name is Hanae and I'm from America."

The old woman lurched and moved her arms sideways. She gave me a long glance and squinted. Then she pushed her stringy hair away from her face and struck the singing bowl. The sound pierced the air and faded into a thin, thread-like ring. With her thumb and index finger, she plucked a piece of incense and lit a small stick. By her jerky movements, she seemed blind. She looked up and grasped at the air as if she was catching flies circling overhead.

"I see war. Your parents will be in a hot and desolate place. Razor points at intervals will confine thousands. A gourd of death will tumble from Hiroshima blue skies. In Japan, glass shards will explode, flesh will burn and the air will be poison. Victors will toss chocolate to orphans. Your outstretched palm will catch nothing. Ushinawareta mono wa, ni do to modoranai. That which is lost, will never return."

Masa exclaimed, *"Nani?* What?" She stood up and grimaced. She was visibly upset and angry. She grabbed my arm with such force that it popped.

"Wow, ow, that hurts," I responded.

"This wasn't a fortune, *dame desu,* just no good." Masa continued, "We need to go home. She told us nothing. Such a bad idea. Never again. Such a bad idea."

Masa's strength was amazing. With ease, she pulled me down the gravel path like a reluctant dog on a leash. Before we left the temple grounds, I heard the psychic:

You'll save two lives but you must dance.

I stumbled and fell. My hands skidded against the sidewalk and were pocked with small rocks embedded in my palm. In shock, I stared at the red spots and indentations as the words of the psychic echoed.

I worried about what would happen to Shintaro if war broke out. He said China or Russia could attack Japan. I thought about my parents being confined. *What does saving lives and dance mean?* I felt like there was an avalanche traveling 100 miles per hour nipping at my heels. What next? I wondered.

The moment was too much. Holding back my emotions, I said out loud, "I want to go home. Masa, I want to go home." But I really didn't know what that meant anymore.

THE KEY

Everything was back to normal the next day. Helping Masa in the kitchen, I cleaned fresh squid and sliced the tentacles. Carefully, I removed the ink sacks and squeezed out the precious egg clusters and pinched the cellophane-like spine free. Black ink splattered the basin and my face. I wiped an itchy spot with my dry sleeve, since my hands were slimy.

Knowing there would be an inspection by Fumi, I cleaned the counter with great care.

When Fumi arrived, she pointed at a spot. In an accusing tone she asked, "What is this?"

It was a question that did not require an answer, but was meant to bite. I picked up a rag and scrubbed the tiny ink mark away.

"Sloppy," Fumi complained.

How easy would it have been for Fumi to wipe it herself? I wondered.

After she left, I threw the towel on the ground. I was afraid to complain, instead I buried myself in schoolwork and chores.

The next day, I was frantic when things became worse. I kept the front gate key around my neck. But in the heat, the cord raised red bumps. I scratched lightly and then more vigorously. Finally, I removed the necklace temporarily and placed it somewhere I could find it easily. After dinner I looked for the key. I thought, *Where did I put it? It had to be somewhere in the house.*

I searched the usual places: the kitchen, my dresser, outside yard, and the living area. Even though my initial efforts were fruitless, I double-checked my clothes, peeked over shelves and then behind furniture. I raised the tatami mats and checked the cracks and prayed, *Dear God, please help me.* I searched the same places again and again before midnight, hoping for a miracle.

How can this happen? I thought. *Surely this is a bad dream.*

That night I tossed my covers and rolled over until exhaustion sent me into deep sleep. The next morning, I hurried off to school and did not mention the key to Fumi. In class, I was distant and preoccupied. Mrs. Tagashira tapped me on the shoulder. "Pay attention, Hanae," she said.

"Yes," I responded and thought that thieves might find the key. My stomach knotted up when I recalled that the key had the family crest on it. To reassure myself, I thought, *It has to be in the house. But what if I'm wrong? A burglar could open the front gate in the middle of the night. Our screens doors were locked but they would be easy to break.*

I worried, *We'd be defenseless. Shintaro is out to sea and only Fumi, Masa, me and Ichiro are home.* The horror of it struck me in the middle of class, and I blurted out aloud, "Oh, what have I done?"

My classmates turned their heads and stared. I bowed and quickly apologized. "*Sumimasen,*" I said and composed myself. Mrs. Tagashira regained control and instructed, "Turn to page eleven in your textbooks."

With a firm look she walked towards me and said, "Hanae, when the bell rings, stay seated."

I cringed and shrank into my seat. *How can I explain this outburst? I hope she doesn't send me to the principal.*

Fortunately, Mrs. Tagashira ignored me during recess. I watched the clock hands click from one minute to the other. To my surprise, she stacked papers and flipped through notes but said nothing.

Back home, I crawled under the locked gate and resumed the search. Fumi asked, "Why are you so dirty?"

"I lost the front gate key," I replied meekly.

"How could you be so stupid?" Fumi exclaimed. "You're nothing but trouble. What if some evil person finds the key?" Her voice grew louder, "Why didn't you tell me sooner? Ichiro and I could have been attacked while you were at school. Then Fumi said, "You're a waste. Did you hear me? Why do I put up with you?"

"Come here," Fumi said sternly. I hated to be humiliated but I followed her orders. It was as if I were a bad dog that made a mess.

"Give me your hand," Fumi commanded. Then she changed her mind. "No, lay down and take off your shirt. Show me your bare back!"

Fumi placed a pinch of *moxa* on my right scapula and set it aflame.

"Don't you dare cry," she threatened, "Or I'll lock you out of the house. You can pound on the door all day and I still won't let you in."

I gritted my teeth as the *moxa* ignited. Before the fire burned flesh, I remembered what Miss McMann always said, "Remember my students, you are Americans." I felt the resolve in her words and brushed the flaming embers to the floor. Fumi backed off with a surprised look.

I snarled and said, "I know what you were doing in teahouse."

I gathered courage and bluffed, "I heard and saw everything. If you touch me again, I'll tell Shintaro."

Fumi's jaw dropped. My anger took her by surprise. She never took her eyes off me and pedaled backwards as if confronted by a wild beast.

"Never mind," she said out of frustration. "Just leave. Do you hear me?"

I clenched my fists and steadied my shaking hands. I was shocked with what had come out of my mouth. With determination, I fixed my shirt properly and brushed back my hair. It took all my energy to say nothing more.

Fumi leaned closer. She straightened up and wagged her finger. "Before you go to bed, clean yourself up, little girl."

I struck back like a samurai. "I am not a little girl and I saw what you did. You should be punished."

In an angry tone, Fumi replied, "Find the keys and if you can't, I'll give you to some other unlucky family."

This was no idle threat. The phrase "Give you to another family" echoed in my mind.

I searched until bed time but never found the key. That evening Fumi secured the gate with a chain and padlock and declared, "It's useless. Tomorrow I'll call a locksmith."

I kept the new key around my neck and vowed never to remove it. Still I had the nagging feeling that Fumi might have found the original so she could hold something against me.

Afterwards, I was thankful that nothing more came of the incident. For the next few days I did my homework even though the tension remained. By the end of the week, I was back into my regular routine.

I wondered how things were at Russell Hotel, Does Mr. Yasui's phonograph still play *Honkon no yoru*? *I could almost hear it now. Oh, how I wish I were walking down that hall.*

The next morning, the streetcar pulled up with a screech. I jumped aboard and peered from the window as it sped past a blur of fences, gates, houses, and stores. A few blocks from school, I saw the woman in the orange kimono. *Oh no! Not again!*

I slid down as the woman boarded. She saw me and stood at the seat next to me. I cringed. Her strong perfume filled the air and almost overcame me. Instinctively I took short, shallow breaths.

The woman bowed and introduced herself, "I am Keiko Tanaka."

I thought she might be a Christian on a mission. But before I could respond, Keiko sat down and opened a silk purse. She pinched out a small black and white photo about twice the size of a postage stamp. It was blurry and torn at the edges.

Pointing to the baby in the photo, she said, "This is you, Hanae, and your father, Toyojiro."

How did she know my name? I wondered.

I squinted and stared at the images as the streetcar bumped and jostled. In the photo, a Japanese man held a baby in front of a building which looked something like the Russell Hotel.

It could have been any man with a baby in front of any wooden building, I thought. I gulped and furrowed my brow. I shook my head in disbelief and covered my mouth in shock. When I dropped my hand, the woman gently touched it. Automatically I recoiled at this unwanted intimacy.

"I am your mother," Keiko said softly.

My voice shook, "My mother? Mother is in Seattle. You can't be my mother."

I leaped from my seat and ran for the exit. The woman screamed, "I am your mother. Don't run away; I have a gift for you."

I looked over my shoulder. The woman held a beautifully wrapped package with red ribbons. My heart pounded as I hit the ground and ran, gasping for breath. The sound of my feet against the sidewalk made me run faster. I scrambled like a mad woman chased by demons.

At school, I was still shaking when the bell rang. It seemed like Mrs. Tagashira was talking in slow motion and the clock hands were frozen. By lunch I composed myself. A little hot tea and rice settled me down. After school, I rushed to the stop and scanned the area. I fidgeted and coiled like a tiger ready to spring in case Keiko appeared. I thought, *Being with other uniformed school girls gave me cover. I could hide in plain sight.*

That evening I recounted the incident to Masa. "The woman on the street car told me she was my mother. She even had a photo!" I said.

This time Masa paid close attention, "I'll talk with Shintaro." Without another word Masa washed her hands and went about her chores. That was the end of the conversation.

Uncharacteristically, Masa fumbled the dishes and dropped one with a crash. The pieces exploded and flew across the room. She swept up every shard. Calmly she put her kitchen knife back in the rack, poured a cup of tea, and sat near the stove. Judging by her strained expression, she knew more about Keiko. By her manner, she wasn't going to say.

"In the meantime," Masa instructed, "Take the early streetcar to school and the late one home. Shintaro will settle this when he returns."

"Okay," I replied, "I'll do anything to get rid of her."

LEAVING FOR THE COUNTRY, 1932

Fumi continued her degrading attacks and insults. One evening she cornered me in the kitchen. "You're a waste of skin," she said, "the laundry is not folded properly, dust specks cover the drawers, the meals are not artful, and worst of all, you are not *yasashii*."

I dropped my eyes and thought, *I hate being called names. That's so mean.*

When Shintaro returned, he brought canned King Crab from Kamchatka, Russia and sugar from Asia. Fumi continued her tirades until the tension affected everyone. At dinner there was a palpable silence. I was afraid to look up from my food and just ate in silence.

Not only were there problems in the house, there was tension in the entire country.

After Japan had defeated Russia in 1932, the military's influence was growing. Given this situation, Shintaro wanted peace in his house because real war was on the horizon.

He asked me to step into the living area and said, "I considered my choices about your situation. After much thought, I've decided to send you to the countryside," he said.

I was expecting this but winced when he actually said it. Nevertheless, I was happy to comply and provide temporary relief by leaving. Shintaro arranged for me to live with Uncle Yosh and his wife Tama on a farm. I thought, *I'm not yasashii so life in the country might be better.*

"Hanae, I'm sorry but we must have peace in the house especially since I'm having stomach troubles and not feeling well," Shintaro said.

"Are you all right?" I asked.

"Yes, just some indigestion," he replied. "Most of all I regret that things did not work out better," he remarked.

I felt like a failure. I wouldn't miss the people at school since I had no friends there. But I would miss the *sento* and Masa.

I nodded in agreement and held my emotions. After some thought I mused, *Time in the country might be good. I can get a fresh start. Maybe the kids there won't call me gaijin.*

It was a sunny spring day when I packed. I folded my clothes and thought, *Packing again. But this time it will be good to leave.*

I squeezed all my belongings into my yellow suitcase and left larger items in my trunk behind with Shintaro. Then I fixed my hair with a small red clip. The bright color contrasted with my straight linen chemise. Shintaro smiled with approval and Fumi bowed politely as if we were strangers. Masa touched my shoulder. She backed away and sobbed quietly. We had grown very close over the last two years and I knew she would miss me, especially our trips to the *sento*.

Shintaro wore a dark suit and black Homburg hat with a blue feather. His glistening shoes were immaculate. They clicked smartly on the cobblestone street as he walked.

There was a rumbling and grinding of metal as the streetcar arrived. We sat on a wooden bench in the back and I held my suitcase tight with my knees. The trolley bumped and periodically lurched.

Passengers climbed on and off quickly. It seemed that they never touched but instead, slipped past each other effortlessly. The ride and commotion kept thoughts about the future at bay. With each turn there was a surprise: a candy store, park with children playing, rickshaws, cabs, and colored banners in front of stores. It took thirty minutes to reach the Hiroshima City Train Station.

My mind drifted to the strange woman on the streetcar. *I remember that heavy perfume that almost made me cough,* I thought.

It was like Shintaro read my mind when he handed me a small picture and said, "She will not bother you again. Everything is okay."

I was puzzled because it was the same photo that the woman showed me. I asked, "Who is she, and how did you get this?"

Shintaro was expressionless. It was obvious that he did not want to discuss the matter. Instead he placed the photograph in my purse.

He put his hand on my shoulder and said, "I'll tell you later, after you get settled. I'll visit you shortly and explain everything."

I thought this was a very odd response because he probably would never have time. Obviously he knew the woman but secrets were involved.

I recalled the teahouse incident and wondered if I should say something. Then I concluded, *now isn't the right time to bring it up.*

In America, I reflected, *white people say what's on their mind. But in Japan, so much is unsaid. I may never know the truth about Keiko, but at least I can do this.*

I reached into my purse, pulled out the photo and handed it back to Shintaro.

"*Sumimasen,* thank you," I said. "Please return it. She must want it."

"Okay," he replied. With great care he slipped it into an envelope as the train station came into sight.

THE COUNTRYSIDE

The three-story train station with its Roman granite columns looked like a Seattle bank. Lines of black Model T taxicabs and rows of rickshaws filled the bustling streets. Shintaro purchased a yellow ticket from a middle-aged man in a cage.

I thought, *The clerk's western-style clothes and green eye shade visor were unusual. His black striped vest, suspenders, and elastics around his long sleeves were classic western garb and out of place in Japan. But obviously he was not a gaijin.*

Under the ornate, domed ceiling, Shintaro read the departure times. Granite floors and high arches with intricate swirling designs decorated the column tops. It reminded me of Saint James Catholic church in Seattle which I visited at Christmas for midnight mass with Kiku and her parents.

The station master's voice emerged from tinny speakers. Arrivals and departures were announced above the noise of locomotives. An old steam engine and train pulled up to the platform. Immediately the crowd rose and lurched like an animal. Shintaro patted me on the back and we merged into the flow. He stood like the military person he was. In a clear voice he remarked, "Work hard and help Uncle Yosh. Make us proud."

I took a deep breath. "I'll do my best," I replied.

Shintaro lifted me and my suitcase in one motion onto the train stairs. I realized then that the gesture demonstrated a sincere sense of sweetness. I wanted to hug him and touch him, but instead maintained my reserve.

He raised his arm and waved gracefully. I acknowledged his farewell and bowed a heartfelt goodbye. Although I was excited to leave, a twinge of abandonment crept in. I forced those feelings aside and gathered myself. *It's my fate to leave, I thought. This is for the best. I must endure.*

Taking my seat, I could still feel the touch of Shintaro's hand on my shoulder. I exhaled, knowing that he and his family were safe in spite of the trouble I caused.

Better that I live in the country, I thought, *than to create more misery. But I will miss Masa and her smile.*

I slumped deep in my seat. In my mind I heard Fumi say, "Sit up straight like a lady." In response, I reclined deeper and folded my arms tight.

Miles of houses lined the tracks; the train wound through crowded neighborhoods and snaked around the rivers and shorelines as it belched black clouds. Like magic, the scenery and people blended into each other, then faded as the train trundled and sleep stole me away.

CHAPTER FOUR

Uncle Yosh and Tama, 1931

The locomotive stopped at a wooden platform covered by a rusty tin roof. Unlike the city, there were tall trees, bamboo fences, and a huge blue sky. The engine idled and blasted steam while people scurried. In the crowd, I saw a middle-aged man jump up and down. He raised his arms high and smiled when he saw me.

"Hanae-san," he shouted. He waved a black and white photo. "I have your picture," he said, "I'm Uncle Yosh!" Immediately he mopped the sweat from his bald head, then bowed and smiled. I was excited and thought of the gifts from Hiroshima but decided to wait.

"Hello, I'm Hanae!" I said. "Thank you for meeting me."

Yosh was brimming with energy. I gestured towards my luggage and he threw my hand bag on the back of his mini truck. Then he secured the suitcase and placed me in the front seat. The three-wheeled truck putted away as I held my hat down.

I was amazed at how green everything was. I loved the lush rice fields interspersed with grazing cows and goats. There was a freshness and vitality in the air. Hiroshima was crowded and dirty in comparison. *I can actually breathe here*, I thought.

The truck chugged up a dirt driveway to Uncle Yosh's farm. His quaint home was like being transported back in time.

The cottage roof was thatched straw. I thought, *This is like a fairy tale.* Yuki, the small white dog, scampered and greeted us. Her tail wagged so hard that her whole behind shook. Tama, Yosh's wife, rushed out and bowed. "Welcome Hanae, please come inside," she said.

How wonderful! I thought. The first thing I saw inside was an open stone hearth with a black cast iron pot suspended over a pit. It served as the cooking area and in the winter was the sole source of heat. Tama slid open a closet door and removed a worn green futon. It was clean but frayed around the edges. "At night," she said, "spread it out near the hearth."

"Oh my, what a comfortable and charming bed!" I said.

I was happy about my new circumstances, especially my escape from Fumi and the strange events in town. After unpacking, I explored the grounds, fields, and compound. There were shallow green ponds with lily pads, willow trees, irrigation ditches, rice paddies, and a large vegetable garden next to a small area for chickens and cows.

Enjoying the serenity, I understood why people believed *Kamisama* inhabited the rocks, trees, and streams. Everything was vibrant and lush. Tadpoles swam in the ditches, which meant there would be hundreds of small frogs soon. Birds chirped and the sun shone gloriously. A large kingfisher stood under a willow tree overlooking the pond. For an instant, my heart pounded.

Oh, I feel like dancing, I thought. I skipped and jumped. *This is such a wonderful place.*

Physically, Yosh was squat, almost like a small tin can. With a shiny bald head, a gray crown, and thick square hands, he looked like one of the seven dwarfs with bowed legs. But he was a serious farmer who took pride in his old style farm methods. With care, he tended the fertile earth and cut straight rows. On all fours he weeded, and tossed the sweetest into a basket for the chickens. Yosh said, "Sweet weeds make sweet eggs."

Indeed, his eggs were fresh and mouthwatering. Often Tama served them raw over a bowl of steaming rice. They tasted of the earth in flavors that rolled around my mouth. Yosh also massaged his cows with his thick hands. He said, "Happy cows make happy milk."

I was surprised that he was in his early seventies, since he worked the fields from sunup to sundown like a twenty-year old. This was his life and he was obsessed with perfection—creating the perfect egg, perfect *nappa*, and perfect cup of milk. This was his purpose—to tease flavors from nature and share the bounty with others year after year. He wanted his products to be known as the very best in the prefecture.

The next day, I began my chores. The primitive conditions were brutal, especially the long hours and back-breaking labor. I rubbed my hands together and felt how coarse they had become so quickly. *Wow,* I said to myself, *I've never had calluses before.* To fight the heat, I splashed water on my face. "Ahh," I said out loud. I wish I could go for a swim."

Back at the cottage Tama grilled mackerel on the *hibachi*. The entire house filled with fragrances that carried me back to the Russell Hotel. I almost heard Mr. Yasui's phonograph and the floor boards creaking under my feet.

The main difference in the country was that when the winds blew from the south, the dust and cow manure odors seeped through the cracks in the cottage. I held my nose. *This is rough,* I said to myself, *but my days are easier than with Fumi.*

Tama was a female version of Yosh, sturdy and solid from strong peasant stock. Her back stooped slightly, and her smile revealed missing front teeth like Masa. She never complained but always showed gratitude. Each morning she prayed before the black-lacquered wood and gold-trimmed shrine. She struck the brass singing bowl and the sound lingered and floated in the clouds of incense. Then she knelt before the altar and began a melodic Buddhist chant.

This is a great place, I thought. I enjoyed being with the couple, their animals, and dog, Yuki. In many ways they were like children, bound to the cycles of nature, the land, seasons and weather. The couple was a part of the environment, like a stream or tree in the forest. I wondered, *Will I ever be like them?* They were self-sufficient in many ways. Yosh took pride in what he could create, especially *sake*. Every night he drank a nightcap with his dog. Often the two of them were up past midnight.

One evening he said, "Join us. Come and drink." Naturally I refused politely. His evening ritual began with a long soak in the wooden bathtub that extracted the day's pain and stiffness, followed by a bout of *sake* drinking.

I smiled and mused, *He and the sake are similar; they both heat for hours in a pot.* I chuckled at the thought.

One evening Yosh and Tama surprised me with a belated eleventh birthday celebration.

Tama said, "Hanae, fresh tuna sashimi and sweet bean cakes. Sorry we were late. In America they celebrate birthdays but not in Japan. But today we act American. *Happy Birthday.*"

Immediately they broke into a slightly off-key rendition. Yuki howled. It was a cheerful event that made me feel at home. During my short time there, the idea of spending many years on the farm emerged. I thought, *This is a wonderful. School will be starting soon and I can make friends my own age.*

A week later I had free time between chores and decided to explore the surroundings. The sun was shining during my stroll into the woods. I loved the fresh air that felt like rain had just fallen. The sunlight blazed straight beams through the trees and my feet squished footprints in the soft forest floor. When I went deep into the woods, the temperature dropped. The brush and scrub became thicker and I heard water rushing nearby. It was a fast-moving river fed by mountain streams. Waters swirled over and around large rocks but slowed at a cove.

Maybe I could catch a sakura masu, a cherry salmon trout, I thought.

They were a colorful species that swam upstream when the cherry blossoms bloomed in May. But I knew they might be gone by now. Nevertheless, I hoped to see an *Amago* trout. I found a walking stick and imagined spearing a fish.

Oh, how happy Uncle Yosh will be if I brought home a trout! I thought.

The clay bank was high so I turned and headed for the sand bar. My brown rubber work boots clumped over the ground. After a few steps, I sank in the sand. To avoid getting mud in my boots, I removed them and tossed them on the bank. I took two more steps towards shore and was held firm like in cement. *I better get back quickly*, I thought. I struggled, but was held fast and sank deeper. *Well this is just silly to be stuck out here.*

The seriousness of the situation, however, struck me. "Oh no, I could be in real danger," I cried out loud. The more I struggled, the deeper I sank, until the sand rose over my knees.

On the verge of panic, I flailed my arms out of desperation. *This is very dangerous*, I said to myself.

I hadn't told anyone where I was going or when I would return, so I could be stuck for hours before they missed me. I recalled a movie where a young boy was swallowed by quicksand. He sank deeper and deeper until he disappeared and only his hat remained on the surface. *If that is true, I'm in big trouble*, I thought.

"Help," I shouted and I waved my arms, hoping someone would hear me. I gulped and pulled my left foot free while pushing down on the walking stick. Sand swirled and pulled back any gains that I made.

If I don't get out soon, I worried, *how long can I last?*

The south wind cut a chill and my teeth chattered. I was losing feeling in my legs. Out of desperation I leaned forward to shift my weight as if to dive forward to break the vacuum. But I was held tight and could only wiggle my right leg to no avail. The forest shadows flickered an eerie glow which distracted me.

I bowed my head and covered my eyes. *I could die here. I'll never see my parents, friends, Kiku, Uncle Yosh or Spotty again*, I thought. Instinctively I screamed, "Help, someone help me."

Yelling above the river's roar was useless. *What can I do?* My eyes searched frantically, for anything to grasp- a limb or stump. But there was nothing. I only had myself and thought.

I must escape if I'm going to survive. If this was shikataganai I would die. If it was "endure," how long could I last?

I pulled my leg right leg again using the walking stick but was held solid. I gritted my teeth and said out loud, "I must fight for my life."

As my thoughts raced, I felt cheated. I am too young to die. I had plans for a future in America and dreams of becoming rich, getting married, and having children. I begged God for help and also the *Kamisama* of the river, sand, and rocks.

"I promise to be a good Christian and raise my future children as Christians," I prayed out loud. "If only you save me."

Tree shadows engulfed me and a cool breeze chattered my teeth. Out of desperation I cried, "Help, someone help me."

My world turned dark and the sound of the river faded like a fly buzzing. I heard voices in my mind. They were clear and gentle as they offered two choices.

"Do you want the difficult path?" they asked. "Then take the left hand extended to you. If you want the easy path, take the right hand."

Easy or difficult, what does that mean? I wondered. *Is this a riddle or trick I'm playing on myself?*

Calmly, the voices asked again. I touched the outstretched left hand. It was full of sadness and hardship. I grasped the right hand, which was warm and gave a sense of contentment.

Life is not easy, I said to myself. *I choose life and not the easy way.*

Instantly I was thrown backwards through space and time, tumbling past galaxies and universes back to the river. I opened my eyes and felt like passing out again until I heard, "Oi, girl stuck in quicksand, I heard you yelling for help in my forest. Don't you know no one understands English here." There is a pause punctuated by a laugh, "Except me!"

Is she a hallucination? I wondered. A rough-looking girl about my age with a huge voice stood in the clearing. She looked like a forest gnome in her black knee-high boots, canvas pants, and bright red hat. Her complexion was ruddy and healthy, something like a female *Momotaro* from Japanese fairy tales. She waved a large machete with a clean sharp blade and steel saw teeth on the spine. There was nothing frail about her, and to my amazement this apparition spoke perfect English.

I pleaded, "Can you run and get help?"

The girl laughed and said, "No need".

This reply brought a chill and confusion as I pleaded again, "Do you understand? You must understand."

Self-assured, the girl smiled and replied, "My name is Koko. I can get you out easily."

I was happy that she was not an illusion. Koko gathered stout branches and piled them on the bank. I thought she would make a bridge from two six-foot walking sticks.

"Take one in each hand and push them down next to your legs," she instructed.

Koko showed little anxiety while she continued.

"Pray to the water *Kamisama* for help, and tell the sand spirits to let loose. Now, push a pole down by your left leg and move the stick to break the suction. Wiggle and raise your leg when the water rushes in. Do the same for the other leg."

I followed her instructions. It was not as easy as it sounded, but eventually my legs were free. Koko said, "Grab this stick." With all her might she pulled. Like a tug of war contestant, she grunted *Yoisho* with each pull, a sound men uttered when lifting heavy objects.

"*Yoisho, yoisho, yoisho*" and finally I was released with a pop. Koko grabbed my hand and pumped it.

"Ha ha, what a mess!" she said with a hearty laugh. "It took ten *Yoishos* to get you out!"

I rubbed my feet and legs to get the blood moving. A few minutes earlier I had been pondering death, and now I was safe. Koko wiggled and then lit a small bunch of twigs for a fire. I sat on a large rock and warmed myself. "How could you hear me above the roar of the river?" I asked.

I rubbed my feet and legs.

Koko smiled, "I know what goes on in my woods. I didn't need to hear you to know you were here. What's your name, girl who bellows in English?"

I gathered myself and said, "I am Hanae from Seattle. I live with my Uncle Yosh and Aunt Tama."

Koko replied, "I know them. I'm Koko from White River near Seattle. My parents sent me here to get a Japanese education. They want me to be a *yasashii* Japanese woman. Ha ha! *Yasashii*, my big toe! I love these woods and I know every big rock, stream, and tree. They're my friends."

She spoke with pride and self-confidence, "The spirits know me. You're lucky they brought me here. I almost went trout fishing upstream, but voices told me to go downstream. When I'm bored, I jump into quicksand for fun. But I wouldn't recommend that. I like to see how long it takes to get out. Sometimes I use walking sticks to break the suction and sometimes I don't. When I saw you, I understood why *Kamisama* sent me downstream to catch a big fish! Ha ha."

I sat in silence and composed myself while Koko chattered. I pulled up my socks and slid my feet into the cold brown boots. With gratitude I said, "Thank you. You saved my life. How can I repay you?"

Koko laughed, "It's nothing, but you're welcome. Most of all it is good to find someone who speaks real English. I'm tired of being called a *gaijin*."

She paused and looked at me like a fish she had just caught.

"Tell me, what do you want to be when you grow up, Hanae?" Koko asked.

Before I could respond, Koko launched a torrent of words. "I want to be a *modan garu*, you know modern girl? I want to wear a chemise, smoke cigarettes, get a secretarial job, travel the world, collect souvenir spoons from every American national park including Yellowstone, do the Charleston, and have a boyfriend who wears a raccoon coat."

Koko laughed loudly, "I can't do that if I'm a *yasashii* Japanese house-wife here." My aunt complains because I do poorly in school. My uncle says I bring shame on the family."

She proudly displayed her left hand. Her index finger had a neat line of incense burn marks. Koko pointed to a large narrow scar and said, "That was when I yelled at the teacher. My aunt burned me good for that one."

Judging by the scars, Koko had a long history of misdeeds. By her attitude, it was obvious that the burns only motivated her to behave poorly, not better. The marks were a ledger of her misdeeds.

She laughed and said, "Pretty soon they'll be sick of burning me and send me back to America! Or maybe they'll run out of spaces! Oh, I can't wait. I'd gladly give up these woods and spirits to be a real *modan garu*. In America I'll be a flapper. You know flappers?"

I rubbed my hands to dislodge the caked-on sand. "Yes," I said, "I saw pictures of them smoking cigarettes and drinking gin. But I think they're out of style."

"It doesn't matter," she said, "because it's the spirit that's important."

I squinted hard and examined Koko from top to bottom. *Was she a real person?* Or was this some type of heavenly drama to ease my soul on the other side.

I pinched myself hard. No doubt this was real.

"Pinch yourself again," she said with a smirk.

"No need," I replied, "and thank you."

A red-orange butterfly with black, eye-shaped spots landed on Koko's shoulder like a pirate's parrot.

"Look," I said pointing at the butterfly.

Koko turned her head and said, "You mean this?" as she brushed it off.
The butterfly flapped its wings and flew off, only to land on the top of Koko's red felt hat.

"It's on your hat!" I exclaimed.

"Oh yeah, they do that all the time," Koko replied with a smile.

I thought, *Never in my life has a butterfly landed on me; even if it did, it wouldn't return after I shooed it away. What a strange day and what a strange person! But I'm happy to be alive!* "Thank you, Koko, for saving my life," I said.

She replied, "You're welcome. Now do something useful with it."

"Don't worry, I will. I promise," I said.

FOXES

Several weeks had passed before I had an opportunity to explore the forest again. The sun was shining and birds singing. I was excited to pick fiddlehead ferns. They were scattered here and there like a breadcrumb trail that drew me deeper and deeper into the woods. Finally, I came upon a clearing and felt a sense of peace. I thought, *Maybe Koko is here so I can thank her for saving my life.*

I pushed the brush aside until I came upon a moss-covered mound circled by large rocks. Sunshine shafts pierced the tree branches. Dark shadows danced as a light rain fell. The wind carried forest fragrances. I inhaled deeply and exclaimed, "This makes me feel alive!" Japanese call it a "foxes' wedding" when rain falls on a sunny day. The legend says that under the cover of rain, tricky foxes marry without prying human eyes.

Butterflies with spots that resembled eyes fluttered overhead. A beam of sunlight cut through the mist and grew brighter and brighter, like a beacon from outer space. The light filled the clearing and dust whirled like a small tornado. Like magic, two silver foxes appeared. They glowed iridescent and moved gracefully as if underwater.

The large male turned and shot an electric beam that pierced my soul. The small female fox looked away. They moved with elegance and grace. I felt their spirits and wild nature.

Frozen like a statue, I watched darkness spread like an eclipse. In a blink, the foxes disappeared. I grew light-headed and sat on a mossy log feeling as if I had fallen from the sky.

I covered my face with open palms. "What happened?" I said out loud.

My basket was upside down on the ground with ferns scattered catawampus. My thoughts spiraled like whirlpools. *I wish Koko were here,* I thought. *She would know what to do.*

A light breeze rose and the clearing was transformed back to normal. I rubbed my eyes. There was no sign of foxes. The sunlight faded and the rain swelled into a tropical deluge. I picked up my basket and ran for cover under a large tree. Hastily I wrung water from my sleeves and rushed home. It seemed like every twig and bramble snagged me as I ran. The hairs on the back of my neck sensed something tracking me. Crows sounded danger calls from the trees. I swiveled and glanced over my shoulder. Finally, I broke through the forest to Uncle Yosh's field. "Home at last," I cried out loud.

Gasping for air, I ran up the path and saw Yuki. "Come here girl," I called. Usually she greeted me with a happy "woof". Instead she whimpered in the shadows, tail between her legs. I was surprised. "What's wrong?" I asked.

I paid little attention to her rebuff since my heart was pounding. I opened the door and hollered, "Uncle Yosh! I saw glowing foxes in the woods, maybe a foxes' wedding." I caught my breath and said, "They were beautiful and strange. I was frozen and couldn't move."

Yosh listened carefully and twisted his face. He rubbed his hands together and sighed.

"Ahhhh," he said in a sad voice. "Foxes' weddings are very bad luck."

I responded quickly, "But they weren't wearing wedding kimonos. They were dressed in white."

"Even worse, white is the color of death," Yosh said. "They're strong spirits that can possess people and sometimes take human form. Maybe it's an evil omen."

I was frightened and wondered, *What have I done now?*

Yosh was shaken and seemed confused. He wondered out loud, "I don't know if this is a threat or superstition." By the strained look on his face, he didn't take the situation lightly. "I'll wait and see what happens," he said.

I had never seen Yosh so troubled. "I'm sorry," I said, "I hope things will be okay."

He composed himself. "It's early but I'll heat some *sake*," he said. "Whatever happens, our crops must flourish and cows must give milk. That must never change."

Yosh grimaced and said, "I sense fear among the chickens and the cows. Maybe it's the moon or a bear in the area, or maybe it's you, Hanae."

A shiver ran up my spine when he pointed at me. Feeling a little dizzy, I replied "Things should be normal tomorrow. I'm going to take a short walk."

"Okay, see you for dinner in half an hour," he replied.

I strolled to the koi pond and called them as usual. *Funny,* I thought, *they're ignoring me.*

Dinner was a meal of teriyaki chicken and brown rice. I smacked my lips unconsciously and felt delight with every bite. The flavors were magical as they danced across my palate. After dinner it was like fairies were assisting me. The dishes and bowls seemed to wash, wipe, and stack themselves.

By the time Yosh began his *sake* nightcap, I was fast asleep. Two white foxes appeared in my dreams. The smaller one wore a wedding kimono and a hat decorated with grape clusters. The large male stood upright with a piercing glare. He looked like a samurai with a *katana* sword that he extended out towards me. I awoke with a cry, rolled over and lay awake in fear.

The days passed and Uncle Yosh grew more and more agitated. "The chickens aren't laying eggs and the cows give no milk," he said. With Tama standing behind him he declared, "I am truly sad, Hanae, but you can't stay. The spirits are unhappy." Yosh believed that I had disrupted the forces that bound nature to man.

This situation was intolerable for someone so dedicated to farming. He took it as an omen and feared that a drought or some disaster would strike. "I cannot risk what I have toiled many years for," he said. "Please understand. I'll write a letter you can take to Shintaro."

I was sad to leave such a comfortable place after only two months. "Can I do anything to stay?" I asked. By the look on Yosh's face I knew the answer. As I packed for the third time in almost three years, I remembered the wonderful time I'd had on the farm.

Oh no, I brooded. *I don't want to return to Hiroshima. Fumi will be angry and bad things will happen, I just know it,* I thought. Her phrase, "You're a waste of skin," reverberated in my mind.

I understood Yosh's fear and did not wish to jeopardize his relationship with the spirits. Nor did I want to destroy his cozy 19th century farm. I bowed to Yosh and Tama. "Thank you for taking care of me and your hospitality. I have a lot of good memories. Thank you again."

Tama packed a basket of fresh *nappa.* She also prepared rice balls with mackerel as a snack for my train trip home. Tama said, "Take care of yourself. We'll miss you." She bowed.

I asked them to stand in front of the cottage with Yuki. "Smile," I said as I snapped a photograph. "I will treasure this picture forever."

Tama pulled a letter from her pocket and said, "I almost forgot. A strange girl delivered this some time ago and I forgot to give it to you."

I gripped the letter tight and tucked it away. In the corner it read, *"From Koko."* I said, "I'll read it on the train."

Yosh loaded the luggage onto the three-wheeled truck while I sat under the canopy. He fidgeted and was not the same solid person I'd met months ago. I managed a weak smile as Tama handed me a jar of pickled plums for Shintaro. The truck chugged and the tires churned dust clouds behind us. To me, the fields and scenery were beautiful even through tears. I cradled the plum jar like a mother protecting a baby.

Yosh was preoccupied. He was not humming or singing, but grasped the steering wheel tight. He pulled up to the covered platform next to the tracks. I checked the schedule and found the Hiroshima express. Yosh did not touch my shoulder, but bowed politely.

"Shikataganai," Yosh said. "Have a good trip, Hanae. We'll miss you and thank you for your work."

I nodded and bowed, "Thank you and tell Tama thanks for her hospitality."

Yosh waited until the train arrived and then waved. There was no anger or joy in his actions. I thought, *this is the Japanese way.* In a trance-like state, I walked to my seat and sat on the hard surface. After the train gathered speed, I remembered Koko's letter.

THE LETTER

Dear Hanae,

Hope you are doing well. I've got great news. Hurray! My aunt and uncle finally gave up. They're sending me to Hiroshima or to Fresno California.

I don't know anything about California but I heard it is very hot. They're still making arrangements with relatives so I won't know for several weeks. I hope it's California and maybe we'll see each other again!

Wishing you a good life!

Sincerely,

Modan Garu, Koko

P.S. Please stay out of quicksand since I won't be in the woods to save you.

RETURN TO HIROSHIMA

It was hot and humid when the train pulled in to Hiroshima City. As expected, no one greeted me. Nevertheless, I could find my way home easily. I claimed my luggage and headed towards the street car. Glancing at the clock tower, I thought, *Masa should be home after her daily grocery shopping by now.* My mind flashed through the last few days. I wondered, *What I would say to Fumi? Maybe I could lie or just not say anything. No, that won't work. I better tell the truth and see what happens.*

It seemed like every stone scuffed my shoes on the way home. I took my time and thought, *Hiroshima streets are noisy and alive compared to the country.*

Waiting under a maple tree, I stepped out when the streetcar's bell clanged. My suitcase was heavy and I dragged it aboard. The streetcar lurched and bounced with each twist and turn. By the time I reached the house, I'd made up my mind to tell Shintaro everything about the foxes.

I hesitated at the metal gate and surveyed the house. Everything appeared the same outside. I gritted my teeth. *Well, here I go again,* I thought as I crawled under the gate with my suitcase in tow. Fumi opened the sliding door. Her eyes grew large and her jaw dropped. She stepped back and almost tripped. It was obvious she was not happy.

Blocking the entrance, she asked in a cutting tone, "What are you doing here?"

"I was sent back to not anger *Kamisama*," I replied.

Fumi furrowed her brow. "What does that mean?"

She hesitated for an instant and I slipped past her like a ghost.

Fumi turned and yelled, "Masa, *Hayaku shinasai*, quickly."

I heard a baby cry. Fumi swiveled and rushed out in a huff, leaving me alone in the living room.

Masa was surprised to see me. "Oh Hanae, why are you here?" she blurted and jumped like a child full of joy. Immediately, she restrained her happiness and bowed politely.

Holding the jar of plums, I said, "These are for the family from Yosh."

With both hands, Masa clutched the container and scampered to the kitchen.

After all that commotion, I found myself alone again in the room. I looked around and noticed that the house had been re-arranged during my absence. The shrine had been moved and even the odors seemed unfamiliar. My old area had been converted into a space for the new boy. I was shocked to see how quickly all evidence of my existence had disappeared. *Do I have a place here?* I thought as I sat on the floor and waited for Masa.

"Leave your suitcase in the corner and I'll serve tea," Masa said as she beckoned with her arms extended.

"Okay, I'll be there in a minute," I replied. I was distracted by the sound of birds chirping and stepped outside for some air. I strolled to the koi pond and the carp were in a frenzy as I approached. *What's happening with the fish?* I wondered. They looked like boiling colors in the water. As usual, I called them but they avoided me. *Am I a stranger now?*

Even the carp are against me, I thought. Out of a dark corner, the silver ghost fish appeared. "*Nani?* What?" I said in amazement. Masa stepped outside and witnessed the occurrence. She covered her mouth in shock.

"The ghost never lets anyone near," Masa said. "Very strange."

She put her hands on my shoulders and examined me closely like a shiny object at the market. "Something is different," she said.

When Shintaro returned that evening, he was surprised. "Welcome back," he said. I bowed deeply. He smiled and said, "You look well. Are you visiting?"

With a sheepish look I replied, "Uncle Yosh thought I angered *Kamisama* and sent me back."

"What? That doesn't make sense," Shintaro said as he squinted and rubbed his eye.

"I saw foxes," I exclaimed. I recounted the adventure in the woods and how the farm animals were unsettled upon my return.

"I see," Shintaro responded. "Country folk can be superstitious. Regardless, Yosh should have told us you were coming."

I pulled out the letter and handed it to Shintaro. "He said to give you this."

Fumi was standing in the shadows and came forward. She bowed to Shintaro. "Please have some tea," she offered.

The house was full of dinner fragrances from the kitchen. I took my usual place at the table and sat in silence while dinner was served.

Afterwards, Masa and I washed the bowls and chopsticks. We laughed and giggled like school girls. *It is like old times,* I thought. *It's great to be back.*

Shintaro motioned for Fumi to join him in the next room. I perked up and listened as best I could. My heart sank when she insisted, "Hanae is a burden and must leave for good. She makes mistakes and loses valuable things. I do not feel safe with her here." Shintaro nodded thoughtfully and stepped away. As was his evening habit, he opened his diary and penned an entry.

After the dishes were done, Shintaro and I had a brief conversation. He folded his hands and said, "This is a difficult time. I've decided to send you back to America. You've done well for yourself. You learned how to read and write and are on your way to becoming a Japanese woman."

My knees shook at the words "You've done well." I thought *No that's not true. I failed.* I dropped my eyes and tears streaked down my face. *Not again,* I said to myself. It was like the whole world was against me. I had no future in Hiroshima.

The temple psychic's warning surfaced in my mind, "A gourd of death will fall from blue Hiroshima skies." *If that is true, it would be good to leave.* But I felt ashamed of my failures and thought about the Aokigahara Forest at the foot of far-off Mount Fuji.

It was called the Sea of Trees and was devoid of wildlife. Many who went to the forest committed suicide by hanging. It was rumored to be haunted or just evil. I composed myself and held my emotions in check. I begged Shintaro to take me to Mount Fuji. "It will be the last time I visit the holy mountain for a long time," I said.

He pondered my request. As a submarine captain, he knew the ebbs and flows of human emotions. Acknowledging my emotional state, he said, "We don't have time to visit Fuji. Right now I need you to take something very important to Father in Seattle. You must be my messenger and carry this book. Only you can do this."

He showed me a box wrapped in a cloth and continued softly, "This is very important since I'm having health problems and my stomach is getting worse."

"What's wrong?" I asked.

"Maybe an ulcer," he replied. "But I'll be fine. Delivering this is important."

He leaned towards me, "Do you understand?" he asked and continued, "Our Father must have this, so please pack it right away."

Shintaro handed me a long, thin object wrapped in cloth, bound with an ornamental tassel-like cord. It was heavy and scary in a strange way.

"This is your great-great-grandfather's sword. It holds our ancestor's spirits. Please deliver this to Father for safekeeping."

My hands tingled as I imagined samurai ancestors marching dirt roads. The blade glistened with a serpentine design and razor sharp edge. The handle was wrapped tightly in a crosshatched geometric design.

Shintaro's deep voice brought me back to reality, "I fear for the future. Father will protect the sword. You're responsible for the sword too."

He touched my shoulder firmly. "Do you understand?"

I bowed under the weight of his hand and said, "Yes. I'll be a good messenger," I said.

Without hesitation I reiterated my initial response which was *Hai*. I felt uplifted since I had an important task. Thoughts of Mount Fuji and the forest fled. Exhilarated, I knew that I must not fail. "I will not disappoint you," I said.

The next morning, a shiny black Model T Ford cab arrived. The driver loaded my yellow suitcase and grunted as he strapped the steamer trunk on the roof. I absorbed every sight and sound on the drive knowing that this would be the last time I saw Hiroshima for a long time. Shintaro had booked a private cabin and paid my expenses in return for my help at the house. Standing tall, he looked magnificent in his blue navy uniform: shiny boots, jacket, and gold braid over his shoulder.

He handed me a bouquet of chrysanthemums along with his diary. "If the situation goes bad for me and my submarine," he said, "there are secrets Father should know." He paused for a moment. His face turned ashen. Slowly his expression returned to normal as he continued. "We may not see each other for a long time, so thank you for your help. I know Fumi is difficult and I'm sorry for the way she behaves. But she is my wife and the mother of my child. Please excuse her."

Shintaro looked directly at me and said, "You'll be traveling with Sanzo and Matsuyo Nakatani, who own Jiro's Five and Dime store in Seattle. They're good friends of our family. They'll take care of you, so don't worry. I sent a telegram and Father will meet you. I must tell you this, even though you may not understand. I've studied history and we are entering a time of world wars, rebellions, revolutions, and strife."

He paused and gently touched my hand. "Japan absolutely must be America's ally. We'd never have a chance if we fight America, no matter what the warlords say. Even though you have a Japanese education, remember that you're American and not Japanese."

With great urgency in his voice, he continued, "You must be a good citizen in Seattle. People in the Japanese community mustn't give America a reason to suspect them if there is war with Japan."

I bowed, holding the bouquet in one hand and the box in the other. Even though I acknowledged his request, I was frightened for my brother and family but did not know what to say except, "Okay."

My only choice was to do as he wished. I understood duty and would keep my word no matter what. "Yes, I'll do this," I said firmly.

There was a brief silence as Keiko came to mind, so I asked, "Who was the woman on the streetcar?"

Shintaro touched me on the shoulder. His face crinkled when he said, "Never mind. She's not right in the head."

I pressed once more, "Who was she? You must tell me before I leave. Please."

He said, "Keiko took care of you in Seattle when you were born. At first she was a good baby-sitter. Then something strange happened." He paused, "Gradually she began to believe she was your mother and she decided to take you to California without telling anyone." He swallowed hard and then continued.

"Mr. Okada, a close family friend, was a redcap at the Jackson Street train station. He saw Keiko behaving suspiciously and asked why she was taking you to California. She panicked and bolted for the doors. He gave chase and grabbed her.

"Okada was big and strong and wouldn't let go. He took both of you back to the hotel. Mother was relieved and Father was so mad that he made Keiko leave the hotel forever. Eventually she returned to Japan."

Shintaro guided me to the gangplank. I smiled and thought, *That story was not half as bad as I imagined.* I handed Shintaro a thank you note addressed to him, Masa, and Fumi. "Also If Masa can find Koko's address; would you have her deliver this thank you note?"

My feet were heavy as I shuffled up the gangplank. On deck I stood at the railing, waved goodbye, and released the streamers.

There was a bitter taste in my mouth. I felt empty, leaving Hiroshima, a beautiful city of seven rivers. I gripped the bouquet and then tossed it into the water. *I'll be back when I'm a woman,* I promised myself. Part of my soul fluttered away with the flowers and my spirit journeyed back to the house by the river and Yosh's farm in the country. *Goodbye, I will never forget Hiroshima,* I thought.

I would miss the narrow streets and meandering turns that brought surprises around every corner. I would miss the cobblestones, the cherry blossoms near the Ohta and Motoyasu Rivers, the sounds of street merchants hawking wares, the bustle of the night market at Hakushima, and the fragrances rising from vendors cooking octopus in open air stalls.

I would miss the night street sounds, the clatter of rickshaws, buses, bicycle bells and the whoosh of motor cars gliding smoothly in rhythm to city life. I remembered the first time I saw people weaving through the narrow streets, never colliding and turning with drill team precision. My mind was carried to the cherry trees in spring along the Ohta River, a short ferry trip away. I could almost see the blossoms fluttering like snow.

I wondered, *Would I stay in Seattle, get married, and raise a family after graduating from high school? When would I return to Hiroshima? Most importantly, what secrets were in the diary? Why should Dad be the only one to know the secrets? And finally, was Shintaro telling me the full story of the woman on the streetcar?*

Those questions will be answered in time, I thought. Meanwhile I dreaded the idea of another bout of sea sickness. To distract myself, I shifted my mind to being reunited with my family, friends, and Spotty. Returning to America and Seattle would be a relief, I concluded. *I cried so much that I'm done crying.* I said to myself, *From today on, I swear I'll never cry again.*

CHAPTER FIVE

Return to Seattle, 1932-1939

My stomach churned for a week on the trip as the Miike Maru steamship bobbed and crashed through miles of whitecaps. During the day I found comfort gazing at the horizon and gulping fresh air near the bow. The refreshing salt spray, however, was a momentary cure. Standing in the mist, I grabbed the rails and hung on tight when the ship rocked sideways. I thought, *there're miles of rolling seas ahead. I must be strong.* When the wind shifted, diesel fumes engulfed the deck and chased me back to the cabin. I said out loud, "This up and down motion makes me thirsty." Before I could pour a glass of water, my stomach rebelled and erupted like a volcano. I grabbed a paper bag and thought, *There is no ladylike way to do this.*

The side to side rolls and up and down motion reminded me of Yosh. I thought, *This is like the time I drank too much sake with Uncle Yosh. That night my futon was spinning like a merry-go-round out of control. Desperate, I stuck my foot on the ground to slow down the spins. Of course that didn't help one bit.*

After two weeks of being seasick, I was overjoyed to hear the steamship's horn blast when the Seattle skyline appeared. *Finally*, I thought, *I'm really home.*

Hallelujah! I don't believe it!

My heart was pounding before I let out a very un-Japanese, "Yeehah!" Immediately, Fumi's words echoed in my mind, "*Waste of skin.*" I imagined peeling it off like a snake and watching it flutter into Elliot Bay. I grinned and thought, *There'll be no polite tea ceremonies or being called 'gaijin' here. I want to play baseball and hit a home run.*

I jumped and clicked my heels when I saw Dad. He and brother Tom watched me skip down the gangplank. Dad held an American flag upright. I leaped and waved my arms.

"Papa!!" I yelled as loud as I could.

Tom wore a small cap, knickers with suspenders over a white shirt. He had a soup bowl haircut like most boys in Japantown. I wore a white chemise, pearls, a white hat, and black shoes. I was overcome with glee and smiled all the way down the gangplank.

I cried, "*Oto-san*, Father," and then hugged Tomokiyo whose American name was Tom. "Tom, is that really you?"

I bowed to Dad and put my arm over Tom's neck. I was hoping to see Mom but she was at the hotel working. Tom turned and hugged me tightly.

"I brought my red wagon for luggage," he said.

"Tom, jump in so it doesn't rattle. I'll pull you until we load," I said.

Dad smiled and patted me on the back. He was a very gentle person who would have made a terrible samurai. As usual, he wore a wool khaki vest with a gold watch chain arching across the front. Since he had never been vaccinated against small pox, his face carried the scars of his mother's forgetfulness.

Dad worked at *Our House Saloon* on Skid Row, where he went by the name of "Frank." He did small repair work around the saloon and cleaned-up during the day. Gamblers, loggers, businessmen, and travelers patronized the tavern. On rowdy Skid Row, *Our House* was one of the few safe places for customers to gamble. Upstairs was the Lyric Theatre dance hall.

Strolling, Jackson Street, Dad pointed at a three story brick building. "I work there," he said with pride.

I recalled stories he told before I left. He witnessed many things both legal and illegal involving the rich, destitute, powerful and famous. Dad claimed that he spoke no English even though he lived in Seattle for thirty-three years. Nevertheless, he could read and write English and understood more than most people suspected.

We continued past Alaskan Way and Tom navigated the rattling wagon around puddles. I took in the sights, sounds, and fragrances of Pioneer Square. "Wow," I said, "this place is a lot smaller than I remember."

The buildings were dirty, but new businesses sprouted where vacant lots used to be.

"The air hasn't changed," I said, detecting a whiff of freshly cut cedar logs.

Tom complained, "I don't like it. No wonder they call it Skid Row."

I smiled and replied, "Still it's nice when the sun shines."

Dad was amused by our small talk. He patted Tom on the head. "This one," he said, "talks a lot."

In the alleys, seagulls squawked and rummaged through the garbage cans. I thought, *Hiroshima isn't like this. It is more lively and less trashy.* But I loved the waterfront creosote odors and fragrances that rose during low tides.

It was a cozy walk with my brother and father. Tom was curious and bubbled with questions: "What was the ship like? What did you eat? How was Hiroshima?" It was a nonstop barrage. I answered as best I could, but just wanted to catch up on the news and take in the sights.

"What's new in Japantown? How are Kiku, Spotty, and my brothers?"

I had forgotten how beautiful the Olympic Mountains were as they stood like a giant pearled chain on the other side of Puget Sound. The craggy, snow-covered peaks were a grand sight. "There's Mount Olympus," I chirped.

For a moment I watched the ferries cross to Bainbridge Island and Bremerton, heading towards the nearby islands below the snow-covered mountains. To the south, my heart warmed at the sight of the Smith Tower building. City fathers boasted that it was the tallest building west of the Mississippi.

I mused, *In Hiroshima, the rocks, trees, rivers, sea, and mountains have spirits. In Seattle, the people don't care.* Seattle poisoned the waters with waste and garbage. I wondered, *Why didn't I notice this before?*

As we continued up the street, I examined the traffic and was struck by how sparsely populated the city was in comparison to Hiroshima. There were vagrants sitting on the sidewalks which made me feel uneasy. I thought, *If I were alone, I wouldn't feel safe here. Whereas in Japan I never sensed that I was in danger.*

When I was a child, the Seattle hobos ignored me, but as an eleven-year old, I drew some undesirable glances. I paused and realized that I couldn't feel *Kamisama's* strength and rhythms. Whatever influence the foxes and other spirits had in Hiroshima, their magic was weak in America.

As we neared Japantown I began to feel more at ease. Japanese kids could knock on any door and residents would know their family, friends or relatives. This closeness provided a sense of security and belonging. But on the other hand, it meant 1,000 watchful eyes ensured that a child did not misbehave. Children knew they must behave and be good citizens or the entire community would risk the wrath of the *hakujin*, or whites.

Walking up Main Street, I recalled wonderful memories, especially of the Nippon Kan Theatre on South Washington Street in the Astor Hotel. I was impressed by the charm of the four-story brick building and the Japanese men and women in their formal clothes attending the evening performances.

I wished the Japanese actors would stay at the Russell Hotel so I could hear their stories. As foreigners, they were easy to recognize. They took shorter steps and had a different attitude, more carefree.

I wondered, *Could I pass as a Japanese visitor in Japantown?* On the other hand, I was curious about what it felt like being white and walking downtown without the stares. Then I made a wish, *Just once in my life I want to feel like I belong in Seattle outside of Japantown. Yes, that would be wonderful!*

Dad interrupted my thoughts and exclaimed, "It's good to have you back. Too many boys!"

Tom frowned at the remark but kept on pulling the wagon.

"Everything is the same," Dad said. "Except you have a new brother, Bob. We gave him an American name."

Tom giggled and tugged his hat. "Bob is a rascal," he said.

We crossed Dearborn Street and reached Russell Hotel. It was worn and tired looking, very much in need of a fresh paint job. But it was a welcome sight.

Mom was outside sweeping. "Toku, look what we found at the piers," Dad joked to Mom.

"Welcome home," she announced out loud. "Come here everyone, it's Hanae!"

Three of my brothers rushed out and surrounded me. In the crowd, a small boy peeked from behind Mom's skirt. "This must be Bob," I said. "I'm your sister."

He ducked behind Tom.

"See what I told you," Tom said, "he's a rascal."

"Come inside," Mom urged as she gathered the family. The living and dining areas overflowed with warm chatter and wonderful aromas.

I took a moment and examined my family and their faces as if they were frozen in a photo. Some brothers were taller and heavier than when I left. Half joking, I asked, "Mom, how many brothers do I have?"

"Yes, Toku how many? I lost count," Dad said.

She scanned the faces but didn't reply. Immediately Tom piped up the answer, "Too many."

The room filled with laughter.

At dinner, a place of honor was set for me. I was tired, but happy to get re-acquainted. Spotty wagged his tail and begged for handouts under the table. Mom made King salmon in a teriyaki sauce, served with Japanese pickles, rice, and tempura vegetables. It was a heart-warming homecoming. Thoughts of the steamship and problems in Hiroshima faded with each delicious bite.

The boys chattered all evening and my eyes grew heavy. I nodded and almost fell asleep at the table. After the long boat ride, I expected my room to rock and roll but I found comfort surrounded by the familiar floral wallpaper design. I yawned and nestled deep in bed. More than anything I was thankful for the steadiness of the earth and the comfort of home.

THE MEDALLION

Dad told stories at dinner about Japantown during the Great Depression when food lines and cardboard shacks sprung up near Skid Row and the tide flats. A shanty town of 2,000 people appeared just south of J-Town called Hooverville. He said, "it looked like the slums of Calcutta."

My first encounter with a Hooverville resident occurred a few days after my return. Mom had warned me about talking to strange men, but this one appeared out of nowhere and caught me by surprise. He was a tall, bearded fellow who carried a gunny sack and looked like a chimney sweep covered with dust.

His shoes were broken and his loose soles were secured with twine. Long strands of white hair flowed to his shoulders from under his brown fedora. His complexion was gray and his teeth were yellow spikes. When he bowed with hat in hand, I flinched at his animal-like odor. He needed a bath and shave.

Usually mother shooed away hobos but she was busy around back hanging wash. He asked, "Please can you spare a cup of coffee?"

As a youngster, my immediate reaction was to help. But I was puzzled by the request because Mom and Dad never drank coffee. Without a word I ran to get my mother. If he had asked for rice or tea, I could have been more helpful. By the time we returned, he was gone. Mom circled the property searching for signs or symbols hobos drew on fences to show that this house was friendly. There was no trace except a musky smell.

She raised her finger and pointed, "Hobos come and take little girls and do very bad things. You're very lucky he didn't put you in a bag and take you. Otherwise you'd never see us again."

My voice shook, "Okay, I'll be careful," I said.

"You didn't give him any food, did you?" Mom queried with an intense look. "They're like stray dogs. Once you feed them they'll come back for more. These men who drink cheap whiskey and sleep in the woods are good-for-nothing."

I nodded and walked towards a shiny object on the ground. It was a bronze medallion embossed with the words "Alaska Yukon Exposition 1909—Utah Exhibit." I wondered if the hobo had dropped it by mistake or left it for me. With care, I tucked the coin into my apron pocket and squeezed it to make sure it was real. I wanted to believe it was a gift from the strange forest dweller.

Back in my room I studied the coin and its high relief design features. I thought it must have been a wonderful exhibition with people from exotic places and visitors from all over the world. I couldn't believe that it had actually happened in Seattle. But the proof was before me.

This might be worth something one day, I thought.

I kept it as a good luck charm and secured it in my lacquered jewelry box. *Why was I the one to receive it? Maybe it was just a worthless trinket to trick a young girl. Or maybe it was a thing of value.* Regardless, thoughts of the coin lifted my mind like a kite up over the trees. *Maybe it has magical powers*, I mused. A crow on a nearby tree cawed and the sound brought my thoughts back to earth.

To my mother, strangers–especially hobos–were an ever-present threat. At the turn of the century, she rarely left the house alone. There were few women and many rough-looking men on the outskirts of Japantown.

Mom said, "One day a stranger banged on the door and yelled, '*Your barn is on fire!*' Not trusting the person, I didn't leave until the fire spread to my room. At the last minute I ran outside and was safe. The person next door was trapped and died before the volunteer fire department arrived." This was a story she told over and over to reinforce her message about how dangerous living near Skid Row was.

KEIKO

As the days melted into each other, I felt more comfortable. Each morning I stood before the mirror to see if had grown an inch. I was hoping to flourish like garden zucchinis which explode overnight. On summer mornings, you could see how much they grew by the pile of dirt they pushed forward. *I wish I could grow that fast*, I thought.

Down the hall, Mr. Yasui's 78 rpm phonograph played *Hon kon no yoru*. The haunting melody about a lost love. "*Hon kon no youruuuu*" were the first lyrics of the bittersweet song.

His door swung open and Mr. Yasui surprised me.

"Oh, good morning," I chirped.

Yasui was a wiry middle-aged man who wore a sleeveless tee shirt. He looked like an elf when he said, "Good morning."

His room was neat, dominated by a dresser crowded with framed photos.

I was drawn to a beautiful postcard full of city lights.

"Ahh," he said with a twinkle, "Hong Kong, same as the song."

In the doorway, I asked, "Were you visiting there?"

Mr. Yasui's eyes watered as he took a breath. "I met my wife in Hong Kong. See how pretty she was," he said, pointing to a black and white photo of a young woman in a shiny silk dress with a high collar and slit in the side.

I replied, "She looks like a movie star!"

Yasui nodded sadly, "Yes, she was very pretty. But she passed away from tuberculosis after we married. She was the love of my life."

"I'm so sorry, Mr. Yasui," I said.

"*Arigato*," he said, bowing. "We can talk more some other time," he said sadly and closed the door.

I felt bad that I reminded him of thoughts that were both painful and sweet. Yes, I thought, *I would like to hear more about his wife someday.*

As the door shut, the hall was transformed from a vision dominated by Yasui's glowing diorama to darkness. All that remained was a shaft of light peeking from under the door. I rubbed my eyes and thought, *Seeing the inside of his room was like lifting a curtain and peering into his private life.*

I shuffled to my room and hummed *Hon kon no youru*. Thinking of the beautiful woman in the photo, I said aloud to the mirror, "I see an older and wiser girl who had many adventures in Japan. What wonders will the future will hold? Maybe I could see the beautiful Hong Kong lights someday."

As days passed, I unpacked and sorted my things. First, I gave everyone gifts from Japan. Then the samurai sword and Shintaro's book to Dad. Still there remained a mystery in my mind about the woman on the Hiroshima streetcar.

After breakfast I invited Dad to the living room. He fell into his over-stuffed chair and wiggled until he settled. As was his habit, he pulled out his gold-chained pocket watch from his wool vest and checked the time. With a small grunt, he snapped the cover shut. I sat directly across from him and skipped the niceties.

"Papa," I asked, "Who was that woman Keiko in Hiroshima?"

Dad smacked his lips and said, "*Ahh*".

He fidgeted and replied. "She's a distant cousin who has no children and is not well in the head. She thinks she is your mother." Dad paused and rubbed his chin.

"When she heard you were in Hiroshima she asked Shintaro if she could visit. Shintaro said, "No." So she followed you until she found you on the streetcar. Don't worry, Shintaro has taken care of it and talked to her family. She will never bother you again. Anyway, you're here and she is in Japan."

I let out an audible gasp "Oh, I'm so glad." His explanation reinforced Shintaro's version.

Satisfied by his answer, I let the matter go. A couple of days later, I decided to reclaim my *kokeshi* doll. I entered the basement and pulled the heavy canvas aside. Dust particles fluttered like fireflies under the naked light bulb. Nearby there was a small shoe box tied with a silk scarf that read "Property of Keiko Tanaka" on it.

What in the Dickens is this? I thought. Knowing she would never return, I opened the box. My hands trembled as I touched each item. I was trespassing but no one would ever know.

Inside were letters and photos of Keiko, Dad, and Mom in front of the hotel. One caught my eye. Keiko was next to a very old Japanese gentleman whose face looked like leather. I thought maybe he was her father. He was smiling happily, but she looked upset. What does this mean and who is the old man? I replaced everything and re-tied the box.

I concluded, *There's more to this story than Dad would say.*

JAPANESE SCHOOL AND REGULAR SCHOOL

As an eleven-year old, I started third grade at Bailey School. I was taller and older than everyone in class. The teacher gave me *Dick and Jane* readers even though everyone else was working on more complex books. Two boys in the back, whispered "Run Dick, run," and snickered as they pointed at me. I tried to hide the books, but all my classmates knew I was the tall girl who read primers.

Because of my age, I was promoted to sixth grade midyear, and then on to Washington Junior High School in the fall. I was happy to leave grade school and be with people my age. But I had a lot of catching up to do. Also I was no longer the tallest; in fact, I was one of the shorter students.

The transition was difficult because of language difficulties. Sometimes I saw an object and knew what it was in Japanese but didn't know the English word. That problem was similar to when I was in Japan and thought some English words were Japanese and some Japanese words were English. I believed, *"Jogo"* was English but found out it was Japanese for "funnel". So I was hesitant to volunteer in class for fear of embarrassing myself.

There were many Japanese students attending Washington Jr. High, so I managed to make many friends. Every day after school I met my best friend, Kiku. We walked to Kokugo Gakko, the Japanese Language School at 14th and Weller Street. I had an advantage because of my time in Hiroshima. So it was not a surprise that I was near the top of my class.

Kiku was happy that I did well and would brag to others about my Japanese language skills. She was an energetic girl who still wore pigtails. Her mannerisms reminded me of Koko in Hiroshima. Both were direct and outspoken.

Kiku worked hard and played hard. Physically, she was shorter than me and a little stockier. Her chatter bubbled like a fountain constantly. Above all, she was just fun to be around.

"Let's go to the Buddhist church bazaar," or "Let's dance in the *Bon Odori*," or "to the Japanese School picnic," or "Let's go downtown window shopping," Kiku urged. Her ideas continued to flow, "The month-end sale at the Bon Marche will be coming up soon. We can find good things cheap! Wanna go?"

At times I found her exhausting. Nevertheless, every school day we walked from Dearborn Street up the hill to the public school and Japanese school after. Typically, I got home about five thirty and then helped with dinner. The restaurant next door was Komatsu Zushi, and the owner, Tomita-san, was from Hiroshima. He was like Uncle Yosh. They had the same stocky build and sense of joy.

In the afternoons, he would call me over from the hotel, *"Hayaku,* Hanae, or Hurry, Hanae."

I understood the routine and ran across the lot with an empty steel pan to pick up tuna fish bones, chicken necks, or some other delicacy he was preparing. Mom cooked the tuna and made delicious soup. Sharing was part of Tomita-san's personality and oftentimes he gave me extra food for a treat. "When my strawberries get ripe," he said, "you pick some." Tomita-san and his wife had no children, so they always tried to do a little something for me.

After dinner I washed clothes for nine people and hung them on the clothesline. The next day, I had a stack of ironing. The process took two days and I was very careful not to get complaints. While scrubbing, I recalled washing my trousers after the Hiroshima quicksand adventure.

I wonder what Koko is doing? I hope she made it back to White River instead of Fresno or Hiroshima. It would be nice to see her again.

Koko would have done well at our annual Japanese school picnic contests. They were summer events I looked forward to. As the only girl in the family, I played stick ball and baseball, but most of all I was a fast runner. In a citywide parks competition, I placed second and won a ribbon. My dreams were encouraged, *I could be a track star*, I thought, *and make a lot of money!*

It was part of my American fairy tale to be recognized and accepted by white society. But as in some Japanese fairy tales, I knew that the hero might not prevail.

Still, Kiku was always positive when it came to the races. She spoke so fast that her words ran together when she said, "We could win first prize–a hundred-pound sack of rice! Our pictures will be in the Japanese newspapers."

"Yes, I hope so," I replied, humoring her as we packed a picnic lunch of rice balls, cold broiled mackerel, teriyaki chicken, and spinach in a miso sauce into our lunch boxes. As in Japan, we wrapped the box with a cloth and carried it like a package. On our way, we walked past the Japanese florist and meat market to catch the Jefferson Park trolley.

Ropes and wooden boundary stakes sectioned off the playfield. Our teachers organized the contestants and officiated the games. They wore white hats, armbands, and white gloves while they shouted commands. Streamers and flags fluttered as a breeze blew from the south. For several years, Kiku and I had dominated the three-legged race. Everyone knew that we were close friends but no one knew that we practiced for months in advance.

I had taken first place in the girls' 50-yard dash the year before, which earned me the nickname "Rabbit" at Japanese school. For the entire year, I enjoyed my status as the fastest girl in school. When I won, my teacher waved his arms. "Good job, Hanae," he said. "Hey, everybody, she's in my class!"

To remember the victory, I clipped a North American Times community newspaper photo of me crossing the finish line. The caption read "Hanae Tamura took first place and won a fifty-pound sack of rice."

Besides the races, Kiku introduced me to the Japanese Presbyterian Church, which was about six blocks from the hotel. It was a modest 1920 brick building where the *Issei* worshiped in Japanese. English services were conducted later for the *Nisei* in the same building. Mom and Dad were Buddhist but did not object to my becoming a Presbyterian. Unsure of what being Christian meant, they nevertheless were happy that I had found a church, unlike my brothers who spent Sundays playing.

After Washington Junior High, I went on to Franklin High School. Miss Sanders, my homeroom teacher, was well-scrubbed and neat. She represented the profession well with her sense of decorum and manners.

At first, I couldn't help but admire her as an example of American liberty, justice, and fairness. I was proud to be in her class and was looking forward to the year.

Taking roll, Miss Sanders looked down the list and said, "Hanawe? Hanai? Hana?"

Sheepishly I raised my hand and replied, "Present." There was a giggle in the classroom.

Miss Sanders smiled politely and with an almost mocking tone said, "Oh, Hana, such a pretty Japanese name, but a bit difficult."

She looked directly at me and asked, "Do you like music?"

I nodded.

"I know what we should do, class from now on we'll call her Viola. It's a beautiful musical instrument. It'll be so much easier for everyone. After all, what's in a name?"

Miss Sanders raised her arm and said, "According to Shakespeare, 'A rose is a rose'."

I was shocked at how suddenly I was changed from Hanae, which had *flower* and *mercy* in it, to a big violin.

Miss Sanders, I concluded, *isn't as wonderful as I expected.*

The Japanese students in class were silent after hearing my new name. They knew the routine since many of them had suffered the same fate. They understood their place as lesser beings: Tomokiyo became Tom, Kenjiro became Ken, Goro became Joe and Misu became Sue. With a few words and a matter of seconds, I was no longer myself. Sanders puffed up with pride after her declaration.

On the way to Japanese school, I complained to Kiku, "Miss Sanders changed my name to Viola."

"What does that mean?" Kiku replied. "I'd complain to the principal. Who does she think she is? That makes me mad!"

I said, "You're right, I'll talk to her tomorrow."

The next day after the bell rang and the rest of the class left, I walked up to Miss Sanders and interrupted her writing.

"Excuse me," I said, "My name is Hanae."

Miss Sanders glanced up and said, "Yes, I know."

"No, I mean my name is Hanae and not Viola," I said, recalling Kiku's anger.

"Oh, okay," She replied and did not look up from her work. Shuffling her papers, she asked, "Anything else?"

I managed a smile and said, "Excuse me." I exited quickly and my knees knocked on the way out.

From that day forward, Miss Sanders never recognized me and never gave me a second look in homeroom.

When she called roll, she merely nodded.

Nevertheless, I discovered that my favorite class in high school was art. At home there wasn't time to draw or paint because of chores, hotel duties, and homework. As a sophomore, I found my artistic talent.

I admired a photograph of the Taj Mahal and painted a picture of it complete with ornate turrets of purple and pink hues. I was inspired by the story of the Maharaja, who built the palace for the love of his wife. It reminded me of Mr. Yasui's wife in Hong Kong.

I said to myself, *I want to marry for love. No arranged marriage for me.*

PIKE PLACE MARKET—1939

On June 10th my spirits leaped when the 1939 Franklin High School graduation ceremony began. There were green and black crepe paper streamers strung from the chandeliers and a huge "Congratulations Class of '39" sign in the auditorium. The room was crowded with families and well-wishers of all ages.

I wore my white Sunday dress under my robe and put French perfume behind each ear. Amid the applause, my heart danced while the orchestra played "Pomp and Circumstance."

"Congratulations," Principal Wilson said as he handed me a diploma and shook my hand. "You can turn your tassel now."

I whipped the tassel around and skipped off stage. Embarrassed by my impetuous actions, I covered my mouth and proceeded to my seat.

After the ceremony, Kiku and I looked at each other. "At last," we said in unison. Then we tossed our mortar boards into the air. I watched them climb and thought, *so much for Viola.*

The orchestra continued to play as Mom, Dad, and my brothers joined me for cake and punch in the commons. I thought, *Masa used to say that It's nice to have something sweet. That way you forget the bitter.*

But I had little time to enjoy my freedom. The next day I went to work at the hotel helping Mom. A few weeks later, Dad called his friend, Mr. Sumida, of *Sumida Farms* at the Pike Place Market. They owned a truck farm on Vashon Island and brought fruits and vegetables to the market.

I woke early and caught the Dearborn streetcar at 6:00 AM. I was like a sleepwalker navigating the streets past vagrants who slept in the store fronts. I was careful to walk past their cardboard shelters quietly. Mr. Sumida opened the grate and welcomed me with a hearty "Good Morning, Hanae."

He was unloading flats of fresh strawberries. They had a pungent and mouth-watering aroma. *I love the smell of strawberries in the morning,* I thought. Then I grabbed my canvas apron and swept the floors, stocked the displays, and served customers.

My interest in farming was piqued as a sophomore when the class took a field trip to the Puyallup Fair. It had horses, pigs, sheep, carnival rides and games. I was attracted to the blue ribbon vegetable display competition. One of the entries had an American flag design made of radishes, zucchinis, green and red peppers, and Walla Walla sweet onions.

Immediately I thought, *I can do that.*

As I set up my own market displays. I remembered the fair. I created vegetable rows and designs arranged so that the colors sparkled under the lights. There were bright waxy green peppers next to shiny red apples and a flourish of orange carrots with green stems. As my skills grew, I experimented and made the flag for the Fourth of July, witches for Halloween, and Santa for Christmas.

Regular customers looked forward to my displays, and tourists took pictures in front of them. I got along well with the crew and was a conscientious worker. Being a recipient of poor service in department stores had its benefits; I knew how to serve people efficiently and courteously. I also made a point to greet everyone with a friendly smile and "hello." Above all, I called the regulars by name.

"Good morning, Mr. Righetti," I said when he approached. He owned a small grocery store on Capitol Hill and had bought produce from the Sumidas for years.

"And who is this?" I asked. His white cocker jumped up with both paws.

"Down boy, this is Charlie," Righetti replied. "He needs some training but is a friendly fellow."

I petted Charlie and said, "Hello."

Righetti continued, "Actually Charlie belongs to my son who is trying to get into the grocery business. He wants to help pay my daughter's tuition at Seattle University."

"Fantastic," I replied. "I wish her luck!"

He said, "When she graduates as a teacher, she will be the first Righetti to get a college degree!"

Just then I heard the familiar clacking a few booths away. It was "Spoons," a street musician. He did a hambone hand-slapping routine and played the silver spoons for tourists. His unmistakable pops and clicks echoed as he smacked spoons against his cheeks, creating a sound that reverberated like an echo chamber. He never said much but would take off his cap and place it on the ground for coins.

Mr. Sumida slid from behind the counter and said, "Good morning, Spoons." Spoons clicked an energetic reply and bowed as he lifted his hat. In his right hand he held an apple Mr. Sumida had given him.

My favorite customer was Timmy, a disabled infantry private who had been blinded in Europe fighting the Germans. He was tall, about six feet two and had light hair. He always wore dark dark glasses. He was single and lived in a First Avenue hotel run by Japanese.

I heard his cane tap and said, "Good morning Tim, this is Hanae. What can I do for you today?"

Because he was special, I saved the best fruits and produce for him. "Wow, what wonderful fragrances!" he said. "They're really fresh."

"Yes, the apples were just picked," I replied. I handed him one of the best and said, "On the house today." I wanted to do something nice since he couldn't see my beautiful displays. As the word spread about my work, more than once the competing Japanese farm stall owners attempted to lure me away. Most gave up and tried instead to copy my displays. But their efforts were nothing more than comical imitations. It was my positive energy embedded in the designs they could never duplicate.

I remained loyal to the Sumidas and was happy that I could work there for years, creating artistic arrangements. Success was sweet and it raised my self-confidence like I'd never experienced before. As a result, my ten-hour days were not drudgery but fun.

Finally, I thought, *I have found a place in America*, even though the newspapers continued to publish anti-Japanese stories. Being like an artist, I was not viewed as Japanese first, but as a creative individual with talent. I recognized my newfound status and marveled at the fact that the market was a door to the larger society.

KIYOSHI

At Franklin High School, I was attracted to boys but nothing serious. Freddy, a young man from White River, worked for Sumida and took an interest in me. He was a little over five feet tall and had a dark complexion. He smiled easily and laughed often.

His arrival usually began with, "Hey, everyone, I'm here to save the day!"

Fellow workers routinely ignored his greeting. He wasn't a lifer like the others, but a junior at the University of Washington who worked part-time. He studied architecture and hoped to get a professional job in spite of the fact that two Sumida brothers had Bachelor degrees and worked at the stand. Determined to succeed in life and love, Freddy asked me to the Buddhist Church dances.

Finally, I said, "Okay, as long as we go in a group and Kiku comes."

Then I remembered he was from White River. I asked, "Do you know a girl named Koko? She is short and stocky and very loud. I met her in Hiroshima and she saved my life."

Freddy laughed, "Saved your life? No can't say that I do. But I'll ask around. If I find her, would you go to the dance with me alone?"

"Maybe," I said. "I'd appreciate your checking."

Many young Japanese attended the Saturday Night Lake Wilderness lodge dances out of town. Initially the Japanese were welcomed. Gradually the news got out in J-town about the lodge and more Japanese attended until the white locals became concerned. They complained about the "invasion" and we were told not to return.

At Sumida's, the young workers discussed the Lake Wilderness situation. Jack, the clean-up boy, said, "It doesn't matter. The music had gone downhill anyway. We still can go to the Buddhist dances and the bands are better."

Freddy remarked, "I'm surprised that the lodge even let us in with all the nasty things in the newspaper. You know, "Yellow Peril," and how white women should be afraid of us!" He said, "At first the lodge owners were greedy and just saw the color of our money and not our skin."

There were no formal complaints or organized protests about the lodge. It was another case of *shikataganai*. We were powerless and there was nothing we could do.

But deep down, all of us, including me, felt the hurt of being second-class citizens. I thought, *Miss McCann was wrong again. This isn't the home of the free. One of these days I hope it will change*, I thought, *but you can't make someone accept you if they don't want to.*

Nearby there was a commotion when a very tiny Japanese woman in a long black fur coat and matching hat arrived. She exuded wealth as she squired a small entourage of two young women and a gentleman escort. I had never seen such wealth. Most of my customers were working folks. This woman was in her 60s and very stylish. She looked every bit like Queen Victoria in full regalia. It was like trumpets sounded when she entered. Her assistant, Mr. Kano, purchase two apples and a pear from Mr. Sumida.

After she had left, a scent of perfume lingered. The clerks in the neighboring stalls gathered and Freddy said, "Holy smokes, that was Sachi Yamada."

He marveled, "Wow, I've never seen a mink coat before."

Sachi and her husband owned and operated three grocery stores, including the very successful High School Market near Broadway. The man who accompanied her was their business advisor, Mr. Hiro Kano. He had a dignified manner and wore a long black wool overcoat and suit. He and the Yamadas had founded, organized, and headed the fifty-member Seattle Japanese grocery store co-op. The association purchased merchandise in bulk and offered prices comparable to, and sometimes below, the chain stores like Safeway.

Freddy said, "I heard that rich lady is looking for a bride for her son Kiyoshi, who operates Elk Grocery Store."

None of them knew Kiyoshi, but the clean-up boy joked, "I betcha he's ugly."

I was amused until the thought occurred to me that Sachi was checking me out. *I want to marry for love and not have an arranged marriage. I'm sure father and mother would agree*, I thought.

Marriage should be done the American way, I said to myself. After all, I was an adult and had a full-time job. As a child my parents had forced me to leave for a Japanese education, but this was very different. I have my own life now. I won't give that up easily, regardless of what my parents said.

Early the next week after my displays were done, a good looking young man strolled up. He was in his 30s, and well-dressed. Mr. Sumida came out from behind the counter and greeted him warmly. He called out, "Hanae, come here. I want you to meet someone. This is Kiyoshi Yamada, owner of Elk Grocery on Seneca Street. He came to admire your displays." I smiled self-consciously and raised my hand to hide my slightly protruding front teeth. Kiyoshi's eyes twinkled when he spoke about the apples. He said, "This is a beautiful."

"Thank you," I replied, "it's fun for me."

He bought a red apple and took a bite. It crunched and he laughed at the loud sound.

"Thanks, the apple is a Delicious and is delicious," he remarked cleverly. He winked, "See you again." He gave me a salute and departed.

Mr. Sumida rushed up and said, "His family heads the Japanese grocery co-op and are good business people. They own land on Mercer

Island in Lake Washington and are sure ferry service will begin, which will increase its value," he said.

"If I had money to burn, I would buy land there too," Sumida remarked. "Also Kiyoshi was a pitcher for the semi-pro Taiyo Eagles, a great ice skater, and amateur boxer. But most important of all, he and his family are from Hiroshima."

His being a pitcher impressed me. But then I thought, *I'm young and not in a hurry to leave the market, my friends, and customers. I have it good here, why leave?*

The unspoken expectations in such a marriage were that the bride would work for the family grocery and the couple would live in the back of the store. I was not sure that I liked that arrangement.

While all this activity was unfolding, Mom and Dad began plans for me to marry a distant cousin from Japan named Toshihiko. He was in the import and export business and wanted to settle in Seattle and establish his own company. "Toshiko is a good person and shrewd businessman," Dad said. "He needs a wife educated in Japan who knows English to help start the business."

When I found out Toshihiko was a distant cousin, I replied with anger, "I want to marry for love. No arranged marriage for me!" I continued to resist because I also wanted time to see what Kiyoshi was planning.

I didn't have long to wait. Over the next six months it was a whirlwind courtship including dances and clam digging on Alki Beach. At low tide we dug a bucket full of butter clams and also gathered seaweed for his mother.

In the fall we went mushroom hunting in the foothills of Mount Rainier. He was proud of his 1940 Chrysler he'd bought with money earned picking Ponderosa Pine mushrooms, or *matsutake*. They were forest delicacies that smelled like pine trees, and brought a great price at market. His reputation was so well known that people called him Matsutake Kiyoshi. Like a fisherman he had many secret spots. Other Japanese followed him in the forest, but he would lead them in circles until they gave up. On one trip with me he said, "I found three under this log last year," and then he lifted it. Sure enough there were four mature mushrooms. *What a miracle*, I thought.

Since he was a pitcher in the Japanese league, he followed the Seattle Rainiers baseball games. I'd never been to a professional game and was eager to go. The atmosphere at the ballpark fascinated me, especially the green fields which were manicured like a golf course. The small band under the announcer's crow's nest played the national anthem. The drummer and tuba players were animated and lively. I thought, *They play the same songs every night but they act like it's their first time.* For the bottom of the seventh it was "Take me out to the Ball Game." Kiyoshi and I held hands and sang. He could carry a tune but I wasn't that good and covered my mouth.

One evening at the Buddhist church dance, Kiyoshi won my heart when he spoke about being sent to Hiroshima as a boy to live with his aunt. We sat on a bench between songs and relaxed. When he misbehaved in Japan his aunt didn't do *moxa*. She went easy on him because he was burned as an infant when he sat in a pot of boiling soy sauce that was set on the porch to cool. He said, "I have a scar that runs down my back to my legs. I was sick for weeks and they thought I would die. Luckily I pulled through. When we go swimming I'll show it to you."

I touched his hand and said, "No thanks, but I'm glad you didn't die."

I knew exactly how it felt to be punished in Japan. I understood those hardships and still carried one scar.

Kiyoshi teared up when he realized that I actually cared for him as a person. He wiped his eyes and said, "The worst part of Hiroshima was that my mother lied. She said she was going shopping in Kyoto when I was eight years old. I knew she was leaving and begged her to stay. But she insisted that she would be right back and left me for three years with my aunt and returned to America."

I sympathized since I had similar childhood memories of abandonment. Because of our shared experiences, I felt I could trust him. We had an unspoken understanding. I thought, *I could spend the rest of my life with him.*

But pressure grew for me to marry Toshiko. Dad said, "You must obey your parents."

I replied, "You sent me to Hiroshima and I had no choice. Now I'm an adult and I won't marry a cousin! What would my friends and especially Kiku say? It would be disgraceful."

The next week Kiyoshi proposed at Maneki restaurant. When he finished the sushi, he fingered a small jewelry box. After chugging two cups of *sake* he said, "Hanae, will you marry me? We'll be very happy together."

I was hoping he would say something more romantic and flowery. I thought, *Okay* and then I leaned closer to him. He took my hand and I felt intoxicated when he opened a blue box containing a gold diamond ring. I had never imagined anything could be so beautiful. Few Japanese women had rings with so many diamonds.

I was thrilled at the sight and had difficulty breathing. "Yes, I will marry you." I wanted to kiss him but resisted the temptation to do it in public in public. Instead I held his hand tight and declared, "Yes, I will."

In April 1941, Kiyoshi and I set the wedding date. Before I opened at Sumida's, Spoons and Harry the Harmonica man strolled up. The help gathered around me, forming a circle and played "Here Comes the Bride." The harmonica was right on, but the spoons accompaniment was odd, though well-meaning. Mr. Sumida had a big grin and proudly hooked his thumbs under his apron straps. Mrs. Borrichini, from the bakery two stalls away, brought a vanilla sheet cake with a bride and groom figurine on top.

"Best wishes, Hanae," Mr. Sumida said. Spoons tipped his hat and the harmonica man played a brief flourish. I was embarrassed and blushed. "Thank you, everyone." I said. "I'd love a piece of cake." Then I called to my friends in the neighboring stalls.

My June 11th wedding date arrived quickly. The ceremony was conducted by a Buddhist priest in a Japanese judo dojo because I did not wish to be married in the temple. I really wanted a Christian wedding, but since Kiyoshi's mother had co-founded the Seattle Buddhist Church, it had to be a Buddhist service. As a compromise, I selected a non-denominational site and insisted that Reverend Anderson, a white minister, give the blessing.

"*Sore wa ikemasen,*" Sachi said with anger about Reverend Anderson. "That is not acceptable."

Sachi stomped her foot and objected, but I replied, "There will be no wedding without Reverend Anderson's blessing."

Sachi looked away for a moment and placed her hand under her chin and pulled the skin tight. The pain seemed to help her reconsider, after all, I could work in the store cheap as part of the family. After a moment, Sachi withdrew her objections. Kiyoshi's family accepted the wedding arrangements grudgingly, but there remained a deep divide.

Originally I wanted Reverend Hori of the Japanese Presbyterian church, but he did not wish to share honors with a Buddhist priest. Not to be deterred, I asked one of my regular Sumida customers, Reverend Anderson. He was more than happy to give the blessing.

Sachi remained uncooperative but did not interfere. So Kiku and I planned the details.

"Kiyoshi's niece, Annie, should be your flower girl," Kiku suggested.

"Also we'll need lots of flowers," I replied, "and a wedding dress. Not to mention gowns for the bridesmaids."

"How about the invitations?" Kiku asked.

"Mr. Terada printed 200," I said, "but the problem is we need help to address and mail them quickly."

"Oh no!" I shouted, "I forgot to order the thank you cards."

"Don't worry. Mr. Terada can print them fast," Kiku replied. "Also I think our church friends can handle guest registration and the gifts."

"Do you think Kiyoshi's sister, Yoko, would help?" I asked.

Kiku replied, "No she's a little too strange."

"Okay, you are right," I replied.

"What about the dinner menu?" Kiku asked.

Things are happening so fast that I'm having a hard time keeping up with the arrangements. I hope it settles down, I thought.

For dinner, I insisted on the Seven Dragons Chinese Restaurant. Mr. Wong, the owner, was a customer and friend from Pike Place market. When he heard I was to be married, he told me, "Come to my restaurant; we'll do a special ten-course dinner."

I replied, "That's a wonderful idea Mr. Wong. We'll have two hundred guests."

"No problem," he responded. "Some Chinese weddings have five hundred. There are always so many Chinese relatives, cousins and more cousins!"

Sachi protested when I discussed dinner. She clenched her fists and said, "Putting money into a Chinese business means they'll send it back to China to help fight the Japanese army! You mustn't do that." She regarded support for Chinese businesses as a traitorous act against the emperor.

I took a deep breath and said, "We live in America. We're not subjects of the emperor."

Sachi grimaced and turned away. She raised one eyebrow and looked like an angry witch. Sachi warned me, "*Bachi ga ataru,* the universe will strike you for your misdeed."

Knowing I'd done nothing to provoke the universe's wrath, I just smiled. The last contact I'd had with the universe was when I was deep in quicksand and had to choose between the hard path or the easy path. Choosing the difficult one prepared me for Sachi's anger, just as Fumi's torrent of insults and belittling behavior had given me strength. I was confident, knowing that I would survive Sachi's wrath no matter what. But it gave me a shiver to be threatened so soon before the marriage.

"Let's go shopping, Kiku," I said. Both of us were excited to look for a wedding dress. She suggested the Bon Marche department store. "The Bon?" I replied. I was afraid that the clerks might call us names because of all the anti-Japanese articles in the Globe newspaper.

Kiku understood what I was thinking by the look on my face and said, "The Bon is a good place. When the store first opened years ago, the owner's wife actually learned to speak Salish to serve Indians when others turned them away. So don't worry. They will be polite. You've more important things to think about."

My fears melted quickly after the bus ride downtown and I found a traditional white gown with a long lacy train. "Look at this," I said. My fingers ran over the gorgeous satin fabric. I lifted the material to my face and caressed it against my cheek.

"Kiku, what do you think about pink dresses? You and the other bridesmaids and my flower girl, Annie, should be in pink."

The wedding day came quickly and the hall was decorated with flowers and ribbons. All the preparations were finished and only the ceremony remained. I was nervous and bit my lower lip while Kiku and I waited in the back. She chatted about the menu and fussed with her bouquet. I thought, *Time is standing still! I want this to get moving!*

The family hired a movie cameraman along with the traditional wedding photographer. This was the first wedding in the community to be filmed. It was a conspicuous display to flaunt Sachi's wealth.

My heart beat rapidly and I began to blush. I clutched the bouquet and waited until the music played. Everything around seemed to slow down, unfolding like book pages flipping.

Little Annie was first to walk down the aisle when the music played. The crowd turned and all eyes were riveted as she tossed rose pedals over the white runner. Kiyoshi lowered his head as if in prayer. He fidgeted in his black tux with tails.

Dad stood next to me in the same outfit as Kiyoshi. I had never seen Dad so well dressed in my life. Both looked especially handsome like a pair of rich gentlemen. When the pianist struck up the *Wedding March*, the crowd stood. Dad and I glided down the aisle towards Kiyoshi.

Behind the veil, I smiled and remembered the time Kiyoshi and I found mushrooms near Mount Rainier. I lowered my eyes when Rinban Suzuki, the Buddhist priest, started to chant. He wore a dark kimono-like coat and sash which reminded me of a monk. Incense swirled when he struck the singing bowl and banged a gong. His voice rose and filled the room. Reverend Anderson stood by his side. After Rinban finished, Anderson stepped forward and said, "May God grant Kiyoshi and Hanae love and contentment for all the days of their lives."

To everyone's surprise he declared, "You may kiss the bride." Kiyoshi lifted my wedding veil. I looked deeply into his eyes and felt a shiver as our lips met. I saw Sachi squirm at this open display of affection; kissing at weddings was not Japanese. Thankfully the music started and Kiyoshi held my hand. We paused and faced the crowd like stage actors taking a bow and I was bedazzled with delight. On the way to the lobby, I felt like we were levitating.

My dress rustled and slipped over the white carpet like Cinderella leaving the ball. At the exit we stopped to greet lines of guests. As the bride, I was like a celebrity surrounded by well-wishers. Ivy Smith, one of Kiyoshi's customers, wore a beautiful hat and hugged me. "You make a beautiful couple," she said, "best wishes."

When the line ended, a path opened down to the sidewalk. I stood at the top of the stairs and saw Kiku waving her arms and jumping up among a group of young women.

Calculating her location, I turned my back and tossed the bouquet high. I peeked over my shoulder. Kiku understood my move and pushed others aside like a football player. I turned and saw her jump. She raised her right hand and snagged the bouquet triumphantly mid-air.

"I'm next," she squealed as she raised the flowers high above her head.

After all the commotion, Kiyoshi and I descended the stairs. The Chrysler was decorated with a "Just married" sign and a string of tin cans tied to the bumper. I screamed when the guests showered me in a hailstorm of rice. I dropped my veil for protection but grains popped into my mouth. Several lodged in my hair and I shook them out when Kiyoshi opened the car door.

In Japan they would be very unhappy about wasting rice, I thought. *America is such a rich country.*

Hormel ham cans were tied to the car bumper. They bounced and some broke free, littering Jackson Street. Kiyoshi stomped on the gas and sped to the Seven Dragons. Pedestrians saw the speeding car dragging cans and jumped back to the safety of the sidewalk. When we pulled up, the restaurant's neon lights blinked and cast an otherworldly hue over us.

I burst out of the car, raised my dress, and leaped. Mr. Wong greeted us with a bow and stood tall in a black tux and tails. He raised his hand and gestured for us to follow. "Hanae and Kiyoshi, this way," he said. He guided us through the banquet hall. Waiters in white coats were bustling as they made last-minute arrangements.

Mr. Wong opened his private office. "Please," he said as he gestured with his hand and motioned us to enter. "Freshen up before the crowd arrives," he offered.

I pushed my veil aside and said, "Kiyoshi, this is best time I've ever had in my life." I hugged him tightly and kissed him. Kiyoshi smiled and said, "This is fantastic. I've found matsutake where no one could, pitched winning baseball games, and danced for hours at parties, but this is the best," Kiyoshi said.

The noise levels rose as the crowd entered the banquet room. We waited for the signal and then took our places at the head table. The room was decorated with flowers and streamers.

Sitting next to me, Kiku was ready to burst with excitement. She chattered, "Wow, I caught the bouquet. Thanks for throwing it my way. I'll be next and he'll be a handsome baseball player. I just know it."

Gracing the table was a three-tiered white cake topped with a pink-faced miniature bride in white and a tall groom wearing a tux and tails. I asked Kiku, "Would you save the little figurines for me? They'll be my souvenirs."

Kiku winked and examined them closely.

Mr. Yamamoto, the emcee, took the mic, "Welcome everyone to this wonderful reception. It's time to toast to the bride and groom." He raised his glass, as did the guests. "Kanpai, bottoms up," he said.

The crowd noise rose and the festive atmosphere grew. Flash bulbs popped from all directions. I said, "All I see are floating blue dots."

"Wow!" Kiku remarked when she looked at the red neon dragon twisting on the ceiling. "This place is a really fancy. How much did it cost?"

I laughed and said, "Mr. Wong gave us a special rate. Wait until you taste the food."

Peking Duck was served after the egg flour soup. Kiku and I stared at the duck slices, white buns, plum sauce, and curled green onions. "How do you eat this?" Kiku asked.

Mr. Yamamoto overheard Kiku and took the mic and announced, "It is okay to use your fingers to eat the duck."

"I'm making mine into a duck sandwich," I responded. I pinched the meat between the soft white buns and added the green onions.

After the chow mein, Mr. Yamamoto invited the audience to sing. Mr. Yabusaki rose and worked his way to the stage. He stood solid before the microphone and hooked his fingers over his vest pockets. Swelling his chest, he announced he would perform *shigin*. It was a type of Japanese singing that consisted of rising, falling, and steady tones that could stretch out and either fade or stop abruptly. It resembled Buddhist chanting. After his rendition, he bowed and smacked his lips with pride. The audience applauded with enthusiasm and he took another bow.

Feeling the champagne's effects, Kiyoshi was not to be outdone. He wobbled to the microphone and bowed to the guests and me. He loosened his bow tie and announced, "I'll sing, *When Your Hair turns from Black to Silver.*" He began slowly, "I will love you always through the years." He glanced down at me with affection, "I will love youuuuu."

I thought, *What a wonderful man. We're going to have a great life together!*

Exhausted, Kiyoshi and I rose and left the banquet room at 9:30 PM. On the way out I thanked everyone, especially Mr. Wong. "It was wonderful," I told him. "I'll never forget the dinner and decorations."

"My pleasure," he replied. "Remember the Seven Dragons will always welcome you. Best wishes. By the way, I had all the cans and decoration removed from your car."

"Thanks again," Kiyoshi said. "We'll come back and have duck!"

We arrived at Russell Hotel and changed our clothes. Kiku and the others gathered in the living room to open the gifts.

"This is just like Christmas morning," little Annie chirped.

We stacked and folded the wrapping paper, saved the ribbons, and catalogued the gifts.

Holding a large silver clock with airplane wings and propellers, I asked, "Who gave us this?"

Kiku read the card. "From the Sumidas and all your friends at Pike Market. We wish you the very best."

"My goodness, I've never seen anything like this before!" I said with amazement. It was a clock with airplane wings and propellers.

It was almost midnight when all the gifts were unwrapped and recorded. Finally, Kiyoshi and I could leave the spotlight and retire for the evening. My mother prepared a special room for us like a wedding suite upstairs. There were flowers and streamers hanging from the light fixtures.

"It looked like the inside of a desert sheik's tent," I said to Kiyoshi.

He smiled from exhaustion and we fell asleep on the bed, fully dressed.

The next afternoon, we drove to Copalis Beach on the Pacific Ocean. After the five-hour drive, we walked the beach and watched the waves crash on shore.

I said, "I've never seen waves this high and sand so smooth in my life!"

Kiyoshi replied, "It's high tide now so when it drops to low in the morning, this beach will be twice as wide."

To celebrate, we returned to the cabin and popped a bottle of champagne. Together we watched a red sun slip into the sea. Kiyoshi fell asleep quickly. I made a cup of tea and stood before the full-length mirror. I imagined holding a beautiful bridal bouquet.

I said to myself, *I see an American in the mirror, not Japanese. Koko would be proud of what I've become, not a modan garu but an American woman. I* smiled at my reflection. *I've come a long way from Japantown. I can't wait for great things to happen.*

I realized that this was my country with all of its warts, in spite of the anti-Japanese news articles. I wondered, *What's next? It will be morning soon and a new day. I hope our future is bright and that we have a nice house and beautiful children.*

Unfortunately, when we returned to Seattle we were greeted by news that I never anticipated about Shintaro. I was crushed and sad to hear he passed away. I remembered how grand Shintaro looked in his naval uniform complete with a sword. He was my oldest brother and I thought, *I still have brothers but I would not have another like him.*

WESTERN UNION TELEGRAM

June 23, 1941

To: Toyojiro Tamura
921 Lane Street
Seattle, Washington

Shintaro passed away yesterday from a heart attack- stop Help. Please come quickly to Hiroshima-stop

Fumi

CHAPTER SIX

1941-1942

Dad grabbed his reading glasses while sweat beaded on his upper lip. After a long silence he wiped his eyes.

"Shintaro is gone," he exclaimed. His hands shook when he gave me the paper. He sat and whispered, "Toku, I must leave for Japan. Hanae, please help with the steamship arrangements."

"This can't be true," I said. "He was such a strong person and so young."

I felt guilty when I recalled my past anger towards Fumi and how I failed. I thought, *Without Shintaro, she, her children and Masa must be suffering greatly.*

After the news, Dad looked like he aged overnight. His shoulders rounded and his stature shrank. "It's not right for a son to pass before his father," he said. "It's not right."

Shaking my head, I thought, *I need to tell the relatives, especially Kiyoshi's sister, Yoko, who may be able to contact Shintaro's soul from the other side.*

I said. "Dad, I'll take the day off and buy the trip tickets."

There was a sadness that permeated the hotel. To me it felt like the universe had taken a good man from this earth. I wondered, "Why and why now?"

JULY, 1941

A month later, Dad returned and settled into his usual routine at *Our House Tavern*. He brought small gifts of tea and pickles, but he seemed to have lost the bounce in his step.

"How're Masa, Fumi and the kids?" I asked.

Dad sighed, "Ahh, they are doing okay."

"Do we need to send money?" I asked.

"Don't worry," he replied, "I'll do it."

Given Shintaro's death and the recent inflammatory stories about Japanese in the newspaper, I worried about our Hiroshima family treasures.

The next day I searched the hotel and found Dad relaxing. I asked, "What did you do with the sword and diary? Are they safe?"

He looked up from his newspaper and said, "Everything is okay."

"Please tell me more. This is important," I insisted. "Shintaro said I was responsible for them too."

"It's a long story, do you have time?" he replied.

I nodded and he began. "In early July I went to Mr. Kashima's house. We didn't play *go* or drink *sake* as usual. Kashima san welcomed me and we went down the creaky wooden stairs to the basement."

Dad paused and smacked his lips as was his habit when he spoke at length. He fidgeted and continued, "Kashima san dragged out a pick and we took turns cutting a channel in the hardpan at the edge of the foundation in the basement."

He grinned and said, "We worked like coal miners. Then we slipped two swords wrapped in canvas side by side under the foundation. I knew war with America was possible and wanted to make sure the samurai ancestral spirits were safe."

Dad's eyes grew misty as he continued, "We tamped down the dirt and dusted it to cover the newly disturbed area. Both of us felt a sense of relief as we marked the area with an oil stain."

Kashima san suggested, "We should write a note to our families about what we did with the treasures."

Dad said that the burial was sad. It reminded him of Shintaro's funeral.

He took a deep breath and sighed. "I told Kashima san it's done. No one will find them except our families."

"What happened to the diary?" I asked.

Dad took out a hanky and blew his nose. "I burned it," he replied.

I thought, *That's unfortunate. It was so beautiful.* I shook my head. *How many more awful things must we do to protect ourselves in these times?*

ELK GROCERY AND SACHI, 1941

The next day, Dad caught the streetcar to visit Elk Grocery. The store was nestled in the First Hill area and walking distance from downtown. It was a mixed neighborhood surrounded by 1920s five-and six-story brick apartments, which provided a steady clientele for the store. There was a Chrysler dealership, retail stores, small manufacturing companies, and a chicken rendering plant about a mile away on Jackson Street.

Kiyoshi worked behind the counter and handled the day-to-day operations such as ordering, deliveries, and stocking shelves. In return he received a salary and lodging from his mother. The store sold canned goods, produce, milk, wine, cigarettes, and eggs, but didn't have a butcher shop. It was not a modern self-service store like Safeway. Instead, the customers told the clerk what they wanted, and the employee got the items from the shelves or bins.

The building was cold and drafty in the winter and warm in the summer. The floors were concrete, and after years of standing on the hard surface, gravity took its toll. Kiyoshi suffered from varicose veins, which bulged unattractively and ached daily. To ease the pain, he wrapped his legs with elastic bandages. The grocery business was tough and making a penny per item was doing well. With sweat and determination, the business grew.

Even though business was good, Sachi and Koemon's marriage was rocky. They had never truly known each other before their arranged wedding. Intentionally their relationship was fragmented by lengthy individual trips between America and Hiroshima. Exacerbating the situation, in 1936 Sachi openly took a live-in lover, Hiro Kano, in revenge for Koemon's Hiroshima indiscretions during a visit. Her defiant act violated the social mores of the tight-knit Japanese community and larger society as well. It was totally unheard of for a Japanese married woman to do this.

The gossip and tension were suffocating. The situation made me feel like a fish in polluted waters. After the wedding, Sachi's real personality as a meddling mother-in-law had emerged. She pulled her strings tight to make Kiyoshi dance. I was hoping otherwise, but worst of all, Sachi didn't pay me. I was trapped. Soon I regretted the marriage with its odd work arrangement and tense family situation. I became depressed and dreaded going to sleep because I tossed and turned for hours.

Oh, what have I gotten myself into? I wondered. *Quicksand would be easy compared to this! Bachi ga atatta, the universe just struck me for a past misdeed,* I thought. *With this awful situation, my past misdeed must have been huge!*

To mentally escape, I thought of the *kokeshi* doll and found it stored away and wrapped in a kimono. It was as I remembered —red lips and that strange smile. I held it in both hands as I did before Hiroshima. I closed my eyes and sent my spirit into the doll for safekeeping. Trouble was coming and I wanted to brace myself for the next wave.

Unpacking the doll, I rediscovered Keiko's photographs. I thought, *I wonder, would this be a good time to ask Dad and finally get all the answers about her? I'll bring it up again shortly.*

THE APARTMENT

Kiyoshi and I lived in the back of Elk Grocery. To make room, Koemon, Sachi, and Hiro moved from the store to a three-bedroom house on Beacon Hill. On some days Sachi and Hiro stayed overnight in the store bedroom, and other times they slept at the house with Koemon.

After the wedding, tensions between Sachi and me remained high. I sensed that she wanted revenge for having Reverend Anderson at the wedding and dinner at the Seven Dragons. But for now there was an uneasy cease-fire, given the distraction of the anti-Japanese agitation. The newspapers spread propaganda and fear about Japanese in America. The headlines said we were spies and the Japanese farmers were selling poisoned produce. The family was concerned. Sachi said, "I hope our white customers keep coming. I worry about what the newspapers say."

"Don't," Kiyoshi replied, "Our loyal customers traded with us for years. We'll be fine." He smiled and pulled out his feather duster.

On cold Seattle mornings, I welcomed the glowing flames that danced in the oil stove in the back apartment. A dented teakettle provided humidity, but was removed on Wednesdays when a portable clothes rack appeared. On wash days, water condensed on the window and blocked the view of the back yard. I picked up a cloth and said to myself, *It would be nice to see the yard.*

Because of the cramped living quarters, privacy was at a premium. I had to overlook many things: snoring, smells from the bathroom, the jumble of drying clothes, and odors from the kitchen. The bathroom was shared, and the toilet bowl had a perpetual rusty ring. The metal medicine cabinet was full of odiferous Japanese medicines, herbs, and salves. When opened, the smells gushed out.

So much to do, I thought. *When will I have time to make this a proper house?*

I cooked on a Glenwood stove that had four ornate legs and nickel-plated trim. It had a flat cooking surface with four round, manhole-like covers and a metal poker to stir the fire and ashes. Wood was stacked nearby, and there was a small ash bucket and shovel. I saved the ashes and sprinkled them in the backyard.

I thought, *the crackling and popping of wood accompanied by the tea kettle whistle is comforting; one small pleasure to be thankful for.* My other pleasure was playing the Baldwin piano. Often, I opened the lid and hit some random notes and listened to them float in the air.

Looking out the window, I asked, "Sachi, can I start a vegetable garden in the backyard? We'll have fresh greens to eat and I can put the ashes in the garden."

With an air of indifference, Sachi turned her head and nodded. Because it was late in the season, I planted vegetable starts: lettuce, tomatoes, and strawberries in mounded rows. The area was transformed and bees arrived followed by robins. The yard exuded a pleasant and comfortable aura that sparkled as if I had lured *Kamisama*. Pea vines climbed the clothesline strings and honeybees worked the purple lavender. *Wow, it's amazing how much everything grew,* I thought. *I have a green thumb that Yosh would be proud of. I wonder how he and Tama are doing and of course Yuki.*

Just for fun I planted sunflowers and named them after the threesome. They grew to over seven feet, and Yosh was the tallest although in real life the plant was taller than he. The plants looked like sunflowers during the day and at night like people standing and chatting. There was a spooky feel in the evening when the wind blew and their heavy heads nodded among the dark shadows. *Kamisama,* I said to myself, *please help my garden grow, especially my sunflowers.*

I felt sad when fall arrived and much of my garden was harvested. I remembered reading a Seattle Globe article about planting a winter crop. With spirits lifted, I scanned the yard in anticipation. The garden became my space to relax and escape from the claustrophobic, tension-filled apartment.

Checking the garden became part of my daily routine which included going to the back porch and opening a metal garbage can containing a sack of Ebisu brand rice. I scooped out the white grains, raising a small cloud with each dip. The grains tinkled and bounced as they hit the cooking pot's bottom. Washing the rice was both a ritual and necessity. The grains made a scratchy sound with each swirl of my hand in the milky water. I saved some of the water for my plants.

Like panning for gold, I swished and washed the rice, removing the starch from the pearl-colored beads. When the water cleared, it was ready. I smiled and remembered Masa teaching me how to prepare food. She would love this iron pot, I thought. Food reconnected me to good memories at Shintaro's house. *I think Masa would be proud of my cooking.*

THE CHICKEN

Dad visited Elk Grocery often and spent time puttering around. When the sun shined, he enjoyed cooking lunch on a small charcoal hibachi. Twelve blocks away was the Rainier poultry plant. One morning, a reddish-brown hen strolled into the backyard. It must have fallen off a truck and found her way under the fence to feast on my vegetables.

Seeing the bird, I dropped the watering can. It bobbed its head and poked its neck back and forth. It glanced at me but was not frightened and made no effort to appear like anything more than a clueless bird.

"Dad, where did that come from?" I asked, displaying a piece of shredded cabbage.

The chicken stripped several different plants, leaving a wake of scattered green destruction.

"So much for my winter crop," I grumbled. "Dad, why is that thing here?"

He shrugged his shoulders. Sachi heard us and peeked out the back door.

"*Shikataganai*," she remarked as she turned her back on the destruction. With a self-satisfied smirk she said, "*Bachi ga atatta.*

I rolled my eyes at her remarks and turned to Dad.

"Well, Dad, are you going to keep it?" I asked.

Like a parent speaking to a child, I remarked, "If you keep the bird, it better not eat any more of my plants. Are you going to cook it now, or wait until it does something useful like lay some eggs?"

Dad smiled a silly grin.

He waved his hand and said, "Yes."

By his gestures, he gave the impression that it might be a good pet. With a stern look, I put my hands on my hip and grimaced.

I chided, "Okay, but if you keep it, you need to care for it and give it a name."

"Ha ha, Okay, Ichiro, number one son," Dad replied.

I laughed and waved my hand, "I've spent time in the country and hens are girls, don't you know. It must have a girl's name."

He had a mischievous look and said, "Sachiko is a good name."

I rolled my eyes, "You can't do that. Sachi would never stand for a chicken named after her!"

With a chuckle he said, "Okay, I'll think of a better name."

I left the yard and thought, *I can't believe he wants to keep that darn thing! Are we running a zoo?*

Dad smacked his lips as he contemplated the fate of the escapee. He rubbed his chin and asked, "Is this a pet or something for the rendering plant?" It peeked through the cabbage and poked its neck back and forth. He laughed. "Oh, I could catch it with a fishing net. That would be a sight!"

Speaking to the chicken he said, "I'll have mercy on you. Do something to deserve it."

Dad waited and watched but the bird was nothing more than a dumb creature. He covered the hole in the fence then asked, "Hanae, why did *Kamisama* send this? Was it a sign or an omen? Was it my obligation to care for one of God's creatures or was this a gift to cook for dinner?"

"I don't know, but you'll have to do something soon," I replied.

Since Dad was in a good mood, I saw an opportunity to ask about Keiko. I said, "Never mind the chicken. A long time ago I found photos of Keiko. In the pictures she's with you and a funny-looking old man. What was going on?"

Dad replied. "You were too young to understand."

"Well, tell me now. I'm an adult." I insisted. "What's the big mystery?"

Dad sat down on a wooden box and paused. "Okay," he said. "Keiko was a picture bride and the old man sent her a photo of a young and handsome man. When they met, she couldn't believe the deception. So she refused to marry him," He said.

Dad picked up a stick and scratched the ground for a few seconds and continued, "She was in debt for the trip and the old man wouldn't pay unless she married him. Keiko didn't have the money, so gangsters paid her debts. In return she worked at a house of pleasure near the Nippon Kan Theatre."

"What? She was a prostitute? How did you get involved?" I asked.

"Well, she was headstrong and they beat her up," Dad continued. "She had nowhere to go and ended up on our hotel steps with nothing but the clothes on her back. The gangsters came looking for her and your mom decided to help. Because Keiko was from Hiroshima, Mom felt sorry for her. We contacted her family in Japan and it turned out she was a distant relative. It took some time, but the Hiroshima people paid the gangsters including a ticket home."

I was shocked and asked. "Was she a prostitute?"

Dad nodded, "Yes, when we found her, she had a black eye, bruises on her arms, and burns over her body. So we took her in."

What next? Every story seems to just keep unraveling. What else don't I know? I wondered. "Okay Dad," I said, "is there any more to this?"

He shook his head and said, "No, that's all."

"You sure?" I asked.

"Yes," he said. As was his habit, he pulled out his watch to check the time and then lifted himself slowly from the chair.

WAR IS DECLARED

Molly, my dog, joined the family at Elk Grocery. She had curly white fur and big dark eyes under her bangs. Her name was engraved on her collar badge. Usually she sat by the cash register and greeted people with a tail wag. Many apartment dwellers dropped by just to say, "Hello". Oftentimes they bought something small like an apple, cigarettes or candy. At first Kiyoshi was against Molly but his attitude changed when he saw how much the customers loved her.

When Molly was not in the front, she was in the apartment with Dad or playing in the yard. She respected my garden and would bark at any invading squirrels or rats. Quizzically she turned her head and had a puzzled look when we ignored her chicken warnings.

On December 7th, the *Globe* truck ground to a halt in front of Elk Grocery. A delivery man jumped out. He tossed a bundle and leaped back on the tailgate and the truck roared off.

The headlines read, "Extra, Extra! Japs Attack."

"Holy smokes!" Kiyoshi said. "Everyone come here! The Japanese bombed Pearl Harbor!"

"Pearl Harbor, where's that?" Sachi asked.

"Hawaii," I replied, "they attacked Hawaii!"

"We worked in the sugar cane fields there," Koemon said. "I know that place."

"Kiyoshi, please turn on the radio," I begged.

We gathered around and waited. I had the strange feeling that every passerby was staring as if *we* attacked Hawaii. For months before, the newspapers warned that Japanese were bad people and now there was proof. The Globe ran stories about unfair Japanese competition in the grocery business and at the Pike Place Market. They claimed we took jobs from white people and that we were really spies loyal to the Emperor.

"Oh my!" I said as I felt my neck hairs tingle at the thought. *Shintaro warned me about the danger of war, and so did the Hiroshima psychic.*

"*Nisei* should be okay," Kiyoshi said. "We're American citizens but the *Issei* aren't because they can't be U.S. citizens."

I fidgeted and added, "But the newspapers say we're all bad. We should write them and tell them we are loyal Americans."

We waited anxiously as radio static cleared and the thread-like voice of President Roosevelt emerged. "Turn it up," I urged.

Roosevelt said it was a day that would live in infamy when he announced war on Japan.

I worried about friends and relatives in Hiroshima. *I hope Yosh, Tama, Masa, and even Fumi and her children will be okay. And what of that girl, Koko?*

I had never experienced anything like a declaration of war. "Japanese are targets," I said. This was not like the nagging fear of possible earthquakes but more like waves tumbling over passengers in a stormy sea. Paralyzed and afraid to breathe, I thought, *I want to disappear.*

For days, the newspapers continued to incite panic among the public and accused Japanese of Fifth Column activities including potential sabotage. They raised fears that we'd help the enemy by sending radio signals and giving secrets to Japan. Community groups like the Chamber of Commerce and Elks Clubs called for our removal while others threw stones at Japanese businesses and homes.

Dad had withdrawn the family savings from the Sumitomo bank, based on the warnings in Shintaro's diary. Others burned Japanese possessions in bonfires. Many people were frozen in denial and failed to do anything except wait.

Dad said, "Our treasures are safe." He gave a sigh of relief knowing he and Mr. Kashima had buried their swords. Fear spread that Japanese who owned guns, radios, and swords would have the items confiscated by the Seattle police. Shortly orders were given for all Japanese to turn in contraband items regardless of whether they were American citizens or not. Kiyoshi checked the list, and among other things he turned in our overseas radio in exchange for a slip of paper. Without our radio, we had a hard time keeping up on the news until he found a regular radio in the storage shed. It was an antique but it still worked. "No one will think this old thing can receive messages from Japan," he said. "We'll keep it in the store."

Others predicted that martial law would be declared soon. Tensions increased when many Japanese community leaders were taken by FBI agents.

We have nothing to hide and are loyal. But what can we do and why am I so afraid? I worried.

DECEMBER 11TH, 1941

Kiyoshi removed the padlock and pulled the metal scissor gate as usual. He flipped the "Open" sign and turned on the lights. I wiped the counter and picked up a feather duster. Kiyoshi turned on the radio and paused to hear the latest news.

"Maybe there'll be more about the attack," he said. He rolled up his sleeves and pushed a broom in time with the music. He swept quickly pushing dirt from the sidewalk into the street.

Everything seemed normal as office people rushed to work. The green trolleys glided by, transporting passengers who were chatting and reading the morning newspapers. Kiyoshi dragged out four empty wooden crates and set up the fruit display. He grabbed the *Globe* newspaper bundle and dropped it on the counter. With care, he snipped the packing wires and arranged the papers on the counter. His eyes caught the screaming headlines, "Japs Plan Seattle Attack".

"Oh no! Bad news," he said. His hands shook as he covered the word "Jap" in the headlines with a red brick. Then he bunched the wires and placed them under the counter.

Following his normal routine, he calmly unpacked a box of California oranges and stacked them. "Wow Hanae, this is a great shipment even though they were in storage," he said. They were fragrant and exceptionally beautiful. Kiyoshi inhaled and smiled. He separated the purple wrapping tissue and stacked them flat. The Durante song, "Make Someone Happy" played on the radio. Kiyoshi hummed along as he worked.

The 10:00 AM news broadcast blared: *"We interrupt this broadcast with an important news bulletin. Adolf Hitler declared war on the United States of America today. The president is expected to declare war on Germany shortly. The United States is now at war with Japan and Germany. We will interrupt our regular transmissions as more news breaks."*

"Hanae, This can't be true!" Kiyoshi remarked. "I hope it'll be business as usual," he said as he puffed on an orange and polished it with his apron. He tinkered with the display and placed the price signs in the boxes.

Then the gravity of the news struck him. He yelled, "Criminy sakes, Hanae, we're at war with Germany and Japan."

"Kiyoshi things are getting worse. With so much fighting I am beginning to worry," I exclaimed.

I wondered out loud, "What's going to happen if Japan attacks Seattle? Would you fight the Japanese?"

The thought was like a whizzing hummingbird diving and I imagined Sachi being taken away by the US government and Japanese soldiers with bayonets marching up Jackson Street. Then I shook my head and came back to reality. *No joy in thinking about that!*

"I'm too old to fight," replied Kiyoshi, "so I guess I'll just stay here in Seattle. I'm sure business will be good."

Kiyoshi held up an apple for inspection and spoke as if it were a person. "How can they resist you?" he asked. "Just one look and customers will want you. As Grandma always says, 'Hunger starts with the eyes'." He continued, "You beauties will keep on flying out the door, and in a few years I'll be able to afford a fresh meat counter. Safeway will have big competition from Elk Grocery."

CHAPTER SEVEN

Before the Evacuation, 1942

The shop bell rang and Kiyoshi's niece, Megumi, entered with a flourish. She was a seventeen-year-old student at Garfield High School. Shucking off her hat, she unwound her scarf and dropped her schoolbooks on the counter with a thump.

Visibly upset, Megumi fumed, "Uncle and auntie, the FBI is taking ministers and priests including Rinban Sasaki from the Buddhist Church. Also they took Kenji Mayeda and all the board members of the Japanese Language School yesterday. What's happening?"

Kiyoshi stiffened and rubbed his chin. He said, "I heard about the FBI visits but didn't know that they'd taken Buddhist priests."

"Who will conduct the church services and run the Japanese Language School?" I asked.

Megumi's face flushed red. "It isn't fair," she replied, "They didn't do anything. They're loyal to America. As for me, everyone knows I love my country. This shouldn't happen. It's just not right."

Kiyoshi put down his broom. He said, "Cousin Sue called me yesterday because they took her father and others on December 8th. Right away Reverend Andrews, the pastor of the Japanese Baptist Church, looked for them. He went to the police and FBI. Finally, he found them locked in a cage at the Dearborn Street Immigration Center."

Kiyoshi looked down at the floor and continued. "Sue said that all the Japanese men were unshaven, so she brought a shaving razor. Her father passed it around until everyone was clean-shaved. Otherwise, in a few more days they all would have looked like hobos."

"How could the FBI do that?" Megumi fussed. "It's unconstitutional. This is America and we have rights. The government would never betray its own citizens." She shook her head and slammed her palm down on the table.

"These are strange times," Kiyoshi, said. "War with Japan is especially bad for *Issei* because they can't become U.S. citizens. But we're American citizens. Personally I'm fine as wine. I got a shipment of oranges today and I'm making a beautiful display. The store will be busy as always. My regulars in the apartments have been loyal for years. They know Hanae, grandpa, grandma, Molly, and me. They're friends and will keep coming. Just wait and see."

"I hope you're right," I said. You remember we even invited some of our best customers to our wedding.

"I know," Megumi said, "the rumor mill says we could all be taken like the *Issei* leaders. But I can't believe that!"

Her voice cracked when she continued, "I'm still in high school and Dad runs Legion Hotel. Uncle, you know my Mom takes care of my brothers, sisters, and me. My grandparents both need heart medicine. How can we live if they take us to God knows where? Who would take care of Sammie, my cocker?"

Megumi wiped away tears and said, "What of Mr. Chin who is Chinese with a Japanese wife? What'll happen to him? Uncle, would you go with your wife and kids or would you stay here separated from them?"

"This is not Nazi Germany," Kiyoshi snapped. "This is America and we are loyal. We trust the government. Anyway, where would they put us - at the Olympic Hotel in first class rooms? No, they'll leave us alone. We're small potatoes. We're nobodies."

"I'm still afraid for the *Issei* farmers," replied Megumi. "They don't speak much English. It must be frightening for them. How will their families bring in the crops?" Megumi sighed and said, "I hope they'll be released for harvest. Otherwise, the crops may never be planted or may rot in the ground. We should do something to help. Maybe a fund drive? Uncle, would you put a donation box in the store for them?"

Kiyoshi raised his hand as if to signal "halt" and said, "No, not here. I don't want to call attention to what's happening. We're Americans." Kiyoshi groaned, "For a young girl, you have strange ideas."

Megumi gathered her strength and said, "Rinban Sasaki taught us that every living thing is important. We must take care of each other. We must keep everyone's spirits strong."

I put down the duster and stepped away from the counter. "That's a good idea," I said. "We should do something for the families whose men and women were taken. They'll be too ashamed to say anything."

Kiyoshi turned and asked, "What kind of store do you think I'm running? This isn't a charity." His body tightened. "I sell groceries to white people. We need to make money, not give it away. I know the Japanese farmers are having a tough time, but we have problems of our own making a buck."

I insisted, "Kiyoshi, just do it. It'll be fine. The white customers will understand because they're used to seeing the Red Cross donation boxes."

Kiyoshi backed down and replied, "Okay, we'll have a collection box for a week or two. We can give the money to Reverend Andrews. The FBI won't bother a white minister. Okay girls, you ganged up on me. Are you happy now? Here's an empty Prince Edward cigar box," he said and thumped it on the counter. "Megumi, make a donation sign."

She wrote, "Please give to Japanese families whose breadwinners were taken by FBI." Megumi proudly propped up the sign. "Oh, it looks great!" she exclaimed. "Now, Uncle, can you put a couple of quarters in there?"

"What?" he replied.

Megumi pointed at the box. He reluctantly dug into his pocket and pulled out some change. "This is good enough," he said.

He rolled his eyes and dropped two nickels into the box. "Some days," he joked, "that would be half my profit."

Megumi was pleased, then continued in a playful voice, "Just one more thing, Uncle. I see you stack the nice fruits in front and you give the customers the ones from the back. I know your tricks. Would you let the customers pick their own fruits in future?"

"All my oranges are good, front or back," Kiyoshi insisted. He rearranged the display with care and said, "You need to hightail it to school. Anyway, don't worry. Our prices are good and so is the quality. Isn't it time for you to leave?"

"I have an appointment with Doctor Kimura so I'm out early," she replied, straightening her hat and scarf. "A lot of my Japanese friends at Garfield High School are taking the day off. They're afraid of getting hurt. Some are saying they're Chinese or Korean to avoid trouble. But everyone knows the truth. The Chinese are wearing 'I am Chinese' buttons so they don't get beaten up."

"That doesn't sound right," I said. "We're all Americans. We didn't come over on the Mayflower but we still have every right to be here."

"There are rumors about a curfew," Megumi said. "I need to get an 'I am Chinese' button so I can sneak out." Megumi gave a sly grin, "I'll do it, just wait and see." She frowned and looked down at the floor. "But I hope things will be okay. I want to go to college and become a teacher or nurse. I've never left the state so I want to see the Grand Canyon and

New York City. I'm tired of *podunk* Seattle. There's just nothing happening here; same old people, same old friends, and same old Japantown. I want to see the world and cities like London, Paris, and Rome."

I perked up. "Before the war I traveled to Hiroshima and stayed with my brother and uncle in the country. Oh, I remember getting seasick on the ship. Our family house is near the river in the center of Hiroshima. It's beautiful there."

I thought for a second and continued, "I've never been to New York City but I'd love to see it. The first stop will be the Empire State Building and then the Statue of Liberty. I dream of looking out at the city from her crown. You can climb into her torch too. Anyway, that's what I hear." The phone rang. "Excuse me, I'll get it," I said and rushed to the back room. It turned out to be a crank call about Japanese. Returning to the front of the store, I knelt to tie my shoes.

The shop doorbell chimed and I saw a six-foot tall white man wearing a brown overcoat and fedora. Feeling a little queasy, I decided to rest on a milk box. Immediately I heard a "whack" as the customer smacked a *Seattle Globe* on the counter. He examined Megumi as if she were an insect. Then he peered over his glasses and shot Kiyoshi the hate stare.

Megumi swayed side to side.

I thought, *Maybe he's FBI.* Then I got up and walked towards the cash register.

Unsure of himself, Kiyoshi grinned timidly. "Good morning sir. Can I help you?"

The customer's eyes were inflamed. He spat in Kiyoshi's face. "That's for bombing Pearl, you dirty Jap."

The customer shook his fist. "I'm warning you. Go back to Tokyo or worse things will happen to you and your family."

With a crash, he dumped the orange display, spilling them over the floor. "You can't sell Jap oranges here. This is America."

The man raised the newspaper and said, "By the way, I ain't paying for this. So call the cops if you want."

The customer turned and sauntered out as the shopkeeper bell sounded. Kiyoshi's hands shook.

Megumi was frozen.

I put my arm around her. "You okay?" I asked.

Kiyoshi caught his breath, "Holy man!! He is crazy." Kiyoshi put his hand on his forehead. "I hope he never comes back and thank goodness he didn't break the door. Anyway they're California oranges." With a sigh, he picked up a rag and wiped his face.

Megumi had a strained look, "I can't believe it. This is horrible. Things like that don't happen in Seattle."

I guided Kiyoshi to the mirror and wiped his face. Kiyoshi said, "That guy was a jerk. I was born in Goldbar, Washington. I'm 100% American. I'm not a Japanese citizen. And we're from Hiroshima, not Tokyo."

He threw the rag down. "Oh well, the spit is gone."

Kiyoshi gritted his teeth and twisted his face. He tried to reassure us and said, "Everything's okay. Hanae don't get upset, okay? He turned to Megumi and told her, "Hanae is going to have a baby in August. We just found out."

Megumi blinked and was taken aback by the good news. "Congratulations to both of you. I hope it's a girl," she replied and buttoned her coat in haste. Then she scurried around the displays and picked up a few scattered oranges.

"Never mind those, I'll get them," Kiyoshi said and grabbed a broom. He swept madly working off the adrenaline. "That creep has come in a few times for milk and bread. He never says much. Usually he just gets what he wants and there's no commotion."

Megumi shook her head. "Oh, Uncle, I'm sorry he did this."

He twisted his mouth and replied, "Don't worry. People like him are not our friends. But we might need some extra protection if things get worse. The cops and the government won't turn on us. We're citizens; you have nothing to worry about. Now go and study hard."

He shooed her out and then hollered. "Hey, wait a second. Have a Hershey bar. Now scoot before I call your mom and tell her you're playing hooky."

I waved to Megumi, "Tell your mother 'Hi'," I said.

She pulled her scarf tight and opened the door. A cold wind gusted when the shop keeper bell rang. "Thanks, Uncle, and goodbye, Hanae."

Kiyoshi rested on a crate. He had a dejected look and leaned on his broom. "Boy oh boy, the day's just begun and I'm exhausted," he mumbled. "I should just flip the open sign over."

He pulled himself up and turned the radio off. The silence created an eerie mood in the store. Slowly he turned the sign and bolted the door. "Are we closing early today?" I asked.

He slumped in a chair and lowered his head between his knees. As if in a trance, he stared at the ground and said, "Never mind, just give me a minute."

Not sure what to do next, I stood by the cash register and picked up the duster. Out of the corner of my eye I saw a black Ford pull up in front. Two men in suits jostled the store door and checked their watches. I could see their faces when they knocked firmly.

Kiyoshi hollered, "I'm closed. Can't you read?"

The tall agent replied, "FBI, open the door. We're looking for Mr. Tamura."

Hearing their voices left a sharp pain in my stomach. "I'll let them in," I said. Quickly I flipped the sign and unbolted the door

Kiyoshi rose and scurried in a panic, "Okay, okay, we're open."

There was a strong fragrance of Old Spice cologne. Both agents stared at the oranges scattered over the floor. One caught a glimpse of the newspaper wires under the counter.

The smaller agent examined the tangled wires and asked suspiciously, "What's this?"

Although these men looked official, Kiyoshi was not taking any chances. He stiffened and said, "Can I see your identification?"

"Yes of course," replied the tall one. They presented official-looking gold badges. "I'm Agent Tibbs, and this is Agent Miller."

There was no question that these men were real FBI. Kiyoshi gulped and sighed.

Righting himself quickly, he called out, "Hanae, get your dad. The FBI wants to see him."

"Okay," I said and fussed with my apron.

Nonchalantly, Kiyoshi maneuvered to the counter and closed the lid on the collection box. Agent Miller noticed Kiyoshi's sly move and looked with suspicion.

After securing my apron I rushed to the back living room. I told Dad, "Put down the newspaper. The FBI wants to see you." In response, he glanced out the window and folded the newspaper. I said, "Hurry, don't keep the FBI waiting."

The phone rang. I thought, *Probably another crank call. I'll just ignore it.*

FBI

I hustled to the front and stood next to Kiyoshi. The agents scanned the shelves as if they expected an ambush. In a clipped tone, the taller one asked Kiyoshi, "Are you the owner of the store?"

Sweat dripped down his face, Kiyoshi put down the broom and replied, "Yes, that's me, but everyone calls me Ernie."

The taller one, Miller, asked again, "Is Mr. Tamura here?" He attempted to pronounce Toyojiro, but it came out as Toy oh Jiro. However, he was not flustered by his bad pronunciation.

Miller continued, "He also goes by the name Frank and works at Our House Saloon. We checked at the Russell Hotel today and they said he's here."

Kiyoshi wiped his brow. He avoided eye contact and replied, "Toyojiro, yes, he should be coming from the backroom."

Dad entered and stood motionless next to me.

Agent Miller asked, "Ma'am can you bring him closer? We want to ask him some questions."

I felt a chill down my spine. My knees shook when Dad bent over and adjusted his slippers.

I told him, "Forget your slippers, FBI men want to ask you some questions." He looked up and pulled his khaki wool vest tight.

He said, "*Hai.*"

"He doesn't speak English," I explained, "so I'll interpret."

"What does *Hai* mean?" the short one asked.

"It means 'Yes' in Japanese," I replied.

The situation was like being in the eye of a tornado. Everything whirled around me and the FBI agents behaved like machines. There was nothing sympathetic about them.

Miller asked Dad, "Was your son, Shintaro, in the Japanese Navy before the war?" He paused and craned his neck waiting for an answer.

Dad hung his head and did not make eye contact.

I was unsure how the FBI interpreted Dad's body language. I looked straight into their eyes and imitated their mannerisms to quell their suspicions. I'd never taken this type of approach before, but instinctively I knew Dad's welfare was at stake. My eyes locked on Agent Miller.

I explained, "Dad went for Shintaro's funeral in Hiroshima and he did nothing wrong except to bury his son. He did what was expected of a father."

I added, "You would do the same if you were in his situation."

The smell of Old Spice cologne gave the situation a degree of incongruity. These sweet-smelling men had their minds made up. This was just a formality and they seemed surprised by my resistance. With quizzical looks they glanced at each other.

Agent Miller said, "Toyojiro must come with us."

Without any other explanation, each took an arm and walked out with Dad in tow.

"Dad is not a community leader or threat but a janitor at a saloon," I said as they walked away with him. My heart beat wildly when I realized they were actually leaving. I was determined to save Dad and threw my apron down and ran after them.

When they were about to put Dad in the car, I grabbed his arm and said, "I'm an American citizen born in Swedish Hospital on Capitol Hill and a graduate of Franklin High School." I held Dad's arm tight and gradually pulled him towards me as I spoke.

"We are not the enemy and my father is a simple man. He's a janitor and he's done nothing except to go to Japan and bury his son." I drew him closer and the men loosened their grip. "My brother died and his wife is a widow with three children. Dad went back to help them settle the estate so they could survive."

I gripped Dad's left hand and gently pulled him closer. The FBI agents looked at each other as they began to realize they had lost control. Their nonverbal reactions acknowledged their weakened position when confronted by the steel in my eyes.

Dad turned his head and said, "*Daijobu*, everything will be okay," in Japanese. I didn't acknowledge his remark but only gripped tighter, dragging him into my orbit.

My words were filled with iron and my manner had a calming effect on the situation. To my surprise they released Dad's arm. The agents stepped aside and talked near the back of the Ford. People watched and the street traffic slowed. It was an odd sight to see two tall white men in suits standing next to a small Japanese man tethered by his daughter. The agents turned to me and I feared the worst. I tightened the grip on Dad's hand, while giving the men full eye contact. Miller had a thin tight smile and tipped his hat.

He said, "Sorry for the trouble, ma'am. Today's a very busy day and we must be going."

I wasn't sure what the remark meant and wondered if they were going to just take Dad.

Instead, the Ford drove off in a cloud of exhaust. Dad and I stood in disbelief. Kiyoshi stared in amazement. I wanted to make sure they didn't change their minds, so I watched until they were out of sight. Relieved, I took Dad's hand and walked back to the store. I was shaking and upset at the thought of losing my father to who knows where and what.

"Let's go inside, hurry," I said.

Dad nodded and showed no emotion. He slumped down on the sofa and picked up the Japanese newspaper. I saw the newspaper shake so badly that I was sure he couldn't read a word. I remained anxious, wondering what secrets Shintaro had in his diary. I thought, *If the FBI knew about the diary, they would have ransacked the house.* I said out loud, "No, they didn't know. But they could return."

So I asked again, "Dad, what did you do with the diary?"

He pondered the question and folded the paper. Without looking at me he said, "Ahh, I burned it."

"What was in the book?" I asked, "This is important. What were the secrets?"

He replied, "I couldn't read the old *kanji* and destroyed it."

"What about the cloth that it was wrapped in?" I asked.

"I burned that too," he said.

I was relieved that the FBI would never find the book, but was saddened because my last connection to Shintaro was gone.

Leaving the living room, I caught my reflection in front of the full length mirror and thought, *I see a tired woman wearing a grocery store apron who will be a mother soon.*

I shook my head. "What a day," I said out loud. "What's next?"

To celebrate Dad's freedom, Sachi prepared a special dinner of teriyaki chicken served on her best Imari ware. The wings and drumsticks glistened with a sticky shine. Sachi, Koemon, Kiyoshi, Hiro, Dad, and I sat down to the feast.

Sachi was beaming when she said, "The Rainier Poultry Company just put young hens on sale today."

She bowed slightly and served everyone. In response, I took a meaty bite.

"*Oishii desu*, delicious," I said wiping the sticky sauce from my mouth.

I suspected this was the chicken from the backyard since it was gone. At first I hesitated but then recalled my mirror reflection and chomped hard on a drumstick, followed by a deep moan of satisfaction.

"Good, Sachiko, very good," I said.

Dad smiled, knowing that I was talking to the chicken and not my mother-in-law.

CHAPTER EIGHT

Camp Harmony and Minidoka, 1942

In April 1942, army soldiers fanned out over Seattle's Japantown. There were hammering sounds as soldiers pounded black and white evacuation posters on telephone poles. Japanese were given one week to pack, settle their affairs, and assemble at designated street corners for evacuation.

The notice read, *All persons of Japanese Ancestry, both alien and non-alien …*

I tapped my fingers and wondered, *Non-aliens? Are we now without a country? Can we still vote? Must we pay taxes?* But most importantly I worried, *Where are we going and how long will we be gone?"*

To me there was a symmetry to the orders. *We are obstacles, like the Seattle hills that were sluiced down or like the Chinese who were driven out of Tacoma years before.* The pattern was familiar. This time it was President Roosevelt who saw us as a problem. The first to be taken in the entire U.S. were Japanese from nearby Bainbridge Island. They were sent to Manzanar, California.

Fear spread among the community and many disposed of Japanese possessions. Fifty-gallon drum bonfires burned Japanese books, photos, and other personal items. From the Yesler Street hill, it looked like Japantown was smoldering. Molly sensed the tension and lost her appetite. At Elk Grocery, Kiyoshi had a going-out-of-business sale with "Everything must go!" signs in the window.

As hard as it was to sell and pack at the same time, there was no time to get angry or grieve. Everyone in the family pitched in. Kiyoshi and his dad sold groceries while Sachi and I sorted through old photos, memorabilia, clothes, and valuables.

"We need to keep this antique vase," Sachi said.

I sighed, "We can take only what we can carry. How badly do you want it? It's hard to make up my mind. We have so many things." Fully realizing our predicament, I almost panicked. *What do I need for the baby? I don't have diapers or baby bottles.*

After packing and sorting, I said, "Okay I have my one suitcase done. Kiyoshi needs to do his."

Sachi replied, "Some things can go to the Buddhist church for storage."

I hope they will be safe there until we return, I thought. Then it occurred to me that maybe we would never return. I shuddered at the possibility.

I thought. *I don't want to sell the piano but where could we store it?* I pushed the thought out of my mind and cleared the sheet music stacks from the Baldwin piano. I shed a tear and I placed my fingers on the ivories. The notes echoed and lingered. I recalled Kiyoshi's birthday when I played an impromptu concert. I sorted through the sheet music and picked a simple Bach piece for my last rendition. The music took my spirit to a peaceful place for a moment. It was a pleasant distraction.

Kiyoshi had bought the piano for me even though there wasn't much space. Sachi complained constantly that it was an extravagance because we needed a new stove and hot water heater instead. But he held firm. "Thank you Kiyoshi for the piano," I said. But most of all I was proud of him for standing up to Sachi.

On the first day of our going out of business sale, there was a long line of white people, many of whom we had never seen before. Some just gawked like a crowd watching a building burn. Kiyoshi gritted his teeth as he witnessed the slow destruction of everything he'd worked a lifetime for. "We're not good enough to remain here but we're good enough to take advantage of," he complained.

We opened the back living area and roped off sections for people to walk through. Molly was uneasy with the streams of strangers wandering through. "Easy, Molly," I said and hugged her tight.

A little girl walked up to the piano and banged out a quick rendition of Chopsticks. I walked over and closed the lid.

"How much for the piano?" a well-dressed woman asked. "I'll give you five dollars for it."

I was flabbergasted at her offer. I was angry at myself and thought, *Why did I think we would get a fair price?*

I closed my eyes for a minute and took a deep breath and played a few notes. "It's a very good piano and only a year old."

The woman, replied, "How about seven dollars?"

I turned my back and said nothing.

The woman moved closer. She lifted the lid and tapped a few keys, then stood back for a second look.

I was thinking, *We should just push the piano out on the sidewalk and let anyone take it rather than suffer this humiliation.*

At that moment Mr. Righetti stepped forward. He was a friend I met at Sumida's who operated a grocery store nearby. "Hanae," he said, "You and your family have been helpful even though we were competitors. We always appreciated your friendship so I'll buy the piano with the store. When you come back to Seattle, we can talk about its return."

I bowed politely and shook Righetti's hand. "That would be wonderful. Thank you. If you buy the store, will you take Molly?"

"Yes of course," he replied, "I was thinking about doing that anyway. She is a wonderful dog."

I realized that even though I loved the piano, it could be replaced. But it meant little in comparison to losing Molly. "Thanks again. We appreciate your help."

I turned to the well-dressed woman, "I'm sorry, the piano is not for sale."

"How about twenty-dollars cash?" she replied.

"No thanks, it belongs to Mr. Righetti," I said.

There was a sense of satisfaction among the crowds as they peered at our misfortunes from the safety of their own lives. The lure of bargains was irresistible; it was like feeding frenzy. People pushed and crowded around sale items. They were shoulder to shoulder in our living room clutching and poking items.

I heard a loud crash. A vase fell. I looked and no one claimed responsibility. The crowd parted and I grabbed a broom to sweep up the shards. Ivy Smith, our regular customer, stepped forward and picked up some pieces.

"I'm so sorry to see you and Kiyoshi leave. If there's anything I can do, please don't hesitate," she said.

"Thank you, Ivy, and let me take care of this," I replied. "I don't want you to get cut."

Ivy hugged me tight. She had tears in her eyes when she turned and disappeared into the crowd. I looked up to say something more but noticed that two glass figurines on the piano were missing. "Sachi, did anyone buy the figurines?" She shook her head.

Damn it, I thought. *They're stealing. How could we be so stupid to trust strangers in our home?*

Mr. Righetti bought Elk Grocery and the store equipment including the piano for $200. After our wedding, I convinced Kiyoshi to help out the Righettis by passing on some of our cost savings from bulk purchases. Righetti was grateful and once a month his wife made us meatballs.

Sachi hated the idea of helping the competition, but Kiyoshi did it anyway. She said, "You worry too much about Hanae's white friends from Sumida's stand. You should think of family first."

I thought, *I don't get paid for working at the store, so I deserve something in return. Ironically, Righetti is buying the whole store.*

For the sofa, bed and furniture we received ten cents on the dollar. I thought, *for so little money, we would have been better off giving everything away to hobos.*

Kiyoshi's hands shook when he said, "Mr. Righetti, here are the keys to the gate and the front door. We might need one more day to finish so I keeping the duplicates for now." Righetti replied, "No problem, I understand."

I petted Molly and said, "I'll really miss you. You've been a good friend. The Righettis will take care of you now." Molly wagged her tail.

With the gate locked and our goods sold, we spent the night at the Russell Hotel with my Mom and Dad. Kiyoshi and I stayed in my old room on the third floor. *Odd being back here again,* I thought. *This place is so familiar and comforting. But I'm frightened about what will happen next. I wish tomorrow would never come.*

Since all the hotel guests were Japanese, everyone was packed and ready to leave. Mr. Wong, from the Seven Dragon restaurant, said he would arrange to have some laborers board up the vacant hotel to keep the hobos out. I was surprised by his generous offer. I thought, *At a time like this you realize who your real friends are.* I almost cried. Of course Dad agreed and accepted Mr. Wong's help.

"Thank you Mr. Wong," I said. "We'll see you when we return."

He bowed and said, "Years ago, they tried to chase the Chinese out of Seattle. I know what it is like."

The sky darkened the next morning and a light rain fell. It was as if the angel of death had swept over Japantown. Higo's Five and Dime was shuttered. A hand painted sign over the door read, "Thank you to our many friends."

Nikko bathhouse's iron grate was pulled and doors padlocked. Very quickly, Japantown's empty door wells became magnets for windblown leaves and trash that swirled in corners.

Japantown took on a ghost town look. What remained was a disquieting pall, something like a cold fog rolling in from Elliott Bay.

The morning we left the hotel, I remembered looking down at the streetcar and all the great memories growing up. For the evacuation, each of us wore layers of our Sunday best so that we could bring as much as possible.

I was almost overcome with sadness as we walked to the designated assembly area. We were numb like herd of cattle marching. *"Gaman,"* Dad said hoping to give us strength on our journey.

The Righettis brought Molly to the corner of 10th and Lane to say goodbye. Kiyoshi loaded the luggage and several small wooden Japanese boxes. Dad packed a bento of rice balls and salmon.

A group of onlookers gathered across the street on the hill, staring as if watching a parade.

"Make a line and sign-in here," an army officer commanded. "These are your ID tags, don't lose them."

I examined the white paper tag imprinted with my number, #11557B. Kiyoshi was 11557A as the head of the household. *We're all just numbers and letters,* I thought. *It's worse than school where the teachers give us American names.* I felt like crying.

Kiyoshi turned to the gawkers and said, "What are you looking at?" In response there were no hate stares or obscenities. Standing next to the truck, I lowered my eyes and covered my mouth. Molly broke free and scampered to the truck. She hopped onto the back tailgate and wagged her tail and licked my face. I held her one last time and explained that we had to leave. How could I make Molly understand that she wasn't being rejected for anything she had done?

"Goodbye, dear girl," I said and held her tight.

Kiyoshi lifted Molly and cradled her in his arms, then released her to Mr. Righetti, who apologized for losing his grip. With tears, I waved goodbye and the truck rumbled away. Molly was pulling hard on the leash, barking and whimpering. She stood on her hind legs and raised her front paws in the air.

Molly became smaller and smaller, until the truck turned a corner. I had been hoping that she and the baby would be friends, but that would never happen. I sat down and dropped my face into my hands. I was sorry to leave a loving friend who could not understand. "Sorry to leave you," I said out loud while my head throbbed.

The *Seattle Globe* newspaper story claimed that the evacuation was a necessary precaution. On the front page, Japanese smiled and posed for pictures wearing their finest clothes next to uniformed army soldiers. I thought, *Never would I smile for the camera even if they paid me.* The photo caption read: "Japanese were grateful for army protection on the way to the assembly center."

HIGHWAY 61 SOUTH

Our army truck rattled down Highway 61 South. People whispered about our possible destination. Many speculated that it would be Fort Lewis. I grabbed the wooden braces in the truck and recalled the incident when a customer spit on Kiyoshi. It was as if it had happened yesterday. I wondered what I would have done if he'd come up to me? I thought, *What could I do? Nothing, I guess, just like the evacuation.*

The canvas roof flapped and diesel fumes filled the covered area. My thoughts wandered to mother's good friend, Mrs. Nishimura. She would say whenever something went wrong, "It was all in your mind."

I was hoping that this was a bad dream. But this ride into the unknown was real. I gripped Kiyoshi's arm and asked, "Where are they taking us?"

He had a blank look and hung his head. We were prisoners and Kiyoshi could no longer protect us nor did he have any authority as a man.

I was worried for my family and the baby in my womb. We bounced around in the truck at every rough patch and remained resigned as if waiting for a firing squad.

Are we on death row? I wondered. *So what is my last wish? Oh, I would want Chinese dinner at the Seven Dragons.*

Few people in the white community spoke up in opposition of the president, chambers of commerce, newspapers, and business people. It was inevitable that we would be removed. I had a revelation that came to me. The Globe said we were a threat to white people but the truth was that powerful white people wanted our businesses, jobs, and land. We were the ones threatened and not vice versa. I thought, *I wish we were a threat and then this would make sense.* I had a knot in my stomach and cursed President Roosevelt under my breath.

As the caravan rolled south, I suppressed my screams. Jesus must have felt like this when Judas kissed him. It was the same sense of betrayal I'd experienced when Shintaro told me to return to Seattle. *It's happening again*, I concluded.

What did I do to deserve this treatment? I could think of nothing. The newspapers made us out as lepers that would contaminate others. Only later would a few brave Quakers step forward and offer a hand of kindness. But by then it was too late.

TWO AMERICAS

I bounced up and down on the bench as the truck rumbled. My mind raced. This would be my first child and I wondered, *How could I be a good mother in prison? Surely the government will let me keep the baby,* I thought. *This is not a case of white people giving smallpox blankets to the Indians. But if it is smallpox, would anyone know? Who would report that we died and were never seen again?*

I felt my blood pressure rise and heart beat rapidly. This stress had to be hurting the baby. Would there be a hospital for the delivery or just a first aid station? How sanitary would it be, and would the doctors take care of me and the baby? What kind of America would my child live in when so many were against us?

I could withstand rudeness and hate stares, but I dreaded the idea that my innocent child would suffer. He would face that ugly word "prejudice." I wondered. *Would we survive, or did the government want all of us dead?*

In seven months it would be Thanksgiving. It was a wonderful time when the house was filled with the fragrance of turkey.

How will we spend Thanksgiving, Christmas, and the New Year? What will we have to be thankful for? Maybe just being alive, I thought. *How things have changed so quickly.*

There were so many questions and no answers. I said a prayer, "Please God, give us strength and take care of my child. Thank you for letting us be together as a family and not be split up like some." Deep inside, I still had faith that America would recognize the injustice and someone would come and rescue us. *Maybe Eleanor Roosevelt would help,* I thought.

The truck groaned up a steep hill. Black fumes billowed from the upright exhaust pipes, filling the back canopy. It gave me the same feeling as on the steamship from Japan. "I can't breathe," I said to no one in particular.

"Ouch," I cried, when the seat jiggled and pinched my hand.

The truck jerked and the gears made a loud grinding sound. Like cattle we swayed back and forth in a herky-jerky whipsaw motion. I pulled down my hat and gripped my baggage.

Mentally I felt deflated when I realized that there were really two Americas and I lived in the one with less justice. *Almost everything I learned about America was a lie,* I thought.

I touched my belly. "My dear baby," I said, "You will be born in prison and there's nothing I can do about it." The reality made me feel sea sick.

I continued the conversation in a whisper. "Maybe you should not be born in a country that hates us. If we died now, Kiyoshi would not have to look after us. The family would be better off."

I released Kiyoshi's arm. *Please God forgive me for what I am going to do*, I prayed.

I visualized myself flying off the back of the truck into traffic. I took a deep breath and worked to the rear.

It was then that I heard the Hiroshima voices again, "Do you choose the easy way or the hard way?"

"I'll take the easy way," I said out loud and studied the roaring trucks behind us.

When we go down a hill, I could jump in front of a truck. I imagined being crushed by a prehistoric creature with smoke blowing out its nostrils.

The nearest hospital would be miles away, so I would never make it in time. Just as those thoughts were swirling, the truck shifted gears. The force launched me towards the tailgate.

I thought, *This is the end, hallelujah.* Midair, I saw images like photographs of Masa, Uncle Yosh, the foxes, Koko, and the wedding when Kiyoshi sang.

I glimpsed the ground moving fast like a wild river below. Close to the edge, my coat belt snagged a brace. It held me tight like some heavenly force. "Ugh," I groaned as it pulled me tight and whipped me around.

I grabbed the support and banged the gate with my knee. "Ow, that hurts," I cried as I smacked it a second time. When the gears shifted, the momentum threw me backwards towards Kiyoshi. He grabbed me.

He growled, "*Baka ne*, what are you, stupid? Just sit down or you'll get killed. Now don't move," he chided.

"We'll need to have a doctor check you," he said, trying hard to remain calm. "We have to make sure the baby is okay."

After all this effort and banging, I concluded that the universe wanted me to live. There was no easy way out this time. This ordeal must be suffered from beginning to end. I had no choice but to endure.

"Sorry," I said to Kiyoshi. "I needed some air. The exhaust made me car sick."

Kiyoshi handed me a lunch bag and said, "If you need to throw up, use this and stay away from the back gate."

Megumi slid over and put her arms around me. "Are you okay?" she asked.

"I'm mad," I replied. "Just last month I had a life. I grew vegetables in my garden and was looking forward to my first baby. Now what?"

"Yes, I know. It's true for all of us," Megumi replied, "Last week we were normal people."

I straighten up and replied, "The newspapers said it was for our own protection. Where has reason gone?" *I want to go home and have everything back like it was*, I thought.

"Megumi, I promised myself that I would never cry again. But look at me," I said as tears welled up. *I'm a failure, I thought, I can't even kill myself and worst of all I can't protect my baby.*

"Don't worry, Hanae," Megumi replied, "The courts will help us."

I sighed, "I hope so." Then I prayed, "Dear God, please make our punishment swift." Then out of anger, I asked *Kamisama* for the universe to strike the Roosevelts, *bachi ga ataru*.

When the wind blew through the canvas, I began to shiver. Megumi held me close.

I said, "I don't know what's going on anymore. I wish I did. I'm confused and am at the point where I can't even trust myself. I have no confidence in what I think, feel, or see. Megumi, what kind of human being is that?"

"Hanae, we've all become that way. At least we are together," she replied.

"Oh never mind. Thanks Megumi, I'll be fine. I just think too much." My mind played tricks until I wondered whether I had died falling off the truck and whether everything from that moment on was an illusion.

I thought, *Maybe your past doesn't flash before you when you die. Instead, it flashes forward and you imagine being alive for years, having children, working until retirement, collecting a pension, and all those everyday moments with friends and family compressed into seconds. That way, a person who dies suddenly could pass on without regrets. I could be unconscious by the side of the road, dying, instead of in an army truck. Like a dream within a dream, this thought could be part of my flash forward.*

The truck rattled sideways and my thoughts cleared, *No, that's too confusing. I'm here and will be on this earth much longer.* "Thank you God, for the second chance," I prayed out loud.

Clouds gathered to the south. There were sun breaks with flashes of whites and grays, looking like El Greco's *Storm over Toledo*. It rained all the way to the Puyallup Fair Grounds, our temporary living quarters. It was renamed Camp Harmony by some War Relocation person who thought giving it a good name would lessen the pain.

The fairground gates swung open. Last year I paid admission and went through these same gates to see the livestock and vegetable exhibits.

Today everything was different. The noise level rose as young people jumped off the truck and chatted. The elderly looked like ragtag soldiers heading for the stockade. We dragged our luggage to the side of the road and lined up at the processing center located in the 4 H Exhibit Hall. Announcements blared from the cone-shaped speakers, "New arrivals must register and be given room assignments."

Just a few months earlier, the Puyallup Fair midway had been crowded with fairgoers. There were Ferris wheels, garden exhibits, and animal stalls. Today one overhead sign remained that read "Famous Fisher Scones."

"Oh, what I would give for a scone with blackberry jam and hot coffee with cream right now," I said to Kiyoshi.

In the reception area, white men in suits moved officiously with clipboards in hand. There were lines to sign forms and more forms and more lines. Kiyoshi was given two US Army wool blankets and two mattress tickings to fill with straw. I scanned the Japanese community interpreters who assisted the army, hoping to see a familiar face.

"Megumi," I said, "Where did they find these people?"

"I can't even guess," she replied. "They're Japanese but they look different."

They checked identity numbers and sent families off to their quarters.

"So much humiliation, for what?" I asked Megumi.

The fairground was surrounded by barbed wire. We were in a foreign country with fences, guard towers, latrines, and lines everywhere. Kiyoshi looked at the chaos and said, "The whole world has gone nuts."

"What's a latrine?" Sachi asked.

"It's a toilet with rows of seats," I replied, "and probably no partitions." Sachi held her nose in disgust.

"I smell stinky food," she said, "maybe cabbage."

I pointed at the source. "It's coming from that building," I replied.

Sachi surveyed the grounds and remarked, "*Shikataganai.*"

Unfortunately, there was nothing we could do under the shadow of machine guns. The young soldiers held the power of life and death over us.

"Megumi," I remarked, "One soldier even asked me if we were people since we dressed like humans."

I didn't show emotions when I told him, "I'm pregnant and will have a child soon just like your mother." I thought, *What can I lose? He isn't going to shoot me for telling him I'm a human being.* Not taking any chances, I scooted away and disappeared into the crowd. My knees were weak and I felt a sharp pain in my stomach. I doubled over for a second and then stood up straight and hobbled back to the Exhibit Hall area. *I need to see a doctor,* I thought.

Recalling my childhood vow to never cry, I bit my lip. There was so much to worry about that I couldn't decide on what was first. Ironically, I knew I had nothing to worry about because we were no longer responsible for our lives. The government had taken ownership of us.

Feeling the full weight of the situation, I had the urge to throw something. "There's not even a rock!" I said.

Maybe it would be better if we were dumb animals, I pondered. Then the revelation struck me. *The government could lead us to slaughter and we'd be too dumb to know. After all, some of us live in stalls.*

At night, there was a curfew and movement was restricted. Residents were ordered to pull down the blinds after "lights out." Mothers with newborns and infants had special permission to switch on lights to feed and change their babies. I thought, *At least I can feed my baby when it arrives. But if I run dry, will there be enough formula available? And where will I deliver the child?*

Mom and Dad were especially upset about their living conditions. Like other normally uncomplaining *Issei,* they found it hard to adjust. Out of frustration, Dad and his friends presented a list to the block captains that included serving organ meats that Buddhists wouldn't eat, cramped conditions, the use of horse stalls for bedrooms, and the guards who whistled as they walked past their barracks at 2:00 in the morning.

On a Thursday, Vienna sausage, beans, and canned vegetables were served for dinner. Later, it was discovered that the sausage was spoiled. I wondered, *Do our captors really care if the food is poison? That's what the Globe newspaper accused us of doing to white Americans.*

Hundreds contracted dysentery and lined up at the latrine. I saw Megumi. She stood crooked and her eyes were downcast. Like many, she held an umbrella to shield herself from the horizontal rain while standing in the mud. Others were pale and gaunt, waiting their turn.

Because of my pregnancy, the wait was difficult. Fortunately, one area manager walked past and said, "If you are elderly or can't wait, go to the head of the line."

Two white-haired women moved forward without looking up and took places at the front. I did the same, with my head bowed saying, "*Sumimasen,* excuse me." No one challenged or acknowledged me. The line automatically opened. I was grateful that I didn't feel their eyes. After using the latrine, I went to the back of the line because I knew I would have to go again.

LETTER TO IVY SMITH

April 25, 1942

Dear Ivy,

We are in Puyallup at the fairgrounds. They call it Camp Harmony.

Kiyoshi and I want to thank you for your friendship and store patronage over the years.

I hope you know we have not committed any crimes but must be taken for our own protection, they tell us. It was good to see you at our closing sale.

Also thank you for the character reference on the government forms. We sincerely wish you the very best and when this is all over, we hope to see you again. Thank you again for your friendship.

Sincerely,

Hanae and Kiyoshi
Camp Harmony-25-75
Puyallup, Washington

MAY 14, 1942

My skin was warm and hands trembled. I had a fever and grew dizzy. I was apprehensive about the poor conditions and how the baby might be harmed. "I need to go to a real hospital," I remarked out loud.

Megumi said, "Oh no!" Then she relayed a story about Jerry, a young boy in barrack 12, who had a fever of 102 and was taken to Tacoma General. After much paper work, his mother was able to visit him. He was crying and could barely breathe from fright. Jerry overheard the nurses when they thought he was asleep.

The head nurse instructed the night shift, "Don't do anything for this little Jap; let him die in his sleep."

So Jerry stayed awake all night. Even though he still had a temperature, he said, "I want to go home, take me back to the barrack."

Megumi shook a thermometer, placed it in my mouth and said, "I hope they'll treat you better since you are an adult and pregnant."

When my fever rose above 101, they took me to Tacoma General accompanied by my sister-in-law, Yoko, and a guard. Kiyoshi stayed in camp because of severe dysentery.

The doctors treated me and started an IV. I watched the saline drip into the IV tubes and wondered, *What has become of us? My whole family is in prison and we are eating rotten food.*

I took a deep breath and recalled the ride on the army truck. *Maybe it would have been better if I'd died,* I said to myself.

The curtains opened and a doctor poked his head in. "Okay, miss," he said. "Vacation's over. We're sending you back to where you came from."

With a smirk I replied, "Am I going back to Seattle?"

The doctor didn't get it.

LETTER FROM THE RIGHETTIS

July 28, 1942

Dear Kiyoshi and Hanae,

Helen and I hope you are doing well. My son is operating Elk Grocery and many of your customers have dropped by to send their regards to you and your family. Ivy Smith wants you to know that you and your family are in her prayers.

I am sad to say after you left, Molly wouldn't eat. We tried everything but she just didn't respond. Then a few days ago we went back to the yard and there was a hole under the fence. We put up posters and told all of our customers. We also checked the animal shelter. We're heartbroken and hope someone finds her.

Hopefully she will come back soon.

Sorry for the bad news.

Sincerely,

Mark and Helen
Elk Grocery Store
9th and Seneca
Seattle, Washington

———————————————————————————

CHAPTER NINE

Off to the Minidoka, Idaho Relocation Center

Gripping Righetti's letter tight, I felt my heart pound and tried to bury my emotions. But I couldn't stop grieving. *Oh my,* I said to myself. I thought, *It would be impossible for Molly to find us given the miles of dangerous roads and highways. Even if she made it to the gate, the military would never let her in.*

The thought of her being turned away crushed me. I removed my glasses and covered my face. I wondered, *How long did she wander?*

I chose to imagine the best. *Maybe some generous people found Molly and gave her a good home.* Hammering noises outside diverted my attention. The block captains posted notices that Camp Harmony would close and we would be sent to permanent camps. We heard rumors for weeks but now we knew for sure. "Bainbridge people are in California so we might go there," Megumi said. "I've had it with this place. Anywhere is better than this dump."

"Ah," I moaned. "I'm very pregnant and a train ride to California is not something I look forward to. I've never been there and don't know what to expect. Wherever they send us, there won't be palm trees and movie stars."

Holding back my emotions, I packed our treasures and clothes which now included worn underwear and socks. I sat on my suitcase and crammed in as much as I could. "I'm tired of packing, unpacking, and moving from place to place." I said to Megumi.

She replied, "Why is it always raining when we move?"

Kiyoshi said, "Well I won't miss all the mud and awful horse stall smells."

The loudspeakers crackled and a scratchy voice called barracks numbers. "Block one to the Green Gate." The line of people was sprinkled with umbrellas. It snaked around corners and spaces where people huddled under eaves.

"Here we go again," Kiyoshi said, "Hurry up and wait." We loaded the deuce and half trucks and climbed aboard. Diesel fumes belched when the engine roared, "Where are they taking us this time?" Kiyoshi asked.

I examined the front bumper with its large metal grille and cable winch. *If I got hit by this monster at fifty miles an hour, I would surely be killed,* I thought. It was almost as if Kiyoshi read my mind and said, "Sit in front."

Rain fell on slick streets and the tires sizzled. We entered downtown Puyallup and drove past candy cane barber shop poles and mom and pop grocery stores. There were few pedestrians walking the streets. Mostly there were lines of uniformed armed guards. Quickly we were escorted to a rickety Northern Pacific train car. The guards said, "Pull down the blackout curtains and don't open the windows."

Dad frowned and wiped his brow with a handkerchief. After the delays, he dropped his head and let out a loud "Mooo."

I said to him, "Quiet, Dad, this isn't a joke." He nodded and chuckled at his lapse into temporary insanity. The cow sounds were oddly appropriate for this Alice in Wonderland world.

I was angry, "Dad, what were you thinking? You've never behaved like this before! Have you lost your mind? Have we all lost our minds?"

Dad smiled and waved his right hand.

After four hours on the train, the toilets were plugged and overflowed. We held our noses and covered our faces with makeshift masks. "Disgusting," I said. The odors crawled up my nostrils.

Periodically there was "ka chunk" when the wheels crossed bumpy sections. The train accelerated and headed east for hours until the sky filled with stars. Being six months pregnant, I squirmed. *Will I ever find a comfortable position?* I wondered. Out of boredom, I pulled the window curtains open. There was nothing but darkness.

The locomotive climbed the Cascade mountains and fourteen hours later, it stopped at an unmarked place in the Idaho desert. Rumors spread, "We'll be shot and killed, then stacked and tossed in some ditch." Dad scanned the barren sagebrush and tumbleweed. He muttered something in Japanese.

I thought. *We have to obey the guards no matter what. If they are going to kill us, I hope it's a swift death.*

Everyone exited and we marched to the parked deuce and half trucks. After a one-mile ride over a ridge and into a valley, the Minidoka, Idaho camp appeared. The trucks passed through the stone entry gate and I saw what appeared to be an army base with blocks of black tarpaper barracks. Later we heard that this was land so harsh that the government could not give it away to homesteaders before the war.

"Wow!" Kiyoshi said. "It looks like a military camp with barbed wire, guard towers, and machine guns." As large as it was, the camp was not visible from the highway because it sat deep in a ravine.

We left Puyallup in the rain. Here the sun was scorching hot. The tarpaper buildings radiated heat. We were not used to these conditions and many were at risk of heat stroke. Megumi was perspiring heavily and collapsed. I tried to bend down and help but was hampered by the baby bump. Two ladies rushed over. Shortly an army medic arrived and cleared the crowd. He announced, "Heat exhaustion. We'll cool her down and get her hydrated." They carried her to the ambulance and the siren sounded.

I hate this place, I said to myself. In the meantime, Kiyoshi got our room assignment. He found me and said, "We're in Block 26, barrack two. It's that way."

Slowly I opened the door to the tarpaper barrack. "It smells funny," I remarked.

"For sure this isn't the Hilton," Kiyoshi joked.

The barrack was a large barn-like space. Inside were open rafters with exposed wiring and naked light bulbs hanging. "We're supposed to share this with other families," he said. "But it's better than the Camp Harmony animal stalls, "he quipped.

Grime covered the floor and window sills. A gust of wind blew grit through the floor. I wrapped my scarf over my face and swept the dirt into neat piles. Dust inside and rattlesnakes outside. *Could they have found a worse place?* I wondered.

"We'll hang blankets on the beams for walls," I said. I stared at the "U.S." emblazoned on the olive drab blankets. *"U.S." is us. Us blankets for us! This bent reasoning makes perfect sense*, I thought.

We shared our space with four other families. It was crowded and there was little defense against smells and sounds that traveled freely. Kiyoshi scavenged wood and cobbled together makeshift stools and a dresser. He showed off a wobbly three-legged stool. With pride he said, "Hanae, this is our first piece of furniture."

He unpacked an old metal pot. "We'll keep this in the corner, something we can use as a chamber pot. I'll cover it with a wooden lid," he said. "Tonight I'll steal toilet paper from the latrine."

Within a few days, we established new routines. *We are like Gypsies that move from one terrible place to another,* I thought. We were accustomed to the mild marine climate of the Pacific Northwest and the closeness of the sea. The Idaho weather and temperatures challenged the hardiest souls. "Minidoka is horrible," Kiyoshi blurted out. "They must think we are a bunch of lizards."

Every morning for breakfast, Minoru, Kiyoshi's brother, did an imitation of a cowboy chuck wagon cook. He donned a white chef hat and struck the iron triangle. With a "yee haw" he whipped the steel rod round inside the triangle. The clangs signaled our mealtimes which gave a temporary reprieve from the barracks.

Aside from cooks, there was a need for additional help to operate the camp of 8,000 residents. Block captains distributed occupational surveys and conducted interviews. There were jobs in the motor pool, construction unit, road maintenance section, the elementary and high school and many other areas. Because of his background, Kiyoshi was hired as a manager of a canteen store. My relative, Dr. Matsui, did dental work, and others were clerks at the camp high school. Kiyoshi's brother, Minoru, was a butcher, which got him a job as a cook.

For me, being unemployed was okay. I was over eight months pregnant and moved slowly. Still I did the housework and the wash. When there was a shortage of clothesline, the guards cut the barbed wire to dry clothes. The fence gaps were tempting but the odds of a successful escape were low. I thought, *What chance would a Japanese escapee in Idaho have wandering around Twin Falls like a stray? Anyway where would you go? I smiled and said to myself, If I weren't pregnant, maybe we can walk to Twin Falls to buy donuts!*

I could joke about escaping but the inhumane conditions continued to wear on Dad. *Since we can't fight or escape, my only hope is to write Eleanor Roosevelt.*

During the incarceration, Dad lost ten pounds and declined mentally. "Dad, what was your blood pressure?" I asked.

He fussed and ignored me. "What was it? Tell me!"

"It's normal," he replied.

"What?" I prodded.

"I think it was 190 over 120," he said.

"Good grief, that can't be! Have them check it again," I urged.

"Okay, I'll go to the first aid station today after lunch," he said.

"What's that?" I asked when a cloud of blue smoke rose in the corner. Mom had begun smoking cigarettes in Puyallup after finding a carton dropped in the mud. I told her to return it but she just decided to smoke them instead. Every morning she lit a Lucky Strike to calm her nerves before breakfast.

"Mom, that's a filthy habit," I complained. At first it was just a few cigarettes and gradually it grew into a two-pack a day habit. Her new purpose in life was to see how much she could smoke. Without having to cook and take care of the hotel, she was adrift.

Dad said, "Toku, stop this. It brings shame on our family." Mom ignored him, which was unlike her. She continued as if it was a religious act. "Shame" meant little in comparison to the habit that became her best friend. "Waste of money," Dad said. She persisted and finally he gave up nagging.

To keep his hands busy, Dad scavenged pans, tubs, and other brewing supplies. His apartment was crammed with makeshift *sake*-making materials. Fermented rice odors filled their barrack. No matter how hard he tried, the dust corrupted the rice and the Idaho mineral water spoiled every batch. The yeast is bad," he said. He walked to the door and spat out corrupted *sake*. "Not good," he declared.

Dad almost cried when he dumped his brewing supplies and materials in the dirt. He was a great *sake* maker, but not here. "Everything is terrible," he said to no one in particular.

"Dad," I replied. "Don't worry, Eleanor Roosevelt will help us. I sent her a letter yesterday. I just know she'll do something. Don't give up hope. Also, I heard the Quakers took our case to the courts. I'm sure the courts will get us released!"

"Things are no good, *dame da*," he replied. "Only when Japan wins the war will we be free. You wait and see."

"Oh no, don't say that. There are plenty of spies everywhere," I said. "You and your pro-Japan friends need to be quiet and just play *go*. Otherwise, there will be trouble. Don't worry, America will make this right. Come on and pick up your brewing supplies before someone claims them. We'll try again after I have the baby. I'll help you."

LETTER TO ELEANOR ROOSEVELT

July 30th, 1942

Eleanor Roosevelt,
The White House
Washington, DC

Dear Mrs. Roosevelt,

My name is Hanae Yamada and I voted for your husband as did all of my family. As you know, there are thousands of loyal Japanese Americans in camps scattered around the country. We want to thank you for helping us get the new fire engine. It is wonderful and we feel safer. Also we would like to ask you to release the Japanese Red Cross shipment to Minidoka so we can enjoy the soy sauce, magazines, seaweed and pickled plums. Many of the people are looking forward to the arrival of musical instruments from Japan.

As an expectant mother, I want to make sure my baby will be healthy and happy. Residents are grateful that most families have been able to remain together. But everyone hopes that the people in FBI camps can be reunited in WRA camps. Many Buddhist priests and community leaders and their families are in this situation.

We're living from day to day and conditions are harsh with rattlesnakes and scorpions. Even though we complained about the food to the administration, dysentery has broken out several times. Improvements are slow. For the women, it is very embarrassing to use the gang latrines without privacy. Some ladies cover their heads with paper sacks or go in the middle of the night.

The summer heat is unbearable and doing the wash with a scrub board is backbreaking. Once something is clean, the wind blows dust and grit everywhere. It is not sanitary and it is difficult to care for babies.

My father was a janitor in Seattle and is used to working hard every day but has little to do here. He lost his pride and feels useless. The bounce in his step is gone and he is going downhill mentally. My mother ran a hotel in Seattle but her life now is just eating and smoking. I haven't seen her smile in months.

Please come visit us to see our living conditions. I understand how busy you are but we need help and would like the government to make our life easier. We are loyal Americans and are having great difficulties. Almost everyone has lost their homes, property and jobs. Your visit would be a great thing that would raise camp spirits.

You and the President are in our prayers. Thank you.

Sincerely,

Hanae Yamada
Block 26, Barrack 2
Minidoka, Idaho WRA

MESS HALL

I hope Mrs. Roosevelt will reply to my letter, I thought on the way to lunch. Dad stood in line and I joined him at our mess hall. It was a double barrack with open rafters and a wooden floor. Heavy picnic tables were neatly arranged in rows. Naked light bulbs hung from the overhead beams. There was one long counter area with Japanese men in aprons serving the daily fare.

"What are they feeding us today?" Dad complained, recalling food they were served in the past that he could not eat.

"It's probably something with potatoes," I replied. "They have plenty."

Sitting behind me was Haruye, my aunt, who sat motionless on the next bench. She was almost unrecognizable because of her weight loss. She wore a scarf to cover her long unkempt hair. At first I thought she was a ghost. I walked over and leaned towards her.

"Is that you Haruye? How are you?" I asked.

"Fine," she replied, "still a little weak from food poisoning."

"Yes, anyone who ate sausage got it," I replied.

"Did you hear that the Japanese Red Cross is sending us packages? Is that true? Rick told me that," Haruye asked.

"Yes, I heard about a shipment from a block captain. By the way, how's Rick? Is he in high school now?" I inquired.

Haruye almost whispered, "I feel sorry for him. He is a good son."

"Yes, a good boy," I replied. "The rumors about the packages are true. The supplies are being delayed by Customs but hopefully we'll get something soon. I even asked Eleanor Roosevelt for help."

"That's good. Something to look forward to," she replied softly.

I glanced up at the serving line, "Oh there's Kiyoshi's brother, Minoru. I want to say 'Hi' to him. Take care of yourself. I'll see you later."

Minoru worked hard with his inexperienced crew. Few had prepared meals for hundreds of people at a time. As a result, the quality was uneven and there were many mistakes which they just served up.

When food overages occurred, Minoru instructed his helpers, "Dig a hole around back and bury any left-over ham, roasts, or turkey parts. We don't want our next food allocation to be reduced."

Mealtime was important since there was little else for many to do. *We're like trained animals waiting for a handout*, I thought. *This is what my life has become--eat, sleep, do the wash and go to the latrine. Maybe the soldiers were right to ask if we were human beings.*

Kiyoshi's six-year old niece, Annie, became a hoarder and pilfered food. In the winter, she used the drafty window sills to hold treasures like Spam, wieners, and other small morsels wrapped in waxed paper. She cradled the food as if it were treasures. "Mrs. Joyce, the Quaker lady from Twin Falls, gave me this can of Spam," she told me as she licked her lips. "I'm saving it."

Pointing to a tricycle parked in the corner. I asked, "Hey where did you get this?"

"Mom brought it instead of packing a big suitcase. I begged her to bring it. She warned me they might take it away. But they didn't."

"You mean Yoko carried the trike to Puyallup and on the train here?" I inquired.

Annie smiled and said, "She brought my toys too! I couldn't leave without them. I'd rather l have them instead of clothes."

I looked askance and wondered, *Yoko did that? It was totally out of character for this strange woman with premature white hair who communicates with the dead.*

"That was very kind of your mother," I said.

Ignoring my remark, Annie put the Spam back on the sill.

"Will you share that?" I asked.

She cocked her head and swung her body back and forth. "Not the Spam," she replied. Carefully she unwrapped a greasy Vienna sausage and inhaled the scent. She exclaimed, "I'll share this."

"No thanks," I replied.

For adults, hoarding was a form of resistance and their stashes served as security in a world out of control. Old saltine cracker cans and cast iron pots held mess hall leftovers for late evening cravings. Food caches were like pirate booty. Since we were already in prison, we knew the administration could do little to stop it.

"Who cares if we waste food?" Dad said. "It's free, not something we worked for."

"You taught us to respect food and here you are throwing it away," I complained.

Dad smiled and said, "The taste is no good."

"We've become like *hakujins*," I said, "We live wasteful lives and no one cares anymore. It's *mottainai*, needless waste."

Kiyoshi chimed in, "It gives me the willies to eat from four-sectioned metal trays with bent forks."

I agreed, "It's like fingernails on chalkboards." At the mess hall, internees stacked dirty trays at the cleaning station window until the piles slid, creating small avalanches.

I mused, *Masa in Hiroshima would be unhappy about metal utensils and trays. Wooden chopsticks and porcelain dishes are much more civilized and comforting.*

Under these circumstances, the children found their own tables away from families and parents. They formed groups and claimed their space like a pack of dogs marking territory. "Boys only, no girls allowed," the young ones would say.

"Big game tonight," the high school boys yelled as they left their dirty trays on the tables. Cook-san hollered, "Hey, boys, bus your trays!" In defiance, two youngsters smashed peanut butter sandwiches under their tables and walked away. I thought, *Back home they wouldn't dare do this!*

FOOD POISONING

A few days later, dysentery ravaged the camp again. My stomach growled. I jumped into my slippers and grabbed a bathrobe. I shuffled outside into the dark. The searchlights caught me in a bright beam and illuminated the latrine line. As in Camp Harmony, the young soldiers thought the gathering was a midnight revolt or protest, and spotlights shone on the huge masses of people.

The guards were confused and yelled, "Hey, what's going? Get back to your barracks."

They stood at the ready with their M-1 rifles and machine guns. By now they knew we were people but the fear in the voices indicated doubt. Out of the darkness, an internee yelled, "Food poisoning," and another voice blurted, "diarrhea" and still another, "We got the trots. Don't shoot us!"

The soldiers shouted, "Okay, okay," and they put down their rifles.

Searching for a short line, I hustled by a standing group of men and boys bundled in heavy clothes. They were grim and hugged themselves while they waited. They resembled derelicts in a soup kitchen line. Their foggy breaths rose like steam pouring out of a sidewalk grate.

I'll bet there's a line of women around the corner. I moaned when my thoughts were confirmed. "I can't wait," I mumbled out loud. Determined to find a latrine, I reasoned, *Block 28 might be better.*

I waddled towards the next latrine and took one look. Immediately, I knew that they had suffered the same fate. I took a deep breath and doubled over, fighting the cramps. I couldn't last much longer but the thought of soiling myself was unimaginable.

How disgraceful that would be, I thought.

"Should've used the chamber pot in our apartment," I said out loud.

I was very close to panic when a light fog rolled in and crept along the ground. I held my stomach and painfully jogged on to the next block listening to the sounds of my labored breathing.

The cold air enveloped me. My arms were freezing and my teeth chattered. Talking to the baby, I remarked, "Silly, I should have worn a heavy coat. It's cold." I rubbed my hands together and exhaled. "I hope you'll be okay."

Desperate, I wandered a dirt road that looked like the one I'd just left. My head ached and I felt dizzy. The wind kicked up dust, pelting my face and glasses. Every turn led in circles. I wanted to sneak in to the nearest barrack and use their chamber pot.

If I did, maybe no one would notice me, I thought. It wasn't unusual for confused old men and women to wander into barracks thinking they were home, especially at night. The pain increased and I felt like collapsing. My knees buckled and I stooped over to ease my muscles.

Can't last much longer, I thought. I looked up and saw a glowing red dot moving in the darkness. It rose and fell slightly as it grew closer, I breathed a sigh when I recognized it as a soldier's cigarette.

He asked, "Are you okay?"

The soldier pulled me upright. I stared at this tall young man who looked like all the other guards. His voice was gentle laced with a southern accent.

I coughed and struggled to catch my breath.

"When is your baby due?" he asked.

"Soon," I said, "but right now I have to find a latrine."

The private gripped my arm and half carried me. He said, "Don't worry, you and your baby will be fine."

I stood and shuffled my feet. It felt like two people were supporting me. After a short distance, he placed my hand on a rail and unlocked the staff latrine. Inside was a sweet and clean smell. I exited a few minutes later.

The soldier lit another Lucky. "Where do you live?" he asked.

I replied, "Block 26, Barrack 2."

"You're a long way from home, ma'am. Don't worry, I know where that is," he said.

I smiled, "Thank you. Thank you very much."

He steadied me and we trudged through a foggy maze of barracks with glowing apartment windows.

In a gentle voice he said, "The army's here to protect you. Everything will be okay."

I wondered how this young soldier could be so wise and compassionate. His accent made his words sound like music. His voice lifted my spirits as if I were in church. "I'm feeling better," I remarked. "Thank you."

Straight in front of us appeared the Japanese rock garden Mr. Kubo had built to remind everyone of better days. As we turned a corner it was like magic. "This is it," I said, "I'm home at last!"

The porch light shone brightly. Smiling like a child, I turned to thank the young man again, but he was gone.

I wondered, *Should I search and thank him tomorrow? He looked like all the other soldiers, so chances are slim. Never mind, I'm safe at home, warming my hands at the glowing potbelly stove.*

HARUYE PASSES — 1942

Aunt Haruye's son, Rick, was in distress when he pushed open our barrack door. He said, "Mom is in the hospital. It's serious. Yesterday she told me where the important papers were and her last wishes."

His voice trembled when he urged, "All the relatives need to visit soon."

"I'll be there in ten minutes," I replied. My hands felt disconnected when I dropped the ironing into the basket. I grabbed my scarf and ran to the Canteen. Inside Kiyoshi was at the cash register talking with a customer. I interrupted their conversation. "Haruye is in the hospital," I blurted.

"She isn't doing well and doesn't have much time," I said. "I'm going to see her now. Meet me after work, okay?"

"I'll see you shortly," Kiyoshi said with a grimace. I wondered, *What can I bring to lift her spirits?* I scanned the empty Canteen shelves and just said, "Bye."

I rushed to Haruye's bedside and thought, *I saw her a few days ago in the mess hall and she looked sick then. Today she looks worse.*

Her skin was clammy and wrinkled. She opened her eyes and said, "Hanae would you help look after Rick, if I die?"

"Of course," I said. "Is there anything else?"

She managed a grin and for a moment looked younger. She said, "I want to go home." Her eyes closed and she began breathing easily.

I sat with her until Kiyoshi arrived. "She is resting and seems okay," I said. He wiped his brow.

"She made peace with God and is ready," I continued. "It won't be long."

Kiyoshi closed his eyes. "Will you be here tomorrow? I don't want her to be alone."

"Yes, I'll come after breakfast," I replied.

"Let's go home," Kiyoshi urged. "There is nothing more we can do."

The next morning, I brought a bouquet of wildflowers and I put them in vase on her nightstand. They brought cheer and brightness to the room. Even though she was asleep I said, "I hope you'll have a good day."

Haruye stirred and touched my hand. "Thank you," she said. "Please look after Rick."

She dropped my hand and closed her eyes. She opened them again and asked, "Will you get me a Hershey bar? I've got a craving for chocolate." Then she turned on her side. Her breathing stopped for what seemed like an eternity. I was scared, "Oh no!" I said out loud. When I moved closer and touched her hand, she stirred and began to breathe.

I gasped and said, "Okay, I'll be right back. See you soon."

Haruye waved weakly and said, "Thank you."

I ran to the Canteen and returned in fifteen minutes. Out of breath, I stomped up the stairs and pushed the door open. Haruye's skin was gray and her breathing had stopped again. "Haruye, are you okay?" She remained motionless. I called out, "Nurse, get Dr. Wilson, hurry."

Doctor Wilson grabbed her hand, searching for a pulse. He shook his head and closed Haruye's eyes.

He removed his glasses, "She passed peacefully," he said. "We did all we could, and now she's in a better place."

Rick was standing at the door and entered quietly. He took his mother's hand and squeezed it. He broke down and lowered his face into a pillow. I pulled him close. Her death was not unexpected but it was faster than anticipated. The day before she was exceptionally cheerful and had a good appetite.

I wondered if Haruye heard voices that asked her to choose.

Then I remembered how difficult the dust, grime, anxiety, and heat made life for her. The other day she asked, "When can I go back to Seattle?"

She yearned to escape the oppressive heat and acidic dust. It was like water torture, a constant dripping on her forehead.

I looked at her and realized that imprisonment eroded her health physically and mentally until her body was no longer fully linked to her spirit.

This is not shikataganai, I thought with anger. *This is not something that Kamisama and the Japanese spirits were responsible for. This is a man-made hell authorized by President Roosevelt.*

CREMATION

Megumi and Rinban Sato entered the hospital ward. Megumi took off her scarf and wiped her nose. She said, "We should pray for her soul."

Rinban chanted a Buddhist sutra, *"Nam myoho renge kyo."* He wore a black robe with a purple sash and his hands clasped prayer beads.

Dr. Wilson said nothing and wrote notes on Haruye's chart. He checked his wrist watch and noted her time of death. She was the first to die in Minidoka.

Rinban struck the singing bowl and continued a high pitched, *"Nam myoho renge kyo..."*

Doctor Wilson turned to me, Rick and Megumi. "You have my deepest sympathy on your loss." He bowed slightly and said, "I'll make arrangements. Shall I cover her face or would you like some time with her?"

"Thank you," I replied, "No—please leave her for now."

I shuffled and turned, feeling the weight of my baby. *Doing her funeral will be a long, tough job in my condition*, I thought.

I turned to Rick and embraced him, "Your mother had a good life. She tried hard even though it was difficult. Thankfully, she passed peacefully. You must be strong. She would want you to be strong—*gambari-nasai*," I urged.

Rick lifted his head and closed his eyes for a second, "I don't know what to do about the funeral and the other arrangements. I'm afraid and Dad's ulcer is acting up so he is no help."

I took Rick's hand, "Don't worry, we have many people who know how to do this. Just be strong and help your father."

With confidence I said, "You'll be fine. We'll take care of everything. You've nothing to worry about. For the funeral you'll need a white shirt and dark tie for both you and your dad. If you don't have them, there are plenty of people who can lend you clothes."

I stepped away from Rick and turned to Doctor Wilson. I waited until he looked up from his clipboard.

I asked, "Will you contact the camp director? Please tell him Haruye died and the family will make arrangements. We have customs that must be observed. Thank you."

Doctor Wilson seemed distracted. "Yes, I'll prepare the death certificate and inform Director Stanford. Since she's the first to pass here, I'm not sure how we're going to handle this. But believe me, we want to do it right. I mean, we need to do it right. Trust me."

I bristled at the word "trust." My face twisted. I pursed my lips and my nostrils flared. My pent up emotions rose as if I was possessed. Word spread and outside a crowd gathered to pay their respects. They stood in silence and waited by the door.

I began to speak louder so the crowd could hear. Doctor Wilson stiffened and stepped back.

I said, "We're in jail and we didn't commit a crime. We shouldn't even be here. Why should we trust you? Give me one reason to trust you or the government for anything except to betray us. Yes, this is our fate but we're human beings and not animals."

I fumed, "Say whatever you will about medicine, but don't speak about 'trust'. We aren't free people."

My voice grew even louder, "We're prisoners of war, POWs. This terrible place has broken Haruye as surely as if her wrists were cut and she bled to death."

By his expression, Wilson was dumbfounded by my outburst. I could tell that he didn't realize the powder keg he was sitting on. Like the other staff, he only listened to internees who supported Director Stanford. His mouth was agape as he folded his arms and held himself tight.

Dr. Wilson stepped back and adjusted his glasses. Sweat beaded his forehead and his neck veins bulged. He nodded and acknowledged my remarks. "I'm sorry," he said, "sorry for everything. I'm sorry for your loss." Wilson paused and gulped. "I need to get back to my office. Please excuse me." He pushed up his glasses and tucked the file folder under his arm.

I took a deep breath. In a way I felt sorry for Wilson. He was doing his best under difficult circumstances. But I couldn't trust or believe he would work in our best interests. Like the other staff, he was a puppet and everyone knew it.

It was obvious that Dr. Wilson was not prepared to handle a confrontation. Instinctively I knew that we had an advantage if disagreements arose about funeral arrangements. *If the situation comes to a head*, I thought, *I'm prepared for a war with the administration.* But I sensed that the administration was not prepared for war with us.

I raised my hand and beckoned Rick, Megumi, and Rinban for a meeting by Haruye's bed.

"She must be cremated," I said, "Every Japanese knows that. We might be here for years but eventually we'll return home. And when we do, we'll take her ashes back. Rinban, we must have the funeral here so all her friends and relatives can say goodbye. Can you reserve the Block 30 Recreation Hall for the service?"

He said *"Hai,"* then quickly collected his papers and singing bowl. Rinban bowed and pulled up his robe as he prepared to walk the dusty path outside. He opened the door and said, "I'll make the funeral arrangements now. We'll need flowers, announcements, and envelopes for koden contributions. I'll tell the block captains and they'll help spread the word."

I had a gloomy feeling as the full weight of events sank in. Shortly, *I will be in this hospital delivering a child. Am I putting my baby in danger by what I'm doing?*

I shook my head in frustration. Quietly I prayed for strength and said, "Wait Rinban, don't leave yet; there are still more things to talk about."

Rinban acknowledged my request and closed the door behind him, rejoining the group.

I said, "No one has much money. If we were in Seattle, we could do this at the Buddhist church. We would have a big funeral with tea and sushi or maybe even a dinner at Gyokyoken restaurant. But here, everything is makeshift. We can only do so much."

Megumi's eyes lit up, "We could take up a collection for flowers. Maybe a donation box in the Block 30 Canteen? I'm sure Uncle Kiyoshi will say yes. The other two canteen managers will agree when they find out."

"No, don't do that," I said. "We need the money but this place must not make us shameless. We won't become beggars with tin cups. We may be desperate, but we still have pride. People will know what we need and they'll bring it without our asking. That's the Japanese way."

I straightened Haruye's sheets and tidied up her nightstand.

Glancing at Haruye's body, I said, "See all the trouble you started. Why couldn't you be strong? You should've lived longer."

Then I told Megumi, "Have the students make paper flowers for the funeral and memorial. We need lots of flowers. If they're short of folding paper, newspaper would be okay, but there must be a lot."

Megumi nodded, "Yes, origami flowers."

"Rinban, will you ask Director Stanford to send someone to Twin Falls to buy real flowers? We should have enough *koden* donations shortly. But the funeral home and cremation will cost a lot so the government must cover that."

"I'll ask the director for the expenses," I continued. "Oh, Rinban, check with the carpenters so see if they'll make a coffin for Haruye's funeral, just in case."

My sadness was replaced by a strong sense of purpose. "The carpenters will do a good job. If they can't find wood, we can pull out some of the barrack boards until we have enough. Are they going to put us in jail for stealing wood?"

"Megumi," I said, "find some fabric or a nice quilt we could use for coffin lining. Something Japanese would be best."

Rinban nodded. "I know Shimizu-san, the carpenter foreman. I'm sure he and his crew would be happy to do it. I'll take care of that, too. We'll do our best."

"On second thought, just tell them to stand by until we find out what the administration is going to do," I replied.

I turned to Megumi. "We'll need some other things. Please get Haruye's best dress and find her make-up kit. Also look for her Japanese lacquer combs. Find out if anyone has a white kimono." Megumi had a tense look and her lip quivered. I continued, "We must prepare and wash her body so we can have visitors. It's time you learned the customs."

"*Hai*," Megumi said and exited quickly with Rick and Rinban.

I surveyed the hospital ward and grasped a clean towel and filled a pan with water. Sadness weighed heavily on me. I paused for a second and looked at Haruye, then dipped the cloth and passed it above her closed eyelids. Taking special care, I wiped around her chapped lips and the corners of her mouth.

I combed her hair with long sweeps, stretching the strands into a French roll. After patting her face dry, I covered Haruye's with a sheet to shield her from the dust. A silence settled over the ward. I was alone with her and took a moment. "We'll get this done," I said. I felt the baby kick as I pulled the sheets tight. I picked up Haruye's hand and said, "Auntie, you'll not just be some piece of trash thrown away in Idaho."

The door banged and Megumi returned with a dress and make-up case. I motioned for her to come closer while I pulled the curtain shut with a screech.

"There is a line outside," she said, "it's almost around the whole building."

"She'll be ready shortly," I reassured, "just give me a hand."

Lifting Haruye into a sitting position, we untied her white smock. Carefully we pushed a pillow under her back. I draped a section of the sheet over her, exposing Haruye's thin arm and small shoulder. I said, "Megumi, please change the water."

We dipped her left hand in the pan and with a tweezer's edge we cleaned under her fingernails. As each area was washed, it was covered and a different section exposed. Megumi dried the fingers and then painted Haruye's nails with red polish. I applied lipstick and rouge with the care of an artist, until she appeared at peace. With great care, we washed her hands and placed one over her abdomen. I put a string of brown Buddhist prayer beads in Haruye's hands. *She looks magnificent, almost like an angel,* I thought. The red of her lips and rouge contrasted with the whiteness of her kimono. We stepped back and admired our work.

"I think she'd be happy now. She looks so beautiful," Megumi said.

"Thank you for your help. I couldn't have done it without you," I replied. "Just one last thing. Did you bring her perfume?"

Megumi inspected the kit and removed a small bottle of French perfume.

I opened it and inhaled. "Oh, this is wonderful," I remarked. I lifted the black flacon of to the light. "Ah, so luxurious."

I dabbed a drop behind Haruye's ears and inside the bend of her elbows.

"Now she's ready," Megumi exclaimed with pride. I created a path for visitors to view the body. Old men and women, young people and children stood patiently outside in the heat for hours. Some waited under barrack eaves and others found shade creating a row of black umbrellas. The line grew longer by the minute. Buddhist prayer beads clicked and chattered.

Mourners entered one by one and bowed to Haruye and then to the family. Rinban chanted, *"Nam myoho renge kyo..."*

Outside on the stoop, a bowl of burning incense fumed. The smoke drifted into the ward and cleaned the air. Mourners left individual incense sticks and fully wrapped bundles. It was understood that no matter how scarce, people would gladly give what they could spare.

"I knew we could count on everyone," I said.

The solemn mood was broken when Director Stanford and Doctor Wilson entered. Stanford was an average-sized white male in a black suit and tie. He scanned the room with a puzzled look.

"What's going on here?" Wilson asked with a frown. There were hundreds of people paying their respects. "Looks like we just walked into a foreign country," Stanford said.

It was obvious that they didn't know what to do. But above all, they didn't stop the process which took on a life of its own.

The Director turned to Doctor Wilson and said in a high-pitched voice, "Goodness gracious, what's happening? How long has this been going on?

Nurse Griffin, the head nurse, rushed up to the Director.

She screwed up her face, "This happened so fast I couldn't stop them. The family asked for some private time with the body and when I came back there was a long line with that blasted priest chanting. I didn't know what to do. But believe me, I had nothing to do with this."

"Okay, don't worry, nurse," Wilson responded.

In the meantime, Mr. Allen, a local mortician and his brother-in-law, Mr. Smith, slipped into the room. Allen was a thin man who sweated profusely. He stood with Smith, who was an overweight gentleman in his fifties with wire rim glasses and a thin mustache. His blue seersucker suit was baggy, and his pant cuffs dragged.

Allen wiped his brow and asked, "Am I late? Oh, this is my brother-in-law, Jimmy Smith, who has a mortuary in Salt Lake."

Director Stanford had a befuddled look. Perspiration soaked Allen's shirt collar. He dabbed his forehead with a white handkerchief embroidered with his mortuary's trademark and adjusted his tie.

Smith stood next to Allen. His ruddy face was slightly pink. In the center of his fleshy visage was a prominent bulge with small spider veins coursing through his W.C. Fields-like nose.

Wilson peered over his eyeglasses, "Nurse, you may go now." He waved her away with a dismissive gesture. It was as if he was trying to control some of the situation. Then he grabbed Stanford's arm and tugged. "We need to stop this, you're in charge," he said. "I can't have all these people coming through here. This is a hospital, not a funeral home."

The Director's jaw tightened. "This is a disaster. It's like an intricate time bomb with gears turning and clicking, something I don't want to stop without an understanding what makes it tick," he commented.

Stanford paused and surveyed the room, "I can't believe so many people are standing in the heat. If we disrupt the line, things could ignite and get worse," he remarked.

The human chain snaked through the waiting area and then cascaded down the stairs. It stretched down the road and around the block. Without many recreational activities or required obligations, this was an event to attend. Some people came from the other side of camp to pay their respects.

I began to perspire and felt light headed. "Excuse me, I'm exhausted," I said and took a seat behind a curtain. There I could hear the doctor and others talking in the corner.

Doctor Wilson said to Director Stanford, "We have to take control. It's a circus and this needs to end."

Stanford replied, "Wait, nothing is out of control. There's order, can't you see? We mustn't be hasty. We're the ones who don't get it. We want to respect what they're doing and figure out what's going on."

I peeked through a space in the curtain and watched the line move slowly. Each person bowed to Haruye and prayed as Rinban continued chanting. The atmosphere had changed and the room assumed an aura of a shrine.

Allen, Smith, and Doctor Wilson looked at each other quizzically.

I continued to watch and listen to their conversation. "We're the only white people here, isn't that obvious to you?" Stanford asked. He continued, "So hold your horses and let's figure this out. Maybe it won't last much longer. Maybe we can wait this out."

Dr. Wilson's voice quavered, "I need my hospital ward in case someone gets sick or is injured. We can't have all these people milling around. It's bad for staff morale and the privacy of other patients."

Director Stanford said, "Babies have been born, but this is the first death. I thought about how to handle death, but was hoping it wouldn't happen so soon. We have 8,000 residents of all ages and conditions. We are the seventh largest city in the state and we need to handle this right. I don't want to do anything hasty that gets people more upset than necessary."

Stanford continued, "Right now the Japanese are emotionally distraught about the death. They're a long way from home, in a prison camp, and have lost their dignity. Truly, it's a dangerous combination. I don't want to give them an excuse to turn on us."

Stanford's veins bulged from the side of his forehead as he spoke. His face flushed and he screwed up his mouth. "We don't want to back them into a corner so we have to call the guards. Someone may get hurt or killed. I wouldn't want that on my watch. After all, I'm not a soldier, but a civilian employee. I see these people every day and I can't have them hating me. What do you think, Dr. Wilson?"

The group turned to Dr. Wilson in hopes that he would have an easy solution. Wilson said, "Okay, I'll start the ball rolling. This is something I can't dodge."

Stiffening up, Wilson said. "Okay, I'll ask the family about their plans. Let's talk to Hanae."

Rinban continued his high pitched, *"Nam, nam, nam,"* chants. His tone varied with each strike of the singing bowl. It was an atmosphere engulfed by incense and the sound of Riban chanting.

The four men walked towards us looking like car salesmen with an offer. I opened the curtain and stepped forward. Immediately the line stopped as if to join the conversation. An elderly woman bowed. She waited while the men approached.

I bowed to the woman and said, *"Sumimasen,* please continue."

"Hanae," Dr. Wilson said, "this is the camp director, Mr. Stanford, Mr. Allen from the Twin Falls Mortuary and Mr. Smith from the Salt Lake Mortuary. They've come a long way."

I nodded and acknowledged their presence. "Nice to meet you," I replied.

Dr. Wilson continued, "We want to make sure everything is handled correctly." Loosening his tie, he remarked, "What are your plans for the deceased?"

Several Japanese in line moved closer to listen. The men sensed this movement and reacted by moving farther towards the corner.

"There are Buddhists and Christians here." I said. "But the customs are Japanese."

I motioned Rick to join us. "Please Rick, step closer," I requested. In response, the line stopped again. Megumi urged, "Please keep the line moving."

Even though everyone knew Haruye had a heart condition. There was angry talk among the residents because they felt that the incarceration had been too much for her. I overheard someone say, "If she'd been in Seattle she would have gotten better care." Others nodded in agreement.

I explained to the administration group, "We prepared the body as Japanese custom dictates. Haruye has been washed and dressed for the funeral."

Mr. Allen adjusted his glasses and carefully examined Haruye, "You've done a nice job so far. But she needs proper care in Twin Falls. The heat will begin to do damage," he commented.

Dust blew in and Rick coughed. Megumi gave him water and also turned the electric fans higher. To keep the area presentable, she wiped dust from the sheets and equipment.

I did not acknowledge Allen's compliment, but asked about the arrangements.

To make my point so all could hear, I said, "Haruye's body should be on display today and tomorrow. We're making arrangements for a coffin and a Buddhist ceremony."

Director Stanford was shocked by my words. In response the line stopped and heads turned. Stanford squirmed, "I can't have all these people in the hospital much longer. We need this space for new patients. It really isn't proper to have a deceased person on display." He wiped his brow and said, "I don't want any trouble or anyone getting hurt." With an anxious look, he peered over his shoulder at the crowd.

Rick and I stared at Stanford and the line slowed, waiting for his next word.

"Yes, we know," I said in a sarcastic tone. "We're your prisoners, but there are some things you cannot control. Don't worry, we plan on moving the body shortly."

His face grew red when he raised his voice; "You can't mean you'll take her back to the barracks! We're just not equipped for that kind of thing. There are health regulations and the heat. It's at least one hundred degrees in the shade."

I played to the residents in line who were waiting on every word. I felt their sadness and thought, *It's like they are not only mourning Haruye but their own circumstances as well. They never had time to grieve properly after the incarceration but this is their opportunity.*

I spoke so everyone could hear, "Our group has made arrangements to have Haruye kept elsewhere until the funeral. Health regulations mean nothing here. Just look at the latrines and the unsanitary mess halls."

Director Stanford's voice became hoarse. "That's why I asked the two funeral directors to attend," he said. Then continued, "We want to take Haruye back to the Twin Falls mortuary today,"

I asked politely, "Who's going to pay for the funeral and services?"

Director Stanford held his ground, "We, I mean the government will take care of everything, including the coffin. Don't worry, we'll handle it."

I continued, "If they take her, where will the services be?"

I paused when a large flock of sparrows flew past the windows. They circled and dived madly. I took this to be an omen. *Kamisama sent them*, I thought. A small one flew into the ward and perched on a beam.

Dr. Wilson grabbed a broom and held it high.

"Stop," I yelled. "It'll be fine."

Immediately the bird landed on a different rafter.

Wilson's mouth dropped and the group was obviously taken aback by the bird.

"That's never happened before," Wilson remarked.

"Where were we?" Mr. Allen asked, "Oh the service plans."

He said to Rick and me, "We plan to transport her and have her body prepared in Twin Falls. Once that's done we'll bring her back for the service."

I knew that the sheer number of mourners gave us the upper hand in negotiations. I stood straight and pushed my belly towards them. I said, "She must be cremated so we can take her ashes home. Also, it's our custom to witness the cremation. At least Rick and I must be there."

Mr. Allen paced and pulled at his collar to cool down. He motioned to the others for a sidebar conference. The four white men excused themselves and regrouped. Ironically, their voices carried from the corner and I could hear their entire conversation.

Allen and Stanford talked about possible options. "I can't cremate her," Allen said. "There are no crematoriums in the entire state of Idaho. But I could prepare the body if necessary."

He looked over his shoulder to make sure we weren't paying attention when he opened up. Nevertheless, I heard them clearly.

"The truth is my people don't want them around," Allen said. "After all, these Japs are the enemy and many good Americans died at Pearl Harbor. It would be bad for business. Having the family at the mortuary is out of the question."

Stanford broke up the meeting and said, "Okay, let's see what they can live with. But don't ever call them 'Japs. They don't like it and I don't blame them." Allen nodded sheepishly.

The four men rejoined Rick and me. The line slowed again when we stepped away for the conference.

Director Stanford explained the next steps. "Mr. Allen will take care of the body in Twin Falls and bring it back to Minidoka for the funeral. Cremation is not possible since no one in the whole state has the facilities. We'll prepare the body in town and Haruye can be buried at Minidoka."

Stanford was out of breath after he laid out the plan. At first, he seemed confident but avoided eye contact. Anxiously his jaws tightened waiting for a response. The seconds continued to tick away, and with each tick, Wilson's group squirmed. Finally, they turned to each other. Allen raised his open palms making a "what next" gesture.

Rick was angry because of the delay. He stepped forward and I held him back. "Mom must be cremated," he insisted. "I want her ashes returned to Seattle and some sent to the Hiroshima family grave," he said.

I added, "Yes, she must be cremated."

Director Stanford's shoulders slumped and he turned his head sideways and moaned, "This has gotten out of hand." His words hung like a dark cloud.

The line lurched after his remark. Then it undulated like a beast as mourners whispered the word "cremation." Like a game of telegraph, the information was passed down the line.

I turned to the crowd and said, "I'm sorry you don't have a crematorium in Idaho, but Haruye will be cremated one way or another."

"We won't release her body to the mortuary unless she's going to be cremated," I declared. Slamming my hand down on the nightstand with a pop, I argued, "If not, we'll keep her here. We have Japanese people who worked in funeral homes and know how to prepare the dead. They'll make arrangements and show respect." I straightened up and emphasized the word "respect."

Stanford's group milled around after my remark. Allen pulled out a white handkerchief and wiped his face. There was a small line of vapor forming at the bottom of his glasses. He took a deep breath and replied to me in a shaky tone. "You can't be serious. You won't be able to keep the body for two days without preparation. And you can't possibly cremate her. That's absurd. It must be done by a mortuary; that's the law. I think you're bluffing."

Allen felt the crowd move closer as all eyes turned to him. There was an ugliness present as the line grew surly. Pressure was building and a *Nisei* man yelled, "We're not good enough. Is that it?"

Emboldened, I faced the crowd. Residents began to glare at the white men as if it was hunting season. Several Japanese gave the piercing "hate stare." To me, this drama was a microcosm of the internment. The disagreement represented an opportunity for the prisoners to reclaim some dignity. The crowd sensed it and became agitated. This was not a small-time act of quiet resistance. As the situation intensified, it felt like war would be declared.

Playing to the crowd, I said, "We won't release Haruye unless she's returned for a funeral in Minidoka and we witness the cremation. If the administration won't do it, we'll honor her last wishes our own way."

I snarled, "Would you deny the dying wish of one of your prisoners? Every prisoner gets a last wish."

There was a rumbling in the crowd and a *Nisei* boy yelled, "Cripes sake, do what she asks!"

Another voice yelled, "Every prisoner gets a last wish."

The mood darkened when it became evident that many acknowledged their status of being "prisoners," a label they had avoided out of shame in the past. Their outcries added strength to my bluff. Buoyed by the mob energy, I raised the ante.

"The firemen will take her body and we'll keep her in a canteen walk-in cooler under watch," I said in a clipped voice. "Our block captains and security will guard her. After the funeral, we'll make a bonfire near the canal and cremate her body."

I couldn't believe what I had just said—words channeled from some power beyond my own. Maybe it was the sparrows and *Kamisama's* presence or maybe it was the crowd that spurred me on.

The heat was so oppressive that it made my brain throb. As outlandish as my proposal sounded, my outburst had an effect on Director Stanford. He began to understand the full weight of his problem. Quickly he realized the need to get control and find middle ground.

Stanford looked at the line, now seething like an animal. A young *Nisei* gestured a symbolic cutting of his throat with an imaginary blade as he pointed at Stanford. It was a chilling sight that conveyed the threat unequivocally.

It was obvious that Stanford was shaken by the gesture. He broke the tension by excusing himself and the others. They huddled in the corner. Rick and I took our places as greeters, and tensions dropped. I excused myself and re-entered the curtained area, knowing full well that I could catch every word of their private conversation.

Allen confessed that he had never seen a situation like this, and had never witnessed so many Japanese in a torches and pitchforks mood. "I could almost feel their breaths," he said. With a sense of relief, he remarked, "Glad I'm not responsible."

Allen asked Stanford, "Is there any way we can just take the body to Twin Falls? This stand-off could take all day."

They looked to Director Stanford for direction. "I'm going to have some water first," Stanford replied. "Damn," he remarked as the cup slipped from his hand and bounced on the floor.

I opened the curtain when I heard the sound. Stanford wiped his mouth and raised his eyebrow and said to Allen, "No—these people have suffered enough. They are not the enemy." He rubbed his chin and continued, "Most of them are US citizens. They're wards of the government. As a representative of the government, I'm asking you to do your patriotic duty during a time of war. Help me out. I'll even pay for the most expensive casket if that'll make a difference."

Smith became animated and said, "I'm sorry I came here. I should be back home in Salt Lake City looking at catalogues," he remarked. "And that pregnant woman, what's her name? Is she ever a loony! What kind of camp is this?" He dabbed his face with a hanky and said, "This is a mess. Sounds like the patients are running this mental hospital." Smith continued, "Call her bluff, man. You can't let her push you around like that."

Director Stanford turned to Smith and said, "Easy for you to say this since you don't have a horse in the race. Don't get funny with me and don't tell me what to do. This is wartime."

I saw Stanford wag his finger and say, "People are going to be born and die here." Stanford spit out his words, "Haruye won't be the last."

Stepping back for a second, Smith raised his arms and folded them over his chest, "I'm sorry, but this is your problem, not mine. I don't even live in Idaho." Smith backpedaled, and then Allen shook his head and urged, "Tell him Smith. Go ahead, tell him."

Sweat dripped from Smith's nose. He paused and twisted his mouth and said, "I didn't think it was important to say at first, but I have a crematorium in Salt Lake City."

"What?" Stanford asked as his voice shook. "Why didn't you say so earlier? This is Idaho, not the Deep South. We don't have *whites only* water fountains, bathrooms, lunch counters or buses here. Stanford pointed his finger and pushed it against Smith's chest, "Instead we have a camp for Japanese. Their ashes won't contaminate white customers here or in Utah. Do you understand?"

Smith locked his fingers together and twisted his hands. "Okay, don't get upset. Take it easy. Yes, I've got a crematorium. But I need to think about my business and how I'm going to support my family," Smith pleaded in a tearful manner. He looked down and said, "We've served the community for years and I don't want to jeopardize their faith and confidence."

Stanford clenched his fists and held his rage. His face flushed and he tapped his foot, "Just one more time, right now I have a stack of complaint letters from the internees to Eleanor Roosevelt about the conditions here."

I heard his remark and thought, *Great, maybe Eleanor Roosevelt can actually help us.*

Stanford said, "There was a kid in line who did the throat cutting motion towards me a minute ago. I worry about my family if something bad happens here. This funeral could be the breaking point." He pointed his finger at Smith and continued, "I don't want some Boise or Twin Falls newspaperman poking around because the internees built their own funeral pyres. Get it?"

Stanford almost spit out his words. "Nor do I want the International Red Cross calling attention to the plight of these people to the whole world. Nor do I want the health department wondering whether we had a body stored in the meat locker for two days. This would be a huge propaganda victory for Japan and it would make my superiors angry."

Stanford took another drink and some water trickled down his collar. He insisted, "This death could turn all internees against us. If we don't do this right, the young Japanese men who cooperate will be in danger. No way could they side with us and I wouldn't blame them if we don't handle this in a respectful manner."

Stanford ground his teeth, "Above all I don't want any martyrs or victims to inflame everyone and destroy the good relations we've worked so hard for. So I don't care whether this woman is bluffing or not. We need to do the right thing."

Smith coughed and wheezed while Allen nodded. It was obvious that they weren't going to fight Stanford. They looked at each other and Smith said, "We got the point. Okay, okay, we understand."

Stanford looked directly into Smith's eyes and said with determination. "Best do it unless you want the US army to escort the body to your Salt Lake funeral home and make you cremate her. Is that what you want? Remember, this is wartime." Stanford took an aggressive posture and clearly looked like he had had enough when he said, "I may be a civilian, but the military will do as I say."

Stanford's chest swelled and he spoke with great determination, "Or if you don't budge, there's another way," Stanford remarked with an evil grin. "There's more than one way to skin a cat. I'll have an army ambulance take the body and family to some other mortuary in Salt Lake City for cremation and you'll have lost my business. Just how many funerals do you think we'll have a year?" Stanford knew he had the upper hand and smirked. "We have over eight thousand people here and many are old. How many deaths would that be? I'd guess maybe thirty or forty or more a year. That's a lot of business for an operation like yours."

Stanford twisted his remarks like a knife in Smith's ribs. "That's a lot of money. Remember, it's your choice. Make the right one. We don't have much time. By the way, we need some flowers, too."

Allen whispered something to Smith who paused momentarily. "Okay if that's how it is, I'll do it for America," Smith responded. "I'll do this for my country. It'll be my wartime contribution. That's something I can tell people in Salt Lake."

Smith relaxed his shoulders and looked up at the ceiling. He seemed to be formulating a strategy, "Anyway I'll say you threatened me with soldiers to get this done if anyone asks."

Allen touched his chin as if he was calculating his profits. "Now, you'll pay for everything including the coffin, is that right? Cash?"

"Yes, that's correct," Stanford said. "You can prepare the body in Twin Falls for the service here and either you or Smith can transport her to Salt Lake for cremation. I'll arrange passes for the relatives to go to Salt Lake." All three nodded in agreement and Stanford slapped Smith on the back.

"By the way, it'll be a US government check, as good as gold," Stanford said. He smiled once the deal was closed. He put his arm on Smith's shoulder and said, "Now, Smith, let's get this done for America." Shaking his hand, Stanford continued, "Congratulations, you're helping the war effort like a GI on the front line. By the way, expect some armed guards with the family for the cremation."

With a sigh, Stanford took a more measured tone. "The family will be on Army trucks accompanying the hearse. As far as your customers are concerned, tell them whatever you want, but don't get them involved or there could be big trouble." Stanford pointed his finger for emphasis. "Also don't talk to any news reporters about this," he warned.

He grinned and said, "I'll tell the family that we've agreed to all of their terms. Call your people and we can start the arrangements." Stanford checked his watch, "It'll be dinner soon, so most people will leave if they know the body will be back later." He ran his fingers through his hair and said, "Thank goodness, we'll finally be able to get this hospital back to normal."

Stanford's suit was drenched with sweat when he exhaled out loud, "Whew! What a day! I need a stiff drink," he said. He turned to me and our group and bowed. "Everything will be fine now, we can do what you asked. Allen will prepare the body in Twin Falls and Smith will cremate it in Salt Lake. Please get ready for a trip to Salt Lake. I'll arrange the passes."

"Thank you," I replied, "we'll stop the line shortly and take our dinner break. You can have your hospital ward back."

"Megumi, can you go with Rick to Salt Lake?" I asked. "His father is ill and I'm about to deliver."

Megumi replied in a shaky voice, "Okay, I'll pack some things."

"Rick, you need to pack as well," I instructed.

He nodded in agreement.

I pulled the curtains wide open and sat down. I relaxed for a moment and thought, *This is what real victory feels like. It's winning for others. I need to savor this moment.*

Megumi chirped, "Hanae, please talk to Yoko to see if she got any messages from Haruye."

"Good idea, almost forgot," I replied.

CHAPTER TEN

Hanae and Block 30 Canteen

By the time Rick and Megumi returned from Salt Lake City with the ashes, rows of chairs filled the recreation hall. Floral wreaths stood by a table with a photo of Haruye next to an urn. Rinban Suzuki presided over the ceremony and lines of mourners bowed before her picture. Each dropped a pinch of incense into a bowl.

I sat in the front row with the family. Rick and his father wore white shirts with black arm bands. Kiyoshi borrowed a black tie and I wore a dark dress. Even though the room was uncomfortably warm and stuffy, I was happy to see the results of our hard work. I held Kiyoshi's hand and thought, *Rest in peace, Haruye. I promise we'll take you home for a proper burial someday.*

In a dream, Haruye came to Yoko the next evening. She was well and wanted to thank everyone for their prayers.

BABY ALAN

In the morning, I grabbed my toothbrush, Ivory soap and towel for a trip to the latrine. I was shocked when I felt fluid running down my leg. I yelled, "Kiyoshi, my water broke, the baby's coming!"

Yoko, his sister, was standing nearby. She ran outside and banged the fire alarm. Immediately I heard sirens and the roar of the engines.

"Where's the fire?" a volunteer fireman hollered. Yoko pointed at me. "Can you take her to the hospital?"

"Lady, you're supposed to call an ambulance," he said. The crew waited anxiously for instructions. The captain shrugged and said, "Ah what the heck, we'll do it!"

Four burly *Nisei* jumped out and placed me on a litter. "Lady you're going for a twenty block ride so hang on," one fireman said.

I was concerned because I was going to the hospital where I had made a scene after Haruye's death. *I'm sure they haven't forgotten.*

I turned my head and said, "Thanks, Yoko, please tell the others where I am."

The truck bounced along the dirt road. The contractions started and my mind was running fast. I thought, *Baby are you ready? Welcome to America such as it is.*

The delivery was surprisingly quick. Just a few hours in labor and it was over. I remembered mother used to say, "Eat a lot of greasy foods so the baby just slips out." I laughed at the thought.

The boy was seven pounds and healthy. I cradled the baby and was surprised he had so much hair. My first thought was, *You're a fine looking fellow.*

The nurse came and said, "Wow, your baby is a little cutie! Oh, by the way your husband is here."

Kiyoshi was out of breath. He jogged all the way from the Block 30 Canteen to the hospital. Sweat poured down his face. He leaned over and took a peek at the baby. "It looks like he won't be bald like me," Kiyoshi joked.

"What's his name?" the nurse asked, "he can't go home without a name!"

Kiyoshi and I had girl's names picked out but we hadn't settled on a boy's name.

"How about Reo after the truck?" he suggested.

I said, "How about Alan? Kiku had been suggesting it for weeks."

Kiyoshi and I looked at each other and nodded in agreement. "Yes, that'll be his name, Alan Yamada," I said. "We should give him a Japanese middle name. I like Takeo."

Kiyoshi declared, "I think we should name our next boy Reo."

I furrowed my brow after hearing Kiyoshi's big idea, "No, Larry would be a better name," I insisted and said, "Also we can give him a Japanese middle name. I like Yutaka after Grandpa."

"Okay," Kiyoshi replied. He sat and reviewed the hospital birth information. "It says he was legitimate. Well thank goodness for that!" He smiled and continued, "Birthplace is Hunt, Idaho! I never imagined we would have an Idahoan in the family. Isn't that what they call people from Idaho?"

"It doesn't say he was born in a prison, so that is good," I replied.

Outside my room was a small ruckus. I heard a singsong voice say, "I want to see the little baby!" *Only one person barges in like that*, I thought. Not *Kiku but Megumi!*

She removed her hat and gushed, "Oh he's so sweet. I knitted a small cap." She wiggled her fingers, made her eyes big, and gurgled small baby sounds.

"Thanks. Nice hat," I replied.

"So cute," Megumi said. "By the way, everyone thanks you for help with the funeral. It was beautiful. I think Haruye would have been happy."

"Oh, I almost forgot with all the commotion," I said. "I was glad to help. After all, what else was I doing?"

"Ha ha," Megumi laughed and said, "well, having a baby silly!

LAUNDRY

Two weeks later I bundled Alan for a trip to mother's barrack. The smell of bacon frying on the potbelly stove drifted into our apartment. I wished our neighbors would stop smelling up the whole place. *There is no getting away from that odor,* I thought.

I opened the door of Mom's barrack, wiped my feet, and knocked on a post to announce my presence.

"*Ohaiyo gozaimasu,* good morning," Toku said. She waved her hand to fan the smoke as she snuffed out a cigarette in a coffee can.

"Good morning," I replied and placed Alan in a wooden box with his teddy bear. Mom had all his necessities, plus I left his bottle and toys.

I said, "Thanks, I'll be back in an hour," and pulled my scarf tight for a trip to the laundry barrack. My daily fashion statement included: brown and white saddle shoes, white bobby socks, blue and white dot-patterned cotton dress, and neckerchief. Since I didn't have many clothes, I wore the same things for several days in a row.

For a second, I stopped and studied my image in the mirror. *Worn-out woman like an old dish rag. Not young, not old, but tired and haggard. This is what I've become.* I exhaled and covered my mouth. *Not good,* I said to myself and walked outside. The laundry was like the other barracks except it had lines of faucets and deep sinks for washboards.

I pinched my nose and pulled soiled diapers from my bucket. My supplies included a bar of Ivory soap, wooden clothespins, and the grooved metal washboard. I thought, *Scrubbing clothes on a small washboard is like torture.* My back ached just looking at it.

The wind blew dust which lodged in my mouth. Spitting was not ladylike, but under these conditions everyone did it. I grumbled out loud, "How crude."

In Seattle, I'd never considered spitting. But this anti-social habit was almost like an act of resistance here. I wiped the grit from the corners of my mouth and remembered to stay positive and greet the day with the Lord's Prayer:

Give us this day our daily bread....

But deliver us from evil...

I began scrubbing and humming.

I thought that instead of daily bread it should be daily dust.

America had trespassed against my family. I wondered, *How could I forgive a faceless government? Can I be a good Christian if I never forgive?* It was a point of confusion that I dealt with every day as the monotony and boredom of camp created crevices where strange thoughts leaked in.

Christians are wrong, I decided and said, "Deliver us from evil, and what does one call this prison with scorpions, snakes, and stinky latrines?" I asked myself, *In jail without privacy, what are the temptations?*

Still mulling the pledge of allegiance students recited at the camp elementary school, I thought, *liberty and justice? I wish.*

I pounded my anger out on the diapers, torturing them until they were spotless. I would not win any awards for my victory over grime, but instead would be greeted with another dirty pile shortly.

My back ached and throbbed. To ease the pain, I put my hand on my spine like an old woman. Then I folded and stacked the wash neatly. On the way back, I heard dogs barking. Strays were a welcome addition to camp. It didn't take long for the adults and children to adopt them. Whatever breed they were, they all had short legs and long bodies.

Around the corner was a circle of boys holding sticks. They prodded something while the dogs snarled and jumped.

I yelled, "Hey, what's going on?" The boys turned and stared at me.

"Toshi, Ricky, Stan, George, what are you doing?" I hollered.

They dropped their sticks and ran away. I knew their parents so the boys could expect a paddling if they were doing something bad.

The dogs, however, continued to growl and bark. At first I thought they had cornered a rat. But on a closer examination I saw a kit fox. It must have crawled under the barbed wire. I knew that most wild animals did not risk coming into camp unless driven by hunger.

The fox had large ears and a brown bushy tail. Its eyes had vertical pupils like a cat. It was feisty and held its ground. His head bobbed as he searched for an escape route. I gathered some sticks and threw one at the brown mutt who whimpered and ran off. The other three dogs recognized my anger and backed away, but they were not willing to fully relent without a sign of aggression. They wanted to make sure I understood the injustice of the fox's trespass.

I snarled and raised a stick. They immediately understood their new circumstances and backed away, moving side to side barking and showing fierceness as they retreated. I yelled, "Shoo, get away!"

The dogs scampered around the corner. I looked at the fox and expected that it would've been gone by now. Then I wondered if it was injured. *That will be a problem*, I thought.

I bent down and spoke in a gentle voice. "You okay?" I wanted the fox to know that the danger had passed. Upon closer examination, it was clear that he was unharmed. I was surprised when it locked eyes with me. I sensed its cunning and wild nature. This was a free spirit who was not bound by barbed wire.

"Go now," I said, "before the dogs return."

The fox licked the dog dish to show it would be willing to eat in my presence. The wind swirled a dust cloud and the fox ran into the desert. "Goodbye, be safe," I said.

I took the diaper bucket, lifted the box, and headed back. *No harm done. No need to report the boys*, I thought. They knew a thousand eyes were always watching. Any real wrongdoing would be punished.

I wondered about the kit fox and its life, and how hard it must be to survive the heat, cold, and harsh desert conditions. Then I recalled the foxes in Hiroshima. There was a sharp contrast between Yosh's lush farmlands and the stark desert scrub of Minidoka. *Had I not seen the foxes' wedding, I might have remained on the farm. My life would be very different.*

I hope Fumi and the children are well now that Shintaro's gone. And Masa, oh how I miss her.

The next day I dressed and checked my watch. Recently the administration granted temporary medical passes. I got one for an ophthalmologist appointment in Twin Falls. If the exam was quick, I'd have time to make a side trip to the bakery and Dingwall's department store. I had heard how great those stores were.

My enthusiasm subsided when I wondered, *Will the white people ignore me, or will dogs bark and their children poke sticks? Will it be safe to take my baby to town or should I leave him in camp?*

I had an epiphany. At that moment, I decided, *I'll teach Alan to speak Japanese. That way he can live in Hiroshima after the war if Seattle is unsafe.* If we lived in Japan, we wouldn't have to worry about evacuations or anti-Japanese prejudice. The thought stayed with me as I caught the bus to town.

Twin Falls was a very clean and tidy small town. It reminded me of Puyallup where we caught the train from Camp Harmony. There were mothers pushing baby carriages and old men relaxing on benches near the post office. I stayed on the edge of the sidewalk out of the foot traffic paths. I glanced up at each store front, hoping to find a bakery for a chocolate chip cookie.

Oh, there's the Twin Falls funeral home owned by Mr. Allen who took care of Haruye, I thought. It was a brick building on the corner with a black hearse parked at the curb.

The eye doctor's office was next to the drug store. When I entered, the bell announced my arrival.

"Hello, I'm Hanae Yamada," I said to the receptionist.

She smiled and said, "Please fill out these forms. Did you bring your sunglasses?"

I nodded, yes.

Doctor Carey will dilate your eyes so you'll need dark glasses for a while.

He was a pleasant gentleman in his fifties and was all business. After the exam, I was anxious to do some shopping. Unfortunately, my vision was a little blurry.

I walked to Dingwall's Department store and tried to focused my eyes. I squinted and finally found some white socks. I was hoping to buy them quickly and explore the rest of town before the bus came. I stood like a blind person in the aisle when I heard, "Can I help you?"

I pushed the socks forward as if to hand them over, but the clerk moved past me. It took a second to realize that she wasn't talking to me. I withdrew my hands and smiled. I was embarrassed and searched for another clerk. Not seeing anyone, I managed to the reach the register.

The clerk rang up three sales while I waited. After the third customer, she walked away. *I get it*, I thought, *I don't exist.*

I've been in this situation before and was angry for thinking someone would actually serve me. I felt stupid and pondered the choices: say something, walk away, or stand there wearing my dark glasses. Then I remembered selling my Baldwin piano, the dances at Lake Wilderness, and the loss of Molly. *This is not right*, I said to myself and made up my mind to do something. "God forgive me," I uttered out loud.

I placed the socks on the counter neatly and grabbed a nearby blouse and set it next to the socks. Then I added a couple of scarves and stacked them with the blouse. Moving away from the register, I fingered every item on the way to the exit. I pushed open the door and left. A cool breeze hit me in the face, and I thought, *Oh, my old socks are still good. Why get new ones?*

KIYOSHI AND THE BLOCK 30 CANTEEN, 1944

The next morning, I hustled to the Block 30 canteen. "Kiyoshi, you forgot your wallet," I said.

He patted his back pocket. "Wow, how did that happen? Thanks."

"Have a seat and make yourself comfortable," Kiyoshi invited. He pointed to the potbelly stove. "I can make some tea if you have time," he said.

"No thanks, I've wash to do," I replied.

"Okay, see you after work. It's inventory today, so I'll be late for dinner. Go ahead without me. I'll grab a bite later."

I nodded and said, "I've got tons of diapers! See you later." Then I reconsidered, "On second thought, what's the hurry? The laundry will always be there. A cup of tea sounds good."

Kiyoshi gestured with his open palm and said, "Sit by the stove."

Not wanting to get in the way, I replied, "No, I'll drink it alone in the backroom."

I walked to the storage area and found a cozy spot on a 50 lb. bag of potatoes. *Sitting down will make my sore back better,* I thought. The tea warmed me and made me grin. From my location I could peek out and see most of the retail area.

The Block 2, 15 and 30 canteens were like old country stores where farmers gathered around the cracker barrel. Inventories were always low. When rumors of shipments like soap or fruit surfaced, residents lined up in anticipation.

Kiyoshi was the Block 30 canteen manager. His supervisory job was an opportunity to establish himself away from his mother and Elk Grocery. Wearing a canvas apron, he dusted the shelves as he did in Seattle. He became so consumed with his work that I was sure he forgot about me in the storeroom.

The radio played the tune "Be Positive," and he hummed along.
"Be happy, be free, it's a wonderful day!
It's time to spread the joy!
Beee possss iiiii tive!"

From a distance I saw Kiyoshi grab a yardstick and do a Charlie Chaplin "Little Tramp" imitation. He popped on a fedora and pulled it tight and bowed his legs. He walked pigeon toed down the aisle, twirling the yardstick like a cane.

I'd never seen Kiyoshi clowning at work before. Nor had I ever seen him do the Chaplin imitation. I laughed and felt like an audience of one about to break into applause.

After his routine, he put down the yardstick and tossed his hat on the counter. Back to normal, he placed a teapot on the stove and picked up an old *Life Magazine*. The shop doorbell chimed and Kenji and Jimmy entered. Shoji, followed them. He was a mystery because he never said much and always wore a frown until those lines cut deeply into his face. I recognized all three men since they lived in Block 26. My curiosity grew.

Kenji was usually cheerful and happy. He was a strawberry farmer from Hood River, Oregon who also operated a small orchard of peach trees with his wife and four children. His skin was like leather and his hair was parted right down the center. Wearing overalls and mud-caked boots, he looked like a good-natured person.

Jimmy was a young man on the high school baseball team. He was about to graduate in June. As an athlete, he moved quickly but with an odd shuffle.

Shoji remained quiet and walked over to the stove and extending his hands in front of it.

Kiyoshi greeted them, "Hey everyone, good morning!"

Kenji took off his hat and scanned the shelves, "When's the apple shipment due?"

Kiyoshi shrugged while he continued dusting. His expression and tone turned sour when he complained, "We wait for everything–lines at the latrine, mess hall, and Sears catalog mail call. Our time is worth nothing." He nodded and said, "That's the God's honest truth or–if you're Buddhist–it's ah, you know."

Kiyoshi chuckled and said, "I've got some news today. We are *kawaiso*, pathetic. The Japanese Red Cross is sending us charity. Some Swedish ship carried the cargo but they wouldn't let it dock in the US."

Kenji and Jimmy looked at each other in amazement. "You're kidding," Kenji said, "that can't be!"

"It's true," Kiyoshi continued. He moved to another shelf and dusted while he spoke. "Finally, the Spanish Consul helped end the SNAFU. Maybe we'll get some Japanese pickles or soy sauce after the camp committee divvies it up. They also sent us bandages. Can you imagine that?"

Kiyoshi walked to the counter and placed both of his hands flat against the surface, "But to answer your question, no apples today. Maybe they'll switch out the order and give us something else like potatoes."

"That's what I figured," Kenji barked. With amazement he asked, "Red Cross shipment from Japan? I never thought I'd see the day."

He wiped the dust from his hat and continued, "We sent packages to Hiroshima after earthquakes. But I never expected they would send charity back to us. I didn't know Japan had anything to spare." Staring at the stove, he asked, "Hey, you got tea?"

Kiyoshi pointed to the blue enamel pot next to some white mugs. "Help yourself. Tea bags are from yesterday so you'll have to let them steep longer than usual. It's Lipton."

He turned to Jimmy and asked, "What can I do for you, kid?"

Jimmy lurched from the sudden interest. "Do you have any Ivory soap, please?" He asked, knowing this would be a long shot.

Kiyoshi gave Jimmy a sideways glance, sizing him up as if he was ready to toss a curve ball. "Hey kid, I've seen you play baseball. You're pretty good." Kiyoshi grinned, "Sorry, we've got plenty of potatoes but no soap yet. Maybe tomorrow."

Jimmy's shoulders slumped. He adjusted his baseball cap and screwed up his lips muttering, "That's what everyone says. Maybe tomorrow, what can you do?"

Kiyoshi laughed, "Well, it won't come any faster, no matter what. I used to count my days here, but gave up. Right now maybe we're at day 600 or something. All we've got is time: hard time or easy time, but 24 hours each day, nothing more and nothing less."

"Yeah," Kenji laughed, "time is the great equalizer. No one can get more than 24 hours in a day!"

Kiyoshi nodded and sipped his tea. He continued, "Time doesn't matter here. We have nothing to look forward to." Kiyoshi turned to Jimmy and said, "Anyway, without soap, try some cologne. It'll make you smell pretty for the girls."

Jimmy hung his head and walked to the teapot. He dragged his feet and kicked up dust from the floor boards. He paused, "Oh, by the way, my name is Jimmy from Block 26," he said.

With a strong grip, Kiyoshi shook his hand. "Nice to meet you, kid. You're a shortstop, right? It's a hard position."

Jimmy's eyes lit up.

"At short, the ball just comes right at you fast," Kiyoshi continued. "You need a good arm to sit deep in the hole and throw to first. I've seen you hit. You're pretty good for a little guy."

"Thanks," Jimmy said and then replied, "I want to be the next Joe DiMaggio, the Yankee Clipper, wear the pinstripes and play in the house Babe Ruth built. I just can't figure how to get there from Minidoka."

Kiyoshi had a skeptical look when he picked up the duster and said "I pitched for the Taiyo Eagles, semi-pro. My specialty was the submarine pitch." He motioned a sidearm, almost underhanded pitch. Kiyoshi's voice filled with pride.

He continued, "Ever see anything like that? I got them every time until they caught on in the later innings. Then the coach brought in Shigano, who threw fastballs." Kiyoshi puffed on his finger nails and rubbed them against his shirt proudly. "We were so good we even beat the white teams. Take my word for it, no matter how good a player you are—no Japanese will ever play in the bigs. Japanese are too small and the owners won't give you a break."

Kiyoshi continued in a playful tone, "Oh, by the way, when we have soap, it'll be on the second shelf. I wouldn't want our shortstop to offend other teams. Ha! Ha!"

With a bounce in his step, Kiyoshi picked up a potato and threw it at the potbelly stove. There was a "Thunk" that echoed and the potato ricocheted into the corner.

"That was a strike," he said. "Just like the old days."

Kenji shook his head and pointed in an accusatory fashion and then said, "*Mottainai*, wasteful, you shouldn't waste food."

"Ha ha," Kiyoshi laughed, and walked back to the counter. "This isn't waste. It knocks soot from the stove pipe. Idaho is full of potatoes. No one will miss this one. Anyway it's a government-issued potato." Kiyoshi smirked, "You know how you can tell?"

"How?" Kenji responded, snatching the bait like a hungry bass. Kiyoshi smiled, "They've got a big G stamped on the top." He continued with a loud belly laugh. "Ah, gotcha–that's a joke!"

Kenji had an annoyed look and pulled down his dusty fedora. "What's wrong with you? *Mottainai*. That wasn't funny. My dad was a farmer in Hiroshima and he taught me well."

Kenji lit a cigarette. It stuck to his lip and moved up and down with each remark. "Dad would waste nothing. I remember his shirts were patched, but clean. After the shirt wore out, it became a rag. Then it became a mop head and finally into the trash."

Kenji exhaled a cloud of blue smoke. "Dad taught me everything I know. He'd never waste anything and could make this desert bloom." Forcefully he asked, "Why do you think we dug the canal to the vegetable fields? Next year I'll bring cabbages to sell, just wait."

He paused and then said, "Kiyoshi, don't roll your eyes, It's true."

Having everyone's attention, Kenji continued, "Even the little kids are wasteful. They don't eat with their families and no one watches them.

Once I saw some boys pouring milk down a knothole in the mess hall table. They would never have gotten away with that at home. Boy, oh boy, their dads would tan their hides."

As Kenji spoke, his anger rose. "We have no pride," he said. "Yesterday cook-san buried a whole turkey to prevent the rations from being cut. He did it away from the administration spies. "I hate those spies. They're filthy dogs, *inu*. At Manzanar some of the *Nisei* caught two *inu* and beat them up."

"You talk about wasteful," Kenji continued as his voice grew louder, "last week some young bucks from Block 16 set off a false fire alarm and went on a joyride. They were whooping and hollering full speed until they hit a pothole and broke the axle. Those young punks left the truck in the ditch and walked away." Kenji's face turned red as he growled, "What would have happened if there'd been a real fire? We'd lose everything again."

MEGUMI

I felt guilty listening in on the canteen conversations. Nevertheless, I enjoyed witnessing the drama. I was about to finish my tea and slip out when the front door swung open and the bell chimed. Megumi, now a nineteen-year-old, entered with her friend Mary. Megumi stomped her feet to loosen mud as part of her grand entrance. Heads turned when she smiled and greeted everyone with a whirl of her wool scarf. For a young *Nisei* woman, she was exceptionally outgoing. Her short black hair and bangs made her look like a young Japanese child.

Megumi performed a beauty queen wave to everyone. "Who's wasteful?" she asked. "Anyone I know?"

Kiyoshi laughed and said, "Hi, Megumi, what can I do for you?" He flicked his feather duster and added, "As if I didn't know."

She removed her scarf with a tug and popped off her hat. Knowing she held the spotlight, she peeled off a glove slowly. "Uncle, now you be nice," she said. "My friend, Mary, lives in Block 8."

Mary removed her scarf. She was a slight young woman and very plain looking. Her hair was medium length and her clothes were drab. She looked older and wore wire frame glasses that perched midway down her nose. Her eyes were downcast and her teeth chattered slightly from the cold.

"We're on our way to the beauty parlor," Megumi continued. "I thought we'd say 'Hi' to you great big handsome men! I told her this is the best canteen, better than Block 15. So be nice." She pulled her glove off and waved it as she spoke.

Kiyoshi replied, "Yeah, yeah, we'll be nice."

Megumi walked up and down the aisles looking at the empty shelves. She asked, "Has the Pond's Cold Cream arrived?"

Kiyoshi shook his head, "No, sorry. I told you yesterday it would be a week or more."

She spoke like a radio advertisement and explained, "Most people don't take care of themselves here. The desert dries your skin until it looks like dead leaves."

Her head swayed while she waved her glove like an orchestra conductor, "Skin can shrivel if not moisturized regularly. Cold cream brings it to life. It protects you from the sun and the desert." She stopped and smiled while all eyes were transfixed on her. The men were spellbound by the strangeness of what she was saying. "I put it on every night and every day. But right now I'm down to my last jar."

"Aha!" Kiyoshi exclaimed, "Megumi, I've got a solution for the cold cream shortage." He rolled up his sleeves and clapped like an old fashion pitch man. "How about some vanishing cream? That might be good for you."

Megumi puckered her lips in mock affection. "Vanishing cream? Oh, you like my visits and if I shopped at the other canteens, you'd miss my sunny personality." She put her hand on her hip. "What would you do without me? All the beautiful movie stars like Betty Grable use cold cream. I read it in the *Silver Screen* magazine."

Kiyoshi snickered and raised his hand as if to brush off her remark, "At night I bet you have a white face with only your eyes and lips showing. Maybe a towel wrapped around your head. You know, over the metal curlers that roll and snap on a red rubber bead. I bet you're a sight."

Jimmy laughed and pulled down the bill of his cap. "This is quite a show!" he said.

Megumi glanced at Kiyoshi and turned away in a huff. "Why are you so mean, Uncle? If you came by the barrack at night, I'd hit you with a frying pan. You bad man, I'll tell Hanae, *warui ne*, bad man."

I covered my mouth and held back a laugh. *I should leave but this is getting good*, I thought.

Continuing her scolding, Megumi crossed her arms and then pointed her finger accusingly. She fumed, "You dirty old man. Just like Mr. what's-his-name, you know, that old man with the skin condition who walks to the bath everyday wearing his robe so the wind blows it open. I mean, the little girls get scared to see such a sight."

Taken aback, Jimmy laughed so loud he almost fell out of his chair. I'm sure he'd never seen such a brazen display from a Japanese girl. He raised his eyebrows in surprise.

It was then that Megumi noticed Jimmy. She looked him up and down as if he were a piece of new merchandise. Then a glint appeared in her eyes and her attitude changed. "Hello there," she said. "Where have you been all my life?"

Jimmy squirmed, realizing that he was now the center of her attention. He squinted and stepped back after her remark. He swallowed hard and managed to ask Megumi, "Do you live in Block 26?"

Megumi replied, "Yes, of course. That's the best block" and then she paraded to the potbelly stove. Jimmy, Shoji, and Kenji made room for her. Like a little girl, she tilted her head sideways and threw back her hair. "Guess what?" she says, "I'm going to Twin Falls today." She waited for the gravity of her remark to be realized. "It took a month to get a pass to see the eye doctor. And the best part is, I'll have time to go to the drugstore and find some real cold cream." She pursed her lips and looked at Kiyoshi.

He said, "You mean you won't be coming around here in the future? What a loss." Kiyoshi slapped his hand to his forehead. "But I'm sure Twin Falls will appreciate you." Pausing for a second, he said, "By the way, you should ask Ross about town. He goes every week for the US stamp bond program and the Minidoka annual photo project. He's a good guy and picks up vitamins for the pregnant women while in town."

Kiyoshi smiled, "Bright boy, that one. He has the administration wrapped around his little finger. Smart, yes sir."

The door swung open and Ross entered. He looked like a rah-rah college boy with gold wire rim glasses and hair slicked back hair full of Dixie Peach pomade. Wearing a wool pullover argyle vest and a white shirt, he resembled a cheer leader. Ross was exceptionally tall for a *Nisei*. He was so handsome that a group of teenage girls formed an informal fan club. They giggled and cooed whenever they saw him.

Moving towards the stove, Ross declared to no one in particular, "Holy smokes, it's cold out there. Hey, did someone just call my name or was it my imagination? That's my name. Don't wear it out."

He chuckled at his own corny joke and knocked on Jimmy's head and said, "Anyone home?" He looked around the room and wiggled his shoulders. He unzipped his jacket and showed off his aloha shirt. "I'm wearing my glad rags and will be off to wow the big city. Well, not a real big city, but Twin Falls."

Kiyoshi lifted his cup and took a sip. He said, "Hey, Ross, you go to town every week, don't you?"

Ross smiled and nodded, "Of course, someone has to do it. Might as well be me."

Pointing to Megumi, Kiyoshi continued, "You should help Megumi. It's her first trip. You know my niece don't you? She's from Block 26." Kiyoshi pushed Megumi towards Ross. She smiled and batted her eyelashes.

Rubbing his arms from the cold, Ross said, "I'd love to help her, but I've got important things to do." His face glowed as he said, "I've raised $1,000 for the war effort. The money will support our troops and maybe end this war sooner. Remember, even we can do our share."

"Yeah, yeah," Kiyoshi said as he grabbed a potato and massaged it. "You can save that old college stuff for the girls. You better be careful. People are suspicious of your privileges. They're calling you an *inu*. They might beat you up and no one will squeal, teacher's pet you know."

Kiyoshi picked up the feather duster and bent the handle as he talked. "If someone breaks your leg, that's just too bad. Remember there are a lot of tough old *Issei* who still think Japan's winning the war and all this victory stuff is baloney. Those old guys could rough you up and that's not counting all the *Nisei* who think you're a phony."

"Woweee! You sure know how to make a guy feel right at home," Ross said, "I'm no phony. I'm as real as a heart attack!"

After his display of bravado, Ross turned on the charm. "Man alive, I'm no *inu* and I'm not afraid. The good people know I'm doing right and that I'm not a traitor."

Ross's enthusiasm grew as if he were a jazz musician hitting his stride, "When I go to Twin Falls, it helps everyone, and the war effort, too. Hey, if I didn't bring back vitamins, how many babies would have rickets? I know some *Issei* still think Japan will win but they don't bother me. They won't look me in the eye and say anything. It's all hunky-dory."

Ross broke into a little celebratory dance with a spin to emphasize his point. He kicked up his feet and waved his arms and his shoes thumped the floor.

Kiyoshi said with a serious look, "They'll sneak up on you at night on the way to the latrine. The next morning you'll be in the mud and in the camp hospital with a broken leg." For emphasis he bent the feather duster handle almost to the breaking point. Everyone watched and held their breath as the handle creaked. Kiyoshi continued, "There's been talk, so be careful. You need to behave more like a Japanese and not like some white college boy from Alpha Phi Alpha or whatever."

Ross paused and turned sideways. His easy manner faded when he zipped his jacket. Kiyoshi pulled him aside for a private conversation. Nevertheless, I could hear every word. Ross put his arm around Kiyoshi's shoulder and remarked, "You know a lot of people. So get the word out that the vitamins help camp children avoid deformities and weak bones. If they put me in the hospital, no one will go to the Twin Falls drugstore and the children and mothers will suffer."

Kiyoshi nodded and acknowledged what Ross said. "Hmm, okay. I understand. I'll make sure the right people know. Don't worry about it."

After their talk, both rejoined the group around the stove and warmed their hands.

Megumi smiled and sized Ross up with a sideways look. "Ross, did you really belong to a UW fraternity?" She touched his shoulder softly and remarked, "Wow, I've never met a fraternity man before."

Ross glanced at her hand and stepped away from Megumi's touch. With an uneasy smile, he said, "Kiyoshi was just kidding. Everyone knows that Greek fraternities don't accept Japanese, even if you're a genius. The only way you can get into a frat house is if you wash their dishes or do their lawns."

"Oh, I didn't know that," Megumi said as she cooed, "Anyway, would you take me to town today? It'll be my first trip."

Ross rubbed his chin, "Sure, why not? We'll catch the 10:30 morning bus. Don't worry, Twin Falls is so small you won't get lost."

Ross announced, "I need to buy war bond stamps for the fund-raising campaign and also go to the print shop and check on our Minidoka photo annual."

He ran his fingers through his hair, "You can tag along or go shopping on your own. The white people won't bother you. Some don't like Japanese but most won't do anything except give you a dirty look. He tightened his lips and then warned, "But you need to take care of your business and not dilly-dally. Come find me right away when your appointment is over."

Ross pushed up his glasses. He said, "Hey, any wonderful people interested in buying some savings bond stamps?" Immediately he pulled out a small booklet of stamps and waved it above his head. "It's a sensible way to build a nest egg. It's so painless and in no time you'll have a whole book."

"Oh no, not again," everyone groaned in unison.

In spite of the negative reaction, Ross continued, "If you bought $18.75 cents worth of stamps you could get a Series E Savings bond worth $25 after ten years. I think that's a great investment since it supports the war."

The group shook their heads and avoided looking at Ross. Kenji scowled but did not interrupt the pitch.

Kiyoshi blew on his tea and took another sip. "Hey, Ross, help yourself," he said and motioned to the pot. "We know about the stamps. You've told us a thousand times. Hanae has a book and she thinks she'll get rich. That'll be the day. First we need to get out of here."

Ross pushed up his jacket sleeves like a pitchman. The group moaned, "Don't tell us again!"

"Okay, I'll have mercy on you" Ross said, "Kiyoshi, would you get my stamp money from the safe? That's actually why I came."

Kiyoshi pulled out a heavy canvas bag of coins and placed it on the counter with a thud. "Here's your money, son. Plenty of silver there. Take care of it and remember where it came from. We had to sacrifice for every quarter." The unmistakable sound of coins in a bag echoed when Kiyoshi smacked the bag with his hand. "By the way, do you need a bodyguard? You must have a hundred dollars there.

"Wowee," Megumi said, "the stamps will really help America win the war."

Kiyoshi looked up, with a serious expression. "Is flirting with guards part of your idea to save the world and help America win? I see you smiling at them." Kiyoshi's face tightened. "I see how they stare at you. Especially that tall, pimple-faced private. His looks like death warmed over. Do you really believe they're interested in you?"

Megumi bristled and replied, "Uncle, why are you saying these awful things?"

"For your own good. *Nisei* girls and white soldiers don't mix," Kiyoshi said. He picked up the feather duster and bent the handle to make his point. The group held their collective breaths as the bend grew. Before it snapped, he stopped and said, "The soldiers may like you, but remember, if they get orders to march us all out into the desert to shoot us, they'll do it. You can't trust them. We're the enemy."

Kiyoshi's voice rose. "They have rifles and guard towers. We're not their friends or pets. Get it straight, young lady."

Kenji joined the fray. "Megumi, what's the matter with you?" he asked. "*Baka ne*, stupid! You can't trust the guards. They think we're gorillas. They're stupid." Kenji grimaced and almost spit out his words, "Worst of all, they will follow orders if told to kill us."

"That's crazy talk, and you know it," Megumi replied. She folded her arms tight, "They'll never do anything to harm us. Anyway, I'll be leaving soon." Megumi continued. She picked up her scarf and sashayed sideways. "Mary and I volunteer in the hospital and we've sent out applications to join the Cadet Nurse program."

With a smirk, she said, "I'll return when I have my uniform and then we'll see who's a gorilla." Megumi pulled her scarf tight. "When I get accepted, I'll go to school in Minnesota and become a nurse and help in Europe. I'll be part of the Army and serve my country, just like men from Minidoka. I'll make $16 a month plus free room and board. That's almost as much money as a doctor makes in Minidoka, and probably more than you, uncle. Put that in your pipe and smoke it!"

Kiyoshi scowled.

Megumi continued, "Karen Koura in Block 23 was accepted to the Seton School of Nursing in Colorado. I applied there. Maybe they'll take me too. Who knows?"

Megumi stood tall, like a soldier. "This would be an opportunity to prove my loyalty. On my applications I always write the Japanese American Citizen's Pledge." She continued, "I say it every day: 'I am proud to be an American and I believe in its values of justice and equality for as long as I live.' Can't you feel the power and spirit? Robert Mukai of the American Japanese National Federation wrote those sacred words which will help us win the war and rebuild America after."

Shoji, the loner, frowned and dragged his chair with a scraping noise. Usually he just sat and would come and go randomly without a word. Few paid any attention to him since he said so little. He was too old to be in the army and was a bookkeeper for Northwest Coat Manufacturing in Seattle. After Megumi's recital, he stirred and spoke.

"Words are words," he said.

Kiyoshi's mouth dropped in response to Shoji's awakening.

Shoji continued, "Where did you find that garbage anyway? Just more government baloney." He motioned with his arms, "Just look around you. You and your whole family are behind barbed wire." He snarled and grimaced. "After losing years of your life in jail, you speak of trusting America. What a laugh." He stood up and pushed his chair aside, "I lost over $3,000 in wages. Who's going to pay me back? If you were a real patriot, you'd say what Patrick Henry said—*Give me liberty or give me death.*"

Shoji stretched as if he had awakened from a deep sleep. "Death is what governments bring in times of war— death to Japanese civilians with the fire bombings of Tokyo. Luckily most of us are from Hiroshima and our relatives are safe."

He continued, "Death is no stranger to the 442nd Regimental Combat Team. The US government gave our Japanese American fighting boys the liberty to face German tanks and bullets. Where's the justice and where's the liberty? Freedom for us means being dead in a grave." Shoji raised his fist. "Even the federal courts ruled against us. Your high-sounding words and nurse uniform may impress some silly army private from Arkansas, but they mean nothing to me."

Megumi stiffened, and her face grew red. She said, "The Japanese American Pledge is famous. Where have you been? There is more to life than this canteen." She shook her head and continued, "Oh, you men are impossible!"

She continued with a faraway look, "After the War, I'll marry a doctor and we'll have a wonderful life. Maybe I'll settle down in New York or Minnesota. I've never left Seattle except for camp. It'll be exciting and fun." She raised her eyes up to the ceiling and blinked. "I can't wait to see the Empire State Building and the Statue of Liberty. You wait and see how successful I'll be."

Posing like a cultured lady with a teacup, Megumi crooked her little finger and said, "Of course, my husband will be handsome and rich. We'll buy a big house with a white picket fence and have three kids and two cars."

Kenji replied, "Two cars, why do you need two? *Mottainai.*"

She ignored the remark, "I won't ever think about this place– canteen, barrack, guards, or barbed wire." She postured as if addressing a large crowd, "When my children ask about the War, I'll just say that's when I met your dad. I won't talk about the sand blowing through the cracks or the knee-deep mud or the awful flies in the summer and the stinky latrines. I'll tell them I became a nurse during the war, that's my American story." Megumi paused and said to Shoji, "Why are you frowning?"

Turning to the group she announced, "Why do I shop here? You don't have any inventory. Your tea always tastes bad and you never put enough coal in the stove." Her nostrils flared when she said, "I'm sorry I bragged to Mary about how good this canteen is."

"Oh, come on, Megumi," Kiyoshi said with a grin. "You know we really like you and would feel lost if you stopped coming." For emphasis, he picked up the duster and waved it like a wand. "This is the best canteen because of all the great customers."

He chuckled and continued, "The other canteens are boring. Remember when we had that WRA photographer taking pictures? I think her name was Lange, and she came to my Canteen, not theirs. Don't forget that." His eyes brightened when he twirled the feather duster. "One of these days you'll see my picture in a book. Then you can say, 'There's my uncle'."

"Anyway if you can't find any cold cream in town, I'll give you a scoop from Hanae's jar. She won't miss a smidge," he said.

Kiyoshi wound up like a pitcher and threw an imaginary pitch.

"Just picture this," he said, imitating a radio announcer. "It's the bottom of the ninth and the count is three and two, two outs and we have a one run lead over the Nippon Giants." Kiyoshi touched the bill of an imaginary cap and shook off the catcher's sign. He pushed his tongue against his cheek to imitate a wad of tobacco.

"The catcher gives the curve ball sign. I shake it off." Kiyoshi shakes his head. "Then a fastball and I shake him off again. Finally, he gives the submarine sign. I take a deep breath and chuck that ol' rock."

Kiyoshi pitched a potato at the stove; it smacked the front grate and careened around the room. Puffing up, he said, "Strike three! Game's over and we win. The submarine works every time."

He strutted as if he had really done something significant. "Great pitch, huh?" Kiyoshi reached behind the counter and said, "Megumi, have a Hershey bar on me. Get ready and catch this."

Kiyoshi lobbed the candy high in the air near the rafters. The group held its breath. All eyes focused on the candy bar. Megumi tracked it and caught it with both hands.

She said, "Got it. Thanks, Uncle, say hello to Hanae. Ross, I'd meet you at the bus stop."

Ross hollered, "Ten o'clock, we'll catch the bus on Hunt Road."

"See you girls later," Jimmy said. Mary grabbed her coat and hat and opened the door. The wind rushed in and they headed out.

Kiyoshi looked at Ross, Shoji, and Kenji while he twirled a yard-stick, "Anyone up for a card game tonight? I'll give you fair warning. I'm always lucky when Hanae is pregnant."

I thought, *He thinks I left a while ago. So this is how Kiyoshi acts when I am not around. He's like a different person!* Without a sound I put the teacup down and headed out the back door.

I was angry, not at what he had said, but I wished I could sit around all day and throw potatoes. I've been pregnant the entire time in camp. Alan was born in Minidoka after two hours of labor. Five months later, I was scrubbing diapers when I felt had a sharp pain that doubled me over. An ambulance rushed me to the hospital but it was a miscarriage. At the time, I wondered why it took Kiyoshi so long to get to the hospital. I mused, *I'm expecting again. So Kiyoshi is lucky at poker is he? He should have won a ton of money by now.*

LETTER TO KIKU

July 24. 1945

To: Kiku Kashima
816 Lane Street
Seattle, Washington

Dear Kiku,

Happy belated 4th of July!

Please thank your parents for offering their basement for us to live in. We will be leaving camp soon! They say late August. As you know Kiyoshi was in Seattle looking for an apartment two weeks ago and couldn't find anything. Everything, including the Seattle public housing was full.

We were desperate when the administration told us that the camp would be closing soon. So we really appreciate your father's generosity.

Right now I am packing and cleaning our barrack apartment for the big day.

Dad will be happy to see your father. He misses drinking sake and singing songs like they used to do. Camp has been hard on him. But he is happy that our relatives in Hiroshima are safe.

Are the rumors true? We heard someone burned down a Japanese farmer's house on Vashon Island and Japanese are still unwelcome in Seattle. In Hood River they have a petition telling Japanese not to return. Is that true? We are hoping that we can return peacefully like you and your family. I am afraid for my kids.

I hope our trunks stored in the Buddhist Church gym are still there. Kiyoshi plans to get a grocery store going but things have changed. There is no Japanese co-op anymore and Safeway has taken over the customers.

Looking forward to seeing you soon, and thanks a million.

Sincerely,

Hanae

Minidoka WRA Camp,
Block 26-2
Minidoka, Idaho

CHAPTER ELEVEN

Return to Seattle, 1945-1961

There was a loud bang outside the barrack when Megumi stomped up the stairs and flung open the door.

Pulling open the room divider curtain, Kiyoshi asked, "Megumi, What's all the racket about?"

She held a copy of the August 7th Twin Falls Times and cleared her throat, "Hiroshima was bombed yesterday!"

Kiyoshi grabbed the newspaper. "It says the city has been destroyed." He said, "That can't be true."

"Let me see the paper," I insisted, "not the whole city!"

"It's a lie," Mr. Fuji, our neighbor, exclaimed. He pulled the paper away from me and declared, "Japan will win the war. This is a just a made-up story!"

If it is true, I thought, *then Fumi, Masa, Ichiro and others might be dead or wounded. What of the train station, vendors, trolley, temples and everything I knew?* I couldn't imagine our family home being gone. *Dear God,* I thought, *please help my relatives, if this is true.*

"Fuji-san, please give me the paper. I need to know more," I begged. I sat down and stared at the headlines. But the words just seemed to dance.

"What can we do?" Megumi asked.

"I don't know," I replied, "They could be in bad shape."

Holding back panic, I said, "We need to contact Director Stanford or people at the high school, they would know what really happened."

That morning, Director Stanford posted a special announcement about the bomb. His bulletin recounted the news article and said that additional details were coming.

On August 11th, he wrote Nagasaki was bombed on the ninth. It was like the earth flipped on its axis. With the inclusion of Nagasaki, few doubted that Japan would win. The news hung heavy over the camp. I thought, *Our relatives could be starving and we can't do a thing. Even if we could help, we have so little to give.*

Dad frowned and said, *"Shikataganai."*

I bit my lip and declared, "Dad, don't say that. I'm so sick of hearing that word!" There must be something we could do.

Kiyoshi almost cried when he asked, "How many more cities will be destroyed?"

Who will take care of the dead? I wondered, *what of our family grave?*

But Uncle Yosh and Tama should be okay in the country, I thought. But who can we contact?

Even though Kiyoshi earned low wages at the Canteen, I managed to save about fifty dollars. In addition, I had ten dollars in US savings stamps. We could send some money to our relatives. But how?

Waiting for the next event to happen, most residents mindlessly followed their daily routines. The dead time was unbearable. I had cabin fever and was on edge. Kiyoshi was in a sullen mood and no longer talked about leaving camp since the bombing occupied our thoughts.

The next bulletin from Stanford came on August 16th and announced that the Emperor surrendered. There were VJ-Day parades across the country. It was like New Year's Eve celebrations on the outside.

The mood was somber as more details emerged about the bombings. Old folks, children, and workers were killed instantly and many were injured. Both Hiroshima and Nagasaki were damaged beyond recognition.

I wondered *what happened to my school made of concrete? It might have protected the children. I hope they didn't die.*

Director Stanford understood our concerns and contacted the Red Cross. Limited mail service to Japan would be restored but wouldn't be available in the bombed areas. I thought, *I'll contact Uncle Yosh and see if he knows what happened to the family.* Also, I wrote the Quaker headquarters in Philadelphia for help.

After years in camp, we learned to live with Minidoka's lack of freedom. But the bombings resurfaced the depressing aspects of confinement. Fear was visible in the eyes of the residents. They moved aimlessly like schools of fish in a stagnant pond. There was a palpable sadness that enveloped us. Even the mess hall was quiet. I was afraid I would break down and cry at any mention of Hiroshima.

We'd become used to hard times: the weather, bad food, and mindless routines but the bombings broke our spines. The moment was too big to comprehend. Women wept openly in church and even the guards went out of their way to be polite. Residents who gathered around the pot belly stoves in the canteens did so in silence. It seemed even the sparrows stopped chirping.

I didn't know what would be worse: sinking in grief and anger here or living freely on the outside like Kiku and her family. Anxieties increased when rumors spread that the camps were closing sooner than planned originally. We didn't know whether to cheer or cry because we had nowhere to go except to Kashima's basement. Instead I kept busy doing the wash and sorting our possessions.

"Kiyoshi," I said, "We should keep this iron pot. It might come in handy."

"That's our chamber pot," he replied. "It's disgusting. We can't use it in Seattle."

"Are you sure?" I replied. "I can clean it and make it sanitary."

"No," Kiyoshi sputtered. "Never, just leave that stinky thing here for the government. We'll live in a good place where we won't need it."

In September, Kiyoshi visited Seattle again to find proper housing. He hoped for something better than Kashima's basement. He searched J-town and other neighborhoods we could afford where people would rent to us. Kiyoshi found nothing that would accommodate both of us, a child, and newborn.

Kiku sent a letter that the basement remodeling was finished in late August. I stuffed some baby clothes into a box and pulled out my yellow suitcase. When I touched the case, a flood of Hiroshima emotions erupted. I could almost see the Hiroshima rivers, cherry blossoms, streetcars, and bustling merchants. But that was years ago and far away. I could not imagine all that being destroyed in an instant.

I was lucky to be here, I thought. But being released was frightening. *Can we make it on the outside? We need help,* I worried.

I thought, *Leaving camp is worse than being taken. At least in Minidoka we have housing and meals.* We would have little money plus the extra burden of two kids. In addition, we had our Hiroshima relatives if they survived. *How can we deny their requests for help?*

Uncle Yosh mailed Kiku and reported that the family home by the river was destroyed. Fumi and Masa died in the blast but Ichiro and his sisters were alive. He and the youngest were in the country when the bomb fell. But Akiko, the middle child, was at home and required medical care for severe burns. He asked that we send goods and not money for them to trade on the black market. My cousins had no income and were begging for their lives.

We must do something, I thought. *Japanese are so proud. Things must be very bad for them to beg.* My brothers and I chipped in and sent money and packages. *Thank God for Yosh*, I prayed. *We couldn't have done anything without him and his little truck.*

The next day, I continued to sort through our possessions. I found a laquer comb and remembered preparing Haruye's body. Four hundred died in camp. Ironically well over 400 were born including my two boys. I packed and waited. Then I unpacked because we hadn't received our authorization to leave. As I re-sorted our belongings, I wondered, *Will we be welcome in Seattle and can Kiyoshi re-start the business?*

Many had left camp before us and the nights in the half empty barrack were strange. The usual sounds of snoring and babies crying were reduced and what remained were echoes like ghosts. Many barracks were shut down completely and Kiyoshi's canteen was closed along with two mess halls.

Our circumstances had changed rapidly and even the guards behaved differently. Before they watched us with suspicion and always stood at the ready. Now they barely seemed to notice us.

Finally, the day came. Mom, Dad, Kiyoshi, me and the kids lined up for the trip to Twin Falls and the train station. We wore our best clothes for the trip. Residents got $25 and a bus ticket. I was fuming, *This is sure a measly amount for three and one half years in prison. Worst of all, they didn't even apologize.*

I shook my head and inquired, "Dad are you and mom okay?"

"*Sumimasen*," he replied with a nod.

I packed a lunch and for all to share and said, "Dad, in Seattle you can make *sake* and play *go* with your friends." His eyes lit up and smiled.

"Mom, when we get home, you should stop smoking," I insisted. "It's not good for you."

She said nothing. Instead she unwrapped the lunch and took a peek. "Looks good," she said happily.

We boarded the bus and waved goodbye. Kiyoshi's brother, Minoru, stayed and would resettle in Salt Lake later. My younger brothers, Tom and Bob, were going back East for college.

I was anxious and worried that the government would change its mind at the last minute. I took shallow breaths and exhaled until I looked over my shoulder and saw the gate, barbed wire and guard towers behind us.

I said to Kiyoshi, "I hate Idaho. I won't ever return."

"Same with me," he said. "I just want to be gone."

I thought, *Being in prison is miserable. I'm so angry I could spit. I'd never wish this punishment on anyone, even my worst enemy. But I'm grateful that at least they didn't kill us.*

"We should celebrate when we get home," Kiyoshi said. "We can go to Seven Dragons."

"I feel more like screaming than celebrating," I growled. "We never should have been there."

"*Shikataganai*," Dad responded.

"Dad, don't say that," I urged. "It's like giving up!"

Kiyoshi added, "Hanae just put it behind you."

I gritted my teeth, "Never mind," I said.

The landscape trundled by my train window. I reflected on Hiroshima and Nagasaki which were vibrant cities instead of rubble when we arrived here. Before camp, I had never been to the desert nor did I dream that I would have two children and one miscarriage in prison.

When the evacuation began, Sachi had a great deal of influence as a business woman. But the incarceration destroyed her base. In Minidoka she was just another unemployed *Issei* woman, a status that remained after the war.

Hiro, Sachi's not-so-secret lover had his life upended. Originally, he was assigned to the bachelor quarters away from the family. He petitioned to join the family but was denied. As a last resort, he beat and threatened Sachi, who pleaded with the administration on his behalf. But her actions were to no avail. Nevertheless, when we were released, Hiro physically rejoined the family.

After we returned, Kiyoshi scanned the *Seattle Times* want ads and landed a janitor job at the Acme Hotel on Madison Street. "I can't get the store going, so this should be okay for now," he said, grateful for a job, no matter how menial. He vacuumed the halls, did handyman work, and helped with bellmen duties. The work was honest, but a step down from operating a grocery business. Nevertheless, it was a way to support us and earn money.

I managed to make the Kashima basement comfortable while the rest of the family was in public housing including Hiro. Other families lived in the Japanese school, which served as temporary living quarters. Being away from his parents brought a lightness to Kiyoshi's step as Sachi's control had diminished.

I was grateful to the Kashimas for their basement which was near Kiku and her husband, Kaz, and family on Lane Street. Kiyoshi gathered scrap lumber to cobble together makeshift shelves. Like camp, we used blankets to create privacy. Although we were in new circumstances, Kiyoshi felt the effects of being re-exposed to the corrosive rumors about his mother and the daily humiliation of arguing with hotel maids. He was no longer the wise-cracking Kiyoshi who held court in the canteen.

Very quickly his ulcer erupted and his mood darkened. "Hanae, the house is a mess. Can't you keep the kids quiet!" he yelled. "They leave their toys scattered around and I stepped on a toy tractor. Do something," he urged. "Larry smashed a window accidently and Alan and his friends broke the bed. How are we going to pay for the damage? It is shameful."

"We'll manage," I replied, "like we always have."

I stayed at home and rarely ventured outside of Japantown. One day I took a break and left the kids with grandma and walked downtown. I put on my Sunday clothes and thought, *I just want to enjoy the day and the city.*

I had walked past the fancy Olympia Hotel many times but never looked in. It was the best in Seattle and the president stayed there once. The sun was shining and my spirits were high. *Just a short turn and a couple of steps, I will be able to see the magnificent interior. Maybe I can see the famous French ballroom with lights outlining a castle wall.* I took a deep breath and entered. I was in awe of the dark chairs, gold staircases, and ornate railings in the lobby.

For a moment I thought, I *feel like a genuine person and not a foreigner.* I was spellbound by the grandeur and elegance. The ornate ceiling looked like a church. There were Filipino and Japanese bellboys in snappy uniforms, white gloves, and pillbox caps who rushed by officiously. I smiled, but none responded. Standing in the lobby, I was mesmerized by the beauty of people in motion, fancy luggage, elevator bells chiming, and well-dressed men and women coming and going. It was like I was on a movie set and the actors were in front of me in gorgeous costumes.

All of this beauty was a few miles from Japantown and I had never thought to walk through the hotel's magnificent brass doors before today. Inside, it was like a wonderland. I marveled at the world that swirled around me. My eyes fixed on an older white gentleman and his wife who relaxed in leather chairs next to a small end table. They were a perfect couple in their tailored clothes and fine shoes. He smoked a black cigar and wore a three-piece linen suit with a gold watch chain. She had a large hat and a long white dress with lace trim.

I thought, *What an elegant sight. They must have traveled the world and are now off to some exotic destination.*

As if alerted by my attention, both looked up. They did not say a word but frowned. I felt like an insect floating in a glass of milk. They glanced at each other and shot me the hate stare, a piercing bolt of pure evil, like snake venom spitting. The room seemed to collapse until only the three of us existed. I felt like an insignificant smudge, glowing in a spotlight.

The stares ripped through me like rifle bullets. I wondered, *Did the hate stare need to be taught? Or was it second nature like their tailored clothes?* I knew they felt I had no right to be there, or to even exist. Without a word they had degraded me to the point of numbness. Hanging my head, I walked away defeated.

One Japanese bellman noticed my situation and gave me a sympathetic look. But other staff ignored me and moved efficiently about their business. The ornate elevator doors opened and closed while operators wearing white gloves cheerfully greeted the guests. I retreated to a corner and thought, *If I were wearing a black and white maid's uniform and carrying an armful of towels, I would have been invisible. I could have passed through the luxurious surroundings without a glance or raised eyebrow.*

After that experience, I swore that I would never take that type of degradation from anyone again. But those were hollow thoughts of a woman grasping for courage after being released from a government relocation center.

I knew I could rationalize the hate stare away: *They weren't looking at me. Or, maybe they think I'm Chinese and not Japanese. Or I'll never see them again. Or, it was a big mistake, and they thought I was someone they knew.*

Mentally I scratched and clawed for any reason to believe that it was an error, although I knew the truth—it was pure prejudice and hatred. It was something that these people thought was their right and indeed their obligation.

Leaving the hotel, I encountered two white children on the sidewalk. They taunted and spoke mock Chinese like, *"Oyung Oyong ching chong."* The children pulled their eyes into a slant and bucked their front teeth and reacted as if they had said something profound. This behavior wasn't uncommon. Naturally I was angry. But most of all, I fumed knowing my children would have to endure this treatment. In addition, I understood that no white person would intervene on their behalf.

LETTER FROM UNCLE YOSH

December 1, 1946

Dear Hanae,

This is Uncle Yosh. I am sorry for being a burden. I received a box yesterday. Thank you for the packages and money for Shintaro's children.

Since the bomb, Tama and I have gone to town to help clear the rubble many times. We finally gave up our search for Fumi and Masa. The whole area near the river was destroyed and the neighborhood was burned to the ground.

Ichiro was safe with me in the country. After the bomb, he helped search for his mother or her remains. With so many people gone and so much confusion, we found nothing. The police and city government were not helpful and the hospitals were full. Many doctors and nurses died. We are hoping that the Red Cross would send help.

Ichiro's sister, Akiko, survived the bomb. She was burned badly and needs medicine for the pain. So please send more packages to help her. I am poor and have no money to spare. Thank you.

I'm sorry for being a burden and sorry I sent you away earlier. Please forgive me.

Uncle Yosh

NO GOOD, 1946

Uncle Yosh's letter was another sliver of information about Hiroshima. Seattle friends also shared news they learned. As I read Yosh's letter, my hands shook and I unconsciously chewed my lip.

I handed Kiyoshi the letter. "Please read this. We must send more packages," I said.

He read every line carefully. "Things are worse than I thought," he whispered. "Yes, we must send more."

"We don't have much but we'll do the best we can," I promised. "We've saved a little while living at Kashima's house." I thought with the bad Hiroshima news, *it feels like we're being slowly eaten alive with each piece of news.*

After six months with the Kashimas, we packed our clothes and household items. I sorted through our belongings and set aside clothes we could send to Yosh. I worried about Hiroshima every day.

It was sunny when we moved and I was happy to leave the damp basement full of mildew odors. Our new house was a rental south of the old Japantown on Lane Street near Kiku. It was more spacious than the basement but still cramped. Alan and Larry slept in the dining area and Kiyoshi and I in the bedroom. Dad and Mom lived upstairs. Including Kiku, three other Japanese families, the Shigas and Katos, lived in the semi industrial neighborhood.

The Italian landlord, Mr. Merino, had chickens in his front yard. Every morning the rooster crowed. Kiyoshi groused, "I wish they would kill that noisy thing. I haven't had a decent sleep in ages." Our houses were an island surrounded by a sheet-metal factory, tire warehouse, clay bank hill, and glass window warehouse. Regularly, trucks rumbled by and the sound of screaming metal saws in the nearby shops filled the air.

Kiyoshi complained, "Hanae, everything's no good." This included the University of Washington football team which lost a game through a "bonehead play". The Seattle Rainiers baseball team who were cellar dwellers, our house in the industrial area, the rainy Seattle weather, and the maids at Acme Hotel. He grumbled, "The boys spend too much time outside and their skin is too dark."

When they misbehaved, Kiyoshi would not burn them with incense, he took a more expedient path and just hit them. He was miserable and angry being a janitor. His ulcer flared and he was placed on an even stricter diet that involved eating bland foods and drinking milk. His dinners were one step above baby food. No matter what he tried, he had very bad breath.

During one of his tirades, he complained, "When will your Hiroshima relatives stop begging?"

The remark struck a nerve, I lashed out, "They're desperate and could starve to death. We must help. That's our duty."

Alan heard and asked, "Why do you give all our best Christmas presents to Hiroshima? I want to keep some this year."

"You don't understand," I replied, "They were bombed during the war and live in shacks. When you get older, you will."

"Mom, I didn't like the fruitcake you saved last Christmas. You should have given that to Hiroshima," Alan replied.

Kiyoshi insisted, "See even the kids complain."

"Okay, okay," I replied. "Next Christmas we won't give away so many of the presents we get."

Kiyoshi's negative attitude and rants about work and life continued for years. It was 1950 when my youngest, Larry, entered Bailey Elementary School and Kiyoshi's ulcer erupted.

The ambulance delivered Kiyoshi from work to the house. He was in bed and his face was ashen. It was like he was in a casket resting at a funeral home.

"Is he alive?" Larry asked.

I told the boys, "Kiyoshi has a bleeding ulcer."

"How could they stop a stomach from bleeding? A bandage wouldn't work," Larry said.

I replied, "He collapsed at work so they gave him medicine."

Larry asked, "Is his stomach filled with blood?"

"I don't think so," I replied. "Doctor Johnson will be here soon."

I thought, *How are we going to pay the doctor bills, rent, and grocery bills? How long can we last? We'll have to use our savings and what about the Hiroshima relatives? Who'll take care of them?*

I never told the boys what deep trouble we were in. Instead we took it day by day. I avoided thinking about the consequences and just remained in denial as long as I could. There was no reason to believe things would work out. Reality struck after we ran out of money and our bills stacked up.

I told the Merinos we would be late on the rent and I got a part-time job at the Rainier Market. Kiku agreed to babysit. At least we could get groceries on credit until I got a paycheck. I made ends meet by putting off some bills and making partial payments on others. Luckily I bought enough time and stalled until Kiyoshi returned to work. But the fear of falling off a financial cliff into who knows what remained for months.

After Kiyoshi recovered, I packed his lunch and sent him off to work. Every day, I thanked God for his health and our squeaking through.

During the ordeal Sachi told me more than once, "You need to work full-time to save Kiyoshi." But I resisted and chose part-time work so I could take care of the boys.

Nevertheless, she continued to meddle and insisted, "Bachi, Kiyoshi's illness is 'bachi' and the universe is unhappy with you." I thought, *What did I do? I have done nothing to deserve this.* Unfortunately, Kiyoshi's health incident marked the beginning of a long string of hospital visits that lasted for years.

In between his bouts of illness, I was exhausted and mentally tired. One morning after breakfast, I felt a sharp pain in my abdomen and doubled over. Something I ate, I thought. *Ow, I hope this will pass soon.* "My God," I said out loud, "I'm spotting blood." I wondered, *Now what?* I recalled the miscarriage in camp. *No, that can't be. I'm not pregnant. I hope this is nothing.*

I put off calling Doctor Johnson, believing things would improve. In the bathroom I glanced in the mirror and saw bags and dark circles under my eyes. *What a sight,* I thought. The intensity of the attacks grew and became more frequent. Then I knew it was not indigestion.

I sent the kids off to school and called Dr. Johnson for an emergency appointment. I took the bus downtown to his office. After an exam he said, "This is very serious. You need a hysterectomy. I'll make the arrangements. It needs to be done soon."

I was afraid of surgery and how much it would cost. But what could I say?

"Are you sure?" I asked. *How are we going to pay for this?* I fretted.

"Absolutely necessary," was his response. "We'll probably have to remove everything out so you won't be able to have any more babies."

I wasn't able to grasp what that meant. I thought, *I'll have to think about that later.* Reluctantly I replied, "I'll tell Kiyoshi right away and make arrangements for the boys." I worried about how much money we had in the bank and asked "Doctor, how long will it take to recover?"

"At least a month," he replied.

"Oh my, that's a long time," I said. I saw dollar signs.

A week later I underwent surgery at Swedish Hospital. *I'm so tired,* I thought when my gurney reached the operating room. It was cold inside so I asked for a blanket. Shortly, I heard the doctors' voices fading as the anesthesia took hold. My last thoughts were, *This is going to be like a long boat ride across the Pacific. There will be days of pain, bad food, and bed spins like in Hiroshima.* In my mind I recalled the steamboat's horn blast and the word "*gaman.*" I shook my head and thought, *I chose the hard life in Hiroshima and unfortunately my wish is coming true.*

MINIDOKA BLOCK 26 REUNION

By summer of 1947, I had recovered from my hysterectomy and was back at Rainier Market working. Every July, I took the boys, Alan and Larry, to Block 26 reunion picnics at Kubo Gardens. It was a working Japanese garden owned by the Kubo landscaping family. It included *koi* ponds, a small waterfall, Japanese bridges, a bamboo grove, and a large picnic area of grass lined with flowers. Kiyoshi never attended the gatherings. He said, "Crowds make me nervous."

Hundreds gathered at the twenty-seven-acre garden for the annual celebration. To an outside observer, it must have appeared like an ordinary picnic. Few would have realized that it involved former prisoners gathering to socialize, sing, and play games. In addition, most attendees had relatives in Hiroshima. As a result, there was always an additional layer of sadness during our merriment. I worried about Shintaro's children who were rebuilding their lives without parents or significant resources. My mind couldn't accept the fact that Fumi and Masa were never found.

At the picnic, a 78 rpm phonograph record blared Japanese music through speakers hung next to dangling red lanterns. Picnic blankets were spread near galvanized metal tubs that held ice cold Rainier Beer and soda pop.

I found a place in the shade. "Boys put your stuff here and don't go running around," I said. Then I unpacked the lunch: teriyaki chicken wings, rice balls, and hot green tea in a long black thermos. In the center of the field was a free standing mic where people took turns singing and making announcements.

Kiku brought her children and sat next to me. She tugged my arm and said, "Sing something, Hanae!" She pulled me up and dragged me towards the microphone.

"Okay, okay," I replied. With each step, I felt like a different person. I climbed the hill, and thought about what song I should sing. The mic whined and then settled down.

I adjusted the microphone, put my arms behind my back and stood proudly.

"I'm Hanae from barrack two. My parents, Toyjiro and Toku Tamura were in Block 26 and we are all from Hiroshima. I will sing *Hong Kong Nights* in Japanese. *Honnn konnn no yoru, Honnn …*" It was the song I remembered from Russell Hotel when I was a child and Mr. Yasui showed me the picture of his wife.

When I finished, I was pleasantly surprised and soaked in the applause. I took a bow and then another. Returning to our picnic blanket, I told my sons in a very serious tone, "Block 26 was the best. Mr. Kubo made a beautiful rock garden in our block. People in Block 33 were not good."

Their eyes grew big when I told them. They actually believed they were better than kids from the other blocks. It became a point of pride for them.

For many, which camp you were in was very important. Whenever I was introduced to new Japanese Americans, I would ask, "What camp?" If it was Minidoka, then the next question was, "What block?"

If they were among the residents of Minidoka, they were immediate friends. Better yet, if they were from Block 26, they were like relatives, and if their family was from Hiroshima, they were like gold.

It was only later that I realized the exclusive club I was in—group imprisoned because of of race whose relatives suffered a nuclear attack. As such, we were indeed very special and unique, but not in a good way.

Once at the dentist, I found a magazine with black and white pictures of Hiroshima and Nagasaki. Both cities looked like a moonscape of twisted steel and broken concrete. Victims with scabs and bald patches wandered the streets. Piles of rubble were strewn with corpses. One survivor pushed a wheelbarrow through streets lined with debris. I imagined my cousins in shacks begging for food. I thought, *It's been almost two years and images of the destruction continue to leak out. Will the bomb victims ever be normal human beings again?*

SHINY PENNIES, 1952

After camp, Sachi plotted and tempted Kiyoshi with gifts to maintain control over him. "If you take us mushroom hunting, I'll buy you a brand new 1952 Chevrolet," she said.

I protested, "We don't need a car that badly. If you do, we'll never see you on the weekends." I recognized the ploy to pull him closer and away from me and the boys.

But the temptation was too great. "New Chevy," Kiyoshi said. His eyes brightened, "that's pretty fancy for a hotel janitor." Sachi paid cash for the car and Kiyoshi took delivery. It was a brand new two-door blue fastback. He washed and waxed it regularly. "It will run forever if you change the oil every 1,000 miles," he said.

At first, the outings with Sachi were sporadic but gradually they increased. Because the car could only accommodate four, usually Sachi,

Hiro, Koemon, and Kiyoshi's sister, Yoko, were passengers. The boys and I were not invited. I pleaded, "At least take one of the boys. Why do you have to take Hiro? He's not family!"

Kiyoshi just mumbled and avoided the subject. "Okay, okay," he said insincerely. That just meant he heard me but wasn't going to do anything. After regaining a foothold with Kiyoshi, Sachi attempted to pull the grandkids into her web. Naturally I was her biggest obstacle.

Sensing an attack, I took immediate action. The next Sunday I told the boys, "Wear your white shirts, bow ties, and sport coats to church."

I called them out of the Sunday School building and escorted them to the brick church next door where the *Issei* and *Nisei* worshipped. It had massive pews and stained glass windows. The pulpit was ornate and the stage was draped with blue velvet bunting and curtains. A piano and organ sat in the corner.

Reverend Hori stood in a dark robe. He looked over his glasses at them and sprinkled holy water. In a very firm baritone voice he said, "I baptize you in the name of the Father, the Son and the Holy Ghost."

My heart soared when I saw the boys in their Sunday best. Their faces beamed and their untamed hair was slicked down. I said, "You two look like shiny pennies. Now you're safe and secure." I almost danced because their souls were now out of Sachi's grasp.

As expected, Sachi ignored their baptism. The boys asked, "Why does grandma offer us money to join the Buddhist Cub Scouts?"

To my delight, the boys refused her offer. Alan said, "We're Christians and won't change." When the boys got older, she tempted them again, "There are many pretty girls at the Buddhist Church."

Alan and Larry were horrified. Sunday school taught them that Jesus was their savior and Buddhists were on the road to damnation. They were puzzled and asked, "Why does grandmother want to send us to hell?"

"I don't think she believes that, but you boys must decide," I said. "Anyway always remember you were baptized in the big church." Both understood and nodded in unison. It was obvious to them that grandma Sachi's was putting their prospects of reaching heaven in jeopardy.

To their bewilderment, she persisted and complained, "Who will take care of my grave after Kiyoshi is gone?"

The thought of an untended grave caused her anguish. As a last resort she turned to me. I ignored Sachi's overtures and stayed busy working full-time at Rainier Market. By October 1952, we managed to save a little and could afford to leave Lane Street. For the kids, I wanted a residential neighborhood with parks and fewer industrial noises and trucks. "I'd love to get away from that damned rooster," Kiyoshi insisted.

We searched the city but most real estate brokers would not sell to Japanese. Finally, we found a 1914 four-plex on Beacon Hill through Hamre Realty. It was near Sachi's old house before the war.

"Kiyoshi, Hamre will sell us a house. Halleluiah! But no bank in the city would lend us $14,000 to buy it," I complained.

Totally beside myself, I asked friends, customers, and former customers from the Sumida Produce stand, "Where can I get a home loan? Washington Mutual, Peoples Bank, Seattle First, Seattle Trust and Loan and many more said 'No'." I fretted, "What can we to do?"

Mr. Okada, a Rainier Market customer, overheard my conversation and said, "Check banks in Bremerton. I know some Japanese got loans there."

Bremerton, I thought, *that's a long way away. Why would they lend to us in Seattle?*

But I was desperate. As a last resort, I made a long-distance call to the First Bank of Bremerton and talked to a loan officer. I was hoping that this was not like Lake Wilderness Lodge where they welcomed Japanese and barred them later.

Mr. Gill, the loan officer, was friendly over the phone and willing to meet us. The next day, we got dressed in our Sunday clothes and took a bus to Pier 52 for the forty-minute ferry ride. We brought all our recent income tax forms and proof of employment.

"Are you sure he said it was okay?" Kiyoshi asked, when we boarded the ferry. He continued his rant, "I had to take the day off. This is costing money!"

"Our chances are very good," I replied in a calm voice. My heart was racing because I wasn't sure whether we could trust Mr. Gill. *I hope no last minute things will come up to squash the deal*, I thought.

Kiyoshi was antsy when the ferry horn blasted as it pulled away into the green waters of Puget Sound.

I enjoyed seeing Mount Rainier looming in the south through the clouds. *The mountain reminds me of my trip to Hiroshima when I crossed Elliot Bay in a steamship.*

Kiyoshi wore a blue suit and looked his best. I thought, *He hasn't dressed this well since our wedding.* He was uncomfortable and loosened his tie. Kiyoshi fidgeted and asked, "Does the person know we're Japanese?"

I bit my lip and replied, "Must you say things like that?" Then I composed myself and responded, "He knew we were Japanese by our names. What else could we be? White people don't have names like Kiyoshi and Hanae."

Kiyoshi ran his palm over his bald head, "Something will go wrong, just wait. I know it."

The ferry rocked and doubt crept into my mind. *I hope Kiyoshi is wrong*, I thought. *I don't want to live at Lane Street forever. Anyway, why would Mr. Gill lie?*

Kiyoshi's face tightened, "Did he say it was for sure?"

By now my mind was churning. "He said our chances were good," I replied with less confidence and more irritation.

"Will the bank be crowded? You know I hate crowds," he whined.

I stomped my foot and said, "Yes, it will be crowded," I said, "Now I'm going to the bathroom so just stay put. Don't move."

The ferry slowed and docked. We joined a line of passengers and walked up Main Street. The bank was a two-story granite structure with pillars and concrete stairs. "First Bank of Bremerton" was carved in stone above the entry. I said, "This is it, let's go."

Kiyoshi tensed up.

I tugged his arm, "Hurry," I urged.

I had butterflies when we pushed open the ornate metal doors. It was a magnificent cathedral-like space. I felt insignificant, like a country mouse slipping on polished floors. The bank was spotless and shiny. Large tables with heavy carved legs dominated the open area. Ornate wrought iron cages held the well-scrubbed tellers. It was institutional in every sense. The white employees moved with confidence and their heels clicked over the floors.

Nothing bad or unusual could happen here, I thought. *This is not anything like the fancy hotel where they gave me the "hate stare."*

Obviously we were out of place but no one gave us a second look. One customer actually smiled as we passed. I returned the greeting and felt elated. I was taken aback because our best clothes looked drab and tired. I pulled Kiyoshi to the closest teller. She was courteous and directed us to Mr. Gill's desk. I knew Kiyoshi was thinking we would be turned away after our long journey. But I had come too far to give up.

A moment later, Mr. Gill arrived. He was a thin man with a light mustache and three-piece suit. He had a quick smile that filled his face. He said, "Do I have the pleasure of meeting the Yamadas?" Pronouncing our names perfectly he continued, "Let's see, Kiyoshi and Hanae?" I nudged Kiyoshi with my elbow as if to say, "wake up."

He continued, "I spent some time in Japan in the military after the war and learned something of your culture and customs. I had a great time. It's really a 'man's country'. They sure know how to treat men."

Kiyoshi was nervous and didn't seem to hear a word but I understood perfectly. *I must be yasashii to not upset the transaction.* I tried to imitate the behavior of Fumi in Hiroshima. Purposely I spoke sweetly as if talking to a superior.

Gill examined our income tax information and commented, "The temples in Kyoto are beautiful. But I didn't like the bustle of Tokyo," he declared. With each word, legal papers were pushed across the desk, back and forth until everything was signed in a matter of a few minutes. Purposely I imitated his movements and mirrored his mannerisms.

With a faraway gaze he said, "One of these days I want to go back. It was great duty for a kid like me from Minnesota out of high school. The Orient was exciting."

I remembered all the young army guards I'd seen in camp. *How naïve they were with their pimpled faces and ill-fitting uniforms.* Quickly these thoughts fled. "Are we done?" I asked.

Gill glanced up at the lobby clock. "Yes, it was my pleasure." I relaxed and was drawn to a family photo with a Japanese woman.

"Is she your wife?" I asked.

"Yes, that's my Kimiko," he replied with pride. "Everyone calls her 'Kim' and we have one boy and one girl. She's a wonderful mother who keeps our kids clean and neat!"

"Is she from Hiroshima?" I inquired.

"No, she's from Kyoto," Gill replied.

"She looks like a lovely person," I said and moved closer to the photo. "May I see it?" I asked.

"Of course," he replied and he handed it to me.

I examined it closely. With two hands, I returned it gracefully. I said, "Thank you for letting me see your photo and thank you very much for your time. It was our pleasure."

Kiyoshi said, "We really appreciate it. You won't regret it. We'll pay you every month on time. I promise, thank you again."

"You're very welcome and congratulations on your new house," Gill replied and shook our hands.

"Okay Kiyoshi, the ferry leaves soon!" I said. I grabbed him by the arm and pulled with all my might. I wanted to leave before he said something regretful. With the loan approved, I felt like we were bank robbers escaping with money bags. "Hurry before he changes his mind," I urged.

Rushing out the door, I jumped up and said, "Hurray, we got it!" The guard stared at us suspiciously.

I couldn't believe how easy it was. "Can't wait to tell the kids and people at work," I said. "Thank goodness. What a joy! Yeah! We can have a new house at last."

Kiyoshi blinked several times. He didn't seem to understand the full gravity of what happened. Mentally he was a step behind and asked, "He has a Japanese wife?"

"Who cares," I said. "Let's celebrate. I want Chinese food tonight at the Seven Dragons! Yippee! We've got a new house!"

1953

The new house was actually a four-plex instead of a single-family home. We occupied apartment B. The three other units were rented to single people and a couple. It was a small 750 square foot one-bedroom space. The boys slept in the living room on the couch and Murphy bed. Kiyoshi and I had the bedroom. The apartment needed painting and the floor sloped slightly. Nevertheless, I was overjoyed to be there.

We stacked my black steamer trunks full of kimonos layered in mothballs up to the bedroom ceiling. I put a green throw rug which was a soft piece of comfort on the cold linoleum floor.

Amid the stacks of trunks and cardboard boxes was my beautiful blond vanity, bench, and a matching dresser which the Righettis had saved for us. The set had lines that were soft and curved with swirls carved on the drawer faces. It had bright orange plastic drawer pulls, and a flawless finish. It was a 1940s quality piece, the kind one would expect to find in a movie star's Hollywood mansion. It was like a jewel sparkling in the clutter. Because the room was so small, the matching nightstand was surrounded by boxes. There was barely enough room to pull out the cushioned bench. But the set reminded me of better days before the war, an extravagant reminder of a different time and place.

The rest of the apartment was worn and tired. The linoleum floors were cracked and faded. The bathtub had claw feet and perpetual rust stains under the faucets. The boys shared a small living space like caged animals and the closeness caused tempers to flare.

The bathroom door had been torn from the frame by Alan because Larry had barricaded it after a fight. Alan rushed the door, breaking it loose. Kiyoshi wanted to burn Larry but could never catch him. But he did manage to snag Alan once for a different offense and knocked him out cold, cuffing him on his temple. I was angry. "The *Reader's Digest* says that parents should not punish children by hitting them," I said. After that, Kiyoshi rarely laid a hand on them in anger.

VARIATIONS ON DEATH, 1955

Gradually, life on Beacon Hill settled into predicable rhythms. The boys were doing well in school, Kiyoshi worked at Acme Hotel, and I was full-time at Rainier Market. Alan began junior high and Larry was close to finishing Beacon Hill grade school. The anti-Japanese agitation subsided and the newspapers no longer featured negative stories about Japanese. The Hiroshima relatives were progressing and Ichiro's sister, Akiko, recovered from burns. I was happy to hear she was about to be married.

The seasons turned from rainy falls, to cool winters and cloudy springs to overcast summers. Starting in October, it was dark early in the morning when I woke at 4:00 AM and dark again by the time I came home. It seemed like it rained every day until the days grew longer and finally the sun appeared briefly in March.

No matter how hard I tried to forget, the lingering after-effects of the forced incarceration and devastation of Hiroshima remained. Some men returned to Seattle and were lost without their prewar identities. A church friend, Mr. Takeda, never could find a job and finally gave up. In other cases, women emerged as family bread winners and raised children almost single handedly. After the war, Japantown was a shadow of its previous self. The population was scattered and many Japanese suffered a low grade sense of paranoia accompanied by fears of being taken again.

"We must be good citizens and never give the government or white people an excuse to remove us," Reverend Hori preached at church. I lectured the boys repeatedly, "Remember, everything you do reflects on the community. So stay of trouble."

We did our best to be good citizens and Americans. The boys joined the Presbyterian Cub Scouts and attended the jamborees. In July of 1955, Kiku phoned and told me that Ben, the assistant Cub Scout master, had died. He was in his thirties and unmarried.

I told the boys immediately. "Ben was doing good deeds because he was living on borrowed time. That was one reason why he drove you two to the Scout meetings at the Nakamura house."

"But we just saw him last week," Larry said, "and he was fine."

During the discussion, Larry said, "It must be a mistake and he'll come as usual on Wednesday nights."

Alan remarked, "It's no mistake but I'd never imagined that he'd die so young."

"His body will be on display at Butterworth's Funeral Home," I replied. "Do you want to see him there one last time or just at the funeral?"

There was a silence as the boys dropped their eyes. That was the only sign of emotion they showed. I wondered, *Did I teach them to be so stoic at such a young age or was it something about being Japanese?* I looked at them intently and remarked, "I'll ask you again in a day or two. It's hard to decide right now."

Larry was curious, "How did it happen? He wasn't old like Grandma Toku."

"Toku was sick and died gradually but Ben committed suicide," I said. Suicide was common among the Seattle Japanese in the 1950s. It was treated in the same manner as a heart attack, stroke, or cancer. There were no further explanations necessary. Just suicide.

Thinking about Ben, Larry commented, "Maybe all of us are living on 'borrowed' time but some get more than others before their pictures are placed in the Buddhist shrine upstairs."

"Larry, you understand, don't you?" I inquired.

He nodded and asked, "Why would anyone want to kill themselves? I'll miss him," he said.

"I don't know," I replied. "If you want to wear your Scout uniform to the funeral, I can wash and iron it."

"Okay," he replied. "Will Dad drive us?

SUMMER 1955

Before summer passed, I pressed Larry on why he'd spent so much time climbing trees at the park. For a month, he avoided his friends and spent hours in the treetops. "Was it Ben's death? Is that the reason?"

Larry hesitated and said, "I asked you many times how Grandma Toku died, but you wouldn't tell me." Visibly upset, he asked again, "How did she die?"

I was puzzled at his response, "You were only three years old at the time, so I didn't think you'd understand."

"But I asked for years and you'd never say," he said with a frown.

"I know," I replied, "But we were ashamed. Grandma started smoking in camp and by the time we left Minidoka it was two packs a day. First, she developed health problems and finally died of lung cancer. That is the truth."

There was a long silence. "You don't remember do you?" Larry asked. "Remember what?" I responded.

"Alan and I made noise when she was sick and we played cowboys on the banister. We whooped and hollered until you came out and told us to be quiet because Grandma was sick." Larry paused and took a deep breath. "We obeyed and went outside and it rained so we came inside. But before we knew it, we were making noise again. You yelled at us, so we stopped. The next day Grandma died, and all the relatives and friends came to the house. I thought for sure that I'd killed her because I made noise."

"Oh, no," I replied as my shoulders dropped. "I didn't know, I'm so sorry." I put my arm over his shoulder.

Larry took a deep breath and his voice shook, "I asked you many times but you ignored me. Then I was sure that you knew my noises had killed Grandma. It's a secret I kept for years. I tried to tell you, but you never listened."

"Oh my!" I said and covered my mouth. "I didn't know. I didn't mean to cause that. Now that you're older you must realize that you didn't kill Grandma Toku."

"Later I realized that I hadn't, but instead thought I'd hurried her death," he replied.

"No," I said with a shaky voice, "She was so full of medicine that I'm sure she didn't hear a thing. Don't worry, you didn't kill her or hurry her death."

"I feel a little better now," Larry replied. "I wish you'd told me sooner. How many years has it been?"

I feared that the damage of carrying that burden had taken its toll. Larry closed his eyes. It was not something he could get over in a day. I realized that it would take time to dig out the tangled roots of guilt.

"I'm okay," Larry whispered, "But not really happy. Dad always says, 'Everything is no good.' I think about that all the time."

"Goodness gracious," I said, feeling the sorrow of my neglect. I asked, "What can I do to help?"

"Nothing," he replied. "It's all done and gone."

"I'm sorry. Will you forgive me?" I begged and hugged him tight.

"Sure, everything's fine. Nothing more to say," he responded

1961

Kiyoshi's health was good and the boys were growing up. I worked part-time and managed to save money. Our Hiroshima relatives wrote and said how grateful they were for our help and even invited us to visit. I was happy to not worry about them any longer.

After Alan graduated from Cleveland High School in June, 1961, he moved to San Francisco. He talked about it for years, but I never expected that it actually would happen. One evening I came home and asked Kiyoshi, "Where's Alan? His closet is clean."

"I guess he went to San Francisco like he always said," he replied.

With anger I asked, "Did you know anything about this? Did you take him to the Greyhound or train station?"

"No, he just left a note on the kitchen table," Kiyoshi replied.

"A note? Just like that?" I said, "We should have seen him off." I banged the silverware on the table and cleared his setting. Without a word I started cooking and held back tears. The fragrance of salmon and rice filled the kitchen. *What kind of family are we?* I wondered.

At Yosh's farm, the crows cawed a warning when I stepped outside and the rabbits scurried into the bushes. Then it dawned on me, *Oh I get it, Mr. Crow you alerted the rabbits. Animals and birds take care of each other, what happened to this family where a son leaves without a word? I'm so mad. I need some time to figure out who to yell at.*

Those thoughts fled when the telephone rang. I picked it up. Without saying "hello" the caller asked, "Hanae, why didn't you see Alan off today? I had to take him to the train station. He was alone. Where were you?"

Taken aback, I replied, "Who is this?"

"This is Yoko," she said.

I replied, "I didn't know he was leaving. Anyway, he said he would be going to school in California and would return soon."

"What?" she replied. "He told me that he was never coming back and was mad at Kiyoshi for beating him up. Did you know that?"

"No, I didn't. They never got along but I thought he stopped hitting the boys," I said.

"I'll contact my brother, Tom, in Oakland and see if Alan checks in with him. In the meantime, I'll try to get ahold of him."

"Is that it?" she asked. "You're his mother. You need to do more. Call me when you find him. Goodbye."

Yoko never spoke to me like this. *Who does she think she is?* I thought as my anger grew. Maybe it was from all the years of stress and chaos that made us numb. I could sympathize with others but when it came to my own troubles, I was distant.

Denial was my first reaction to any problem. It helped me cope with camp memories, Hiroshima, and our family illnesses. My usual excuse was that I would think about it later. It was a temporary solution, but after doing it over and over it occurred to me that I had actually become a person who didn't respond to my personal pain but just put it off. I felt empty after this revelation and decided to confront Kiyoshi. I threw down my apron and walked into the living room.

At that moment, Larry came home and turned on the tv. "What's for dinner?" he asked.

"Never mind," I said, "Has Dad beaten you up?"

With a puzzled look he asked, "What?"

"Turn off the television," I snapped.

"He hasn't hit me in years. Not since I was a third grader," he responded with a puzzled look.

"Did he beat up Alan?" I asked.

"I don't know," he replied. Larry walked towards the kitchen and opened the refrigerator. "Why don't you ask Dad?" he said. "He's in the front yard."

Larry pulled out his dining chair and sat down and asked, "Where's Alan?"

Without emotion I replied, "He went to San Francisco and will be back soon."

Larry squeezed lemon juice on the salmon and filled his rice bowl. But before he could take a bite, he said casually, "He didn't even say goodbye."

Three months passed, and Alan's place at the table remained empty. One evening at dinner, Larry tapped his fingers and asked, "When's Alan coming back?"

I barked, "Soon."

Then he asked, "Have you heard from him?"

I hesitated and replied, "No, not yet."

"Have you tried to contact him?" Larry asked.

My voice cracked when I replied, "He sent a letter but the return address was no good."

Larry frowned, "That's just like him. I hope he's doin' okay," he said.

As the months passed, Alan's table space filled with random items: the salt and pepper shaker, soy sauce, and a Heinz ketchup bottle migrated over until his space was gone.

Trying to make sense of his departure, I asked Kiyoshi again if he beat up either of the boys. He said, "No." I looked at him square in the eye and asked, "Are you sure?"

"Yeah, I haven't hit him in years," was his response. "He'll be okay. Anyway, it's good he's on his own. We have one less mouth to feed."

I felt a pain in my stomach. I realized how much I had twisted my mind to cope with a torrent of obstacles. For years, I had nightmares about barbed wire, mushroom clouds, and stacks of Hiroshima bodies. The more I put things off, the more the knots became permanent. I thought, *I've become a damaged person who doesn't even know how to grieve anymore.*

As usual I concluded, *I'll think about Alan's leaving tomorrow, not now.* Mentally there was so little space left in me to grieve. I wondered about Larry and worried because I didn't pay much attention to him as a child. In the back of my mind I was afraid he would die prematurely like my miscarriage.

With these negative thoughts, I recalled Kiyoshi's saying, "Everything is no good."

Then I heard crows cawing outside. "*Kamisama,*" I said out loud, "are you here?" I stepped out on the porch and watched the birds chatter on the roof tops. Immediately I thought, *Maybe there's a rabbit nearby. In the city that was unlikely but it still could be Kamisama sending a message. After all, Japanese spirits were everywhere in nature.*

OFF TO WESTERN STATE HOSPITAL

Life is full of uncertainty, I thought. In 1942, I was expecting to be happily married and living a good life in Seattle. After Pearl Harbor, Japanese Americans were forcibly incarcerated. I was angry and concluded, *Living in exile for three and a half years in Minidoka should not have counted as time subtracted from our lives. But it did.* This injustice was on my mind for years.

After Alan left in 1962, I continued to work at the Rainier Market on Jackson Street. One morning I lifted a crate and felt a sharp pain shoot up my leg. I was angry at myself and thought, *Why didn't I flex my legs when I lifted?* That one second mistake cost me a trip to the hospital and surgery. Like Minidoka, it changed my life.

After the back operation, I stayed in bed at home and craved sweets, something that made me feel human. My eyes glazed over and my mind went into a slow tailspin. I left most meals uneaten and began to believe that "Everything is no good," as Kiyoshi always said

Larry entered the bedroom and engaged me in conversation. "How are you doing, Mom?"

"I'm fine," I said, slurring slightly.

"Do you want something special to eat?" he asked.

Eat? I thought.

There was a silence as time slowed. My mind slid away from reality.

"I can't think of anything." I replied.

There was a knock at the door and Doctor Johnson entered. Yoko had called him earlier. He was a very tall and distinguished looking man who was our family doctor since after camp.

Larry waved goodbye and excused himself.

Dr. Johnson said, "I sat down with Kiyoshi, Yoko, and Sachi to discuss your condition. How are you Hanae?" he asked.

"I'm okay," I replied.

He rose and said to me, "This is very different from your past operations. We must take quick action before it gets worse. Hanae I'm recommending that you be hospitalized again," Johnson said. I was so tired after hearing his remarks that I just gave up until Yoko entered. At that point I began to argue to no avail.

The next day after lunch, Kiyoshi drove me to Western State Mental Hospital in Steilacoom. I'd never been there or spent much time in South Tacoma. But with a slip of my disk, the hospital would be my new home for months to come.

CHAPTER TWELVE

State Mental Hospital, 1962

The hospital mesh windows and partitions reminded me of camp. Every day no matter how hard I tried, Minidoka was on my mind. *Gaman,* I would say to push the grief and anger from my mind. *At home I could trust Doctor Johnson and my friends. At Western State, I'm afraid because strangers are in charge of me like in camp.*

In contrast with Idaho, the hospital lawn was lush, trimmed, and edged neatly. There were no signs of interloping rye grass in the lawn, or bare stem dandelions standing tall after releasing airborne spores to flutter. I could feel the spirits of nature I'd left behind in Japan. "*Kamisama,* are you here?" I whispered out loud. "Can you help me?"

Across the highway were the hospital farm fields with vegetables, pigs, cows, and fruit trees. "That's a regular farm," I said out loud. "Uncle Yosh would love it."

Residents raised crops and tended animals as part of their therapy. There was no barbed wire, no machine guns or armed guards. In the distance I saw patients with straw hats and blue overalls bobbing among the crop rows. Even though most of the harvesting was over, there was work to be done that connected them to the cycle of the seasons.

With summer over, the campus rose garden showed the effects of a chilly September. The bushes were scrawny and bent, with gaps. Resisting the change in season, a few single stems with red flowers survived. As usual, the sky was overcast, something between iron gray and gunpowder in color.

In high school, I had read about ancient Greece with its clear blue skies and a crystal Aegean Sea. The philosophers and thinkers like Plato and Aristotle could see long distances and ponder great thoughts. They could walk unfettered in light clothes and sandals in comfort. The drab Pacific Northwest, by contrast, encouraged some to take on the gloom of the skies.

A light breeze blew across the hospital's south campus and rustled the rhododendrons. Birch bark peels fluttered, revealing the layer beneath. In this damp climate, changes came quickly: rain clouds cleared and returned again in an instant.

I laughed when Puni, a tanned 30-year-old male patient from Hawaii, celebrated a sunny fall day by disrobing and running on the lawn. I heard him cheer and holler, "The sun! At last the sun!" he cried. The outburst ceased faster than the orderlies could restrain him when he discovered that Pacific Northwest autumn sunshine was cold and biting.

Poor man, I thought and chuckled.

Inside my room, I shuffled to the dresser and picked up a mirror. I ran a straight part in my hair and climbed back in bed. Leaning against the headboard, I hummed a Japanese song.

The tune reminded me of Hiroshima. A year ago, I saw a Japanese magazine that featured Hiroshima's rebirth. I saw photos of new highways, buildings, stores, cars, and bustling businesses. The city had a strange "just built yesterday" look since almost nothing old survived.

I remembered my good times with Masa in the kitchen and *sento*. I thought of Fumi and her harsh remarks. Even to this day, I had difficulty comprehending the destruction of Hiroshima. I almost believed it still existed somewhere around a corner.

But I knew full well my home was in America and longed to see my sons, Kiyoshi, and best friend Kiku. After arriving at Western State, I wondered, *Do my friends really exist or are they like Hiroshima--totally changed in my absence. Will I be here less than the three and a half years I spent in camp? At least in Minidoka I had family and friends. Here I am alone.* I cringed when I thought, *I hope I won't need surgery.*

I felt uneasy. The hospital was in the white world, where the doctors and nurses did not understand my culture or values. They would use western methods and western cures. I worried about being the only Japanese and wondered, *How will I be treated and how will I get along?*

In Minidoka, thousands were depressed or angry for years, but their anger largely remained untreated. The problems simply festered or were denied. *At least here we have drugs and group therapy.*

I peered through the wire mesh windows and the skies darkened. The south wind drove waves of rain lashing against the windows. Strong gusts bent the giant poplars which created the impression of gnarly giants swaying along the road. The hospital turnaround was whipped with sheets of horizontal rain. Green uniformed gardeners rushed for cover as the scent of freshly cut grass wafted across the immaculate grounds.

Perfection is important at Western State, I thought as I pondered my surroundings. The hospital façade was solid and conveyed a sense of permanence and stateliness which belied the reality of screaming mental patients. The red brick and granite stairs were an appropriate shelter for lost and disjointed souls. After sunset, the campus seemed like it was from another era. I imagined men in top hats and dark suits riding horse carriages clopping up the driveway.

A fluttering linen curtain separated me from my roommates. I donned a terry cloth robe and removed my glasses and put it on the bed stand. My breathing slowed and my eyelids grew heavy. Back home I would be up and around this early, but here I nodded after taking medications. My head swayed and bobbed slightly. Radios played full blast and echoed down the hall: syncopated rhythms, drum beats, falsettos, do wops, and big bands cascaded in a mishmash of sounds.

The airways came alive in a cacophony of disjointed flowing sounds: "Pat O'Malley coming to you on 850 AM KJM in Tacoma: Weather today is 52 degrees and cloudy, shop the B&I superstore for everything you need, come by and visit Bobo the gorilla, traffic is backing up on Pearl Street, for the best paint, forever yours—sunny smile—caress my hair, cha cha, boogie woogie, music from the mountaintop...."

Through the jumble, I focused on a thread from the radio. "This song blasted up to number one on the charts last year when Colonel Alan Shepard became the first American in space on the Freedom Seven. A boss golden oldie from 1961–hang on Tacoma—do you remember 'Having a Blast' by the Red Raiders?"

> *"Ooo Wa, Ooo Wa*
> *we're stomping the night away*
> *rocking the hop,*
> *we are jumping*
> *blasting the night away"*

The thumping beat pried open corners of my mind. Before sleep overtook me and dream logic slipped through, I wondered, *What happened to my sweet dog, Molly?*

I felt the trauma of being separated from my beautiful cocker spaniel as if it had been yesterday. My mind was playing tricks. My waking side knew Molly had probably starved to death or been hit by a car years ago. But I still worried.

ROOMMATES

There was joyous noise when my roommates, Franny and Dutch, scooted through the curtain. "Hi, Hana," they chirped in unison.

I smiled and said, "I should have told you when I first arrived, that my name is Hanae– like *Ha nah eh.* The hospital people call me Hana because they can't say Hanae properly."

The girls nodded energetically, "Okay, we get it."

I was wary of my roommates since we had so little in common. Dutch was a nineteen-year-old redhead and Franny was a twenty-year-old blonde country girl. I recalled growing up in my large family: if there was a disagreement among three people, it was always two against one.

I thought, *Being the oldest and Japanese, I will be the odd person out.*

To me they seemed like good neighbors, but I wondered if I could trust them.

The girls were energetic and bounced like children at play. Franny had a cheerful smile and always greeted people with a "Good morning" or "Good afternoon." She was six feet tall and looked like a long-legged college girl who could dance on table tops with a lampshade on her head in Mazaatlan during spring break, tempting the desires of fraternity boys. She had a wildness and worldliness with a soft edge. Franny appeared easygoing but was not someone to trifle with. For a girl from a small town, she was well-read and sounded like the World Book Encyclopedia with her surprising comments. Her crow's feet at the corner of her blue eyes spread wide with each infectious smile.

Franny had a casual manner and often wore baggy blue jeans. "Comfort is cool," she would say as she pushed up her glasses. Sometimes she rolled her pant legs and other times she let them down. Her two upper teeth protruded slightly which made her smile stick to her teeth endearingly. She moved –glided –with long effortless strides. Reclining in an overstuffed chair, her posture was a cross between a slump and a slide deep into the cushions. She became at one with the slick upholstery.

It was a way to mask her height. Her bad posture upset the nurses, who would say, "Franny, sit up like a lady."

Dutch, my other roommate, was a five-foot-tall redhead, about my size. She was an attractive nineteen-year old with huge round wire-rimmed glasses. She could pass for twenty-one. Her red hair was pulled so tight it was like her freckles were ready to scream. Dutch's bright eyes were magnified by the lenses and shone light blue like the sky or green like the waters of Puget Sound, depending on the color of her blouse. A curvature of the spine gave her body a noticeable twist.

"Hey, man, that's really cool," she would say or "That's a gas." Her eyes held mysteries as they glowed iridescent–sparkling portals to another time, place, and dimension. If there was a looking glass to fall through from this world, it would be her eyes. She was not the table-dancing type like Franny, but she held her tequila and could hoot and holler when tavern bands played. More than anything, she was electric. It seemed like if you touched her, you would receive a shock. It was as though she had just rubbed her feet on a nylon carpet and was waiting to crackle a bolt of lightning. Many a young man must have taken a jolt from one of her kisses.

Nurse Olson entered the area and announced, "Okay, ladies, it's time for meds. Please meet me at the window."

Medications were dispensed in small paper cups accompanied by a glass of water. After we had downed the pills, Nurse Olson checked every mouth and even under our tongues. Depending on the person, she used a wooden tongue depressor to search corners.

Afterwards, we strolled back to my area.

"We have a little time before the meds kick in and go *blotto*, so *pleeeze*, Hanae, tell us a story," Dutch pleaded.

Franny was fresh and full of life. Dutch was perpetual motion and her eyes focused like high beams. The girls gathered like children around the bed. Their laughter revived me. Franny wiggled. With a sleight of hand, she produced a pill and flipped it into the garbage.

"Out, damned spot," she said, "That's Shakespeare."

I was puzzled by Franny's trick. "How did you do that?" I asked.

"Hey, Hanae, I'll tell you later. What's cool is that we've never seen you smile," Franny remarked.

Dutch focused on the ceiling then asked for a Japanese fairy tale. "Something we haven't heard before."

I closed my eyes and recalled the stories I had told my own children. "How about Momotaro, the peach boy?" I offered.

Franny pushed Dutch with a friendly shove. "Hey, girl, you like peaches, don't you?" she said with a chuckle.

I raised my right hand and extended it to begin the story. The room grew smaller and cozier as the stories brought warmth and color to our quarters. For a moment the institutional white walls softened, floor tiles glistened, glossy paint mellowed, and the ceilings lowered.

I enjoyed sharing stories. This was part of my heritage and something new for the girls. They, in turn, loved tales that carried them away to strange lands and times.

"Momotaro," I began, "was an answer to an old couple's prayers. They'd always wanted a child but could never have one. One day the woman found a giant peach floating in the river. The couple pulled it out and when they cut it open, a baby popped out."

Dutch asked. "Peach, like a giant beach ball with furry skin?"

Ignoring Dutch, I carried on, "The woman wrapped him in her apron and looked to her husband for reassurance. There was no doubt that they would raise the baby as their own. Quickly the years passed, and Momotaro grew into a strong and brave man."

I wrinkled my brow and with a determined look, said, "To repay the couple, he vowed, 'I will rid the country of the demons and trolls who do evil things'."

"Whoa, that's cool," Dutch said as her eyes grew large.

I waved my arms as I stared at the spellbound girls. I marveled at how quickly stories brought us together. It was like primitive people gathering around a fire sharing courageous exploits and heroic acts.

I said, "Momotaro left to fight the goblins. On his journey he met a pheasant, a monkey, and a dog who joined his quest. The pheasant flew over the wall of the Ogre's fortress and stole the gate key. When the fight began, the bird pecked the demons' eyes, the dog bit their legs, and the monkey fought fiercely. Finally, the demons were vanquished and Momotaro became a hero. Now, that story has a happy ending," I announced with pride.

Nurse Olson entered and said, "Okay, girls, lights out in five minutes and bed check in fifteen. So get ready for bed."

"Okay," we responded in unison. I yawned and stretched.

"I'm gonna' crash. Let's hit the hay," Franny said. "We'll continue tomorrow evening.

THE NEXT EVENING

We gathered again and I continued. "But you know," I added, "There are stories of *tengu* or demons who lived in the mountains near Hiroshima."

In my excitement, I slipped into Japanese and said, "*Honto ni,*" and then covered my mouth in surprise. "I mean it was really true. *Tengu* men had red faces and long noses and raided the villages." I paused and touched my chin. "They stole food and sometimes kidnapped young women. It made sense, because there were shipwrecked Portuguese sailors who hid in the mountains before Japan was open to westerners. The villagers would never have seen white people with long stringy hair and big noses. In the cold, the faces of the sailors would be red like apples. To simple folk they could be easily be mistaken for monsters."

The girls rocked backwards, almost falling off the bed. "If I were shipwrecked in Japan, I could be a female *Tengu,*" Franny said proudly, "and I have a big nose, see." Franny turned and showed her profile.

Dutch fluffed up her hair, "My red hair looks like flames. What would they think of that? I would have been some type of fire demon."

I squinted and replied, "Oh, you'd both would be very scary."

Dutch fidgeted and pushed up her glasses. "Momotaro," she remarked, "was not a bad story, but I liked the one you told us a while back, about Urashima Taro."

Franny rubbed her chin and asked, "Which one was that?" She cocked her head sideways, "I don't remember."

Dutch perked up and her eyes focused on the ceiling.

"Okay, I'll tell you," Dutch said, almost without taking a breath, "Remember, Urashima Taro saves a giant turtle from mean village children and releases him back into the sea. The turtle returns a year later and asks Urashima Taro to visit the underwater palace and a beautiful princess." Dutch took a breath. "He agrees and to his amazement is taken under water by the turtle. He has a wonderful time in the palace."

Suddenly Dutch gasped as Franny hollered, "Breathe, girl!"

Dutch gulped and continued, "After what seems like the passage of several days, Urashima Taro wants to return to his mother and grandmother. Reluctantly the princess says goodbye and the turtle takes him home."

Dutch took another breath. "Back at the village the trees have all grown taller. Urashima Taro looks for his house but can't find it. Finally, he talks to an old man who says he heard a story about a boy who left his mother and grandmother 300 years ago and never returned. After hearing this remark, Urashima Taro begins to age and turns to dust!" Dutch wiped her brow, "Thank goodness I finished. Almost ran out of gas!"

Franny raised her arms and cheered, "I remember that! You really knocked it out of the park, girl!"

I nodded my approval and smiled with satisfaction. "Good job," I said.

Dutch stood and proudly took a bow. Then she walked to her chest of drawers. She pulled out a pair of jeans and tee shirt and placed it against me and said, "You should put these on."

I stared and hesitated. "I never wear jeans."

Franny nodded in agreement, "Yes, but they would make you feel better and not like a hospital patient."

"Okay," I said, "But I better not get in trouble!"

After I put on the jeans, Dutch and I resembled each other in an odd way. I was uncomfortable with my new look, but felt younger. There was a pause and silence when I modeled my new clothes. With a smile, I twisted with hands on my hips as if in front of an admiring crowd. The radio played a rock and roll tune which made me bounce and the wind picked up and rattled the windows in rhythm. Rain splattered against the glass.

The moment was interrupted by Nurse Olson, who entered and said, "Lights out in five and bed check in fifteen."

"Okay," we responded as usual.

"Good night, everyone," I said and picked up my toothbrush. My eyes grew heavy. "We'll continue tomorrow," I said.

Franny yawned and Dutch stretched. "Sounds good," they replied. "Good night."

THE FOLLOWING EVENING

At our evening story time I inquired, "Where were we? Let me think." Before I could start, Franny interrupted and said, "Our American fairy tales have happy endings like Momotaro, not like Urashima Taro. What kind of country would have stories where the hero comes home and everything is changed and he dies? That's really a drag."

"Aha!" Dutch responded, "I know, Rip Van Winkle but he didn't turn to dust immediately."

Then Dutch looked up as if in a trance. Her hair radiated as she shook her head. This time she was very deliberate when she spoke, "The Urashima Taro moral is you can't go home. In a poor country everything changes and not always for the best, so this is the lesson the children must learn."

I looked in amazement at the girls. "My goodness," I remarked. "How did you ever know that?"

The girls put their arms over each other's shoulders and spoke in unison like identical twins, "We are crazy, not stupid! Ha, ha!"

"But then again," Dutch said with anger and determination, "In America, Snow White's mother died. Cinderella was an orphan, Bambi's mother was killed and Dumbo's mom was thrown in jail. There were some real anti-mother things coming down in our stories too."

Her face flushed and she pushed up her glasses with her index finger. "I think I'll bring that topic up in group sometime."

Franny was annoyed and said, "Would you stop that? You know, that arm waving scene? It's like sparks are flying off of you. They feel like little prickly things hitting me, you know those *jiggity jaggety* things. Hanae, can you feel it or is it just me?"

I nodded, "Yes. It's something like sand in a strong wind stinging your face."

Dutch backed off and slid to the side of the bed and lowered her head momentarily. Her eyes looked exceptionally large. Instantly she changed back to normal, as if she had just released some weird energy.

"I'll calm down, so don't get bent out of shape," Dutch laughed and crossed her arms as she draped her legs over the edge of the bed.

"I've got another fairy tale complaint." Dutch pulled herself forward. "You remember Rapunzel? She let down her hair so the prince could climb the tower and they could make out big time." Dutch paused for emphasis. "Well the prince knocked her up. When the woman who was taking care of Rapunzel found out, she kicked Rapunzel out. So Rapunzel was abandoned in the woods to have her twin babies. That's really off the wall, man."

Franny assumed an upright posture. She said, "Well that's why my 'little friends' are so spiffy. I won't have any kids as long as I have my rubbers."

Dutch asked, "What?"

"You know condoms!" Franny replied, "and I don't have to worry about letting down my hair."

Franny emphasized the "my hair" as she pushed it up with her right hand in a comic fashion. Dutch looked straight at Franny with a sharp-shooter's eye, "Yeah, like 'your friend' will do a lot of good here. We're like a bunch of caged animals," Dutch said with a slight grin as she folded her arms and gripped herself tight. She nodded with authority as if she had just spoken a final truth.

"Oh, girls," I replied and reached out to Franny. "Don't say things like that. Babies are good, but a lot of work. I really didn't have a choice like you do now. Alan, my first, was born nine months after we got married, and then we went to the relocation camp. My second was a miscarriage that wasn't even a baby. The third was Larry, my youngest. I really worried because we didn't get good food or good medical care in Minidoka. So far they're okay, but later I had some female problems and had everything removed. I was in the hospital for a week and can't have any more children." The pain of it came back to me, and for a moment I couldn't speak. "I felt I was no longer a real woman. But I'd rather not talk about it."

"Whoa, that's too much," remarked Dutch as she unfolded her arms. "That's terrible. I hate surgery, man oh man. The only thing I've ever had taken out were my tonsils. The thought makes me crazy."

Franny said, "ER".

Dutch replied, "What do you mean 'ER'?"

Franny howled, "*Crazi*ER, get it?"

We all laughed and fell into each other's arms. The smell of Franny's lemon-scented perfume surrounded us.

Like clockwork, Nurse Olson entered and announced, "Lights out."

"Good night, girls," I said and opened my drawer. I thought, *We're magnets drawn together like family, sending each other off to pleasant dreams.*

THE EVENING AFTER THAT

When I first met the girls, I was uneasy with their closeness. I rarely hugged my own children except when they'd been babies. For years, Kiyoshi never touched me with affection. Words like duty, honor, shame and obedience came easier than "love." Showing emotions might shame or dishonor the family. I believed that maintaining honor was my most important duty. Being in a mental hospital was especially hard. It was such an embarrassment that I couldn't tell Kiku where I was. Silence was a face-saving gesture but deep down I knew someone must have told her.

Lord knows, I thought, *the family has been the subject of enough gossip because of Sachi, and her live-in lover.*

Franny leaned back with her palms behind her head. With a superior smile she said, "Fairy tales are like country western music: the girlfriend cheats, the boyfriend lies, and only the dog is faithful."

Franny was surprised at the coherence of her own speech as she huffed on her finger nails and rubbed them against her blouse with exaggerated pride.

"Man, that was righteous," she said, showing amazement. "A real wonderment." With her thumb and index finger, she pinched the bridge of her nose lightly. Then she exhaled.

"We're all like dust," she continued. "Tumbleweeds whirling until we catch a fence. The next big wind blows us down the road. Maybe it's just fate and it's all planned."

She raised her eyes as the music lilted. "I remember my boyfriend, Steve, and I parked in the woods and started making out. He said we were goin' to the submarine races. But we just parked at the lake."

Franny rubbed her eyes and continued, "Country music played on the radio, maybe Loretta Lynn. The tune was romantic, which really put me in a mood. I was ready and willing, and dreamed that I was with Johnny Cash. The truck windows steamed up and it was crazy for my first time. I really didn't know what I was doing and didn't even like it. But I wanted it badly."

She shook out her blonde hair. A darkness crept across her face. "We gave up this beautiful blue-eyed seven-pound, seven-ounce boy for adoption. I called him Buddy. Every year I remember his birthday, December 18th. For his first birthday I got plastered out of my mind. I need to do the same this year but that'll be a problem unless I get out." She was almost out of breath but managed to continue. "He lives in California with a good family. Hope he's okay. He'll be turning two this year."

Her voice broke. There was an awkward silence. She took a deep breath and whispered, "I didn't give him a real name. Just called him Buddy. I remember the day I let him go." Franny grabbed a Kleenex and wiped her nose. "That was the worst day of my life. I held him and told him I loved him."

Dutch put her arm around Franny. "I just cried my eyes out at the hospital," Franny said. "I wish things could've been different, but I was still in high school and my parents couldn't afford to keep him." Franny wrapped her arms around herself. "Buddy whimpered when I let him go. It was miserable. I put most bad memories away, but this one keeps coming back."

I reached out and held Franny's limp hand. Her face was drained as if she was about to collapse.

"Every time I hear a baby cry," she said, "I think of Buddy." Franny's neck muscles tightened. She continued, "And worst of all, he'll never know me. I carried him for nine months. Damn, he was mine. I swear I'll never give away another baby, ever."

Franny raised her head and tears streamed down her nose and cheek. Dutch and I let her fall back on us like a Raggedy Ann. She was shaking profusely.

Dutch pulled a Kleenex from the bed stand and handed it to Franny, who blew her nose.

"I should have kept him," Franny said with fierceness. "He was mine, but I was too young and stupid. Now look at me, I can't even take care of myself."

Dutch gripped Franny tight and urged, "Franny, breathe, remember to breathe!"

Franny reached for another Kleenex. She continued, "I pray he found a good home and grows up to be a good man. Maybe we'll meet someday." She smiled, "I think about that a lot. When I see a toddler, I wonder if Buddy would look like him. Oh, it never ends. It's like my heart is leaking. I did okay for a while but I kept on thinking about him."

Franny crumpled her Kleenex and tossed it in to the wire waste-basket. "Buddy is stuck in my head all day and night. I search for him in my dreams." Franny held back tears, "I hope he wonders about me sometimes." Her voice rose and cracked. "I'm not even sure his adopted parents told him about me. You know, one of these days when I get old, I might have grandkids that I won't even know." She exhaled and blinked slowly. "Oh, that makes me so sad. I'd love to be a grandmother. That would be really cool."

The group was quiet. We were drained but Franny managed to continue. She exhaled a long breath, collected herself, and wiped her nose.

She continued as her voice broke, "I had terrible nightmares. You know, the kind where you think you forgot something important and you can't find it, or you are lost and everything keeps changing and you search for the right path. I used to wake up screaming."

She stopped and clutched her neck with one hand, her habit when under stress. "The nightmares were so real that I got mixed up. Things started falling apart and I thought about killing myself. I dyed my hair so I'd look different. Instead of platinum blond it turned an awful shade of orange." Franny hung her head and continued. "I looked in the mirror and was crushed at my appearance. I couldn't leave the house looking like that."

Franny touched her lips and looked down at the floor. She composed herself and poured a glass of water. She drank slowly, savoring each drop.

"So I put on a wool cap and caught the Greyhound to Portland," she said haltingly. "When I got off the bus, I was a first-class mess sitting on the bench, no food, and no money. Some nice businessman felt sorry for me and gave me bus fare home. I must have looked terrible."

Franny was sobbing. "That's when I decided to kill myself," she said. "I remember it was an overcast day after I got home. I opened the medicine cabinet and grabbed the first bottle of anything. I figured. that an overdose would do the trick." Franny shivered and continued.

"After I made up my mind, I was happy. I walked out to the back yard and the sun peeked from the clouds. I sat in a cedar chair and popped open an Olympia beer. Then I took a couple of swigs and waited for the sun to set." Franny took a sip of water and paused.

"By the time it was dark, I'd swallowed a whole bottle of aspirin. I was hoping it would knock me out but instead I just got sick. I mean really dizzy, barfy sick. I hyperventilated and passed out. My dad found me and drove like crazy to get my stomach pumped."

Franny grimaced, "I always remember the feel of those fuzzy tablets. That's why I can't swallow aspirin now. No matter what, they just won't go down. I tried again with sleeping pills another time, but they wouldn't go down either. So, for my own good, my parents sent me here. I'm doing okay most of the time. But I still miss my Buddy."

Franny's shoulders drooped and her story was interrupted by Nurse Olson announcing, "lights out". Instantly, there was a stillness and silence. We hugged and became one. Franny's troubles spilled into our hearts and we felt her pain as if were ours. Instinctively, we held hands and waited for Nurse Olson to enter.

JIZO

After several months, the hospital routines began to wear on me. I felt overwhelmed and finally understood what confinement really meant. This wasn't Minidoka with its guard towers, but instead a benevolent and stifling dance. I was not finding myself, but losing my identity in a series of prescribed and repetitive activities. I wondered if this was why Franny and Dutch behaved the way they did, always challenging the routines, perhaps as a way to preserve their sanity.

What would they be like on the outside if they were free? What would I be like?

I was not totally committed to the hospital's program, but once the momentum started, I knew there were few choices; after all, I couldn't just check myself out.

Just then I heard the girls slide open my curtain. Dutch's face lit up and she wiggled like a six-year old after eating candy. When she had a revelation, it took over her whole body. She twisted and twitched as she said, "Wow, I have a great idea. We can make apple pie moonshine to celebrate Buddy's birthday! We need some cinnamon sticks and a pot of boiling water."

Dutch glanced at Franny for approval, "Franny, you can make it during your kitchen on-the-job training."

Then Dutch continued, "Combine boiling water with apple cider and alcohol—190 proof will do it. We should be able to get some alcohol since most of the orderlies think we are just stupid and crazy." She checked our reactions and continued, "So I think I can act stupid enough to get some."

Franny smiled and ran her fingers through her hair.

"Dutch, why bother?" Franny said. "Just get some booze from the WSU agriculture students on the farm. The college dudes can get you those small liquor bottles. You know, like they serve on airplanes."

She nudged Dutch playfully with her shoulder. "We would need three or four Jim Beams or Smirnoff vodkas or anything!" Franny gave Dutch a long up and down look as if she was taking inventory. "We've been dry so long, just a little will get us looped. Ask that college guy who is sweet on you. You know—the tall skinny one. He'll do anything for you."

Dutch gave a sour look, "Yeah, yeah," she replied insincerely.

As they chattered, I looked at Franny and thought, *They are my only bright spots here.* When I fully comprehended this fact, my ambivalence about them faded and I decided to accept my roommates unconditionally.

Touching Franny's hand, I said, "Franny, I'm happy that you're still alive and with us. This place would be miserable without you and Dutch."

I thought of my trips to the temples in Japan and said, "Japanese have a ritual for almost everything, even losing babies." I paused thoughtfully. "There are stone statues or *jizos* that are placed at crossroads or sacred places. People put scarves on them and leave toys and playthings to comfort deceased children."

The girls listened carefully. Franny raised her eyebrows. I drew a picture which looked something like a small blob with a bib.

"It looks like this," I said.

"Like Casper the Ghost!" hooted Dutch.

Ignoring Dutch, I continued, "Yes, a birthday celebration would be something to look forward to. We could start with a *jizo* for Buddy even though he's still alive." I felt energized and connected to the project. I continued, "I'll make one in crafts. It could be paper-mâché or we could gather stones in the garden and place small trinkets for Buddy. It's the least we can do."

Franny's shoulders tensed up. To put her at ease I said, "You don't have to worry about whether you're doing it right, just make it the way your heart tells you." I was at ease since I found a project and purpose.

Franny's eyes grew red. She covered her mouth and lowered her head.

There was an honesty and simplicity in my explanation that was not lost on the girls. They realized the actions may or may not actually cure anything, but they were willing to accept a Japanese custom as a solution that dated back several hundreds of years.

Catching the spirit, Dutch said, "We need something special, a trinket or gift for the *jizo*."

I opened my drawer and found one item that was unique. My fingers were drawn to a bronze medallion.

"This will do," I said. "It's a coin from the Yukon Pacific Exposition in Seattle."

The girls marveled at the shiny bronze piece with its beautiful high relief design: Two prospectors were on one side and a Native American in a canoe on the other. A steamship and sun were in the background. They passed the coin from hand to hand. Franny held it between her thumb and index finger and exclaimed, "Holy smokes! It's a 1909 Alaska-Yukon-Pacific Exposition medallion."

Dutch said, "Are you sure? It's so gorgeous. Betcha it's worth a lot."

"It was a gift to me years ago, but it was meant to be yours," I said with a pleased look. "It will work nicely for our ritual."

I gathered the girls and formed a small human triangle on the floor. Franny held the medallion and closed her fingers around it. Dutch and I placed our hands on Franny's shoulder.

"I have an idea," Dutch explained, "My grandmother was part Cherokee and knew about sacred objects. Close your eyes and take deep breaths."

"We'll say a prayer, and Franny's grief and sorrow will be drawn into the coin," Dutch whispered. "Every regret and fear will be absorbed and your mind will be free of guilt." The room grew quiet and only the birds chirping could be heard. "Franny, you can now give Buddy's care over to the universe, to be loved and nourished, knowing all good things will come to him."

We bowed our heads and said, "Amen," in unison. If an outsider were to observe us, they could have mistaken us for Druids gathering under the full moon.

"Place the coin under your pillow tonight," I instructed. "Franny, think about Buddy and how happy he'll be. Dream that your sorrows flow away like a fairy tale with a happy ending. Your tears will turn into streams that reach the sea and become part of the natural cycle."

"Thank you," Franny said and linked arms with Dutch. "Thank you both." She shed a small tear.

I believed we had done something good but wondered, *Is this really a solution in a place where happiness is a pill and the final solution might be a lobotomy? Who knows? But at least we are not helpless.*

The clouds separated and the evening sunshine streamed through the window grates. Shafts of light filled the room. Outside, the poplars swayed and the gardens glowed. For a moment, memories of yesterday's wind and horizontal rain faded. The sun shined and I forgot the rain.

CHAPTER THIRTEEN

Bon Odori and Other Dances, 1962

Sunday morning, my alarm clock sounded like a woodpecker banging. I wiped my eyes, flipped the switch, and replaced the clock on the dresser. The room felt heavy as if I were underwater. Pushing through sluggishness, I began to worry whether I was improving. *I don't know for sure but I sure don't want to be here forever.*

I pulled the hand mirror from my drawer and thought, *I'm beginning to look like the walls of this hospital - drab and tinted slightly green like under fluorescent lights.*

The sight of peeling lead paint, institutional tile floors, and locked metal doors irritated me. I pushed those thoughts away so the day could move forward.

Later that night after dinner, the girls and I gathered in my room. I was tired, but they were cheerful and wide awake. Franny sat on the side of the bed. Dutch jumped up and down in a frenzy. She wanted us to notice something special.

I felt her excitement and asked, "How can you be so active after your meds?"

The girls smiled and looked at each other. "There're many ways. If you want, we'll show you!"

I crinkled my nose, "No, thanks. What's that smell?"

Dutch looked sheepish as she raised three tongue depressors with an "S" written on each in black ink.

"What's that?" I asked, moving closer and examining the sticks.

"It's her code of S," Franny replied, "It means *Something Similar to Sun* which is her way of saying the sun is out and it's time to slather on Coppertone. That's why she's wearing shades."

I had a puzzled look, it was as if I had just walked into the middle of a conversation. "Okay, I sort of understand. Dutch smells like a sunny day at the beach. Why so much tanning lotion?"

Dutch gestured with a half-hearted smile, a "Who knows" shrug of her shoulders. "The forecast calls for sun and I wanted to celebrate the appearance of the great yellow ball in the sky! I need to catch some rays."

"Well, summer's coming but aren't you early or a few months late?" I asked. I looked out the window and said, "Anyway you don't need lotion now. It's evening and the sun has set already."

I longed to see the sun and remembered past summers. I said, "Summer to me is Japanese dance, *Bon Odori*, that celebrates our ances- tors." I adjusted my glasses and continued, "It's the time they return to earth." I spoke slowly and with precision. "In Seattle people wear bright kimonos or *happi* coats and dance outside the Buddhist church. Every summer, even in Minidoka, we had *Bon Odori*."

Franny and Dutch brightened up. "Show us how! We want to dance," they chirped. "Show us pleeeze," they pleaded and jumped up and down.

I laughed, *Moments like these make me feel valued as a person. The trick is to not over-emphasize my Japanese heritage because I'm an American.* Main- taining that duality was a challenge since most white people regarded me as a foreigner.

I curled my lip and focused. "My favorites are the Dai Tokyo Ondo and *Tanko Bushi*," I said. "The most fun is the *Tanko Bushi* or Coal Min- er's Dance. I can teach you now, okay?"

"Wait a minute," Franny said. She ran to her dresser and like a hur- ricane and tossed underwear, shirts and socks helter-skelter over her bed. Finally, she cried, "Eureka!" and pulled out a brightly-colored kimono with a blue and white lotus design. It was long and flowing like a robe. Franny smiled, "Look, everyone, I've got a kimono."

She threw it on dramatically and raised her arms inside the dangling sleeves. Her blonde hair and the kimono were an incongruous pairing especially with her blue jeans and tee shirt underneath.

"Wow, where did you get that? They're really some fine threads," Dutch said. She touched the silk fabric and rubbed it against her cheek.

Franny continued, "This cute guy had the hots for me and promised to take me touring with his band. He gave me this. Ain't it beautiful!!! It belonged to his mother. He wanted me to have something to remember him by. A couple days later, he hit the road for Colorado."

I examined the kimono and held it up to the light.

"This is really beautiful. Very well made," I said.

I was about to ask the person's name, but Franny didn't give me a chance. "No, no," Franny remarked and shook her head. "I don't talk about him."

The kimono was probably pre-war, which meant it could have been in the owner's family for generations.

There's a story here, I thought. *Why would this fellow give Franny something so valuable? Chances are he was Japanese and I might know the boy's mother. What a coincidence that would be!*

I gave Franny a look from the corner of my eye, but decided to change the subject. In a minute everything was back to normal. The breeze began to blow through the windows and birds were chirping. The girls were chatting when I lined them up for the dance.

"Now, settle down for a minute," I said and arranged them in order. I took a position slightly in front of them and to the left. "You are dancers in a long line, so imagine that there are hundreds in front and in back of you." I assumed an upright position. "I'm your instructor, so watch and copy me. It's easy once you get the basics. Are you listening?"

Franny was still swaying her baggy sleeves back and forth. She twirled, then buried her hands deep inside her sleeves. "Sorry," she replied, "We're with you."

"You'll be moving your arms and shuffling your feet," I continued. "Remember this is a coal mining dance and we're miners. I'll hum the music. Okay?"

The room became warmer and the broken radiators hissed. I said, "Imagine you're with three hundred dancers on a cobblestone street and the line goes up the block and curves back down. "The curb is packed with spectators sitting on blankets and lawn chairs. Picture a big taiko drum the size of a large barrel, being pounded by a man in a *happi* coat and bandana, boom boom."

I imitated the loudspeaker announcer and began, "Okay dancers the next is the *Tanko Bushi*, take your places. The music blares and the drum booms," I said.

I clapped my hands once and then again. I reminded the girls that grace and rhythm were more important than precision.

"Each person moves in their own way," I said. "The motions are similar but not exactly the same. Although it's a dance, you mustn't smile." I pointed my finger and continued, "You must be serious. It's not about you. it's about the group that dances together for their ancestors. Okay, now, watch me while I do all the steps. Boom – boom."

I raised my arms up and down and the girls followed the movements. "Now dig with your shovel. Boom–boom. Throw the coal over your shoulder, then push the cart and push-push."

Dutch winked and looked at Franny and asked, "This is a dance? It feels like work. I got lost. Can you do that again?"

"Sure," I said as I went through the moves slowly.

"Once more?" Dutch pleaded.

Franny's arms and legs collided and tangled. Her face flushed pink. She imitated a ballerina and did a jump with her toes pointed and followed with a scissor kick. Dutch and I stopped and watched while Franny did pirouettes and collapsed slowly into a full lotus position.

Dutch chuckled and pulled Franny upright.

I gazed at my students and said, "Okay, get ready and follow me. Let's move through the steps again and Franny, pay attention. No more ballet." I faced north and explained, "The line will be moving in that direction. Turn this way and when the music starts, count to four and clap your hands."

After twenty minutes of instruction, I decided to quit. "Okay, girls, you did well for beginners," I said. They ignored me and continued digging with shovels.

Dutch hooted, "I can dig it, baby!"

Franny looked at Dutch, "Yeah, that's what you say! I wouldn't blame our ancestors for running away if they saw us dance. Next time I want to be the drum."

"Okay, Franny, you can be the drum, but you'll still have to dance," I said, "With some more work, we'll do just fine."

There was a softness in Franny's voice. "Thanks for teaching us. It took my mind off of my troubles. Back home, no one tried to help me like you two," she whispered.

Then Franny grinned, still poking an imaginary shovel into the ground. "We weren't that good, but anyway it was fun," she said. "I'll feel better after a sound night's sleep. This was more helpful than group. Thanks again to both of you."

Down the hall Nurse Olson announced, "Let's get moving ladies."

Franny kissed Dutch on the cheek and turned to me. My first instinct was to draw back. I hesitated for a second, then relaxed and accepted a peck on the cheek.

GUILT AND SHAME

Instead of watching television the next evening, the three of us discussed the *Tanko Bushi*. I praised them. "Good dancing yesterday." The fun in my voice faded when I remembered Franny's loss.

I turned to Franny and urged, "It's okay to remember your child."

Dutch nodded in support and I continued. "It's only natural as a mother to grieve and feel guilty."

Franny stroked her neck slowly.

"But the main thing," I said, "is that you're moving forward and not stuck. After the war, my next door neighbor died from sleeping pills and another hanged himself after they returned from Minidoka." My eyes grew misty.

"I try to forget and forgive Minidoka," I continued, "But there's no escape from the memories. They'll always be with me, like the loss of your Buddy. Franny, you must learn to live with it. In Japanese, this is *gaman*, or bearing the unbearable."

I continued, "I was going to kill myself. But all I had was a pair of scissors. I imagined poking myself in the stomach and then in the eye. Just mentioning that makes me shiver. Pills would be the best for someone like me, I decided."

"Wow," Dutch said, "In the eye? That's just too off the wall, man. You've got to be outta your tree to do that."

"Pills," Franny said, "didn't work for me."

"Our medicine cabinet didn't have much," I responded, "I was in a daze but didn't want my children to find me on the floor in the morning. Those experiences weigh heavy on the family." I cleared my throat.

"Suicide is darkness that continues," I went on. "Some of my friends did it. There is an emptiness in the families for years."

My voice broke and I paused. "No one in the Japanese community questioned it. Suicide was something we never talked about. You don't want to shame yourself or your family because people will gossip."

I slipped my hands into my blue jean pockets. "The worst one," I recalled, "was Mr. Ida, who hanged himself in their new house in Rainier Valley. His teenage daughter came home from high school, opened the garage door, and found him dead, wearing his best suit and tie. No one could understand why he did it. He was a successful businessman."

Franny nodded. "I understand shame," she blurted out. "Whether you deserve it or not, people put it on you and you have to deal with it. When I was pregnant, mothers pointed at me. I wasn't married and they knew Steve wouldn't marry me. I was an example of a bad girl."

Anger welled up in Franny when she said, "I felt guilty, but guilt is better than shame. You can wash guilt away by going to church, confessing or doing good deeds. Guilt is easy. But shame is like a cloud that follows you."

"For me, just the shame of being here is very hard," I said. "I didn't even tell my best friends."

I brushed back my hair, which had fallen over my glasses. "I worry about my youngest, Larry," I said. "His real first name is Yutaka. He's very sensitive. I would tell him over and over he was named after my grandfather, and that Yutaka means bamboo in Japanese."

I squirmed a bit, "I tell him to bend but don't break. One of these days he'll find out that Yutaka doesn't mean bamboo. I hope he doesn't think insanity runs in the family. Was it wrong to lie to him?" I asked.

"What does his name really mean?" Franny inquired.

"It means 'rich,'" I said.

"Nothing wrong with that," Franny replied.

The girls moved and found a comfortable place on the bed. This initial sharing had been one revelation after another.

I said, "It was just a little lie to help him be strong when things got rough. If I died, he would always remember being bamboo. I think it was okay."

I was staring at the brown tile floor, distracted by the patterns for a second.

"Well it was a lie," I said wistfully, "and I hope it doesn't hurt him. Both of the boys were born in Minidoka. All I remember were mounds of diapers, dust, and bad food. I had a bar of ivory soap, a scrub board, and a galvanized steel tub, nothing like today's electric washer and dryer. It seemed I was always scrubbing diapers."

I touched my lower back. The thought of doing laundry had made it ache. "After they announced that they were letting us out of camp, since we didn't have anywhere to live. So we remained as long as we could. We felt hopeless. Finally, we found housing and they gave us a train ticket and twenty-five dollars."

"That's how much they give criminals when they leave prison!" Dutch said with surprise, visibly moved by the story.

Once I had begun talking, there was no stopping. It was like a slow-moving run-away train.

I said, "We heard people were firing bullets into Japanese homes in Seattle when we were released. In Hood River, Oregon, they wouldn't even sell groceries to Japanese. So families had to leave town just to buy food. Can you imagine that?"

Franny and Dutch hung on every word as if it were another fairy tale.

I continued, "My Hood River friends, the Yamamotos, had no choice but to buy groceries out of state. Every Saturday after shopping, they drove down Main Street showing off the goods they purchased. The girls waved and smiled as if they were princesses on a parade float instead of a farm truck. Eventually the grocery people gave in.."

I cleared my throat and took a breath, "Janet, one of the Yamamoto girls, told me there was a 'Japs go home' petition circulated. The names of the people who signed were printed in the newspaper. The minister, neighbors, and even her high school teacher signed. Janet said it broke her heart to see people they knew and trusted turn on them."

"Where could you live and be safe?" Dutch asked.

"Well silly, in America," Franny replied, "Hanae has known hard times, but liberty and justice for all means exactly that. This is her country and it needs to live up to its promise."

What I had described was totally foreign and unbelievable to the girls. They couldn't understand why the government had done it, but they understood the hurt of rejection.

Franny sighed. "I'm strung out. It's been a long day and almost time for Nurse Olson to make her rounds. I'm hitting the sack early. See you in the morning."

ANGELA M. SMIT, AKA DUTCH, 1962

After dinner we gathered as usual. "In grade school," Dutch said, "the kids discovered my mother was part Cherokee. They called her a 'squaw' and threw rocks at me and my little brothers." She raised her fist and her voice shook, "Usually we outran them but one day I made up my mind not to take it anymore."

Dutch sat up with a determined look. "The two Nelson boys and their little sister ambushed us behind a vacant 76 gas station. The boys were just plain mean. You know, the kind that torture cats. But their little sister was like an angel in her white dress."

Franny and I made ourselves comfortable while Dutch began her story.

"I was fuming when they started making fun and throwing rocks," Dutch said. "I grabbed a broken window pane shard and launched it. They ducked and were scared when it crashed and shattered into a hundred sharp pieces."

Dutch flicked her wrist, imitating the motion. "I told my little brothers to get down when I picked up a heavy stick. I shrieked, 'I am Angela, Messenger of God, fear my wrath! God wants you all dead!'"

Franny and I looked at each other in amazement.

"My red hair was flying," Dutch said, "I smacked John, the oldest on the elbow. He howled and cradled his arm. Then I jumped Sara, the smallest. With one hand I threw her to the ground, dragging her by the hair. I must have been more forceful than I thought. Blood was all over her clothes. You'd thought I'd stabbed her. John and his other brother were in shock when they pulled me off. 'You killed her,' John hollered. Her brother lifted her up and said, 'Nah, she's okay. Just a bloody nose.'"

Waving an imaginary stick Dutch said, "I was a Viking spirit like a Valkyrie. My eyes were pulsating like they were going to blow."

Dutch continued as if it was actually happening, "'If you boys ever pick on us again, or any other American Indians at school, I'll break Sara's face. Do you understand? Do you want her to have a face?' The Nelsons didn't say a word but were like a bunch of whipped dogs. They backed off and ran home."

Franny and I were spellbound. This was no fairy tale, but more like an ancient myth.

"I hollered vile words at them," Dutch went on, "and I threw the stick when they reached the top of the hill." Dutch continued, "After dinner, Mrs. Nelson, Sara, and the boys knocked on our door. Mom opened it."

Dutch coughed and took a drink and growled, "Mom looked at them with daggers in her eyes and made them stand on the porch. Mrs. Nelson said, 'You need to pay for Sara's new white dress. It's ripped and blood-stained after your daughter attacked her!' Then she pulled the bloody dress out of a brown paper bag."

Dutch looked directly at both of us and pointed her finger for emphasis as she continued, "I knew Mom would stick up for me. She heard the whole story since my little brothers had told her. My mother's voice sounded like it was full of stones when she raised her voice and said, "I won't pay for anything. Your boys shouldn't call people names and throw rocks. They got what was coming to them.' Best of all, she slammed the door in Mrs. Nelson's face. Even when we were in high school, none of the Nelsons talked to us. But for sure they never threw rocks or called us names."

Franny looked askance and said, quoting Dutch, "Angela, Messenger of God and God wants you dead? Where in the world did that come from? I bet they didn't sleep for weeks with that threat hanging over their heads."

Dutch chuckled and said, "Angela is my given name and it means, 'Messenger of God.' Those kids got the message. Anyway, I didn't go by 'Angela' since there was an Angelina Smit in my class and they got us mixed up."

The air seemed fresher for the telling of Dutch's story. It was magical in the way she seemed to grow larger as she told it. Or maybe it was the violence she found herself capable of in the past that amazed us. Dutch's story drew us closer as we joined hands. It was an odd scene: an older Japanese woman in jeans, a young redhead, and a blonde in a flowing kimono linked together on the edge of a bed.

The girls made my life bearable. I thought, *When I return to Seattle, I won't have anyone to share stories and talk with.*

Maybe this was a lesson that would help me on the outside. Here, I could just talk about anything whether it was meaningful or not. That certainly would be a change: I'd be a different person, one who let life flow through without reservation. *I'll like to be more like that*, I thought.

CHAPTER FOURTEEN

Century 21 and the Cuban Missle Crisis, 1962

The next day we had free time after lunch. "Tonight," Dutch said, "we should all be in our beds when Nurse Olson comes. That would bug her since she's so used to breaking us up."

"Ha ha," Franny replied. "Okay, let's do it!"

Dutch was feeling loose and uninhibited. Her eyes sparkled when she began to tell more tales from childhood. She wiggled and pursed her lips before revealing her big secret.

"Some other bad things happened to me. Get this, I was accused of burning down a barn," she giggled and covered her mouth for a second. "You believe that? No one was injured, not even cows or chickens, but when I get mad, things happen."

She continued, "When my parents were out of town, I had a party at my house. What happened was just stupid. I caught my boy-friend, Jake, in bed with my best friend. I went freak city and started yelling at everyone. I was screaming and things were moving like flashes all around me." Dutch waved her arms and her hair flew side to side. "That's all I remember. I woke in a hay field and the neighbor's barn was burning." Dutch's eyes glowed. "I've always heard voices and they told me what to do, but not bad things. Sometimes I hear them talking through the walls. That's what I told the cops who accused me of setting the fire. But they had no proof."

I was taken aback and interjected, "I heard voices in Hiroshima when I was stuck in quicksand. I think they saved my life. We can talk about it later."

Dutch looked puzzled but continued, "The neighbors insisted that I was bad news. The police found no matches, lighter, or anything. So they were up a creek. My word against theirs." She nodded a "I told you so" look then leaned back and said, "But they charged me with disorderly conduct because I didn't have any clothes on. Can you believe that? I couldn't explain why I was naked. Anyway, my public defender said the case would go better if they thought I was temporarily insane. Dad made bail and I went home."

Dutch paced around the room and said, "The day after the fire, I was feeling pretty good. I decided to attend Sunday service at the Methodist Church and wore my best pink dress." She opened her arms like Christ on the cross and continued, "I sang the hymns and felt taken by spirits. It was like Jesus was bursting in me."

She flailed her arms and said, "So I ran out of church screaming and singing the Old Rugged Cross. I just tore my dress off and fell to my knees. I was free! The church women formed a circle around me. But I stood on the lawn and waved my arms because I saw the Virgin Mary in the clouds."

Dutch jumped up as if rejoicing. "They called an ambulance and I woke up in the emergency room. That's all I remember except feeling wonderful at church. That absolutely did it for my family. I didn't harm anyone but that situation and the fire landed me here. My parents felt safer with me away 'in care', you know, because of the fire and all."

"Holy smokes!" Franny said. "Did I say really say smokes? So what happened next?"

"Anyway, Dad said because I have scoliosis and my spine curves sixty degrees like an 'S', being under state care would be best so I could get the surgery for free," Dutch said. She looked up at the ceiling. "My parents could never afford the operation. If I don't have the surgery, the doctors said, maybe my lung will be damaged or crushed by the curvature. So far there have been no fires, I'm still breathing, and I managed to keep my clothes on." She laughed.

"All that was really nothing," Dutch said. "What happened before was worse. I never told the police because no one would believe me. It was like everyone was laughing at me and I didn't want to talk about it. So, don't ask, okay?" She stared at both of us and nodded her head up and down and asked, "Okay?"

Franny and I looked at each other and managed to say, "Okay."

Dutch walked to her dresser and pulled out a nautical chart of the Strait of Juan De Fuca and the San Juan Islands. She spread the map out on the floor. "I love charts," she exclaimed. "Just look at how cool this is.

It tells you the depths, shorelines, and all the little islands and straits. It's amazing, I could look at maps all day."

I shrugged my shoulders in surprise since Dutch's transition was so abrupt. "Okay, no problem let's look at the map," Franny said hesitantly. With a puzzled look I waited for rest of the story, which never emerged.

Dutch pored over the chart, with her nose almost against the paper. She traced the curved lines with her finger. "This curve," she said, "is what my spine looked like on an x-ray. Funny to see my spine on a map." The silence was broken by Franny since there was no telling where this conversation was going.

"Hanae," Franny said, "We should brush your hair. Where's your hair brush?"

"I think Mrs. Tester took it," I said. "Sometimes she comes around with that strange look. It's like she doesn't have a soul."

"Have you seen her husband?" Franny says. "He's one of those bald-headed overweight goofs. With someone like him, I can see why she is here."

I said, "Is there anything we can do to help that poor woman?'

The girls frowned and said nothing until Franny finally remarked, "Maybe say a prayer."

"Yes we could do that tonight," I said.

"Oh, Franny, I'm going nuts," said Dutch, "We should flee the scene and take Hanae with us. There's a small patch of corn about a mile down the road. We can sneak out, eat it raw, and party in the field. Last time we did that the orderlies found the cobs and became suspicious, remember? We lied and told them it was an art project!"

"That would be okay if there was any corn still standing this late in the season," Franny replied.

Dutch picked up a rag and began dusting. "The orderlies knew we didn't work in the corn fields, but what could they say? I mean we *are* locked up for a reason aren't we?" Dutch's face lit up. "Or if we really get bored we can sneak out and go to Three Finger Jack's Tavern. That'll be no sweat. I can pass for twenty-one. We can meet a lot of nice guys from Fort Lewis or men from McChord air base. It'd be fun."

She continued, "Last month we picked up two army soldiers who bought us drinks," Dutch said as she continued to dust the shelves. She remarked, "Around midnight we asked them to drop us off on the highway. I told them I dared Franny to spend the night in the old abandoned mental hospital wing because it's haunted." Dutch laughed and continued, "We jumped out of the car and screamed as loud as we could and kissed them goodbye. I gave my guy a French kiss, plenty of tongue.

Then we wrote phony phone numbers on their arms and hustled back to our beds."

I smiled and said, "Now Dutch, do you really think I believe that? I'm not that gullible! Sneaking out at night?" I was annoyed and shook my head. "You'd never make it past bed check and all the locked doors. Oh, you girls—what imaginations," I exclaimed. "Next thing you'll tell me is that you dug a tunnel under the fence."

I thought, *For sure they probably dream about escaping.* Even I had considered that. Nevertheless, this had to be fantasy. But if any two girls were capable of escaping just to party, however, these two could figure out how to do it.

But I still wondered about bed check. That was a question I never asked for fear they might have an answer—a response so simple that it might even be believable. I stared at the floor and pondered whether I should believe anything they said. *Are they telling tales or the truth? It must be fiction. Why in the world would they do that?*

I moved away from them and walked towards the grated window. In that instant, I began to recount everything the girls told me. *Were they liars?* A nagging feeling of betrayal emerged. Before I could carry this feeling very far, Franny gave in to the truth.

"Okay, okay Hanae," Franny said. "Enough of this baloney. We didn't escape, Dutch just made it all up. We were wrong to say what wasn't so."

Franny touched my shoulder gently. "We'll never lie to you again, promise. We just get so bored. But all we have is each other and lies come between people." Franny gripped me a little tighter. "We need to be honest with each other." She paused and said, "We can lie to the nurses, orderlies, doctors and group, but we must never lie to each other. Agreed?"

Dutch nodded in agreement. We hugged each other and were quiet for a moment. Afterwards I felt relieved. From that moment on we had a pact to be truthful with each other. Immediately after Franny's confession, everyone could feel the difference. Even the vibrations in the room seemed to have changed for the better.

"Well, Hanae," Franny said, "We may not be able to escape this week, but when visiting day comes, we'd like to meet your sons. Now, that's no lie. You know, the ones in this picture." Franny pointed to a photo on my shelf.

Dutch said, "I like the older one with the nice smile and Franny likes the cute young one."

"Oh, you girls are impossible," I said with a blush. "Alan, the eldest, lives in San Francisco, so he won't be coming."

"Man oh man," Franny said, "I wish we could have gone to the World's Fair with one of them. It's ending this month." Franny said, "I wanted to go up the Space Needle and ride the monorail. We're missing it all. Exhibits about the future, new stuff in science. Sitting here in the boonies is killing me."

Franny stretched and continued, "Good grief, the future's forty miles away and we're like a Model T stuck in the mud. They say diseases like cancer and heart attacks will be eliminated. We'll get free energy from the sun and wind. Gas won't be thirty cents a gallon and it won't cost $3.50 to fill your tank!"

"That's what I call a wonderment," replied Franny. "On top of that, in the future we'll have time-saving appliances. Life will be so easy and convenient with monorails and other wonderful ways to get around." Franny rubbed her palms together.

She said, "Maybe in the next century we'll have personal helicopters. You can talk to your house and tell it to turn up the heat. The laundry will wash and stack itself and you won't have mismatched socks. We'll have plenty of leisure time for hobbies and not mindless chores."

"Whoa," Dutch interrupted, "Hey, that leisure time, reading, and hobbies sounds like living here without the meds! In the twenty-first century everyone'll live like mental patients, but for sure they'll wear better clothes!" Dutch laughed at her own joke.

"How does that sound?" Dutch said. "Boy oh boy, that would be boss."

"On top of that," Franny continued, "President Kennedy promises we'll send a man to the moon. Holy Moly, you believe that? An American walking on the moon! And the next century is only thirty-eight years away. I can't wait."

Tapping her fingers and bouncing, Franny resumed, "I begged the doctors to take us on a field trip to the fair. It would be a once-in-a-lifetime experience." She hugged herself. "They could rope us all together like pre-school kids for all I care. I just want to go." Her voice rose, "They have water skiing shows in the stadium and the Royal Lipizzan Stallions. I love horses."

Franny touched her chin. "I read there's a stack of one million silver dollars on display. Whoa, that is so cool. The Wild Mouse ride is like a miniature roller coaster from Germany that whips around and goes up and down on tracks. What a gas!"

"I heard the best was the Centrifuge ride," Dutch said, "You go into this big cylinder and it spins. The force plasters you up against the inside wall." Dutch spread her arms out like an angel. "The bottom drops out and wallets and glasses go flying and you're held fast. Then your skirt slides up so you better wear clean underwear. Boy, that would ruin your big date. But anyway I really think the fair would be so fab. I can't wait for the next century."

"I wish I could be there with you in the next century," I said. "I'd be in my late seventies and probably won't make it."

My eyes lit up when I said, "You lucky girls have bright futures. I don't know what I'll do when I get out." I adjusted my glasses, "You can go to college and be anything you want. I don't have any real skills."

I felt old and tired. "When I was your age I worked at a produce stand and later sewed projects at home. Maybe I could get a job in a clothing factory. Some of my friends at church work in garment factories. That would be the best I can hope for. But you girls have opportunities. The twenty-first century sounds great."

Dutch's eyes brightened. "Don't worry, Hanae, the state vocational rehab program will get you training. That's what they do. But I have a great idea!" Dutch continued, "Since Hanae may not be around next century, we should meet at the top of the Space Needle, like the movie where Cary Grant agrees to meet a woman at the Empire State Building."

Dutch fidgeted. "The woman never made it because of an auto wreck and the two went their separate ways not knowing what happened. It was so romantic and tragic. We should meet at the top of the Needle in the future since we missed the World's Fair.

Franny jumped up, "That would be fun," she said. "How about Saint Paddy's Day 1970, at noon? We should all be out and be married with children by then. We'll have a lot to talk about."

Dutch interjected, "Yeah, that's a day we can all remember. But we should come alone—no family or friends. Just a reunion for us. What do you think? Yipee!"

"Oh, oh", Franny said as she snapped her fingers. "I've got it," she remarked, "It was Deborah Kerr. She played the woman in the movie *An Affair to Remember* with Cary Grant. It was a great movie."

"You're such a brain," Dutch said. "Are you sure about the movie, or are you kidding? How do you know all these things?"

"I'm sure as the nose on my face," Franny said.

I considered the reunion and thought to myself, *Right now I'm with girls who are my closest friends. But will we have anything in common years from now? What will we say to each other?* Then the thought struck me, *Who cares? It'll be fun and something to look forward to.*

CUBAN MISSILE CRISIS, OCTOBER 16TH-26TH -1962

It was almost dinner time when the wind picked up and rattled the window grates. The lights flickered after we agreed on the Space Needle reunion. Suddenly the radio was silent. Franny walked towards the Motorola and before she could turn the dials, a news flash blared.

We interrupt this transmission to present an important news announcement.

At 7:00 pm Eastern Standard Time President Kennedy authorized a blockade of Cuba in response to the construction of Russian nuclear missile bases just 90 miles from American soil.

Voice of President Kennedy: Good Evening, My Fellow Citizens:

This government, as promised, has maintained the closest surveillance of the Soviet military buildup on the island of Cuba. Within the past week, unmistakable evidence has established the fact that a series of offensive missile sites is now in preparation on that imprisoned island. The purpose of these bases can be none other than to provide a nuclear strike capability against the Western Hemisphere....

Our goal is not the victory of might, but the vindication of right -- not peace at the expense of freedom, but both peace and freedom, here in this hemisphere, and we hope, around the world. God willing, that goal will be achieved.

Thank you and good night.

The DJ came on, "This is Pat O'Malley back on the air. Stay tuned— during this crisis we'll interrupt our regular programming when news breaks. In the meantime, the station management requested ten seconds of silence."

Silence ensued.

O'Malley continued, "It's half past the hour and time to spin some platters. We want to play this real golden oldie to remind us what a great country we live in."

God bless America
Land that I love
Stand beside her, and guide her
Thru the night with a light from above.
From the mountains, to the prairies,
To the oceans, white with foam
God bless America, my home sweet home."

I turned off the radio. There was an eerie parallel between Kennedy's speech and Franklin Roosevelt's 1941 declaration of war.

The girls looked at each other in shock. "Holy Cow! Is this the end of the world? Hanae, turn the radio back on will you?" Dutch asked.

Franny rubbed her chin and replied, "Don't know and maybe."

I stared down at the floor and my voice shook. "I know Hiroshima and the atomic bomb. I grew up there and our family home was near ground zero. The fire, radiation, and blast destroyed almost everything. I lost friends and cousins," I recalled. Then I took a breath and turned the radio back on. I exhaled and said, "Many of my relatives were never found. Ironically, I was lucky to be in Minidoka instead of Hiroshima."

My voice faltered as I continued, "But the Japanese houses couldn't withstand the fire-bombing in Tokyo or the atomic bomb. The blast destroyed our home completely. My teenage cousin, Akiko, was home at the time. It was a miracle that she lived. They said the house fell on her and saved her."

Dutch interrupted the story. She asked, "How did that save her?"

I blinked and rubbed my eye. "Akiko was burned, but no one would speak about it," I replied. "If you were a woman and survived the bomb, there was fear that no one would marry you because you might carry disease. So the family never talked about it."

Dutch and Franny exchanged glances. "This Cuban thing could be another Hiroshima. My head is spinning," Dutch said.

I continued, "Some of my friends and relatives were gone but others survived in the countryside," I said. "People on the way to work, at school, or at home, just vanished. One instant you were brewing tea and the next...." I paused. "No one could find a trace of you."

I took a deep breath and explained, "My cousins said that there were so many dead they just had to walk over them instead of around them. It was karma. It was a bad time to be Japanese. In America we were in prison and in Japan they were bombed."

Dutch and Franny hugged themselves tightly. They looked like two dolls sitting upright, waiting for the next wave of bad news.

"Many died in Hiroshima," I continued as my voice broke. "More suffered from the radiation burns and a lack of medical help."

The room felt colder and the tile floor patterns seemed to swirl slowly. Franny and Dutch furrowed their brows and leaned forward as they listened to each word.

I sobbed for a moment and then resumed, "For weeks we didn't know what had happened to our relatives. The news was slow and no one knew what an atomic bomb was and what it would do to paper houses."

I relived my loss with each word. Then I cleared my throat and said, "Fumi, my sister-in-law and her housekeeper, Masa, were never found. For weeks we didn't know what had happened to the others until my uncle Yosh told us Fumi's son was safe in the country and Akiko survived." I rose from the edge of my bed and looked down at my slippers.

"Akiko, my cousin, suffered burns all over her body. All the hospital beds were full and there was a shortage of medicine. It must have been difficult." My voice quivered and I took a sip of water to clear my throat.

"The Japanese government was helpless and the Hiroshima people had no choice but to take care of themselves," I sighed and said. "Today, even after all these years, they have a real spirit of world peace because of the bomb. They also have a strong belief in themselves since no one helped them rebuild."

Dutch's face drooped. She came to me and threw an arm over my shoulder and said, "Nothing like that's ever happened in America. A few hurricanes, tornados, and earthquakes, but nothing where a whole modern city is wiped out. I'm so sorry about your family. What did you think when you heard the news?"

I blew my nose and wiped my eyes. "In Minidoka there were many people from Hiroshima. We had to wait weeks to find out if relatives had survived. When we got bad news, it hit us hard. But everything seemed so far away," I said. "It was too much to comprehend. We just couldn't understand."

I continued, "The Buddhist priests created memorials in the Block 30 Canteen, which also served as an information center." I caught my breath. "People would gather and exchange news about friends and relatives. Everyone felt helpless. Most could not imagine the complete destruction of a city they knew. Every place they remembered was destroyed and many of their friends were gone in an instant." I twisted my hands. "Many camp residents just didn't say a word, as if nothing had happened. It was *shikataganai*, it can't be helped. Others denied that the bomb had been dropped and that Japan would still win the war."

The girls seemed to feel the grief as if it was their own. The story carried a heavy cargo of loss, something that they had never experienced. Neither of them, however, were familiar with Hiroshima. Nor had they ever met anyone who had relatives there before.

"We held our sadness and emotions inside," I said. "All we could say was, *gaman*, or bear the unbearable."

My breathing grew shallow as I confessed, "The uncertainty was something we all endured. Being in Minidoka helped because we were among friends. But our everyday routines became harder and harder. News was sporadic and unreliable. People didn't know what to believe. Some of the old Japanese men continued to say that the US government was not telling us the truth."

I swallowed hard. "The war was ending and there were rumors every day. No one on the outside wanted to hear our problems. Eleanor Roosevelt visited some camps and the government showed pictures of happy Japanese! What a lie."

I grimaced. "Many *hakujin*, or white people, were not sympathetic." I stopped to choose my words carefully. "After Pearl Harbor, we were the enemy; even white children thought so. For years after the war, they would say, 'Remember Pearl Harbor' when they saw us."

I paused and fingered the bed sheet and continued, "But in Hiroshima the victims were old men, women, and children—not soldiers. Japanese soldiers are prepared to die, but not the children. What did those civilians do to deserve such a horrible death and suffering?"

"I was so angry," I said. "But what could we do? When we finally returned to Seattle we had so little money. We feared that our cousins might be starving, and we had so little to give."

Dutch touched my shoulder and draped her arm around me. Franny lowered her head as if in prayer.

I continued, "Kiyoshi made a list of every relative and put it up on the refrigerator and we waited to learn what had happened to each and every one."

Fighting tears, I said, "I can't tell you how heartbreaking it was to draw a line through a name, especially a child's."

I paused and pulled out a Kleenex. "After we left the camp, my parents visited the Buddhist Church and said prayers every week. They lit incense for the dead and survivors for months."

I wiped my eyes on my sleeve and said, "Finally Dad got a letter from my cousin Isao, who was in the Hiroshima countryside. By then we were in Seattle and I collected money from all of my US relatives. I went shopping at Goodwill and bought underwear, socks, shirts, and jackets to send."

"At Safeway we bought canned coffee, tea, and candy for relatives." I paused and took another sip of water. "I remember the first time I shopped at Goodwill. I was so ashamed to buy used clothes. I wanted to tell the clerk that it was for Hiroshima, not me. Not that they cared, but that would have made me feel better."

I adjusted my glasses and closed my eyes. "The Japanese Presbyterian Church started a fund for Hiroshima and Nagasaki. But most people gave to their relatives, especially those who had spent time in Hiroshima."

"I bought second-hand clothes every month," I said and ticked off the relatives who contributed with my fingers. "My brothers sent money – Shizuo worked for the CIA in Washington DC, Henry for Dell Comics in New York, Tom for J. Walter Thompson in New York, Bob was with the Berkley Book Store, and Kenji at Anderson Dam," I continued. Feeling tired, I put down the glass of water. I kept adjusting it until Franny spoke.

"Wow," she exclaimed, "That's unbelievable. If we were bombed here, none of my relatives would help. We'd be on our own. Since we're here, what will happen to us?"

"Man oh man, this is really scary," Dutch said. "I never thought about it."

I waved my hand back and forth, "The Hiroshima relatives didn't want money even though we sent some," I said, "but asked for things they could trade on the black market." My voice shook. "They lived in shacks made of whatever they could scavenge."

I covered my mouth for a second. "Every month I sent packages to my Uncle Yosh. Later they said the packages saved their lives. Can you imagine that? Also we heard that the bomb was so intense that the river boiled away."

Dutch jumped up. "The river boiled away?" She repeated.

"Imagine being there," Franny said as she grabbed a Kleenex and blew her nose. She waited a second and smiled sheepishly at the interruption.

"Hiroshima and Nagasaki people worried for years about passing on illnesses to their babies," I remarked, "Families would examine every one of their children in hopes that nothing strange would come from the radiation."

I shook my head. "That's what 'atomic war' means. It's living in fear of eating radioactive fruit, fish, and meat and drinking contaminated water. You wonder whether you ate or touched something that would curse you or your family forever." I lowered my gaze and said, "It's the fear you pass on to your children."

"I didn't realize how bad it was," said Franny. She put her arm around me and pulled tight. "Bad doesn't even begin to cover it."

"Hanae, how did you make it with your own babies, resettlement after the war, and relatives in Japan?" Dutch inquired. "How could you wake up every morning and face all that?"

In a monotone I replied, "I don't know how we made it through. We felt it was our fate and we had no choice but to endure."

I scratched my head and said, "Maybe," I said, after considering a way to explain it "The sad Japanese fairy tales like *Urashima Taro* prepared us."

I continued, "But if atomic war comes to America, we need to go home. Dutch, if you don't want to go back up north, you come with me."

The girls had blank faces. "I almost don't know what to say," Franny said. "I can't believe what happened to you."

Dutch spoke and gritted her teeth. "I worry about my little brother and sister up north near the Canadian border," she said.

Franny shook her head. "Too many things to think about," she said. "My family and dog Cookie could be gone in an instant. We just can't sit by. There must be something we can do. I don't want to be helpless, and what of my baby Buddy?"

Nurse Miller entered. Politely she asked the girls to leave. "Hanae has an appointment with Dr. Hansen before dinner," she explained.

The girls got up. "Yeah, Dutch, we need to do something. I can't remember what's on the schedule before dinner," Franny said.

Dutch reassured me, "We'll check out the news in the rec room and tell you the latest."

The girls hugged me and said, "We love you."

"Yes, me too," I said, taking their hands and squeezing hard. Then the girls pushed the curtains open and were gone. Nurse Miller took my arm and escorted me to the doctor's office.

CHAPTER FIFTEEN

The Atomic Bomb, 1962

Doctor Hansen's office was a compact space overlooking the rose garden. The room overflowed with rich odors: a stuffed leather chair, orchid plant, and a pipe in a cut glass ashtray. There was a framed family picture with a palm tree and coconut design placed in the center of the oak desk. In the picture, the doctor, his wife and two young sons wore floral leis and aloha shirts. They stood barefoot on a sandy beach.

Hansen seemed taller in real life than in the photo and slightly older. He wore a white smock with a stethoscope and spoke in a slow, deliberate manner with a faint southern accent. He put down a medical file and removed his tortoiseshell glasses.

"Hello, Mrs. Hanna, my name is Dr. Terrance Hansen, and I have come onto your team. This is just a social call to ask a few questions and do a quick exam. Is it Hanna?"

I shook my head and said, "Not Hanna but Hanae—Ha-na-eh." He moved closer and said "Okay" and established eye contact. "I just want to check a couple of things to make sure everything is up to date. First of all, I hope you feel welcome here. We have a long history of good work. I've seen a lot of changes since 1935 when I first started."

He picked up an unlit pipe and chewed the end. "For many years, people with your condition were thought to be incurable. Our job then was to build communities and provide patients an ongoing life within hospital confines. But that has changed. Now we try to get people back to their lives as soon as possible."

Dr. Hansen took a deep breath and sighed. "We used to have Kiwanis carnivals, harvest festivals, and farm animals like cows. I lived in one of the bungalows with my family and I would play golf on the campus course. It was a good life for my patients and my family."

By his manner, Hansen seemed oblivious to President Kennedy's speech and fears of impending doom. His life was predictable. Things were orderly and well-managed, like the manicured front lawn.

"World War II changed everything," Dr. Hansen said. He placed the pipe in the ashtray and knocked the ashes out with a flick of the wrist. "Many of the other doctors left and joined the military, taking their families. It was a sad time," Hansen said, shaking his head.

"It became difficult to support our patients. But our people stepped up and some patients even volunteered and packed goods for the Red Cross." Hansen smiled and looked out the window. "They picked beans and other crops on the neighboring farms because of the labor shortage. After the war, most of the doctors didn't return. It really was a loss. But I still try to keep in touch."

I listened politely but was preoccupied with thoughts of the Cuban crisis. My mind visualized images of my children, husband, and home in flames. I fidgeted and tapped my feet to calm down. On the edge of panic, I felt like jumping out of the chair and escaping to Seattle. But I had no money or transportation, so I had no choice. I wondered if we would be evacuated and where we would go if Russia attacked.

Dr. Hansen continued slowly, which only contributed to my distress, "But with the advent of new drugs and techniques, many more of our residents are going back home. Do you know Violet Foster, the movie star?"

My eyes brightened and I nodded. "She was one of our patients," Hansen said. "She was here for five years and I was on the team that treated her. She was released in 1955 and went back to the Midwest to be a successful show business person. Anyway, I have a picture of her with me at the recreation center. She was a true beauty."

He opened a drawer and took out a photo where he wore a straw hat and was strumming a ukelele.

I recalled Franny's conversation about a famous movie star who'd had a lobotomy and was released. This was something Hansen knew but did not share.

His words were soft and clear as they flowed toward me. Maybe he'd given this speech a thousand times and his mind was elsewhere.

Dr. Hansen sat up straight, "Oh, enough about the past. Hanna, how are we doing today?"

He looked at me and meticulously cleaned his glasses with a tissue.

"My name is Hanae, not Hanna. It's Japanese," I said.

"Okay, Hanae, I can pronounce that. Thanks for reminding me. Now let's see, according to the chart you were born in Seattle. Is that right?" he asked.

"Yes, Swedish Hospital on Capitol Hill," I said and nodded.

"Tell me more about yourself, won't you?" Dr. Hansen coaxed.

I decided to tell him briefly about my experiences so I could get back to my bed and prepare for the potential atom bombing.

After I told him my past, he replied, "You've had quite a life." He adjusted his glasses and said, "Let's begin the exam. Nothing to be nervous about. It's routine. Right now I just want to check your heart and see how you're doing."

Hansen rubbed the stethoscope on his sleeve to warm it. "This might be a little cold," he said, "Please loosen your shirt. Take a deep breath." Then he moved the stethoscope carefully to check my heart. "Strong heart," he said. "Everything looks good. Have you taken your medications today?"

My voice was shaking, "I took two pink pills with water and later drank a cup of coffee."

"That's wonderful," Hansen replied. "I'm going to check your pulse. He placed his fingers on my wrist. "Your vitals are normal. That's good. I see you spent some time in the World War II Relocation Center in— how do you pronounce it—Minnie doka?"

I was nervous and responded, "Yes, it was the Minidoka War Relocation Center in Idaho but it was forty miles away from Minidoka. My son's birth certificate says Hunt, Idaho, but actually it was near Eden, Idaho."

Hansen lifted his pipe and tapped it in the ashtray. "It must have been a very difficult time. I see you have two children. Both boys were born in Minidoka, one in 1942 and one in 1945."

I continued, "I remember the hard conditions and bad food. I hope you don't serve Vienna sausage. It gave the whole camp dysentery."

Hansen laughed. "No Vienna sausages here. We hope our food is to your liking. In fact, I don't believe I've ever eaten Vienna sausages. I like all kinds of foods including sukiyaki and chow mein but I don't eat much canned meat."

"Would you do me a favor, Doctor?" I perked up and asked. "Would you ask the cafeteria to cook rice sometime? I'd really like Japanese rice, but anything, even Uncle Ben's, would do."

Dr. Hansen smiled and jotted down a note. "I'll do that. Sometimes I eat here in the evenings. A little white rice would be a welcome change. Anything else?"

I relaxed and said, "This place is like Minidoka. I have dividers for a wall, eat in a cafeteria, and I can't leave the grounds. But in Minidoka I did diapers by hand constantly. Here I don't take care of my kids, cook, wash, iron, or mop the floors. Instead I take my medicine, watch TV, read magazines, take art classes, go for a walk, and talk with my friends. I met some nice girls."

"Well, that's good," Hansen smiled. "You seem to be adjusting. But I want to check on something. Do you know why you're here?"

I looked up at the office wall covered with diplomas, degrees, and awards. Hansen was well-accomplished and I felt insecure in his presence.

I tightened up and said, "Depression was what they said. I began to think I would never be normal again. I lost hope and thought about dying. I told my sister-in-law and she got upset and told Kiyoshi, my husband. The family thought I would hurt myself so they sent me here." I rubbed my neck and said, "People back home call this place the crazy house."

Hansen chewed the unlit pipe stem. He nodded and smiled, "This is a hospital, Hanae. I think we can help you. We've helped many people in your situation. But it's important that you want to get well." He paused and leaned forward. "You want to get well, don't you?"

I nodded and adjusted my glasses. "My children need me, so I must get well. We don't live a high-tone life. We have a one-bedroom apartment on Beacon Hill."

Hansen picked up a lighter for his Meerschaum pipe. "Do you mind?" he asked, motioning to his pipe.

I nodded approval and scooted my chair a small distance back since I hated cigarette smoke. But I didn't have much experience with pipes.

Hansen took a puff and said, "Well, that's one good thing about us. You have all the time you need to get well here. We keep you on a pretty tight schedule." A cloud of blue smoke rose. "You can just concentrate on getting better. In the future I want to talk more about how you felt when the government took you away during the war."

He leaned back and turned his head slightly to the side. "Do you hold hard feelings about the incarceration? We need to work those things out so you don't hold them inside." He took a puff and a small cloud rose. "Does that make sense?"

His kind manner and sweet smoke made me feel safe. I began to open up. But I was afraid to share my true feelings and changed the subject.

I said, "Three of my friends committed suicide recently. I went to their funerals at the Buddhist Church and visited their graves. I felt sick when I saw my friend Doris cremated at Butterworths. It was a hot summer evening for her funeral, and the auditorium was full and stuffy."

Recounting the story, I took short breaths, almost like breathing in a hot room. "Doris became a Lutheran and left the Presbyterian Church before she died. The white minister said kind words but you could tell that he didn't really know her."

I dropped my shoulders to relieve tension and said, "She worked in a garment factory. You have to be fast to earn a living doing piecework. The pace is nerve-racking. As I stared at her thin body, I wondered how she managed to do that job for so many years."

I tapped my feet, which were beginning to fall asleep. "I'd talked to her a week before she committed suicide. She seemed okay. She had a son and daughter and had divorced her husband; it's really unusual for a Japanese to divorce. I think her husband used to beat her." I coughed and cleared my throat from the smoke. "Some Japanese men do that. But my husband is okay."

"That's too bad about your friends," the doctor said. "Three is a lot to lose. You must have grieved a long time. I wish we could have helped your friends. It's a shame. But I'm happy you are here. We'll get you well, so don't worry."

Changing the subject, I said, "The other night I dreamed I was back in Minidoka and eight months pregnant. There, I used to listen to music from Chicago's Crystal Ballroom every night before bed. Sometimes I'd walk outside with my baby in my tummy and imagine being in Chicago. I'd dance under the moon next to the barbed wire, listening to Tommy Dorsey." I placed my hands on my stomach, remembering.

"It was Sinatra, Crosby, and the Dorsey brothers back then," I said. "My favorites were Judy Garland and Mickey Rooney. In those days you could understand what they were saying in songs. The music now—*Ooo Wa Ooo Wa*. What does that mean?"

Hansen jotted some notes and puffed his pipe. The fragrant smoke hung like a mist. "Today's music is really something," he replied. "I don't understand it either. But that's the least of your worries. Lord knows you've had some incredibly difficult times."

I pulled my lips tight and frowned. "Our Hiroshima family lived close to ground zero, near the dome and park. After the bomb we sent packages and things to help the survivors."

Hansen looked over his glasses and said, "I can't imagine living through that. It must have been a horrifying experience. I've seen the photographs. Once I saw a newsreel of disfigured Hiroshima maidens coming to America to have surgery."

I replied, "The Japanese government was unable to assist survivors. I spent some years growing up in Hiroshima so I knew all my relatives and the city, too. If I'd gotten along better with my brother's wife, I might have stayed there and not returned to Seattle. I could have married, had kids, and been bombed."

"Ironic," Hansen said, "I guess you were lucky to be in Minidoka and not Hiroshima. That's a terrible thing to say, but at least you're alive and healthy. I assume you found a place to live back home in Seattle."

"Yes, we did," I replied and fidgeted. "I think about Minidoka all the time. Sometimes I dream soldiers are taking us again. I can't see their faces, only their rifles and bayonets. I also worry about atomic bombs falling on Seattle. Right now I think the Russians will bomb the Boeing Aircraft Company." I paused and said, "By the way, can I ask a favor? Just a few minutes ago I heard President Kennedy's speech. There could be a war with Russia. Do you know if it's going to happen?"

Hansen acknowledged the story with a nod, but gave no sign of concern about imminent possibilities of war.

"If there's an atomic war with Russia," I asked, "Can I go home?"

Hansen had a puzzled look and said, "I don't know. It's still early and the US and the Russians are talking, which is a good sign."

"If it did happen, would you send me home?" I asked. "I'd want to go home to my son and husband. My family will need me. If it's anything like Hiroshima." I remembered that Fumi's son, Ichiro, was in the country with Yosh and survived. "You know," I said, "We're in the country and probably will be okay, but Seattle might be destroyed."

Hansen's voice was firm when he said, "If America is attacked and there is atomic war, I'll make sure that you get reunited with your family. You have my word on it."

"It's a long way to Seattle," I replied. "Are you sure?"

"Don't worry," he replied, "You can count on me. My in-laws are in Seattle, so I would want to go there."

I bowed my head and said, "Thank you so very much. You're a good doctor. Also, would you make sure the girls, my friends, get home? You know Franny and Dutch, my roommates? I think they might want to come home with me, so I hope you have room."

"Sure that would be okay. I have a small camping trailer with plenty of room. Now we have that settled," he said, "Just relax." He checked his watch and said, "I have a little time to discuss your situation more today." Hansen picked up his pipe and said, "Make yourself comfortable and tell me more. Start where you like, but most people start with their childhood. Close your eyes, your eyelids are feeling heavy, and let your mind to drift."

I reclined on the couch. "Where are you?" Hansen asked.

"I am a child looking at a mirror in Seattle. My parents just told me that they are sending me to Hiroshima," I replied.

ELECTRIC SHOCK

The next day I was rocking slowly after a treatment. I held my chair tight. It was before noon when Franny entered from her kitchen job. She threw her apron on the bed. Dutch clomped in with her heavy work boots.

"Pumpkins and more pumpkins," Dutch sighed, "I close my eyes and what do I see? Pumpkins."

"Hey Hanae, what happened? You look all torn up," Dutch said.

I mumbled in Japanese. The only words the girls could make out were *haji*, which meant shame and *bachi ga atatta*, or that the universe was punishing me.

"Hello," Franny said. Then she looked at me carefully and asked, "Hey, hey, you there?" Then it dawned on Franny. She grabbed me and asked, "What did they do to you?" She covered her mouth, "Oh no!" she said and shook me. "Did they shock you? Dutch come here quick!"

The girls surrounded me and rubbed my shoulders and arms as if to warm me.

I was tired and felt like a crumpled marionette without strings.

Dutch waved her hands in front of my face back and forth quickly. She asked, "They hooked electrodes to your head, didn't they?"

My speech was slurred as I searched for the words. "Electricity," I said. "They attached things to my head. I twitched and jumped like I put my fingers in an electrical plug. They asked me something but I don't remember what."

"You'll be fine, don't worry," Franny said. "Dutch and I had that done."

"I think I'm okay," I replied, "but I saw a Japanese girl there. Maybe a student nurse," I continued. "She had a striped uniform and looked like a doll. Her hair was straight with bangs. I felt so ashamed that she saw me. That girl might know my family and tell others in the community about my shame. I don't want to see her again."

I paused for a few seconds and continued, "There were machines that looked like radios with big dials. That's all I remember except they told me, 'Don't be afraid.' I woke up wondering what had happened. I was confused and my neck and back were sore. The floor tiles were spinning. I was sick to my stomach."

"Yeah, Hanae," Franny, replied, "they did that to me too. You'll have convulsions and spasms when that juice hits you." Franny made a fist and held it tight. She said, "I was so mad. I swear it scrambled my brains like mush. Most of the time it wears off in a couple of hours, but it's still creepy to have so much voltage running through you."

Dutch chimed in, "You'll get over it. After my treatment, I forgot simple stuff like where I put my coin purse. Thank goodness I have nothing of value." Dutch ran her fingers through her hair and rubbed her scalp and continued, "It was like one of those science fiction shows where aliens take over your body."

Franny interrupted, "Hanae, they'll do it a couple more times. When you get back to normal you need to start acting happy and not depressed. Otherwise they'll keep doing it, and heaven only knows what really happens then."

"The electricity gets to parts of your brain that drugs can't reach," Dutch grimaced and added, "I swear it must have gotten into the prehistoric part. I had a craving for rare meat." Dutch shook and her red hair flew. "Imagine that, and good luck finding rare meat around here. I think they boil everything. Man oh man, after those electrical jolts, one thing for sure is that I won't be going to church and tearing off my clothes again."

I nodded, but nothing fully registered about what they were saying. Pulling myself together, I pushed my hair back with my right hand. "What's for dinner today? Have we already had lunch?" The girls wrapped me in a blanket and tucked me into bed.

"You need to rest for a while and we'll check on you later. You'll be okay," Dutch reassured me. "We'll take you to lunch so don't worry. Also it's meatloaf tonight for dinner."

I nodded, then closed my eyes.

Franny turned to Dutch and said, "It would be great if the treatment took away bad memories and left only the good. Then all that high voltage crap might be worth it."

Franny looked at me bundled in blankets. "Hanae, we'll teach you how to act happy. You know, some of those meds make you more depressed, so you have to watch it."

"Damn it," Franny asked, "Why didn't we warn Hanae about the electric shock? What were we thinking? I mean we're not rookies! We should've known. I'm going to talk to Dr. Hansen at group and tell him that they shouldn't have a Japanese nurse at Hanae's next session."

"Oh, I'm ticked off," Franny said. As she talked, she became angrier and stomped the floor and threw some Life magazines. She continued,

"I'm so tired of people telling us what to do, eat, sleep, work, and take your meds." Franny yelled, "We aren't stupid. It wasn't right to wire her up in front of that Japanese girl."

"Nurse," she called. "I need to talk to Hansen now!"

Dutch grabbed Franny and said," Get a grip or you'll make things worse."

My eyes were cloudy but I whispered, "Franny, I'll tell the doctor. Don't get into trouble because of me."

CHAPTER SIXTEEN

Dutch, 1962

Radio music filled the rooms as usual in the morning when I got up. There was a rustle at the curtains and Dutch and Franny peeked in.

Franny waved a brown hair brush in her right hand. "This one is an extra, you can have it until you find yours," she said with a grin.

I smiled, "Thanks. Oh, good news I forgot to tell you. Dr. Hansen said if the Russians bomb America, I can go home. You two could go home too or come with me."

The girls looked at each other.

"What if we can't make it out of here?" Franny asked. She put her hand over her forehead and said, "I was watching TV and the Russians don't want to remove the missiles. It could be curtains for all of us." Franny ran her fingers through her hair and twisted strands randomly and continued, "I was thinking some of these poor patients wouldn't know what hit them. Ignorance can be a real blessing."

"The end of the world is just too much," said Dutch. "We don't need to be sad. I've got a better idea!"

"Not again," Franny and I moaned in unison.

"No, no, listen." Dutch urged. Her eyes glowed and she waved her hands vigorously. "This is a good one. We could have an *End of the World* party!" Her voice brimmed with enthusiasm.

Dutch said. "I saw a movie where this huge meteor was heading towards earth. She wiggled and continued, "People went out to fancy dinners and spent a lot of money."

"Ha ha," Dutch laughed, "The governments wanted to avoid panic so it downplayed the danger. The public is always stupid and easily panicked in the movies, you know." She crossed her arms and gripped tight. "Hey, what's the difference, panic or no panic if we're all going to die? Anyway, this businessman in the movie lit his cigarette with a one hundred-dollar bill to impress his date. Not to be outdone, the other guy wrote a million dollar check and lit his cigar."

"Okay, I get it," Franny said sarcastically. "So you want us to write million dollar checks and light up cigars? Is that it?" Franny raised her hands straight up in the air in mock celebration.

"Can't you be serious?" Dutch chided. "We can go out in style."

"Oh, Dutch, I'm sorry to rain on your flaming parade," Franny said, "but I've got better things to do."

"Yeah, yeah," Dutch answered, "and what do you think will happen after you buy the big one?"

"I used to be Buddhist and now I'm Presbyterian," I replied softly. "I hope to go to heaven but all my ancestors are Buddhist as is Kiyoshi. My kids are Christians so I don't worry about them."

"Well, this may surprise you, but I was a Methodist," replied Franny with a sunny smile. "But now I'm a Buddhist. Those Christians treated me like dirt." Franny twisted her face and continued, "So when I die I'll reincarnate and come back." Her eyes brightened when she said, "I know what I want on my tombstone: *Franny S. Fox: she was a good Buddhist—now off to a better life.*"

"I don't believe in anything," Dutch said in a serious tone, "When I die, that's the end. I'm going to be just nothing, no sweat." She put her fingers together and opened them like a magician and said, "Poof." I don't like churches and I don't like religion. I told you about the last time I was in church.

I joined the conversation and said, "I talked to a friend who was the son of a Buddhist priest, whose father, grandfather and great-grandfather were all Buddhist priests. Christians said he was going to hell because he didn't believe in God. He said he wasn't going to hell. You know why?"

The two girls perked up. They shared a glance and put their arms around each other. They leaned together in anticipation like twins.

Mimicking the son of the priest, I pointed to myself for emphasis and said, "I'm not going to hell because I don't believe in it!"

"Wow! Absolutely cool." Dutch whooped, "Ooh ooh, I like that. When you die, you go to where you believe. That's out of sight! So Hanae, you'll go to heaven, Franny will be reincarnated, and I'll just disappear!"

Dutch continued, "I love it. But that just makes my head hurt. So if I believe I'll become a flower, I will become a flower. Oh, that is so boss! After that, what would I be? I won't have any brains to imagine what's next."

"Oh, I got it," Dutch said, as she jumped up like a child. "That's when I become nothing. Like my friend Tony used to say, *No brains, no headaches.*" She paused, then remarked quizzically, "But what happens to Zoroastrians?"

"Dutch, you don't give a hoot about Zoroastrians and their obscure religion, and you know it," Franny said.

"Anyway, the way you're talking, Dutch, you don't need to become a brainless flower as a middle step, you can just go straight to nothingness," Franny laughed.

"Ouch that hurt," Dutch said as she crumpled over.

Franny continued, "Maybe you'd be better off if you started planning our *End of the World* party rather than worry about your afterlife. Better yet, why don't you just return home if the bomb drops. That would be like going to hell."

Dutch squinted and pushed her glasses back up the bridge of her nose. She said, "The only way I'll go back to Baker Hills is if everyone in town is dead, especially the high school wrestling and football teams. If I were Urashima Taro and found all the trees grown and all my friends dead, that would be fine."

"I told you," Dutch explained, "I was here to get surgery for my back. But the real reason was to get away. I never told you the whole story. But here goes." Dutch twirled her arms and jumped up. "One night my parents were out of town in Vegas, gambling. They were celebrating their 25th anniversary. Jake, my boyfriend, and three of his jock friends and two girls came over."

Franny turned to me and said, "I think we already heard this part."

I smiled in agreement.

Dutch squinted her eyes and continued, "I popped corn and put on a record. We danced and turned the lights down. Someone lit a cigar and cranked up the music. The whole house took on a smoky and noisy atmosphere."

Dutch twisted her lips and as if deep in thought. Then she raised her eyebrows and said, "Well who cares? Who am I trying to protect? I'll let it all hang out." She continued, "At the party the group began to split up and head for dark corners. That's when Jake started flirting and tickling my best friend, Ellen."

Dutch snarled, "I stormed off and held Tobey my cat. I was really ticked off." She paused and made a sour look and said, "Jake's goofy football player friends, Tom and Craig, opened my bedroom and told me to join the party."

Dutch tapped her feet and said, "They came closer and grabbed my arm and pulled hard. They yanked Tobey's tail and he jumped. I struggled and managed to free one leg and kicked Tom in the face. He hollered and held his chin. Just then I smelled their beer breath when Craig started kissing my neck." Dutch winced in disgust.

Her face flushed when she continued, "He was attempting to give me hickeys and planted a big one right on my forehead. I screamed for Jake, but he never came. Tom held my neck in a wrestling hold like this." Dutch motioned a headlock grip.

Franny said, "It was probably the 'sleeper.' It cuts off blood to your brain so you'll pass out."

Dutch continued, "I didn't pass out and Tom unbuttoned my shirt and tugged it off." I was screaming mad. He twirled it around his head like a cowboy and hollered something like *ride'm little doggies!*" Dutch twirled her arm like a lasso and continued, "I saw red and tried to scratch his eyes out. But he kept tearing at me. I could feel his big nasty chest. Then Craig squeezed my neck and everything went black."

Dutch shook her head as if she was clearing cobwebs, "I had never blacked out like that in my whole life. When I came to, I was groggy. This time Craig was hurting me. Tom held me down. I screamed as loud as I could but Jake never came." She blew her nose and resumed, "I started crying. My shirt was torn and my glasses bent out of shape. I called them perverts and screamed, 'I'm not some dumb farm animal.'"

Dutch paused and continued, "They laughed and said, 'It was all in fun and no harm done.' I threw a beer can at them and stormed into my parent's bedroom."

Dutch tapped her fingers nervously and said, "I found Jake with my best friend in bed. He was smiling with a huge grin and said something like, 'It ain't what it looks like.' I screamed and called him a rat and told him that we were done."

There was a darkness that came over Dutch's face. "I called Ellen a tramp and some other bad things I don't need to repeat," she said. "I threw beer cans and dumped the coffee table over. I was furious. Then I stormed out of the house and ran into the night. What were they thinking? I'm a serious person. It's not like I'm some wimp needing anything from them, she cried."

Dutch folded her arms and held herself tight. "The next thing I knew I woke up in Mr. Nelson's field, watching their broken-down barn burn. The volunteer firemen found me in the yard."

Reliving the experience, Dutch's eyes became bloodshot. Her face twisted and sweat beaded on her forehead as she continued, "I was freezing cold. My lips were purple and I didn't have shoes. My feet were scratched and bleeding. I looked a sight." Dutch rocked back and forth when she said, "The firemen wrapped me in a blanket and drove me home. I was really messed up. And you know the worst part?" Dutch touched her forehead with her index finger, "I had a big hickey right here!"

Dutch continued, "I blabbered all the way, saying whatever came to mind." She shivered when she said, "The firemen thought I was speaking in tongues. When they got me home, they phoned my sister but she didn't answer so they put me in a rocking chair. I just kept rocking and rocking. Finally, they called my brother and he was not home. One fireman was going off duty, so he stayed until after midnight when he finally got hold of my sister, who came over. She made me a cup of chocolate."

Franny said to me, "Dutch is a fire-starter but not with matches. Crazy, huh?"

"She is a pyrokinetic," remarked Franny. "She starts fires with her mind! On TV they showed people bursting into flames from spontaneous combustion. The scientists didn't know what caused it." Franny put her hand on Dutch's shoulder. "Girl, I believe you can start a fire with your mind." Grabbing and shaking Dutch's shoulder, Franny said, "But please don't do it here!"

"Don't worry," Dutch said. "After that incident, I never wanted to go back home. I'd burn the whole town down. No one believed me when I told them what the boys did." Dutch wadded a piece of paper and threw it at the trash can. "They just laughed at me. And the worst thing was that everyone was against me. I even began to think I deserved it and that it was my fault. I was so angry at myself and the whole world. Having hickeys on my forehead didn't help."

"Come here," I said and cradled Dutch like a child. Franny put down the brush, ran her fingers through Dutch's hair.

"Thanks for telling us," Franny said. "Your friends betrayed you. It wasn't your fault. What happened was terrible." Cradling Dutch, she continued, "It took a lot to tell us. Thanks for trusting us. Does your doctor know this?"

Dutch shook her head "No, just you two."

"We'll keep your secret," Franny said. "But you need to let the anger out. I know, believe me. Anger can fester and slowly twist your insides."

Dutch's skin was clammy. I held her tight. "I hope you and Franny will let me stay for a while," Dutch whispered.

Franny grabbed a wool blanket from my shelf, and together we wrapped Dutch like Baby Jesus. We held her and rocked her side to side. In the background, the radio played an Elvis tune.

CHAPTER SEVENTEEN

Flowers and Peace

The sky was overcast and sparrows were chirping in the garden. We gathered in my area as usual before breakfast. There was no mention of the night before, which seemed like a long time ago. The little radio played Miles Davis's *Sketches of Spain*. The trumpet sounded like crying.

Dutch's voice broke through the music. "We've got fifteen minutes before breakfast, so I need to split," she said. "Today I've got to work in the fields and hustle back for group."

"Can I change the station?" Franny asked. "The Russians removed the missiles and it looks like the world won't end right away."

"Yippee skippee," screamed Dutch. She jumped like a child and hollered, "Yoo whoo!!! We ain't going to get bombed, that is unless we drink too much booze. Get it?"

"Yeah, that's funny," Franny said and crinkled her nose.

"Great news!" I smiled with joy and relief. "Wonderful! We won't have a Hiroshima here."

Franny switched stations and hummed an anti-war folk song by Pete Seeger, "This is my favorite. Have you heard, *Where have all the flowers gone?*"

The melody engulfed us and made me sway. I said, "That's a bitter sweet tune."

Franny said, "In the song, young girls are picking flowers and then the girls are picked by young men. The men go off to war and when they return dead, the flowers cover their graves." Franny put her right hand against her forehead. "The first time I heard it, I broke down."

Her voice shook as she composed herself and continued, "My younger brother, Adam, wants to join the army. I mean, there's not much to do in Seaview after graduation – join the Alaskan crab fleet, work for the paper mill, or get a state job."

Franny sighed and said, "You have to know someone to get on with the forestry service or ferry system. So naturally my brother's thinking about joining the army."

"He wants to volunteer and fight commies," Franny said. "That's a stupid thing. Why do our young men go off to die? It's senseless," she remarked, shaking her head. "I thought I'd go to college, then get a job. But there are more important things than money." She slammed her hand on the dresser and declared, "We need to stop killing people."

Franny pulled something from her pocket. With pride she announced, "I made this for peace which we need badly if we're going to have a better world." Franny displayed the medallion with the word "Peace" on it. "For a different project, I talked to our craft teacher about doing tee shirts with 'Peace' on the back."

"Okay, count me in," Dutch said as she raised her hand to volunteer. "I can dig it. Back home I've got a 1955 yellow VW bug that I drive down the freeway at seventy. It has a white vinyl interior and black steering wheel and rattles like a tin can." Dutch imitated clutching an imaginary steering wheel. "I love cruising with the radio full blast. It looks like a half lemon with wheels, motoring down the road blasting music. I could wear that tee shirt then!"

I imagined Dutch zooming down the highway in a cartoon car with her red hair dancing.

"I'll have a raccoon tail tied to the back bumper," Dutch said, "But I think that would look stupid if I joined a commune, don't you think?"

Franny and I shook our heads. "No it wouldn't," we said in unison.

"Oh well forget it, maybe a rainbow on the trunk would be better. I'd drive it straight to Golden Gate Park." Dutch rubbed her hands together as if she was expecting something good to come forth.

"Okay," Franny said, "Back to the real world, if that's what you call this." She clapped her hands to get our attention. "Hello, today's Saturday, just like every other day of the week. The only thing different is what's for breakfast. I think that's sad."

Franny twisted the radio dial searching for news beyond the static and whines. "We need to find out more about the missiles," Franny said.

"Yes, that is a good idea," I said. "What about last night?" I continued, "Dutch, are you okay today?" I touched her shoulder gently.

Dutch twitched in her usual can't-sit-still manner. Her fingers tapped rhythmically on the night stand. "Never better," she said.

I replied to Dutch, "I felt badly for you yesterday." I gripped her hand. "I prayed for you and especially President Kennedy. He and his brother Bobby need strength and all the help they can get. The President is so young with all that responsibility."

I picked up a magazine then put it down as I continued, "Yesterday Dutch, it must have been really hard to talk about what happened. I'm glad you trusted us and weren't afraid."

I squeezed her hand tight and said, "I've never really opened up like that to anyone. Your story brought back memories of my World War II evacuation. Japanese are supposed to endure pain and not complain." I removed my glasses, huffed on the lenses, and wiped them clean. "It's part of our culture. But being here with you girls makes me feel safe. You won't say that I'm bringing shame and dishonor to my family or community for speaking up. I'm grateful for your trust." Putting my arms around the two girls, I said, "Love you both."

MISSILE THREAT ENDS, 1962

The next day, there was sense of peace after the missile crisis concluded. The three of us strolled to my area. We settled in and I decided to tell them my wartime incarceration story. "When the Minidoka administration closed the camp, they turned off the electricity. Then we had to leave," I said. "The government forced us into the camp against our will and forced us out when the war was almost over. In August of 1945, we returned to Seattle and stayed with my friend's father, Mr. Kashima. We lived in his basement until we found an old duplex on Lane Street just north of Dearborn."

I continued, "Sometimes I wake up and think I'm still in camp. It takes me a minute to get back to reality. I still am haunted by my miscarriage in camp. My sister-in-law, Yoko, called it a cluster of grapes. It wasn't even a baby, just an *it*."

Franny said, "Oh, that's terrible. You must have felt sad losing the child. It sounds like a hydatid form mole. It's a fertilization problem." Franny sounded like a medical textbook. "What comes out is almost all placenta and no fetus."

"How do you know all these things?" We asked in unison. "Are you sure there is such a thing?"

"I know, I know. Just don't ask me how."

My eyes got misty as I continued, "Rinban Suzuki, the Buddhist priest, said that people choose the circumstances of their birth and this child chose not to be born in captivity." I removed my glasses. After hearing that, I was happy my boys, Alan and Larry, chose to be born in camp."

I sank down into my chair and took a deep breath.

"When my sons were born in Minidoka, I was worried because the food was poor," I continued. "I was hoping not to get dysentery when I was pregnant. Also I drank a lot of milk so they would have strong bones. Unfortunately, I had to eat canned meats and not fresh food." I paused and moved to brace my back against the bed headboard.

I continued, "After Larry was born, I didn't feel attached to him because I was afraid to get too close in case he died like my miscarriage. I regret not holding my boys more and telling them I loved them when they grew older. Being so open with emotions is not the Japanese way."

Dutch glanced at the steel mesh over the windows and said, "This is nothing compared to barbed wire and machine gun towers."

"After Pearl Harbor," I said, "they took community leaders to FBI camps, and then the army came for us in April 1942. We were helpless. Whole families, old people, and orphans were removed. There was nothing we could do. The government said it was 'for our own good.' Even if you were as little as one-sixteenth Japanese, you had to go."

Dutch's eyes grew large. "Holy Smokes," she yelled. "One-sixteenth? That would mean one of your great-great-grandparents was Japanese. That's a long way back. I know 'cause I'm one-sixteenth Cherokee and look at me! I'm a freckle-faced redhead and look nothing like my great-great-grandmother. I don't even know what it means to be Cherokee."

Franny grimaced and said, "It makes me mad. Aren't you upset, Hanae? I would be."

I shivered and replied, "There's a Japanese saying –*shikataganai*, which means it can't be helped. Japan was a poor country, with earthquakes, tsunamis, and typhoons. Life was hard and starvation was common."

I took a breath and continued, "In Japan when a typhoon or earthquake destroyed your house it was *shikataganai*. No one wanted to hear you complain since everyone was in the same situation. You just needed to endure it and be quiet. In America, a rich country, there's no *shikataganai*. When a bad thing happens in American, people blame someone or just sue.

I wiped my eyes when I remembered the deuce and half truck that took us to camp. *Oh, I vowed never to cry, but here I go again,* I thought. I was reliving the event and remembered the soldiers and bayonets.

"We behaved like Japanese when they came for us. We followed orders. We didn't complain and make our shame public."

Dutch said, "I understand. But it was wrong and I would be angry." Dutch shook her fist in defiance. "I don't know what I'd do. But I'd cause trouble."

I said, "I thought about killing myself when they were taking us."

Franny ignored my remarks and changed the focus to Dutch, "Girl you know what happens to troublemakers at this hospital? This joint is famous for frontal lobotomies. Can you imagine that?"

As Franny was speaking, I began to reflect on the other patients. *Some people seem normal and others are in a daze, almost like the Japanese when the army came with their trucks.*

Franny continued, "Remember that movie star, Violet Foster? Because she was violent, they used insulin shock therapy and electric shock on her. Finally, they pushed a needle through her eyelid into her brain. She was in the west wing."

Dutch and I gasped, realizing that we were so close to the building where the lobotomies were performed. The most shocking part was that it was normal and acceptable. That was what the evacuation had been like. Most of America thought it was reasonable and appropriate.

I looked hard at Dutch, and then at Franny. "I worry about what will happen next. I don't have a plan and I can't escape like you girls." I pushed up my glasses. "I wake and wonder who the good guys are? During World War II, our crime was being Japanese. Were we the good guys or bad guys? I just don't know. Now I am back in jail again, this time at Western State."

Franny grimaced. She said, "But really, weren't you irate? How did you feel when the whole country had turned against you?"

I became distant and silent. The radio music grew louder. "I don't like to talk about my feelings."

With a frown, Franny tightened up. Her voice was firm and strong, "Cut it out, Hanae," she said. "Be honest. You need to tell us." Franny moved closer. "Those things just eat at you. That's what they taught us in group. It's true. I know what it's like to be helpless and lose a baby. You have to get the anger out."

I looked down at the bed sheets and said, "At the time, I was confused and didn't know who to hate. I was mad at everyone because we went willingly. Then I thought it was *shikataganai*. Finally, I thought we just needed to make the best of it. At least they didn't kill us or castrate the men." Franny and I locked eyes and then I said, "Some congressmen actually suggested that."

Dutch responded, "You've got to be kidding!" She put her arm around me. "I'm glad you're sharing now. Who said the truth would set you free? I can't remember."

"It was John 8:32 in the bible," Franny replied. "Have you ever heard of him?"

"Oh, very funny," replied Dutch.

"Okay, okay," I relented. "I was angry with President Roosevelt. I was angry with Earl Warren, the governor of California for being anti-Japanese. I was angry with Eleanor Roosevelt for doing nothing. I was enraged with the Chamber of Commerce, the Elks Clubs, and the businessmen and farmers who took our land and businesses for pennies on a dollar. So there, that's it. I hate them all!"

Tears ran down my cheeks and dripped from my nose. I cleared my throat and said, "I've held the anger for years and never spoken about it outside of the family. Even within the Japanese community, I'd never talked about this."

"Good," replied Dutch in a satisfied voice, "Now can you forgive them?" Dutch said, "I want to move the conversation to help you."

I paused and carefully thought about my response. I knew the girls were trustworthy and would not bring shame on me.

"I don't know how to forgive them. It's too much," I replied. "People whose job it was to protect us, betrayed us. They took advantage of us when we were helpless and lost almost everything." I sighed deeply and remembered my dog, Molly, and the piano.

Dutch handed me a Kleenex. "And how does that make you feel?" She asked, leaning toward me.

"I see red," I exclaimed. I placed my glasses on the bedside table. "But now I'm tired. Can we stop?"

"You mean anger?" Dutch asked.

I looked down and said, "Yes, anger and sadness. I think even my children feel it. That's something I'm sorry for. But who can you blame when the whole country turns against you? Who can I hate? Many of those people are dead. How do you forgive the dead? Some days are better than others, but there are reminders everywhere and every day."

There was an awkward silence. The radiator stopped hissing and the radio music filled with static.

My voice cracked. "When I see a piano I remember the Baldwin we left behind. It was a wedding gift from Kiyoshi. Reminders are everywhere. Talking about it doesn't change anything. No, I can never forgive the leaders and government. Worst of all, most of America is not even aware of what happened."

Those thoughts and emotions I'd denied for twenty years surfaced like a geyser. "White Americans were angry about Pearl Harbor," I said. "They just wanted revenge and we were handy. I'm upset about Hiroshima and the destruction of Seattle's Japantown. This is like Urashima Taro and there's no Momotaro here." I shrugged my shoulders. "I can't defeat the demons. They are the US government, the FBI and the Supreme Court."

Franny moved closer to me. "Just love yourself and what God has given you–the gift of life and this moment. When I think of Buddy and sadness comes, I hug a tree and all my bad emotions run down to its roots and up its branches." She put her arm around me. "I think of buds, flowers and fruit nourished by my energy. Be the lotus. Be pure white in a stagnant pond. Pull the best from the muddy waters." She nudged and shook me lightly. "You're alive, and life is a wonderment. I know this from trying to kill myself." Franny stepped back and looked at me with a sweet smile.

Emotionally, I felt like I was going fifty miles an hour on a flat tire. I slowed down mentally to avoid tearing the rubber and careening into a ditch.

"I'll try to release my anger," I said. "Can't say yes for sure. Both of you are good for me. I don't want to die cursing Minidoka and holding the hate until my last breath. There must be a way to forgive and let go. But how do you forgive the unforgivable? Regardless of what I do, it is my dream to one day be able to walk down the street and feel at home in America. Yes, that is my wish. If I had ten wishes, that would be number one, to be downtown feeling comfortable in this skin with these eyes."

Dutch and Franny looked amazed. "Wow! Really? That's something I take for granted," Franny remarked.

I continued, "Once I was shopping at Goodwill to buy clothes for my Hiroshima relatives. I was pushing a cart down an aisle when a very large white woman with three dirty-faced children stopped my sons and me."

"The woman looked at us like we were trash and said, 'Some foreigners just don't have the sense to get out of a good person's way.'"

"My son Alan, asked, 'What did she say?' I told the boys the woman was ignorant and to ignore her. 'You have to learn to live with this; there will be others as you grow older,' I warned."

Franny and Dutch were exasperated, "It's sad that your kids heard that," Franny said. She continued, "You've suffered more than Dutch and I could experience in two lifetimes." Then Franny's face lit up.

She pulled out a brown leather pouch and opened the laces slowly. She shook it and a blue stone the size of a nickel rolled onto the bed.

"Turquoise," said Franny smiling. "It's the most powerful if given as a gift. So in return for the medallion, this is for you, Hanae. May it bring you peace."

I held the stone to the light. "Oh, I wish it were that easy, Franny. Thanks so much,"

I replied and reached for a glass of water. "I hope it helps."

Most of all I realized that these girls were a blessing. I could not imagine being here without them. Relieved, I embraced Franny and hugged Dutch and wistfully said, "You both make me feel at home. You're my family. When my time comes to leave, I'll miss you both so much."

"Wait, wait, Hanae, don't fade now," Franny said. "Hold on. I think I've finally got it, our purpose for being together here." Franny leaped off the bed. "I was thinking about this for a long time. The question is 'What can we three do together here to improve the lives of everyone?' The answer must be short, one word. Okay?"

"What does that mean?" Dutch replied.

"Just stay with me on this one," Franny urged in a clear voice. "Dutch, put yourself in a trance and we'll ask questions."

Dutch said, "Okay, give me a minute."

"All right, think of one word to improve the lives of everyone," Franny said. "Just one word," she continued, "so take your time."

"That's easy. My one word," Dutch said, "is about rock and roll music. That word is 'Love.' I love music and it can change the world." Dutch smiled and swayed like a hula dancer. "Music can raise spirits and change people. In fact, one day I looked up at the clouds and saw the Virgin Mary. I felt a tingling like a song that filled my heart with love."

I said in a stern voice, "My one word is for Hiroshima: 'Peace.' May we never suffer another Nagasaki or Hiroshima again. May we not have another world war with atomic bombs."

Franny said, "I thought of 'Peace' for wars we have suffered." She held her chin as if in deep thought. "But Hanae you can have it. My other word then is for Buddy: 'Gratitude'. Even though I lost him, I'm grateful for bringing him into this world."

Franny raised her eyes to the ceiling as if channeling spirits. She said. "I think it was Confucius who taught that the family was the most important thing. The elders show love to the children and in return the children show respect and gratitude."

Franny handed each of us three tongue depressors and a pen. "Write your one word to help humanity. So when we're done we'll have three sets of three with our wishes. Each day we'll set up our individual wishes as triangles and send our thoughts into the universe to raise the vibratory level of everyone around us." Rubbing her hands together, she remarked, "We'll create thought forms and send them out to swirl around the hospital, city and the world."

Dutch and I understood the logic. "We'll be like white witches casting spells," Dutch exclaimed. "People wouldn't know why they felt the warmth of love, peace, and gratitude but it would just seep into their beings."

"Outstanding!" Franny said. "That would be a wonderment!"

Dutch and I were silent as the gravity of the thoughts settled in. Franny continued, "This is what we must do. The world is on a scale, and our thoughts will tip it towards love and against hate, towards peace and against war and towards gratitude and against ingratitude. This will be our purpose together. We may not always succeed, but we must keep the faith."

We all nodded and held hands. For a moment we'd become one.

The project connected us to a larger purpose. Most people might find this idea far-fetched, but within the confines of the hospital and in the company of three like-minded women, it was real.

CHAPTER EIGHTEEN

Leaving Western State

The sky was gray-blue, typical of Pacific Northwest spring weather. The temperatures were in the high fifties. A cool breeze rose from the south and rustled the Japanese cherry trees. I was excited to greet the day. May 10th, my release date, was actually here. I could hardly believe it. *Finally*, I said to myself, *I made it.*

My calendar had an "X" through each day. I thought about the past nine months. *Oh what a relief to be going home. I remember when I first walked up the stairs and how afraid I was. That was like years ago.*

I cleaned my dresser drawers and removed all evidence of my stay. I pulled out the liners, which held the scent of old things. Carefully I placed newspaper in the drawer bottoms. I picked up my white Oral B toothbrush, curled from months of brushing, and happily dropped it in the trash.

I thought, *Kiyoshi should have gassed up on Beacon Hill and must be headed down Airport Way to Highway 99. Is his stomach ulcer under control? How is work? Did he do the wash? Are dirty clothes piling up in the bathroom hamper waiting for my arrival? It'll be good to get back to my normal routine and make lunch for Kiyoshi and Larry.*

My mind flashed when I realized how much I'd miss Franny and Dutch, and the peace and quiet of the hospital grounds. I'd miss the walks around the campus, which brought a sense of tranquility. I thought the garden was like an 18th century English painting with women wearing long dresses and bustles and strolling arm-in-arm with gentlemen in waistcoats and top hats. It was unlike Japanese gardens, which mimicked nature. Most of all, I'd feel strange without the predictable hospital schedules and my friends.

I'd miss *I Love Lucy* reruns and reading the magazines. In a way, it had been a vacation. I wore clean clothes that I didn't have to scrub or iron and had no family responsibilities. Overall, time away had been good for me.

I'd never had a real vacation in my whole life. On my honeymoon, the first day had been relaxing after the long drive from Seattle to Copalis Beach. I remembered the hard-packed, sandy soil at the ocean and how I'd walked barefoot. The huge rock spires were amazing and I loved the ocean mist and the way the wind carried it. The curling waves moved hard and fast, noisy like an express train. The next day we dug razor clams that I'd spent most of the evening cleaning and packing in white cylindrical containers. We harvested pounds of clams destined for the store's walk-in freezer.

Scanning the Western State Hospital grounds, my mind returned to reality. *Copalis*, I thought, *odd what goes through your mind in anticipation of new things. I felt a chill when I thought, I'm afraid of leaving. How can that be? I'm going home and should be happy.*

The quiet was interrupted by the sound of girls chatting and laughing. Franny and Dutch peeked around the corner.

"Good morning," Franny said with a broad smile.

Dutch swayed back and forth and waved wildly.

I wanted to say something special to the girls. But I just couldn't manage my mixed emotions. Instead I told them, "I'll think of you always. I loved our friendship."

The girls seemed to have trouble finding the words too. They giggled like twins and said in unison, "See you at the Needle!"

"Yes the Needle for sure," I said. "On Saint Patrick's Day, 1970." There was a pause and I could hear my heart beating. Everything seemed to slow down.

The girls became animated and hugged me tight. "Love you," Franny said.

"Me too, both of you," I replied. "I have a small gift of origami cranes for you. You can suspend them like mobiles."

"Thanks," they replied. "We'll think of you every day."

I felt anxious and worried that there might be a last minute change to prevent my leaving. *Did I sign all the forms? Do I have any bills to settle?* I didn't want to get my hopes up until I was safely back in Seattle. Kiyoshi had no idea how much I'd changed and what a great experience it had been for me in many ways. I knew the family would never admit where I had been all these months. It was understood that this episode would be treated with silence.

After four hours on the road, Kiyoshi turned up the winding road past the stone entry gate.

Franny and Dutch waited with me in the lobby. We held hands until the Chevy appeared. Their faces glowed as they felt my recognition of the car.

"Is that Kiyoshi?" Franny asked, jumping with excitement.

Kiyoshi wore his blue sweater and soft gray fedora. He hustled up the stairs, taking two at a time. The girls released my hands and I rushed to him. I hugged him so tightly that he almost went limp. My public display of affection was something he wasn't used to. Franny and Dutch were all smiles as they walked towards me.

I turned to the girls and said, "I just want to say...".

But before I could finish, the girls said, "We know." They kissed me on the cheek.

"We'll miss you," they chirped. "Don't forget Saint Paddy's Day. We'll be waiting." Like sprites they scooted around the corner.

Kiyoshi stood as if marooned and was unsure how to act. By his expression, my kissing white friends was obviously a surprise to him. He mumbled his displeasure in Japanese, but since the girls had withdrawn, more pressing matters were at hand. He signed the release papers and grabbed my yellow suitcase.

We walked down the granite stairs gingerly. I had been weak and thin climbing these stairs in early autumn, barely able to hold up my head. Today I stood straight with confidence. "You look good," he said finally. My mouth dropped open when I heard the compliment.

"Thanks," I replied, "I feel great."

I glanced over my shoulder at the huge brick hospital, the beautiful gardens and lawn. Spring was coming soon and Japanese cherry trees were in bloom. I thought, *The blossoms are brave to come out so early. Hopefully a late frost will not take them.* On the third floor I could see Dutch and Franny waving from the window. I felt empty when I waved back.

I slid into the front seat of the Chevy and restrained my emotions. I bottled my excitement and said very little the whole trip. I soaked in the scenery as if I'd never seen such sights before–the grocery stores, restaurants, gas stations, and houses. I read the billboards out loud. I was like a time traveler seeing this world for the first time. I wanted to stop at every store and bakery on the way, but resisted as my thoughts drifted to the kids, Kiku, the relatives, and Kiyoshi's work.

I dozed on and off, still feeling the effects of my meds. By the time we reached the house it was late afternoon. Larry would be on his way home from school. Alan would be at the train station, arriving from San Francisco. So I just had enough time to unpack and get ready for the boys.

To my surprise, I found a black and white photo in my purse. On the back was scrawled, "Remember us." I held it tight with joy. *Those girls*, I thought, *always full of surprises*. They had included a note.

To Hanae,

Be well and safe travels.

Love, Franny

Same for me!!!

See you at the Space Needle!! Saint Paddy's Day, 1970!

Love, Dutch

PS- Remember-Love, Peace and Gratitude.

BACK HOME IN MAY, 1963

One by one, I shook out my clothes with a snap and hung them in the bedroom closet. The familiar sights and smells of home were a welcome change. Something as small as touching my pink padded coat hanger gave me comfort. I switched on the radio and immediately thought of my piano. The Righettis still own the Baldwin since we had no room for such a luxury after our return. *I'll probably never play music again and surely wouldn't have to time to practice.*

My thoughts shifted backwards for an instant, I missed the girls and wondered what they were doing. *Was it art or group today?* My mouth watered. *Tonight is meatloaf and mashed potatoes. I'd love one more dinner with them.*

I placed my reading glasses on the blonde dresser and fingered a bottle of perfume. I looked at my reflection and said out loud, "I see someone who needs new clothes and a visit to the beauty parlor." Fully realizing that this was not a dream, I smiled a slow "glad to be home" grin.

I unwrapped the three tongue depressors and placed them on the dresser in order: "Love, Peace, and Gratitude". I sorted through my hospital treasures: Ivory soap bars and Oral B toothbrushes. As if they were offerings at a Buddhist shrine, I made a place for them in the medicine cabinet.

I examined the apartment and was surprised at how small the bedroom was. At Western State the ceiling had been higher. *This will take some getting used to,* I thought.

It was 3:30 when Larry and Alan tromped up the stairs. I opened the door and hugged and kissed them both. The boys were surprised. By the looks on their faces, I could tell that they were wondering if I was really well. Not sure what to say, they just stared with mouths agape. For a second Larry was skittish.

Nevertheless, everyone was happy I was home. But the boys kept their distance like wild animals whose lives depended on being suspicious.

"Hey everyone, let's celebrate," Kiyoshi said. "We're going for a Chinese dinner at the Seven Dragons."

"That sounds wonderful. I haven't eaten real rice in ages," I said. The thought of cooking today was excruciating. I inspected the house and was surprised that the hamper was empty. The clothes had been ironed and hung in the closet. This was truly "a wonderment" as Franny would say. With every chore done, I thought, *I'd love to have some pork fried rice and shrimp chow mein tonight.*

"Bring the Kodak," I said. Kiyoshi grabbed the camera and announced, "We've got six shots left."

It was close to dusk and the streetlights were glowing when we parked on Weller Street. Halfway down the block the restaurant's neon sign was visible with its flashing red letters. A beam of fire shot from the dragon's mouth to a sphere below. Inside was the usual bustle of staff and customers. Our favorite waiter in a white jacket greeted us. He was bald with a black fringe on the sides. We used to kid Kiyoshi that he and the waiter looked like brothers. I searched for Mr. Wong but he wasn't there. "Please tell Mr. Wong we dropped by," I said to the waiter.

I was happy to see that the restaurant was just as I recalled. I had changed, but the world here had kept its former shape.

"You order, Hanae," Kiyoshi said with a smile.

I automatically ordered my favorites: egg foo young, chow mein, barbecue pork, wonton soup, white rice, and fried rice.

"Oh, I've waited a long time for this," I remarked with delight. "Thank you, Kiyoshi, Alan, and Larry, for all that you did while I was gone. I'm so glad to be home."

The boys bent their heads as if in prayer. Kiyoshi had a nervous twitch. Everyone sat, waiting with anticipation for that instant when a switch would be flipped and everyone would feel comfortable together, again.

POWER MACHINE OPERATOR

It was another dreary Seattle morning at the bus stop. I craned my neck and looked down 14th Avenue South, expecting to see the trolley. I clutched my purse, lunch sack, and ever-present umbrella. *I hope it is on schedule, I don't want to be late for my first vocational training class*, I thought.

I knew Dutch and Francie were dressed by now and strolling across the field. I felt their presence and wondered, *What are they talking about? Do they miss me? I sure miss them.*

As the days passed, I became a regular on the morning No. 3 bus. Out of habit, most passengers migrated to the same seats. The routine reminded me of Western State, where patients sat in the same chairs at each meal. If by chance another person sat in their seat, hard feelings and arguments would erupt. Not so on the bus, given the large number of empty seats and a higher level of civility.

On my state job inventory survey, I listed my experiences as produce clerk, grocery clerk, and sewing for a hobby. My new training involved staying away from heavy lifting, so I was enrolled in a power machine sewing course. The high-powered commercial machines sewed thick fabric like upholstery material or canvas.

After completing the training, I got a job at Northwest Garments and did piecework. Working in the dark factory between rows of noisy machines and operators, I thought, *This makes me nervous. I'm so slow. I better not take a break or go to the bathroom if I want to make any money.*

Every day on the job was like a 2,000-meter sprint. As a new person, I was assigned the most tedious work, while the more senior people got easier and the faster projects.

After a year on the piecework treadmill, a friend at church told me, "Go to Roffee's Coat Factory; they're looking for experienced people." It was hourly, and paid union wages, which was above the minimum. I asked Kiyoshi for advice and he encouraged me. Even though working at

Northwest was difficult, I was reluctant to leave and start all over. I was nervous and edgy during the entire day because of the stress, so I reconsidered. *I can't imagine being here for years. I'd never make it to retirement*, I concluded. *It would be better to quit while I have a chance.*

It took some time to get used to my new job. Thankfully the bus route was the same. After a month at Roffee's, I was turning a piece of fabric around a corner when my finger was caught and sliced. "Ow!" I'd screamed. The pain had been excruciating. Blood had poured down my finger; first a little stream, and then my whole hand was drenched red.

Luckily the finger was not as bad as it looked and I was able to return in a couple of days. But when the weather changed the scar throbbed. It was a reminder like *moxa* scars that ached periodically. But it was nothing like Minidoka which crept into my consciousness every day brought on by a familiar song, the odor of bacon, someone mentioning camp or a piano. After all the years, I just accepted the weight of the camp memory I had to carry.

Roffee, however, was a good thing. It was a humane place where I made friends with two Japanese women, Tomoko and Atsuko. Both of them had family in Hiroshima and were married to GIs who were stationed in Japan. We were in the minority, since Chinese dominated the factory workforce.

The Chinese women were friendly but spoke Cantonese and shared food at lunch. I felt excluded because I couldn't understand what they were saying. In addition, they worked on their own private projects during free time. With the factory's permission, they purchased materials at cost and sewed during lunch hours and on breaks. One person did sleeves, another zippers, and still another did collars. After weeks of passing the projects around, all who participated had completed jackets for their entire families. I was never invited to join but instead bought jackets at a discount. I had no hard feelings as an outsider.

At home, I settled into my daily life. My thoughts of Dutch and Francie began to fade like an old photo. At dinner, I smiled with satisfaction when I realized that I was working hard and that I'd come a long way from Western State. My fears of slipping backwards into depression were no longer on my mind.

In 1964, Kiyoshi's brother Harold burned to death in Hiroshima after he fell asleep smoking in bed. Over the years Harold had been a difficult person. Although he'd been born in America, he'd returned to Japan after the war. The family rarely talked about him because he was a black sheep and troublemaker. In Japanese, he was *iji ga warui*, a mean-spirited person. In Minidoka, he burned ants with matches for amusement. He was angry about the evacuation and he openly challenged Sachi. "You and your lover bring shame on the family," he said. "I'm going back to Hiroshima as soon as I can!"

A month after Harold's death, Koemon, Kiyoshi's father, passed away. In the space of two months Kiyoshi lost a father and brother. After suffering through the 1930s depression, forced evacuation, the bombing of Hiroshima, my miscarriage, my hysterectomy, my stay in the mental hospital, and ongoing arguments with Alan, Kiyoshi thought he could cope with these new deaths.

Instead, his ulcer bled and he collapsed on the job. His slogan of "Everything is no good" came true. He literally fell down on the job. Naturally, the hotel let him go because he was not able to work. Kiyoshi took the loss hard and became sullen. Every morning he read the newspaper but stayed in bed most of the day. He began to swear more often and had difficulty walking without losing his balance.

Doctor Johnson referred Kiyoshi to a specialist. The neuro-surgeon examined Kiyoshi and said to me, "Kiyoshi's brain is deteriorating rapidly and he has one year to live." I braced myself after the news. My legs grew weak. For a second I thought, *Oh no, I can't stand steady. It's happening to both of us!* I took deep breaths and pulled myself together and chased out the negative thoughts. I knew Kiyoshi always did what the doctor said, so I didn't share the prognosis with him. It would be a secret that I would share only with Larry.

Immediately I phoned Larry who was in class at Cleveland High School. The student secretary contacted him to take the call in the office. I held the line and was crying by the time he picked up.

"Larry, your father is very ill and I need to talk with you right away. Come home right now. Kiyoshi doesn't have much time to live."

Larry replied, "Okay, I'll be home as soon as I can." He showed no emotions in his voice or inflection. He spoke normally as if our conversation was something routine.

But I was numb and worried, *How will we make ends meet when Kiyoshi dies?* I remembered my promise to Mr. Gill at the bank about how he could trust us to pay the mortgage on time every month. I felt a shiver and sat down.

That afternoon, I composed myself and kept my mind busy. When Larry arrived I dragged a chair to a card table in the living room. "Sit down, we need to talk," I said. Kiyoshi is asleep now. "The doctor gave him one year to live."

Larry frowned. "Are you sure? Is that all, twelve months?"

Holding back panic, I recounted what the neurosurgeon had said, "He has a year so we need to make plans." I pulled out my checkbook and the stack of monthly bills which seemed to be swirling on the table. Larry stayed calm; after living in a family constantly in crisis, this was just another in a series of bad events. He added up what I earned at Roffee and added his pay from a part-time job at Food Giant supermarket. He tallied the expenses for food, the monthly mortgage payments, rent collections from the three tenants, insurance, and everything he could think of including possible tax returns. He examined the bottom line and said, "We're at least $100 a month short, not counting Kiyoshi's anticipated hospital expenses."

I felt a sharp stabbing pain in my stomach. "Are you sure?" I asked. I hovered over him as he added the columns again and again. I was nervous and distraught. "Is it good?" I asked anxiously.

Finally, Larry looked up after re-calculating the figures he said. "Mom, we'll be okay."

I exhaled and said, "Oh thank God! I was worried sick." Immediately, I collected the bills and put them in a folder.

"The next twelve months are going to be bad," I said. "We need to pay the bills plus Kiyoshi's funeral expenses. If not, we'll have to ask for help and get credit at the grocery store."

That day I went through our mail. In the stack was a Mount Rainier postcard from Francie. She and Dutch were released a few months ago and were going through the vocational rehab program. Shortly they would be looking for jobs. I read it quickly and put it in a drawer. *I'd love to see the girls and miss them dearly. It seems like years. But given Kiyoshi's health, I'll get back to her after things settle down and for sure on Saint Paddy's day*, I thought.

After shuffling through the rest of the mail, I was overwhelmed by the unanticipated increase in the water bill and electricity. *Oh I'll tell Larry to be sure to turn off all the lights when they were not in use.*

I was worried and on the verge of panic because I knew just cutting the electrical bill would not be enough. Nevertheless, I decided to wait before contacting Alan or other family members about Kiyoshi's prognosis, including Sachi, who was still living with Hiro after Koemon's passing. The fact that Kiyoshi was habitually ill and in and out of the hospital made it easy for us to not fully disclose the serious nature of this illness.

"Did you see the bills that came today?" I asked Larry.

He got up from the table, stacked the papers neatly and said, "Yeah, I counted them. Don't worry, we'll be okay." Years later he told me, "It was the biggest lie he'd ever told. He expected the truth to be revealed quickly as the tsunami of problems gathered force and wiped us out.

Taking inventory, Larry scanned the apartment: bed, steel furniture, worn linoleum, repaired bathroom door, sofa and knickknacks. "Mom, there's nothing of value to sell. Everything was worn out, beaten up, or worthless."

He asked, "How much is the samurai sword worth and the silk kimonos? Maybe, we could get something for those things. Do we have anything of value to sell?"

I replied, "We have nothing. We lost all our good things during the war. The car is fourteen years old and is worthless."

"At least we can raise the rents on the tenants by five dollars a month, our rents are really too low," he said. "Also we need to turn the porch light on later to save electricity."

"Yes, we'll do that. I'll tell the tenants about the increase. I hope no one moves out," I replied.

Above all we never discussed Kiyoshi's health around him. If it came up in conversation no matter how insignificant, we changed the subject. I prayed every night and went to church each Sunday. We knew he could die any day. Every morning I caught the bus and headed to work as usual. At work I put my head down and sewed eight hours at my illuminated table in the dark factory until the bell rang and did it again the next day.

Larry was mentally prepared for the inevitable. "Will today be the day?" he asked.

I shook my head no and said, "Looks like we've got another."

Because Kiyoshi did not get worse, Larry said, "At least there are no new doctor bills we have to worry about." I 'm sure Larry worried that we would lose the house and be turned out into the street.

Larry carried on his normal school life the best he could, focusing on homework and finding a date for the prom. We had no one who could help. There were no government agencies that would assist us that we knew of. He said, "Mom, if I can make it until graduation, I can find a job and support the family."

When he said this, I felt ashamed and told him to just wait, and see if something good happens. I'm sure he wondered like me, *How long will Kiyoshi last? He looks okay.*

Larry said, "At school, I wait for that note from the principal's office to call home. It's always on my mind." He and I lived like Franny once described, "Like a cat on a hot tin roof." To our amazement, weeks and months passed without any new health problems. The twelve-month date approached and Kiyoshi was still up and about. We checked and he seemed as well as ever insisting that, "Everything is no good." But I thought, *Kiyoshi, you don't know the half of it.*

I developed a nervous tic in my eye. Larry caught several colds and missed school. I wondered, *After all the drama and living on the edge, maybe it would be better if his Kiyoshi just got it over with. At least we wouldn't be stuck waiting.*

Nevertheless, when Kiyoshi complained about any ailment, as he did habitually, we took extra care to listen in case this was the linchpin that would unleash the sword of hanging above our heads.

After a year had passed, I thought, *Finally I could breathe easy.* However, I continued to monitor Kiyoshi's daily activities carefully. Luckily we were able to make ends meet by increasing the rents and cutting costs. One snowy evening, a drunk crashed into Larry's car. The insurance check was like a gift from the universe to cover some of Kiyoshi's medical bills.

To my surprise after twelve months, Kiyoshi was employable and alive. I truly believed he lived because we never told him his prognosis. If we did, he surely would have died because he always followed the doctor's orders.

One evening after dinner he announced proudly, "I passed my janitor's interview. Seattle University has me on the list!" Larry and I were caught by surprise. He looked at me and I looked at him and we both shrugged our shoulders. It was like a miracle, but we were suspicious and waited. Larry said, *"Oh wow, we should have a celebration, Mom!"*

I knew what Larry was talking about but never acknowledged the real reason. Instead I said, "Sounds good but we should wait."

Kiyoshi overheard us and said, "Celebration? Yes, we should go out and get some Chinese food. I'm going to get a job."

We ignored his remark. He probably never suspected that the proposed party was about his not dying. So I thought, *he's living on borrowed time like Ben the cub scout leader. But borrowed time is better than being dead.*

Kiyoshi's Filipino friend from the Acme Hotel was able to get Kiyoshi hired as a janitor in the Seattle University gym. Larry and I shared a knowing look. I was overjoyed but kept my feelings guarded in case he started falling down on the job.

At work Kiyoshi went by his American name, Ernest or Ernie. Like a cat with nine lives, he emerged as a new man with a new identity. Finally, he had work, a schedule, and a place in the world.

One evening he came home and boasted, "At breaks I would lean on my broom and watch the coed square dancing class. It reminded me of parties at Lake Wilderness before the war."

A large Cheshire cat grin spread across his face, "Today the class was short a boy, so the girls hollered and pulled me out of the corner. 'Ernie, come dance with us.' they said. What could I say to these young coeds except, Okay!"

Kiyoshi's chest puffed up. I didn't miss a step after all these years, "I put down my broom, and do-si-doed." For weeks Kiyoshi came home and bragged, "I danced with some pretty girls again today!"

Judging by the look on Larry's face, he like me, was not impressed. Larry simply would respond with, "Please pass the vegetables." For me it was hard to listen to Kiyoshi's achievements since we'd considered him a "dead man walking" for over a year. Nevertheless, Kiyoshi was proud of himself which was a new feeling for him.

As a child, Sachi had stifled Kiyoshi, and treated him as a weakling because of his scarred back. In a way, he was like the tree on Vashon Island with a bicycle embedded in it. Legend has it that a young man chained the bike to the tree and went off to war. He never reclaimed the bike and over the years, the tree grew around it and raised it off the ground. Kiyoshi was the tree and Sachi was the bike he could not discard. The two grew older together, forever entwined in their strange dance of possession, illness, and control.

I sensed that Larry found it difficult to adjust to Kiyoshi's frequent visits to the hospital. But I always reminded him, "Remember your name means bamboo. You bend but don't every break." I hoped that those words helped him.

After over a year, I had a chance to breathe as Kiyoshi's health found a solid footing. I thought about work, Larry, and how much I had to be thankful for. *Truly I am a power machine operator, both at work and at home. I wish Dutch and Franny could see me now. I'm looking forward to how much they changed when we meet at the Space Needle on Saint Paddy's Day in a few years. I have so many questions for them and so much to tell.*

CHAPTER NINETEEN

Saint Paddy's Day, 1970

I put a big "X" through the 17th on my calendar and took a deep breath. I had been looking forward to this day for eight years. Life was good for me. Kiyoshi was working at Seattle University and was reasonably healthy. Nevertheless, he made his usual trips to the doctors for his ulcer, bunions, varicose veins and other chronic ailments.

Every month we paid our house mortgage and had no outstanding bills. *I hope Mr. Gill at the bank is happy*, I thought. It was a miracle we made it through the bad financial times. I was glad that Larry didn't have to quit high school and get a job to support the family. Instead he was attending the University of Washington in the education program.

With everything in order, I looked forward to Saint Paddy's Day. I phoned in sick at work. *I can't wait to see them*, I thought. I primped and selected my Easter hat and outfit.

I hope they won't forget! I worried. Over the years I lost contact with them and was just going on faith and a promise. I thought, *Eight years is a long time and I would guess we all experienced many changes. Are they married with children? Have they settled down? Are they even alive? Finally, what of our efforts to save the world? At Western State our mutual goals sustained us but on the outside there have been so many distractions.*

Today, I wouldn't miss the factory noise, dust, and loud machines. Some afternoons my work station was pleasant when sunlight shone through the saw-toothed skylights. But most of the time, the area was littered with cardboard boxes overflowing with bolts of colored cloth that surrounded my table. *Today,* I mused, *I'll escape and be 500 feet in the air enjoying the company of friends.*

I thought, *I can't wait.* I hadn't had a postcard from them in years but I was confident they would show. I wrote Franny a while ago but the letter came back marked "Return to Sender."

With great care I positioned my Sunday hat with its white veil and inspected my satin blouse. I wore a silk scarf with a little green streak. I stared in the mirror and admired the reflected image of a mother and wife on her way to the Seattle Center. I wondered, *Am I on a fool's errand? We were mental patients so can I count on them? This is not like the Minidoka reunions where we had a lot in common. This is different.*

My mind raced in anticipation. I know, I'll give the girls a big hug, I thought.

Near the blonde dresser, Kiyoshi stacked my overseas trunks. They were full of precious things that had survived camp. *Maybe I should give Franny and Dutch a kimono.*

The silk kimonos were folded and preserved under a layer of moth-balls waiting for the day I would give them to my daughters-in-law. My heart was racing with excitement as I thought, *Today I'll ask Franny and Dutch if they want one.*

I checked my makeup drawer and applied my special Revlon lipstick, something I never did for work. I searched my photo album and popped out a black and white picture of us from Western State Hospital during Dutch's birthday.

I caught the No 3 trolley which had plenty of room. Out of habit I sat in the same section just like in the early morning. My seat was next to the window towards the front of the bus.

I enjoyed the scenery from the driver's point of view. Sachi's home before the war was on the bus route. The two-story wooden house with its large porch held many bad memories. I thought, *That place was miserable.* The bus lurched and turned down Massachusetts Street and down to the 12th Avenue Bridge near Jackson Street. It proceeded west towards Chinatown and what remained of Japantown. The short ride seemed to take forever. I tried to relax but my feet tapped uncontrollably.

I stepped off at Westlake Street near the Nordstrom store and climbed the monorail platform for the trip to Seattle Center.

The tracks were elevated above Fifth Avenue and the monorail moved smoothly past the office buildings and apartments. When it turned, the train tilted like a carnival ride. I held onto my hat, feeling a pull of forces. The trip was surprisingly short. *I'm almost there,* I thought. *Will I be able to recognize them? What will we talk about?*

The station awning loomed directly ahead when the train slowed. The side doors opened with the sound of a pneumatic whoosh, and I stepped onto the walkway near the Space Needle ticket booth. "Goodness gracious," I said out loud looking directly up at the Needle overhead. "It looks like a flying saucer on stilts."

My mouth dropped open when I extended my neck. I had butterflies and couldn't believe that I was actually under the famous symbol of the Century 21 World's Fair.

I thought, *Have the girls changed? I can't wait to hear what they're doing now.* Occasionally I received a few postcards from Franny's travels but it was hard to put together a coherent picture since she never included a good return address. Maybe they moved, Dutch wanted to go to San Francisco and Franny had a boyfriend in Colorado. Reflecting on the past I had a warm feeling. *Since leaving the hospital I've thought about them a lot.*

The restaurant completed a full 360 degree rotation in an hour, five hundred and fifty feet above Earth. The foundation struts were massive, and they rose and curved together in the middle and split apart, cradling the restaurant like a diamond set in a prong. I looked around the ticket area in case the girls were waiting and then joined the line that snaked around the stanchions. *Wow, $1.50 for an elevator ride. Pretty steep price*, I thought.

I entered the scenic glass elevator which climbed the core structure. Struts and braces whizzed by and buildings below grew smaller and smaller. I felt sick as if I were shot from a giant sling shot.

The elevator stopped at the observation deck above the restaurant and the doors opened with a lurch. I stepped out five hundred feet off the ground, my stomach churned. I walked around the inside and exited to the open-air balcony. The wind was so strong it chased me back to the enclosed area inside.

I fixed my hair and strolled past the souvenir store with its racks of Made in China magnets and Seattle postcards. Anxiously I searched for any signs of the girls. I thought, *It would be just like them to hide and sneak up on me.* A white man in a suit noticed me searching and said, "If you are looking for some of your countrymen, I saw them on the deck."

I nodded, and politely replied, "Thank you. I saw them. They aren't my friends."

After walking the around entire inside, I sat down. *Should have brought something to read or knit*, I mused. Queen Anne Hill, with its three television towers were to the North. To the northeast was Mount Adams; to the south, the Smith Tower, downtown, and Mount Rainier; and to the west, the Olympic Mountains and Elliot Bay. The view was magnificent and I absorbed it all so I could tell Kiyoshi and Larry. Watching the clock, I had butterflies.

I'm a few minutes early, I thought. I found a bench near the elevator doors so I could see who was coming up. I said to myself, *Today is Saint Paddy's Day and it will be noon shortly.*

Time seemed to pass excruciatingly slow. I wondered, *Are they downstairs at the restaurant? Would they be coming up or just waiting there?*

If they don't show up by a quarter after twelve, I pondered, *I'll go downstairs and check the restaurant.* But I worried that if I did, they might come up to the observation deck. "My oh my," I mumbled. "What's keeping them?" I asked out loud.

As the minutes ticked away, I began to worry. *I'm sure the girls won't forget. This was a big deal. We made a promise.* I remembered Kiyoshi's prediction that morning, "They won't show up! They're crazy and you are too if you believe them!"

"Quiet, Kiyoshi," I told him. "They'll be there unless they got hit by a car."

As I waited, I thought of Hiroshima. *This would be a terrible place to be in an earthquake.* I shivered when the wind gusted and the walls swayed.

I imagined, *The Needle would rock side to side in a quake.* It gave me a chill thinking about whipping back and forth five hundred feet in the air for thirty seconds or more. Seattle was earthquake country like Japan and Hiroshima. So I grimaced and thought, *First there would be a hard jolt and this place would swing like a pendulum. Of course the elevators would not work. Being trapped, watching the whole world sway would be horrible.*

I almost worked myself into a state of panic when the elevator doors opened and a group burst out. I examined them carefully: parents, children, and a small group of tourists from Japan. But the girls were not there. "Not there!" I said anxiously.

I wondered, *Maybe the girls have children and they'll bring them. Who knows, anything can happen.*

My mind slipped back to the earthquake risk when I heard "Hanae! is that you?"

A beautiful six-foot tall young woman in a suede coat, baggy white blouse, and jeans stood before me. Her smile was like sunshine. She looked like a girl from a wild west show with her jeans and cowgirl boots.

I stood up and gasped in relief. "Franny, I'm so glad to see you," I exclaimed. She absolutely glowed when she extended her long arms.

"Is that really you?" I cried, feeling engulfed in Franny's presence. When we embraced, I kissed her on the cheek.

"How are you? You look like a million dollars," I exclaimed. My heart jumped. I tried to write you several times but your return address was bad."

"Yeah, I know. Sorry, I was moving around a lot." Franny bit her lip and frowned, "Sit down, it's about Dutch. I'm afraid she won't make it today. She had a serious accident."

"What happened?"

"We got out of Western State in January 1963," Franny began. "Dutch went home but was having a hard time. She applied for a City Parks job but nothing came up. She loved working outside and hated desk jobs, so she got this big idea that she'd join the Peace Corps." Franny paused and looked down and continued, "President Kennedy was her favorite so she volunteered. They put her through all kinds of physical endurance tests like swimming and running. But I think it was the interviews."

Franny took a seat beside me and held my hand. Her voice shook. "Dutch never said why she was 'de-selected.' That's what they call being rejected. She took it hard because she was rooting for Kennedy since she was part Irish. But when he was assassinated in November, she really went to pieces and started doing pain killers, speed, and alcohol."

"Is she okay?" I interrupted. "I mean she isn't..."

Franny looked up and her voice cracked, "Hanae, our Dutch died."

I sobbed and covered my face.

"No that can't be," I whispered.

Franny pulled out a Kleenex and handed it to me. I had been looking forward to seeing her and could not imagine her being gone. "That's just very sad and such a waste," I remarked. My grief was tinged with anger. It didn't seem fair.

Franny continued, "After the Peace Corp situation, Dutch started hanging out with a leather jacket crowd at local taverns. They weren't Hells Angels, but a rough group." Franny took a deep breath.

"Dutch said they acted tough but were sweethearts. Man, she must have been looking really deep, because all I saw was scruff, bad attitudes, and motorcycle boots. She met this dude named Rick. Now he was trouble, a real greaser. I think he roughed Dutch up a little, but she seemed okay with him." Franny blew her nose and then continued, "Dutch said she loved Rick and her heart was full of joy after finding her soul mate." Franny beamed, "She said it was like seeing the Virgin Mary in the clouds every day! She even quoted a poem from Raymond Carver about being loved. So she died happy. Most of all she wanted us to know it."

Franny swallowed hard and said, "It was near twilight in mid-January 1964, when Dutch and Rick hit an icy patch on the road near Mile High Pass. They lost control and smashed the guard rail at 100 miles per hour."

"She broke her neck and was gone instantly. Rick survived with just a few cuts and scrapes." Franny made a fist and pounded the chair as she continued, "He blamed the ice and not his speed, alcohol, and stupidity."

"I thought I'd write you but just never got the courage. I had your address, but writing would have made it final in a way I just couldn't bear."

Franny let out a slow steady sigh and pursed her lips. "It would have been like admitting she was gone forever. There was a part of me that still wanted to believe she would come walking through my door someday. What a shame, that girl was bright and good-hearted."

Franny put her arm around me. "You just can't go home and expect everything to be the same. You can't go home and pick a fight with people who did you wrong. Time passes and they aren't even the same people. I learned that from you, the way you forgave and went on."

Franny broke down again and wiped her nose. I put my arms around her. Our sadness spread like a fog inside the observation deck. The tourists paused for a second as they seemed to sense our grief. There was a pause and the room became silent. The ding of the elevator bell reanimated the situation and a crush of tourists rushed out.

Words flowed from Franny as if she were channeling a wise being. "I thought of rooming with Dutch after Western State. If I had, she'd be alive today. But there was a whole lot goin' on and I just couldn't do it." Franny glanced down at the floor.

"Had I gone home," Franny remarked, "I'd have been like Hester Prynne in *The Scarlet Letter*. I asked myself if I should walk around town wearing a scarlet letter for having a baby in high school and do good deeds to redeem myself? Then I'd have to wait until the community forgave me or until my punishment time was over." Franny's voice quivered. "No way was that going to happen."

"Hanae, why is it that the women always carry the guilt and shame?" Franny remarked with a frown. "The men can be angry, victorious, or even seek revenge, but the women carry the shame." Franny's jaws tightened, "No one said anything to my old boyfriend."

Franny shrugged and said, "Man alive, I didn't even know much about sex. I don't carry that guilt anymore and don't seek forgiveness. Those people in town judged me but I have to live my life and look at myself in the mirror in the morning. I am not Hester Prynne," Franny said with anger. They blamed me for being weak." Her eyes looked up at the ceiling. "If I went anywhere in town, I had to put on my mental armor to be safe," she said.

"After being released, I was still messed up, so I really couldn't live with Dutch. I hadn't made peace about Buddy yet. Even to this very day I think of him. He would be about ten years old now." Franny stopped for a second and focused on the nearby children chattering and laughing. "But I can't do anything about him or Dutch, other than say a prayer and try to move on with my life. That's the best I can do."

I replied, "Yes, I know what you mean. We were in a very special place at a special time, the three of us. After we were released we couldn't help but be different. We couldn't protect each other in the same way. It's sad but true. Maybe if we were less busy, we could've done more for Dutch."

There was a ruckus as the elevator opened and another group of school children tumbled out. They were noisy and called to each. One child spotted a ferry from Bainbridge and yelled, "Look a boat!"

Franny turned for a moment and watched. "Maybe Buddy could be here," she said. "Anyway," she continued, "I know Dutch wanted to see you. She was going to thank you for the depressing Japanese fairy tales!"

We looked at each other and laughed, experiencing the essence of Dutch again. "Once she told me those fairy tales and stories about your past really made her thankful for what she had," Franny said. "It helped her through some real tough times."

"She's resting in peace now," Franny whispered. "We were hoping we could make it to century twenty-one together, not the World's Fair, but the year. You know, all three of us crossing the finish line together. She found 'Peace.' It's odd her word on the tongue depressor was 'Love,' which she found as well. What was that Japanese word you used to say?"

I said, "*Shikataganai*."

"Yes, it can't be helped, how can I forget?" she responded. She pulled out another Kleenex and continued, "I heard her parents were upset because she wanted to be buried in Port Angeles in a cemetery that over-looks the Strait of Juan de Fuca. You know, the winds come off the water and it's a chill you can't believe. I don't know how she picked that place."

Franny rubbed her eyes and removed her glasses. "It's a ferryboat ride and long drive away. I guess she just didn't want to be near her home-town. But her parents buried her in town with the rest of the family."

"Hanae, do you remember the night we heard about the Cuban mis-siles? We were really scared. *Man oh man*, I was about ready to blow a cork. But at least we didn't crawl into bed with a cookie and wait for the bombs."

Franny smiled as she re-lived that night. "Dutch and I had an *End of the World* party. She sneaked some medicinal alcohol and got salt and limes from the kitchen." Franny chuckled, "It wasn't a martini or a margarita but it sure made me feel like the world was ending right then and there. Maybe it was just poison, I don't know. We figured you wouldn't want any of that craziness so we left you alone. I've always wondered how you got through those days when we were so upset."

Sadness overcame me when I recalled that time. "I was on anti-depression drugs, so those days were like a dream. But I knew no matter what happened and how bad it got, there'd always be people who lived. I prayed my kids would survive like some of my cousins in Hiroshima."

Franny said, "Hanae, Dutch always wanted you to know how grateful she was for you being her friend, same goes for me. I mean everyone on the outside rejected us."

"You girls brought a clarity when we were trying to regain our lives," I remarked. "But I want you to know how much both of you meant to me," I said. "You made me happy. You showed me how to hold people and tell them you loved them. These were things I rarely did before. You girls made the hospital tolerable."

My face tightened as I remarked, "It would have been fun for me if you two had been in Minidoka. Of course that's absurd, but if you'd been there, you would have made the desert and barbed wire less... oh I don't know, less something. But I wouldn't wish that on anyone."

I took a deep breath and continued, "But I didn't forgive and forget. Instead I pushed the shame and anger deep inside. One more thing," I continued, "It's all about shame like in the *Scarlett Letter*. The heroine carried her shame on her dress, but I carry it on my skin and eyes. Minidoka shame became like a tattoo that seeped into my soul. I tried to ignore and deny the past, but it was no use."

I shared a revelation. "After Western State, I decided it was not my shame, but the government's. That made it worse, because who is the government? —the government is everyone and no one." I curled my lip.

"I told you some of my feelings at Western State, I hated President Roosevelt for the internment; Earl Warren, Governor of California, for his anti-Japanese opinions; and President Truman for bombing Hiroshima. There was no end only frustration," I said.

"Years later," I continued, "I realized that you girls taught me simple things matter. Life is too short to keep the hate inside. You gave me the gift of love. I was a Japanese person who was the enemy a few years earlier and you showed kindness. You became my friends, yet I felt unworthy." I took a deep breath, "You brought me joy, and above all, showed me that I have hope."

"Wow," said Franny, "All along I thought you'd forgiven, and that was how I tried to live my life. Oh well," she said, "my mistake, but it worked for me."

Franny continued, "Do you remember at Western State when I told you were like a cat on a hot tin roof like from the play? It must have been excruciating, always jumping and being on guard when you stepped outside. Dutch and I had a hint of it in our lives, but when we saw the world through your eyes, we knew what it was like as an everyday event."

"One other thing," Franny said, "you talked about Hiroshima and Minidoka. Dutch said afterwards that she could see Hiroshima even though she'd never been there. It confused her, and afterward she wasn't sure what to believe about America, or where she belonged, as she carried your memories. It took her months to work out."

Franny ran her fingers through her hair, "When we were feeling really low after you left, Dutch hummed the coal miner's song and I did the drums. We danced until we pushed our coal carts over a cliff." She paused and smiled for a second.

"Take a look and let's check out the view," Franny invited. We walked to the window and gazed down at Lake Union. "The city looks great from here," I said.

"Yes," Franny replied, "It's beautiful, but I really don't like heights. I think it was Dutch's idea to meet at the Needle."

"Okay, let's leave," I said. "The height makes me uncomfortable too, like I'm falling. I know we probably won't have an earthquake today, but I'd rather be on solid ground."

"Sounds good, can you imagine working here? It gives me the willies," Franny said. "An earthquake would be too much. Let's get moving." Franny took my arm and chirped, "We can go to the Food Circus for a cup of coffee or to eat something. Dutch would say, 'Eat something exotic for a change'."

The elevator doors whooshed and the operator stepped out. A group of school children raced out. "Going down," the operator said.

"Yes, we're going down," Franny replied with a sigh, "Back down to earth and all those things we left behind."

The ground zoomed closer and the support beams whizzed past like race cars. Just slightly off kilter after the ride, we stepped out. Long lines serpentined around the lobby. Then something odd happened: it was as if a light had been turned on, and for an instant, everything became quiet. There was a strange electricity crackling and a whiff of lemon perfume. The air felt clean, like after a summer rain.

Franny bounced and asked, "Did you feel that electricity, Hanae? Did you catch that perfume? Holy smokes, that could only be one person! Dutch is here, I just know it."

The crowd came back to life and the noise level returned. "Well, I'll be darned. That's a wonderment," Franny said. "She just dropped by."

Franny pushed her glasses up the bridge of her nose. "You know how she used to write things on tongue depressors? After Western State she wrote and told me something you could not get onto a tongue depressor. Guess what?"

"I can't imagine," I said, gazing at Franny.

"Okay," Franny whispered as she raised her arms like Dutch used to do. "Our girl had 'Love' tattooed on the inside of her left arm and 'Peace' on the inside of her right arm."

"Oh no!" I replied, "you've got to be kidding."

Franny remarked, "The best one was where she put 'Gratitude'. It was smack on her behind. What a clown! This world would have been a better place if she were alive."

I smiled, "Sounds like her. Did she say whether 'Gratitude' was on the right side or left side?"

"Knowing her, I would have guessed it was like a broken word," said Franny. You know like 'Grati' on the left cheek and 'tude' on the right.

Franny chuckled, "But who knows? If not broken, then I would guess the left bum since she was a lefty. By the way, do you drive?"

I shook my head, "No I don't," I said.

Franny replied, "Never mind. But think about coming to my place on the Fourth of July. I live about an hour away. It would be fun if you could make it."

"I'd like that. Write your name, address, and phone number on this postcard," I said. Then I insisted, "This time leave your correct address!"

"You do the same on the Space Needle receipt," Franny replied, "When we get to the Food Circus let's drink a toast to Dutch. She wouldn't mind an Orange Julius toast."

Franny turned, "Love you, Hanae."

I had forgotten how special those words made me feel, "I love you too. By the way," I replied, "There's a photo booth downstairs. It takes quarters and you get a strip of four photos. I want a picture of us, something to remember."

KIYOSHI, 1983

In 1983, Kiyoshi retired from his janitor job at Seattle University and spent most of his time fishing for trout at Green Lake and steelhead at the Ballard Locks. His moment of fame came when a KING TV reporter interviewed fishermen at the locks about Hershel the sea lion. Actually there were several sea lions and the press named the largest Hershey. As a protected species, he camped out in front of the fish ladder and feasted on steelhead trout.

If the fishermen hooked up, they had to be quick. Otherwise Hershel would rip the fish off their line. He was captured several times by Fish and Game and shipped to California but returned in a week. Many blamed him for depleting the entire Lake Washington steelhead, salmon, and sockeye runs. The TV reporter saw Kiyoshi fishing and asked his opinion.

Kiyoshi was proud of his ten second television interview. On camera he said, "They should just shoot and kill Herschel." He was so pleased that he called all our relatives to watch the late evening news.

Larry chided Kiyoshi, "You can't do that! It's illegal. Don't say stuff like that. What will people think?"

Kiyoshi responded, "It's the truth. They should kill it."

I snapped at him, "*Bachi ga ataru*, for saying bad things. What will the white people think of us? We don't want to be sent away again. Don't say bad things on television."

Kiyoshi gave his standard response when challenged, "Never mind, it's the truth," he said.

Steelhead fishing declined and Kiyoshi's health also deteriorated. His trips to the hospital increased as his ulcer and internal bleeding returned. Years ago, we thought he was living on borrowed time which in reality turned out to be twenty years. *Pretty good*, I said to myself, *for someone who was supposed to have died years ago.*

After he passed at age eighty-three, I told Larry the story of Kiyoshi's funeral, when his body was on display at Butterworth's Mortuary. His cousin Shizuko from San Francisco had slipped Buddhist prayer beads over his hands. I discovered them and put them in his suit pocket. Over the next few hours, I checked to make sure no more beads appeared. I believe they were cremated with him. *Good riddance to those beads*, I thought.

I cried after his death knowing he had had a tough life. Having suffered severe burns on his back as a child, being abandoned in Hiroshima, losing his business, going to camp and returning to work as a janitor was difficult. His mother constantly tried to manipulate him at the same time he suffered her adulterous shame. He had more than his share of problems including his health and my health. But in the end, he found happiness as a fisherman until the fish runs declined and the seasons were closed.

He was never sorry about the way he behaved on TV or in real life. In the end he was the same angry person who just became old and died. More than anything, I felt sorry for him. He endured, but never became a whole person because of his physical and mental scars. Because he was on the verge of death so many times, I was relieved when he passed. During his many false alarms, I mourned and cried. So when he finally passed, I didn't have many tears left to shed. It wasn't until I saw his pallbearer fishing buddies, that I knew it was for real. He was gone and I could finally cry for him.

I buried his ashes at Fairhaven Cemetery in the Japanese section near his mother and father. Every Memorial Day for years, I put flowers by his grave and pondered the Buddhist philosophy about choosing one's birth. "Kiyoshi, why did you choose to be born to your mother and father? And why did you choose a challenge that would defeat you? And finally what did you learn from this life?"

I had no idea what the answers might be. But asking made me think, *Why did I choose to be born to Japanese in America during the depression, to experience prewar Hiroshima, to be sent to a camp, to suffer illnesses and now Kiyoshi's death? I wish I could talk with Franny and Dutch about all my experiences. They would have some ideas.*

1983-1994

After Kiyoshi's death, I had time to unclutter and focus on the future. I sat on the front porch and watched the sun set and heard the birds chirping. I felt *Kamisama* close by and imagined I was back at the Western State garden.

My thoughts drifted. Things were taken care of, the house was free and clear, and I saved enough for his funeral and cemetery plot. *Now that he's buried, I don't have to live in fear of his dying at any moment anymore. My children are safe and secure. I don't have to carry Kiyoshi's psychological baggage, and his mother's shame.* But Minidoka fears still lingered and I irrationally worried about being taken again. I told myself, *I don't need to look over my shoulder for something bad to happen anymore.* With all that behind me, I decided to enjoy what time I had. "Love, Peace, and Gratitude" were the words that brought me clarity and direction.

I re-examined my old habits that held me like chains and discarded those I no longer needed. First, I lit incense and released the Yamada family shame brought on by Sachi. As the smoke rose and dissipated, I disconnected myself from the shame. It was so simple I wondered, *Why didn't I do this sooner?* Next I vowed to never exercise *gaman* and bear the unbearable. *Gaman*, though noble sounding, was an excuse to suffer needlessly and promote inaction. Without it, I could stand up and speak my mind.

As the sun set behind the Olympic Mountains, I discarded *shikataganai*, and swore to never say that word again. We are in America and almost nothing is *shikataganai*. Someone or something is always responsible in America. There is no "it can't be helped." People are at fault and something always can be done to address it.

As I shed my old behaviors I thought, *After all what could I lose? I've already served three and a half years in prison, was treated with electric shock, and lived with Kiyoshi for twenty years after the doctors gave him a year.*

Feeling the strength of my decisions, I rose from my chair and went inside the house. I decided to write Franny a letter even though eleven years had passed since my last attempt. In 1983, I mailed her Kiyoshi's funeral information but never got a reply. This time I was hoping the results would be different.

As I thought about what to write, I recalled moments that occurred since our last meeting. In Hiroshima, I chose the hard route and definitely got my choice. *What a thought!* I said to myself. *A difficult life, I got exactly what I wished for. If I ever have a choice in my next life, I would choose less hardship. That would be a welcome change.*

LETTER TO FRANNY

September 24, 1994

Dear Franny,

I hope you are doing well. It has been more than twenty years since we meet at the Space Needle. I sent a letter in 1983 after Kiyoshi died but did not get a reply. I apologize for not writing sooner but please know I think of you often. Time flies and I have missed you, I meant to write again, but I felt embarrassed after waiting so long.

Anyway, I want to catch up with you since my health has not been good. I'm at Kamada Nursing home this summer and was thinking of you and Dutch. I don't have much time. Over the years I prayed for you both. As I write this letter, I think about

*what I asked God and also my conversation with the Japanese
spirits. Sometimes I wonder if I am being a bad Christian when
I talk with the spirits.*

*Also, I'm writing because I asked my son Larry to deliver the two
photos we took at the Seattle Center booth on Saint Paddy's Day.
I want you to have them and I want you to meet him. Maybe you
can become friends.*

*So here is my story for the last twenty years. I retired from Roffee's
coat factory years ago and volunteered at Kamada Nursing Home.
Ironically I'm now a Kamada patient and enjoy the activities.*

*My father-in-law Koemon died in 1972; my mother-in-law Sachi
passed in 1975; and Kiyoshi died from congestive heart failure in
1983. My father went back to Hiroshima in 1973, and his health
failed quickly. During his last year, he lived on sake because he
had difficulty eating.*

*Doctors told me I had non-Hodgkin's lymphoma in 1988. I had
two operations at Swedish Hospital, one last year. The surgeons
were very nice but the tumor kept coming back. I had chemo for
a while and lost my hair. I got a wig and it looked okay. But
this is funny, one day I put it on backwards and went shopping.
People were staring at me and finally someone told me. I was
embarrassed and turned it around. Ah! How Dutch would have
laughed to see that!*

*Both of my sons are doing well. Alan married a Mexican woman
and they have two girls. Larry married a nurse and they have one
son. I hope you get to meet Larry and my grandson Matthew soon.*

Love,

Hanae

CHAPTER TWENTY

Kamada Nursing Home, 1994

I felt a chill and pulled the crocheted coverlet up to my neck. As my lymphoma became exceptionally aggressive, I knew it was time to check in to a nursing home. I ate well, but was not getting nourishment because of an intestinal blockage. After two operations to fix the condition I thought, *It's time for hospice care.* My life force began to fade and my plastic name bracelet which once was tight hung loose around my left wrist.

After I settled in at Kamada, I phoned Alan, asking him to visit me. The next day Larry came, bringing his son, Matthew, who stood by my side. My hands shook as I reached for a glass of water.

I smiled and said, "Hi Matthew."

My eyes were cloudy. It was a pleasant surprise to see him. I took Matthew's hand for a moment and asked, "How are you?"

He replied awkwardly, "I'm fine."

Matthew smiled shyly and said, "When I was small you took me to Beacon Hill Park and pushed me on the swings and merry-go-round. For lunch you'd cook kasu cod. It was delicious."

I said, "Do you remember the Japanese fairy tales and origami? There was Urashima Taro and Momotaro and the sad story about a mean man who killed his neighbor's dog."

I mussed his hair and said, "Matthew, please wait outside for a few minutes."

He waved goodbye and sat in the waiting room.

I sat up. "Larry, I need to tell you the family secrets before it's too late," I said. "You need to know these things."

"Okay," he replied and sat down. His face showed nothing but dread at the prospect.

"First, you have my birth certificate and will?" I asked. "I gave them to you a month ago with the box of valuable papers."

Larry nodded, "Yes."

My eyes cleared and I gathered strength and spoke. "Your father never could cut the apron strings from Grandma. She always found some way to keep him tied. You know, she bought him the Chevy when we couldn't afford a car."

The sun broke through the clouds and filled my room. Dust particles floated in streams of light. The air felt stuffy and thick as I continued, "That's why Kiyoshi was always away on weekends. If it wasn't the beach, it was *matsutake*, and then it was *warabi* and then *fuki*. I finally gave up and just went to the Japanese movies with Kiku."

"We knew that, Ma, that's no secret," Larry said. "Sometimes we would go on the trips with Grandma and sometimes not. But we didn't care. It was okay."

"Oh," I replied. "That was just how it was. I told Kiyoshi not to do it but he wanted the car and that was that."

"No big deal," Larry replied, "I want to know more about Hiro, Sachi's lover. Would you say something about Hiro?"

Larry exhaled and said, "When I was young I thought it was funny that we had two grandfathers on Dad's side. As I grew older, Alan and I asked about their sleeping arrangements. The answer was that Hiro was a very capable business advisor and he slept in the guest bedroom. But to our teenage eyes it looked like our own grandfather was the guest. This was our family secret that the entire community knew until we got old enough to figure it out."

My mouth was dry. "Please hand me some orange juice, Larry."

He continued, "I couldn't remember when Hiro wasn't with the family. His face was in every family photo."

He turned his head sideways and asked, "Are you going to say anything?"

I shook my head and took a sip of juice, then replied, "I have nothing to say. None of that means anything anymore."

My lips were chapped and ached. "Never mind," I said. "Would you please open the drawer and take out the book wrapped in Japanese cloth?"

I took another sip of juice and continued, "It's my brother's diary. Grandpa said he burned it before the FBI came in 1941 but he actually hid it, and sent it to Uncle Tom in Oakland after the war. Since Tom couldn't find anyone to translate the old *kanji*, he returned it to me. Just look at the pages and how nicely the characters are written."

Larry untied the patterned silk cloth and uncovered the book inside. It had gold leaf around the edges with elegant print that reflected great care and an artistic flair. The *kanji* characters looked as if they had been done by a printing press instead of Shintaro's actual hand.

I said, "Tom mentioned the possibility of war. But the rest was everyday stuff written in outdated kanji that even Tom's translator couldn't read. I believe Shintaro wanted me to think it was important so I'd have a purpose when I returned to Seattle."

I moistened my lips and opened my eyes wide. "You know how I always used to say, 'When we get rich we can buy a new house or go on a nice vacation'?"

Larry smiled. "Yeah, I remember. You used to say that all the time. We all wanted a new house and leave our cramped one-bedroom apartment. It was so small that Alan and I used to argue over who could stand on which side of the stove in the winter and whether my underwear warming on the stove crossed the line to his side."

I responded, "I never told you this, but Grandpa Toyojiro was a good friend of the famous gardener, Mr. Kubo. Grandpa loaned him money to buy Kubo Gardens. You remember the garden where we had the Block 26 reunions for years?"

"Yes, as kids we played on the Japanese bridges and in the bamboo groves near the waterfalls. There were big rocks in the pond and we used to play leapfrog," Larry replied.

"One year you fell into the pond and had to be pulled out," I said. "You said the carp bit you. Everyone just rolled their eyes saying you were too active to run on the bridges. Luckily the water was only two feet deep."

Larry squirmed and said, "How could I forget?"

"Anyway, Mr. Kubo promised grandpa ten percent of the garden in return for the loan," I continued. "There were no papers, only a handshake. That's why I always used to say 'When we get rich.' That was what I meant. Now that the Kubo children are selling the gardens, they'll make millions. We could get a lot of money finally. I hope you and Alan get some."

Tapping his fingers on the table Larry said, "Mom, didn't you hear that some South Seattle community group is protesting the sale of the garden? They called it a public treasure and killed the sale so the gardens would not become condos."

He almost growled, "They say it should be a public park. Isn't that just like America, you work all your life to make a beautiful Japanese garden and when you try to sell it, the neighborhood is up in arms? I thought this was a free country. It's like the camps, and Japanese are victims again."

Larry's voice softened when he added, "Mom, it was a nice thought to get rich someday. That helped us through some tough times but it was only a handshake, and we can't get money on a sixty-year old handshake."

He cleared his throat and said, "Never mind, Mom, we always thought you were dreaming when you talked about getting rich. There are no records, so we won't get anything — but that's okay with me. Anyway, what was in Shintaro's diary that was such a big secret? Surely it was more than just everyday stuff. Tom must have said more than that."

"Much later I finally found someone who could read old Japanese script," I replied. "Shintaro said war with America was coming and Grandpa and Grandma should go back home to Hiroshima since they were not US citizens. He said we'd be okay in America since we were US citizens."

Larry subdued his anger and said, "Man oh man, he was right about the war. But was he ever wrong about going back to Hiroshima! And he was really wrong about how our family would be treated in the US."

"Oh, none of that matters anymore. I had a good life and I can't complain," I said, turning down the radio as the news came on.

"Does that mean you've finally forgiven America for what it did to us during the war?" Larry asked.

"No, it just means I don't care anymore." I took another sip of juice. "It's not Christian, but you can live a good life and not forgive someone or the government. In the time left, I will not forgive them. Never."

"I guess that makes sense," Larry said with an edge to his voice. "But I just don't want you burdened with it. Can't you let it go?"

"You know, if not forgiving the government keeps me out of Christian heaven, so be it. I'll end up somewhere else," I responded, "maybe with Kiyoshi."

Time slowed and I closed my eyes. A jet plane flew overhead and it was like the clock's ticking filled the room.

I broke the silence: "I told you about when Kiyoshi was on his deathbed, didn't I? I called the Presbyterian minister because Kiyoshi wanted to go to Christian heaven and be with me and not his mother. The reverend came to the hospice and said a prayer, but he refused to baptize Kiyoshi. I was angry." A tear fell from my eyes and then I resumed, "But what could I do? Right after the reverend left, Kiyoshi died. So I don't know where he ended up, maybe reincarnated as a Buddhist. But I tried."

Larry said, "I visited Dad before he passed. I'd never seen him act that way before. He didn't apologize or ask for forgiveness for not standing up to Grandma or the government. Instead he said, 'Larry, I wasn't a good father, but I didn't damage you too much.'"

He continued, "Mom I was shocked by the remark because I didn't think Dad had enough self-awareness to even know where he was. Nor did I think he knew who he was talking to, since he'd suffered from delusions about being in Hiroshima for days. I was amazed that Dad actually realized what he'd done to our family. Later he asked if I would take him home. I told him that I was sorry but I had a job and family and couldn't take care of him."

I replied, "Kiyoshi asked me to take him home, too. He was unhappy with the food and complained, 'Everything is no good.'"

Larry remarked, "I'm going to do something I've been thinking about for years. I'll remove Hiro's pictures from the family album." He added, "I'll return the German porcelain statutes to Saint Vincent. You know the six-inch young boy in lederhosen with a blue hat. He's playing a violin with a dog sitting at his feet. It's what Hiro brought home and was so proud of."

For years the figurine held a prominent position in Sachi's knick-knack case.

"That's a good idea," I commented. "After the war," I said, Hiro worked for Saint Vincent DePaul and stole treasures until he was caught and fired. After Grandma Sachi and Hiro had passed away, Kiyoshi kept the items as if they were family heirlooms."

I continued, "Sachi convinced the Buddhist church to keep Hiro's ashes since he didn't have a burial plot with the family." I paused and gave a sly look, "This is the good part. About ten years ago I got a call from the church because they wanted to know what to do with the urn. It had been left there for years on a shelf, after grandma had passed. So I contacted Hiro's relatives in Japan and they refused his ashes. They knew what he'd done and did not want to be part of his shame. As it turned out, the Buddhist church didn't want Hiro either."

I chuckled slightly. "I'm sorry; this isn't really funny. I told the Buddhist Church what his relatives said and the priest asked for their address. They were so fed up that they sent the ashes back to Japan. Heaven only knows what happened to him. He deserved that." Even though I began to tire, I said, "One more thing though. Do you ever dream of foxes?"

"No, not at all," Larry said. "I've dreamed of a lot of things and had nightmares, but foxes never came into it. Why do you ask?"

"No reason," I said. But I wondered, *Did the fox spirits from Hiroshima bother him?*

"Also I heard several sansei committed suicide recently. You aren't thinking of doing that are you?" I asked. "I know you did not have an easy life."

Larry replied, "No I am fine. Everything is okay. Just take care of yourself."

With a burst of energy, I changed the subject. "Larry, Remember, you are a Christian and I'll see you in heaven. Don't ever become a Buddhist. Promise? Remember, you were baptized by Reverend Hori in the big church and that lasts forever."

"Okay, sure that's fine," he replied.

I wiggled in my chair. My eyes closed until the nearby sounds of the *Bon Odori* taiko drums called my spirit to the cobblestone street in front of the Buddhist Church. I had danced there for years under the colorful paper lanterns strung between the telephone poles.

From the stage platform, Mr. Kaku had announced the dances when I was a young woman, a mother, and now a grandmother, to celebrate the summer festival commemorating returning souls.

The drums pounded a loud rhythmic beat in time with the scratchy 78 rpm records of high-pitched Japanese folk tunes.

Taken by the urge to dance, I said, "Take me to the *Bon Odori.*"

At first Larry hesitated, and then said to my surprise, "Okay, but you can't stay too long. Hurry, put on your robe."

He helped me slide into a wheelchair, laced my low top tennis shoes, secured each foot, and pulled a blanket from the cupboard over my lap. Although it was July, the Seattle evenings could get cold. He checked on Matthew in the waiting area.

"Take your time, I'll watch some TV," Matthew said.

I was quiet as Larry wheeled me to the elevator and down to the lobby. We checked out and headed to Collins Playfield a block away. The viewing area was on a ridge above Main Street which looked down at the line of dancers in bright red and blue kimonos decorated with lotus, crane and floral designs.

The dancers would raise their arms in unison to the music, turn in, turn out, step forward and step back, then resume ahead. Most were women or girls, but there were men with twisted towels around their heads like sushi chefs wearing bright *happi* coats, and even people in street clothes.

Families and individuals sat on nylon-webbed folding chairs at the curbside. Others moved in groups on the sidewalk like fish schools migrating and pushing into each other as the dancers weaved up the street. Dancers slapped their fans, turned their heads, and shuffled their feet forward and backwards as darkness set in and the paper lanterns glowed.

The line twisted single file up the street, near the end of the block. It turned and came down the street towards the bandstand which loomed like a guard tower. When more dancers joined, there were double and triple lines like the swirls of a snail shell.

It was not unusual to take a half an hour to complete the entire elliptical path. Most performed with little or no facial expression as their movements were left to convey their emotions. The entire group moved like a centipede composed of individuals who displayed their differences in styles, gestures, grace, and enthusiasm. This celebration was what the ancestors returned to witness—subdued joy executed with grace. Ideally, the rhythms pushed the dancers' egos into unconsciousness, until only the dance and the moment existed.

I raised my right hand and pointed to an open green space on the edge of a hill above the street. Larry pushed me towards the spot and two families pulled their blankets aside to make room.

"*Sumimasen*," I responded to their act of kindness. My eyes brightened as I recognized the families. It was Mrs. Kato and her two sons from Block 26.

Mrs. Kato smiled and said, "Hello, Hanae." She turned to her children, "This is Gordon, and my youngest, Cary, and his daughter, Jean."

I bowed slightly at each name. Then I said, "I remember when the boys were born. This is my son, Larry. He was born in camp too."

I turned to Larry and said, "Please, get me some *somen* noodles. It's my favorite."

He had a look of concern. But I smiled and said, "I'll be okay with the Katos."

Mrs. Kato nodded, "We'll take care of her."

"Listen," I said with excitement, "That's the *Dai Tokyo Ondo*. Oh, I wish I were out there!"

Larry hustled down the slope and merged with a stream of spectators. It was a traffic jam. He turned and looked back over his shoulder to make sure I was okay. I waved happily at him and he turned into the crowd.

He weaved and slipped through openings to the somen noodle stand. By then the *Dai Toyko Ondo* was over and the dancers were taking a break. The wind rustled the trees and kimono sleeves fluttered. The dancers headed for the booths that sold roasted corn, sushi, shaved ice and soft drinks. I thought it was amusing to see female dancers in beautiful kimonos eating corn on the cob.

I watched Larry stand in line for that precious plastic bowl of cold white noodles. As was the tradition, the servers wore white tee shirts and white chef hats. At that moment, I imagined them plunging a ladle into the dark liquid and scooping out cold broth of soy and bonito, then pouring it over the noodles sprinkled with chopped green onions.

As a child, Larry used to slurp the white strands and end with a lip-smacking sound. This was the same technique I learned from Masa many years ago.

"Nothing was better on a summer's evening than somen," I said out loud. Looking at the mass of people, I was able to see Larry rejoin the crowd and work his way upstream like a salmon. I waved my arms and felt full of energy when he neared.

Larry climbed the grassy hill and sighed with relief when he handed me the noodle bowl. He pulled the chopsticks from their paper wrapper and split them with a snap. Immediately he rubbed the sticks together to remove splinters. My hands were shaking when I managed my first taste.

I slurped with satisfaction and moaned, "Oh this is delicious, some things don't change." It reminded me of past *Bon Odoris* and Hiroshima where I savored somen on hot summer evenings.

It was as if the flavors had carried me back to when I had danced for my father, mother, and more recently, Kiyoshi. It was a homecoming as the drums pounded and the music blared. I felt fortunate to be there on a warm summer evening under a clear sky.

"Larry," I said, "This may be my last time. Kiyoshi's spirit comes back every year and I'll be with him next year. Anyway, I have something to ask. Will you dance for me next year?"

He stepped back and replied, "Mom, you're going to live for a long time. They take great care of you at Kamada."

"I know," I said. "Dance for me, okay?"

The music ended and the announcer's voice blared, "Dancers take your places for the *Tanko Bushi*."

"Oh, the Coal Miner's Dance. It's the best," I said. "Dance for me next year," I pleaded.

Larry replied, "Mom, you know I don't do things like that and I can't dance."

My mind slipped slightly when I referred to Larry by his Japanese name and said, "It's okay, Yutaka. It's easy to dance." I began to shift my feet and raised my arms. "Just do this and clap your hands three times."

TAKE ME HOME

The next day when Larry visited, I felt weak. I had some things that I felt were very important. I held his hand and said, "I want to apologize for making your life so hard. When I was carrying you in camp, I was always afraid. I was scared you would be stillborn. Later I worried that you wouldn't get nourishing food and good hospital care in camp."

Larry straighten the items on my nightstand. He said, "What brought all this on?"

"I didn't hold you or tell you that I loved you because I was afraid you would be born dead or die quickly," I continued. "But I was wrong. Kiyoshi and I were the ones always in the hospital. I'm sorry we couldn't give you a stable life."

Without expression, Larry said, "You were just fine. It was the only situation I knew."

My voice quivered when I said, "I'm sorry I used to tell you that I would leave you kids if you didn't behave." It was a threat I vowed to never use on my children. But I did in a time of weakness.

"I thought you said that because you knew I'd killed Grandma," he replied.

"Oh, that's another thing. I'm sorry I didn't tell you sooner how she died. I'm sorry that I never thanked you for keeping the house running and paying the bills when Dad was sick. I'm sorry that Kiyoshi gave Alan a concussion when he knocked him out and forced him to move away. It must have been difficult. Can you forgive me?"

Larry nodded unemotionally. "Mom this is all old news, and nothing I want to hear again. Living through it once was enough. You did the best you could and I'm glad I didn't let you down."

I replied, "You've done well, becoming a teacher, getting married, and having a nice son. You should be proud."

Larry took a deep breath. "Mom," he said, "Let's talk about something else."

With tears in my eyes, I replied, "I'm sorry that we forced you to be like an island to protect you from Grandma's *haji* and my Western State Hospital shame. I wish I could wave a magic wand and change it. Will you forgive me?"

Larry clenched his teeth and I continued, "I wish that you could become more trusting."

He responded, "For all our family's faults, I don't think less of you."

"Thank you, Larry," I said with relief.

Larry rubbed his chin and continued, "Dad was trapped in anger, living in a desert of his own making. It was like he was another casualty of war. He carried Minidoka with him always. I don't want to be like him."

Larry paused for a second and took a deep breath. He said, "Dad couldn't handle what the government did, so he dumped it on us kids. But we were too young and really couldn't deal with it. That's why Alan misbehaved in school."

I covered my mouth and replied, "Oh I always thought Alan had trouble because he only spoke Japanese and not English when he went to school. I felt guilty for years about that, but you've done well."

"We spoke English to you," I said. I never fully realized how deeply he had thought about our family's problems. I thought, *He obviously had a strong desire to create something positive that could be passed on to Matthew, unlike his father. How did he figure this out at his young age and how did he make peace with Kiyoshi's anger?*

I reflected on my revelations and thought, *When I was at Western State I picked "Peace" and sent money to Hiroshima. I should have chosen "Love" and given it to my children to make up for Kiyoshi's behavior.* I was overcome with grief when I realized my mistake.

Larry looked at me with a sideways glance. "What are you thinking, Mom?" he inquired.

"Nothing," I said, "I'm proud of you. You'll do just fine."

ROSES

The next day I felt weaker and had a hard time staying awake. I was nodding when the door opened and Larry brought in a bouquet of roses. He said, "Someone sent you these. There's a note, do you want me to read it?"

"Yes," I replied.

He opened the small envelope and said, "It's from someone named Franny. She was sorry that she never contacted you after Kiyoshi's passing. Her father died at that time and she was grieving for months. She left you her phone number."

"Thank you," I replied. "The flowers are pretty. I sent her a letter last week but wasn't sure it would reach her. Is today Tuesday?" I asked.

"Friday," Larry responded. "Alan will be coming to see you tomorrow. He'll be on a morning flight from San Francisco."

"Oh, good," I said, "I miss him. What month is it?"

"July," came his answer.

My voice carried a sense of urgency as I wrapped up loose ends. "Did I tell you where to find the samurai sword?"

"Yes, I have it," replied Larry. "Also I have Shintaro's diary. Don't worry. I'm used to taking care of things."

I pushed a small lump of turquoise across the bed. "Keep this for good luck. I've had it for years. Turquoise is best if given as a gift."

"Thanks," he said as he held it up to the light.

I gathered all my strength and said, "One more thing. My last wish. I want to go home, okay?"

"Mom, you can't go home. We can't take care of you. That's impossible," he said.

I smiled, "I don't mean Beacon Hill. I mean Hiroshima."

Larry raised his eyebrows. He turned instinctively toward the door to exit as if to escape this assignment.

"Remember years ago you went to Hiroshima," I said. "The family grave was near ground zero, surrounded by tall gray buildings. There was a stone monument with a drawer that opened like a mailbox. It contained the family ashes."

He replied, "I would need help to find the grave. Why Hiroshima?"

I whispered, "I tried to be American. Before the war and after there was discrimination and I felt more at home in Japan. I walked Hiroshima streets and felt like I belonged."

"But mom, you are an American," Larry said insistently. "You aren't a foreigner, why go back? Anyway you told me they treated you badly in Japan and called you *gaijin*."

I touched my eyebrow. "Yes, that's true. With maybe a day to live, it doesn't matter to me anymore." I said, "I tried to be an American but never made it. I'll come back in the summer for *Bon Odori*."

"*Wakarimasu ka?* Do you understand?" My words relieved me of a burden that I had been carrying for years. I felt lighter, even invigorated. "No more *gaman*. *Wakarimasu ka?* No more."

Larry nodded, "*Wakarimasu.*" But asked, "Why didn't you tell me earlier you wanted to be in Hiroshima? Why such a sudden decision?"

I replied, "I've been thinking about it ever since Kiyoshi died and wasn't baptized. But I didn't want to say anything because it would've upset you. I'll meet you in Christian heaven and my ashes will be with Buddhist ancestors. Maybe Kiyoshi will be there. I would have told you sooner about wanting my ashes in Japan, but you would've tried to change my mind."

My hands shook as I handed Larry a wrinkled envelope. "Yutaka, here are the names of my Hiroshima cousins. They will take you to the family grave. Use the money I am leaving you to make the trip."

"*Wakarimasu*," he replied. By his look, Larry was surprised that his Japanese language skills were coming back from childhood.

My vision blurred. "Promise that you'll dance for me at the *Obon* festival next year. And promise me that you'll take me home to Hiroshima. This will make me happy. America was okay because of you and Alan. America is your home and times have changed for the better. What happened to me will never happen to you. Be strong, remember your name means 'bamboo,' so you can bend but not break."

Larry nodded and closed his eyes. His face contorted as he tried to comprehend what had been asked of him.

I continued, "Take me home. Yutaka, take my ashes to Hiroshima so I can rest in peace. Do that for me, won't you?"

He said nothing, but bowed his head and tightened his lips. "Okay, I'll take you home. But you really should be buried here. That's only right. What about the family plot at Fairhaven cemetery? What about the family already buried here? What about your grandchildren and me and your great-grandchildren yet to be born?"

My eyes lost focus for a second and then I replied, "None of my relatives are Christians except for you and Alan. So it doesn't make any difference where I'm buried since they will be in a different afterlife," I swallowed hard and continued, "Anyway, I don't want to be in the Japanese section of the cemetery with all the people who made us ashamed of your grandmother and Hiro. Take me home, Yutaka. I'll come back every summer."

My eyes brightened, "My friend Franny can teach you. She knows how to dance. I taught her."

I pulled an envelope from under my pillow. Written in shaky letters was the name Franny S. Fox.

He asked, "Her name is Fox. Is that why you asked me about foxes the other day?"

This took me by surprise. "No," I replied, "I never thought about that. Would you take this to my friend Franny in Black Diamond? She's the woman who sent me the roses."

Larry found two black and white photos of a younger me and an attractive white woman. Both of us were smiling and having a wonderful time.

"We took the pictures at the Seattle Center years ago. Each of us got two and now I want her to have all four," I said.

"Who is she?" Larry asked.

"Franny and Dutch were my best friends at the Western State Hospital," I said.

"The first time I visited," Larry said, "there were two girls with red lipstick. Was she one?"

"I think so," I replied. "She said she saw you so that must have been the time.

"Yeah, I remember them," he replied.

I continued, "The three of us used to have a lot of fun together. I want her to have these pictures. Can you deliver them tomorrow? I already phoned her and told her you might come."

Larry tightened his lips and said, "Tomorrow afternoon is already taken. I wish I'd known you needed this done so soon. I need to drive Matthew to soccer practice and it's about thirty miles to her house in Black Diamond. Plus, Alan is coming."

I begged, "Please, just do this for me tomorrow."

Larry said, "Okay, we'll get an early start to beat the traffic and get back to meet Alan. So call this person and tell her we'll be there at 8:30 tomorrow morning. Matthew and I will come back and see you in the afternoon after soccer."

"Okay," I said. Larry got ready to leave.

"Wait," I said, and held out my arms and gave him a hug as he bent down. "See you soon," he said.

Matthew popped his head in and I smiled.

"Bye-bye, Matthew." I raised my arms. "Come here," I said, "give me a big hug."

"Love you, Grandma," Matthew said. "Love you, too," I answered.

"Oh, one last thing, Larry. Promise you'll dance for me at the *Bon Odori*?" I asked with determination.

"Mom, I told you. You know I don't dance," he pleaded.

"Don't worry," I whispered and repeated, "Franny will teach you."

Larry hesitated and tightened up, "Okay, I'll dance if you do something for me. Leave half your ashes in Seattle."

I squinted and paused. "Okay, half here and half in Japan," I replied. "Maybe toss half into the Motoyasu River where our family home was. That way I can ride the Japanese current back to Seattle. "*Wakarimasu ka?*"

"*Wakarimasu,*" he said, "Yes, I understand."

I recalled my words to Franny years ago about things coming full circle, "Your tears will become streams that reach the sea."

I relaxed and remained calm, "On second thought, it would be better to put half in the Strait of Juan De Fuca so the Japanese current takes me."

"Where did that idea come from?" Larry asked. "That current will probably go south towards California not to Japan."

I blushed. "That's okay," I said. "Never mind Japan, just leave half in Seattle at Fairhaven and half in the Strait. But tell Franny what I said about Juan De Fuca. Okay? Be sure to tell her."

"Okay, that's a deal," he replied and exited.

"See you tomorrow," he said and closed the door.

I shut my eyes and sighed. In that space before sleep swallowed me, I heard an airplane pass overhead. The sound faded and then grew into Taiko drums pounding. *Must be Bon Odori time*, I mused. I laughed, when I realized it was my heart. "Be quiet," I chided, "I need my rest."

"Rest, Hanae?" I heard voices ask.

"*Kamisama* is that you?" I replied. Their presence made me feel light headed. One voice inquired, "Hanae, from your time on earth, did you get what you wanted?"

Without hesitation I replied, "Yes, thank you. I got what I was promised, a hard life. But I regret that I never felt like I belonged in America after all these years. Maybe that will be in my next life."

The voices were full of kindness when they asked, "Hanae, do you want to take the easy or hard path?"

I recalled Hiroshima when they offered me the same choice. Images of Mom and Dad, Shintaro, Masa, Uncle Yosh, Kiyoshi and the boys flashed. I smiled and said, "This time I'll take the easy way." I took a deep breath and continued, "I'm ready now."

LETTER FROM FRANNY

Dear Hanae,

It was so good to receive your letter. I'm happy that your family is doing well but sad to hear about your condition. I sent roses to you yesterday. Today I got your phone message about your son coming tomorrow. I'm looking forward to meeting him and will give him this letter.

After bouncing around for a few years I got a job with the National Parks and now work at Paradise at Mount Rainier. Can you imagine me in Paradise every day?

Anyway, I never married but I have four wonderful dogs and a five-acre piece of land. I have a good life. It's funny. The other day I was thinking of you and Dutch. Remember that time she was so excited and told us there was a Macy's Thanksgiving Parade outside? She dragged us to the porch and pointed to the sky.

It was a windy day and the sun was shining bright. The clouds were billowy white mixed with dark streaks. Dutch said, "That cloud looks like a bear." Then she found a Frankenstein monster, a race car, a blimp, a loaf of white bread, and a tiger's face. We all laughed because the clouds actually looked like those things.

I told her that we should not stare too hard or our energy would dissolve the clouds. She laughed and we spent the whole afternoon staring and pulling them apart like cotton candy.

Even to this day I look up and see animals and explosions of brightness. Once I saw Dutch wearing her round glasses hovering in the clouds. She was smiling her electric smile. Then I realized someday all three of us would be there with the puffy bears, swirling monsters, fuzzy dogs and cat faces. When it's sunny I'll look for you next to Dutch.

Until then, I hope your days are filled with love, peace, and gratitude.

Love,

Franny

END

Glossary

Bachi - like karma, or the universe will strike you
Baka - stupid
Chibi - a small person or child
Daijobu - everything will be okay
Dame desu - no good
Dorobo - a thief
Ii desu ne - good or sounds good.
Furo - bathtub or bath
Gaijin - foreigner
Gakko - school
Gaman (gambarinasai)- the act of bearing the unbearable with dignity
Gambare - endure or be strong
Gasa gasa - hyperactive
Genkan - entry alcove
Geta - wooden slip-on shoes similar to flip flops
Giri - duty
Hai - yes
Haji - shame
Hakujin - white person
Hayaku shinasai - hurry up
Hambun - half
Iji ga warui - mean spirited
Issei - First generation
Kamisama - spirits that inhabit all things
Kanji - Chinese characters as opposed to hiragana and katakana, which are entirely Japanese
Katana - samurai sword
Kawai so - sad
Koden - money given at funerals
Kokeshi - wooden doll usually given to a girl at birth
Matsutake tori - hunting for pine mushrooms
Mochi - sweet bean cakes or sticky rice dumplings
Modan garu - modern girl
Mottainai -wasteful

Moxa - a form of punishment involving burning the offender with small tuffs of burning matter

Nani - what?

Nappa - a leafy vegetable

Nihonmachi - Japantown

Nisei - Second generation

Obon - the period of time which celebrates the return of ancestral spirits and Bon Odori which is the dance celebrating the event

Yoisho – a word normally used when lifting or pulling something heavy

Onsen – hot springs

Otosan - father

Sake - rice wine

Sakura masu - cherry trout

Sansei - third generation-Issei is first and Nisei is second

Sento - bath house

Shigin - a type of singing

Shikataganai - It can't be helped

Shogi - Japanese chess

Shoyu - soy sauce

Soba – noodles, usually buckwheat

Somen – very thin noodles made of wheat flour served cold

So desu ne - It is so

Sore wa ikemasen - It's not acceptable

Sumimasen - excuse me or thank you

Taiko - large drums

Tanko Bushi - Coal Miner's Dance

Tsukemono - pickled cabbage or nappa

Ume - red pickled plums

Wakarimasu ka - Do you understand?

Warabi - fiddle head ferns

Warui ne - bad isn't it

Yasashii - mild, gentle or very polite manner

Yurei - a type of ghost

Notes

Seattle History Sources
Morgan, Murray: Skid Road-An Informal Portrait of Seattle. University of Washington Press, 1982.
Brief history of Seattle-https://www.seattle.gov/cityarchives/seattle-facts/brief-history-of-seattle
Seattle riot of 1886 -https://en.wikipedia.org/wiki/Seattle_riot_of_1886

Japanese American History
https://densho.org/
https://en.wikipedia.org/wiki/Densho:_The_Japanese_American_Legacy_Project
https://en.wikipedia.org/wiki/Internment_of_Japanese_Americans
https://www.britannica.com/event/Japanese-American-internmen
Recently the statistic that 50% of the internees were children has been questioned. Wikipedia states that 30,000 of 120,000 were children.

Other Sources
Page 214, 215, 217, & 294 – Tanko Bushi various YouTube sources
    https://www.youtube.com/watch?v=LEJiRvGLEv8
    https://www.youtube.com/watch?v=G5hEGhchl-E
Page 229 – Excerpts from President Kennedy's Cuban Missle Crisis speech from Wikipedia.
    https://en.wikipedia.org/wiki/Cuban_Missile_Crisis
Page 230 – God Bless America lyrics excerpt from Wikipedia
    https://en.wikipedia.org/wiki/God_Bless_America
Page 277 – Reference to Raymond Carver's Poem *Late Fragment.*
Pages 270 & 281 – Reference to Tennessee Williams's play *Cat on a Hot Tin Roof*

Acknowledgements

Many thanks to Roger Shimomura for the cover illustration "Searchlight" and Alfredo Arreguin for his portrait of the author.

Special thanks to Jeanie Okimoto for having faith in my work. Thanks to Jay Rubin for his editing and critiques. Also thanks to Ann Butler, Carol Barton, Danielle Vermette for their editing work and Tess Gallagher for her comments and support. The final editing, however, was done by the author.

Thanks to Erin Shigaki for her layout work and to Dorothy Mann, John Gordon Hill, Ellen Hill, Kathy Kirkland, Peg Cheng, and Sue Tomita for reading and commenting on my early drafts.

I am indebted to: Linda Ando, Barry Grosskopf, Wendy Lustbader, the late Professor Nelson Bentley, Joe Okimoto, my wife Karen Matsuda, my son Matthew Matsuda, daughter-in-law Jesika Matsuda, Mary Matsuda Gruenewald, Alan Matsuda, Jane & Larry Briscoe, Carol Benge, Lynn Arakaki, Mark Johnson, Vivian Lee, Louise Kashino, Grant Kunishige, John & Binko Bisbee, AC & Jerry Arai, Marjorie Young, Pam Krute, Tom Yamada, Betsy Wilson, Anna Tamura, Tetsu Kashima, Carole Kubota, Evelyn Matsuda, Melissa Matsuda, Viviana Matsuda, Vince Matsudaira, Brad & Allison Joseph, Karen Maeda Allman, Rick Tanigawa, Jan Johnson (Panama Hotel), Jean Nakayama (Maneki Restaurant), Ann Aoki, Gary & Carrie Dodobara, and Lauren Iida.

Information about the barracks and structures were obtained from Gary Bohlen. In addition, he supplied stories that informed the poem about homesteaders in my previous book of poetry, *Glimpses of a Forever Foreigner.*

About the Author

Lawrence Matsuda was born in the Minidoka, Idaho Concentration Camp during World War II. He and his family were among the approximately 120,000 Japanese Americans and Japanese held without due process for three years or more. Matsuda has a Ph.D. in education from the University of Washington.

In July of 2010, his book of poetry entitled *A Cold Wind from Idaho* was published by Black Lawrence Press in New York. In 2014, *Glimpses of a Forever Foreigner* was released, a collaboration between Matsuda and artist Roger Shimomura, who contributed 17 original sketches.

In 2015, Matsuda collaborated with artist Matt Sasaki, and produced two graphic novels: *An American Hero - Shiro Kashino* and *Fighting for America: Nisei Soldiers*, funded by the National Park Service and available through the Nisei Veterans Committee Foundation or the Wing Luke Museum. The Shiro Kashino animated version won a 2016 regional Emmy and is available online: https://www.seattlechannel.org/CommunityStories?videoid=x59988.

Also in 2016, he and Tess Gallagher collaborated on *Boogie-Woogie Crisscross*, a book of poetry developed from e-mails they exchanged over a period of three years, when she was in Ireland, and he was in Seattle.
It was published by MadHat Press.

Matsuda lives in Seattle with his wife Karen, his son Matthew, and his wife, Jesika.

CPSIA information can be obtained
at www.ICGtesting.com
Printed in the USA
FSHW011021040520
69885FS